image® comics presents

SKULL KICKERS™

FIVE FUNERALS and a BUCKET of BLOOD

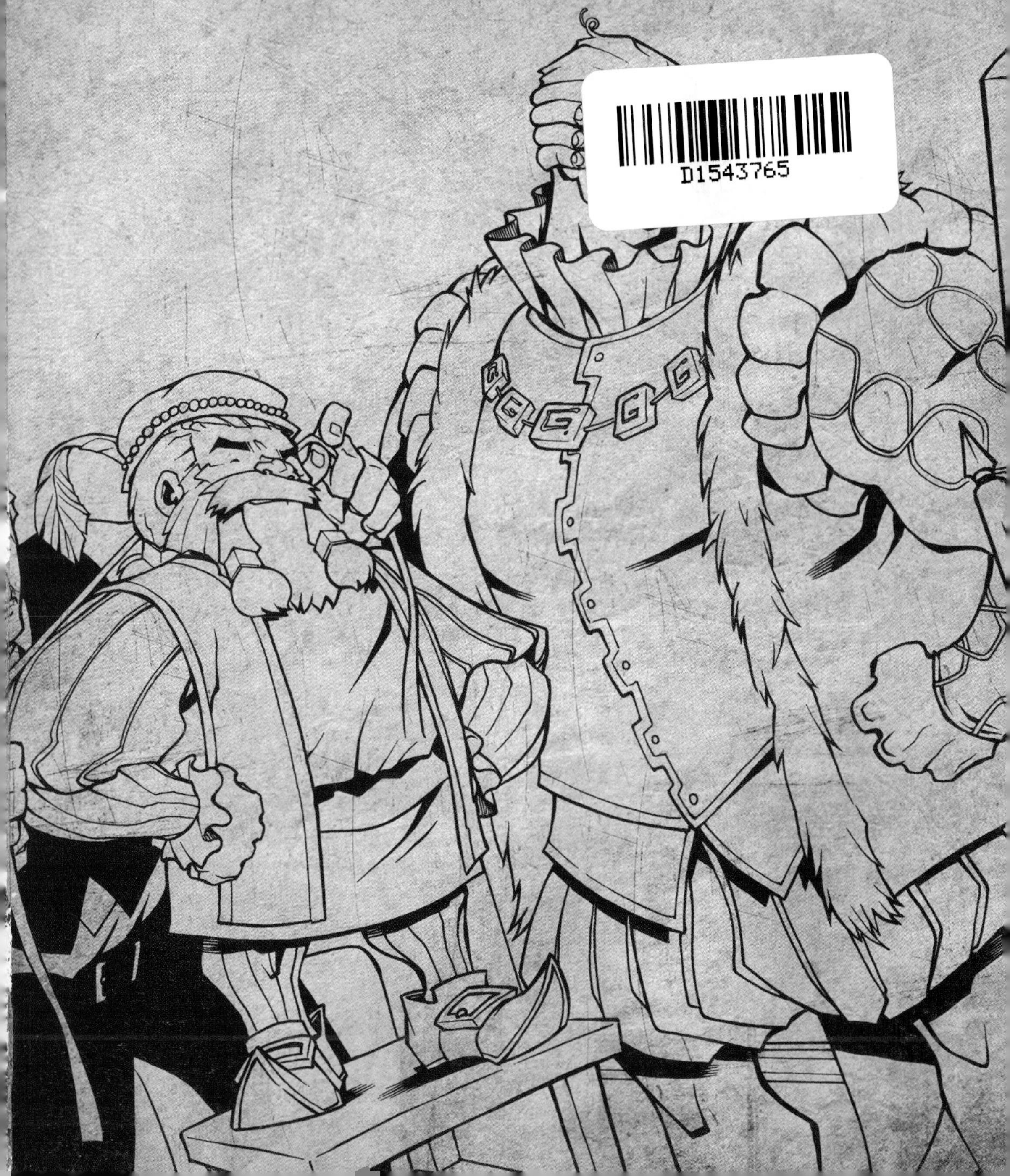

SKULLKICKERS, VOL. 2
ISBN: 978-1-60706-442-8
First Printing

Published by Image Comics, Inc. Office of publication: 2134 Allston Way, 2nd Floor, Berkeley, California 94704. Copyright © 2011 JIM ZUBKAVICH. Originally published in single magazine form as SKULLKICKERS #6-11. All rights reserved. SKULLKICKERS™ (including all prominent characters featured herein), its logo and all character likenesses are trademarks of JIM ZUBKAVICH, unless otherwise noted. Image Comics® and its logos are registered trademarks and copyrights of Image Comics, Inc. All rights reserved. No part of this publication may be reproduced or transmitted, in any form or by any means (except for short excerpts for review purposes) without the express written permission of Image Comics, Inc. All names, characters, events and locales in this publication are entirely fictional. Any resemblance to actual persons (living or dead), events or places, without satiric intent, is coincidental.

International Rights Representative: Christine Meyer (christine@gfloystudio.com)

PRINTED IN THE U.S.A. For information regarding the CPSIA on this printed material call: 203-595-3636 and provide reference # EAST - 411207

IMAGE COMICS, INC.

Robert Kirkman - chief operating officer
Erik Larsen - chief financial officer
Todd McFarlane - president
Marc Silvestri - chief executive officer
Jim Valentino - vice-president

Eric Stephenson - publisher
Todd Martinez - sales & licensing coordinator
Sarah deLaine - pr & marketing coordinator
Branwyn Bigglestone - accounts manager
Emily Miller - administrative assistant
Kevin Yuen - digital rights coordinator
Tyler Shainline - production manager
Drew Gill - art director
Jonathan Chan - senior production artist
Monica Garcia - production artist
Vincent Kukua - production artist
Jana Cook - production artist
www.imagecomics.com

Writer
JIM ZUB

Pencils
EDWIN HUANG

Inks
EDWIN HUANG
MIKE LUCKAS
KEVIN RAGANIT

Colors
MISTY COATS
ESPEN GRUNDETJERN
MIKE LUCKAS
JIM ZUB

Art Assist
TOM LIU

Lettering
MARSHALL DILLON

"Tavern Tales" Writers
CHRIS SIMS
BRIAN CLEVINGER
RAY FAWKES
ADAM WARREN

Artists
JOE VRIENS
JIM ZUB
SCOTT HEPBURN
IAN HERRING
JEFFREY "CHAMBA" CRUZ

Issue Covers
CHRIS STEVENS
SAEJIN OH

Trade Cover
EDWIN HUANG
ESPEN GRUNDETJERN

Graphic Design
VINCENT KUKUA
JIM ZUB

Skullkickers Logo Design
STEVEN FINCH

Skullkickers Created By
JIM ZUB
CHRIS STEVENS

Special Thanks

CULLEN BUNN
NATE EDMONDSON
ELAN FREEDMAN
STEVE JACKSON
STACY KING
RON MARZ
PHIL REED
CHARLES SOULE

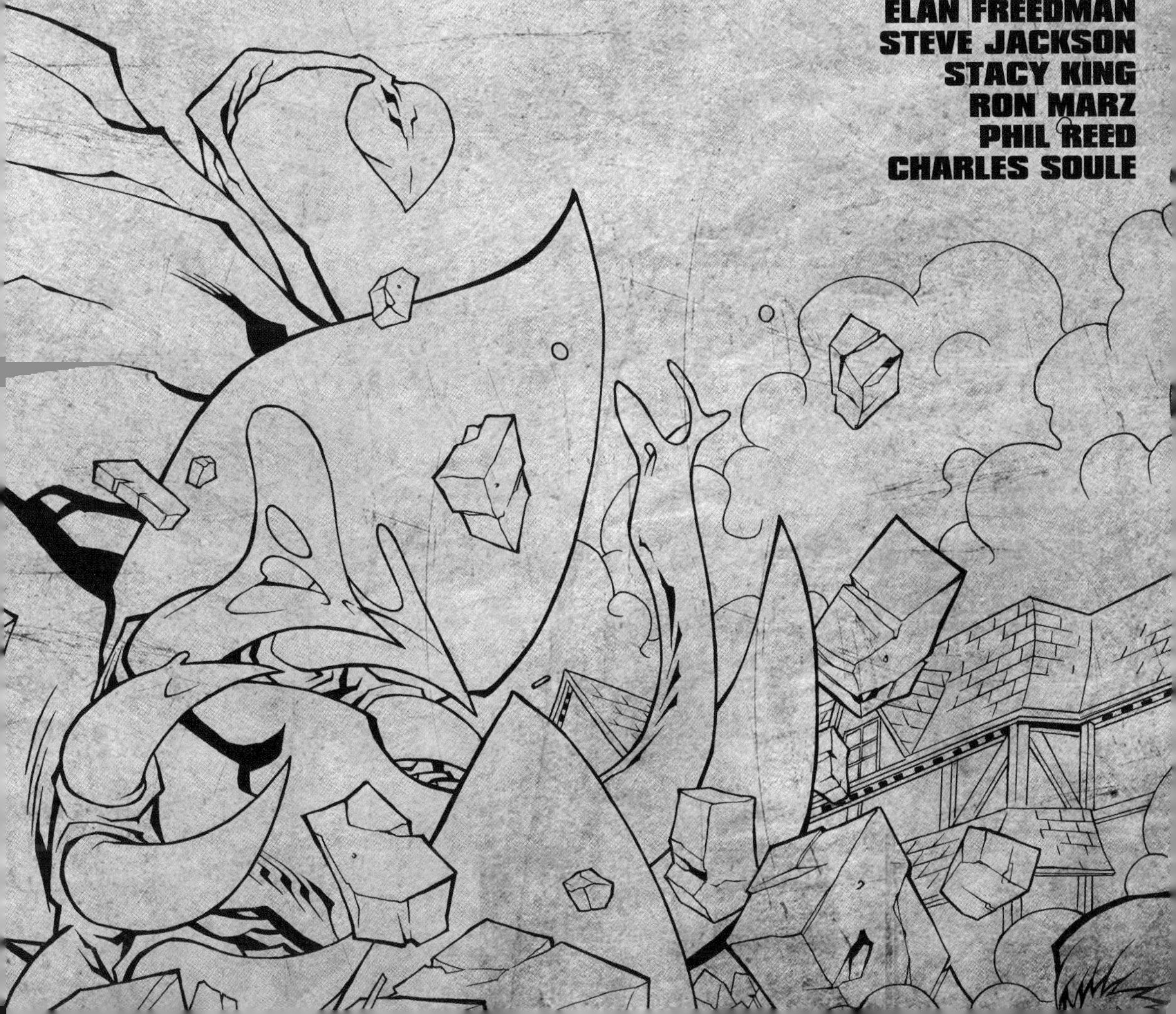

Baldy, Shorty and a Bullet for Hamlet

Once upon a time, a black-robed wizard, a fairy tale princess and a demon familiar walked into a bar. The wizard says to the bartender, "What can we order 'to go'? We're in a hurry." So, the bartender says to the black-robed wizard "That depends... what's your back-story?" and the wizard says,

"Well..."

Suddenly the demon's head explodes from a gunshot from the far end of the bar. An enormous bald guy, not previously part of the joke, rushes forward, tossing the princess across several tables for her own safety as the dwarf mercenary roars toward the wizard, kicking in his skull.

Hamlet, if you really think about it, didn't end any better than that. Many critics ... most of whom favorably reviewed the first edition Advanced Dungeons & Dragons Dungeon Masters Guide as 'compelling' and 'well-plotted'... actually prefer this ending to Hamlet as it involves fewer soliloquies or, in other words, 'breaks between combat rounds.' Indeed, I personally recommend that a comparative analysis of Shakespeare's entire body of work and Skullkickers be offered at Harvard; largely as a means of actually motivating students to come to class.

My recent book 'XDM: Xtreme Dungeon Mastery' was an attempt at returning the concepts of 'play' and 'fun' to role playing games. In that epic tome, we identified three types of approaches to fantasy. These were specifically related to gaming but may translate generally as well:

> • **TYPE 1:** If it moves; kill it. If it doesn't move, kick it 'til it moves. Get treasure to buy bigger weapons to kill bigger things to get bigger treasure. (Logic loop)
>
> • **TYPE 2:** If it moves; talk to it. If it doesn't move; talk ABOUT it. Stay in character, pretend you're in a LARP and speak in an affected voice. (Emotion loop)
>
> • **TYPE 3:** If it moves; what do I do to WIN! If it doesn't move; what do I do to WIN! ('The Man' loop)

If you find yourself weary of dealing with Type 2 and Type 3 people all the time, then I heartily recommend a sojourn with Skullkickers. Here you will find solace in a place where subtlety is measured in minimizing body count, where nuance is determined by which part of the wall the target's head penetrates and where restraint involves not firing a 120mm handgun with infinite ammo more than five times in any given frame.

These two guys would kick Hamlet's skull all the way into Prince Fortinbras' lap in Norway. Take THAT, poor Yorick!

--Tracy Hickman
October 2011

Tracy Hickman is an international and New York Times Best Selling novelist with over fifty books in print. He is best known for his 'Dragonlance' and 'Deathgate' series. At this writing, he is completing his next book, 'Wayne of Gotham' -- a Batman novel for DC Comics.

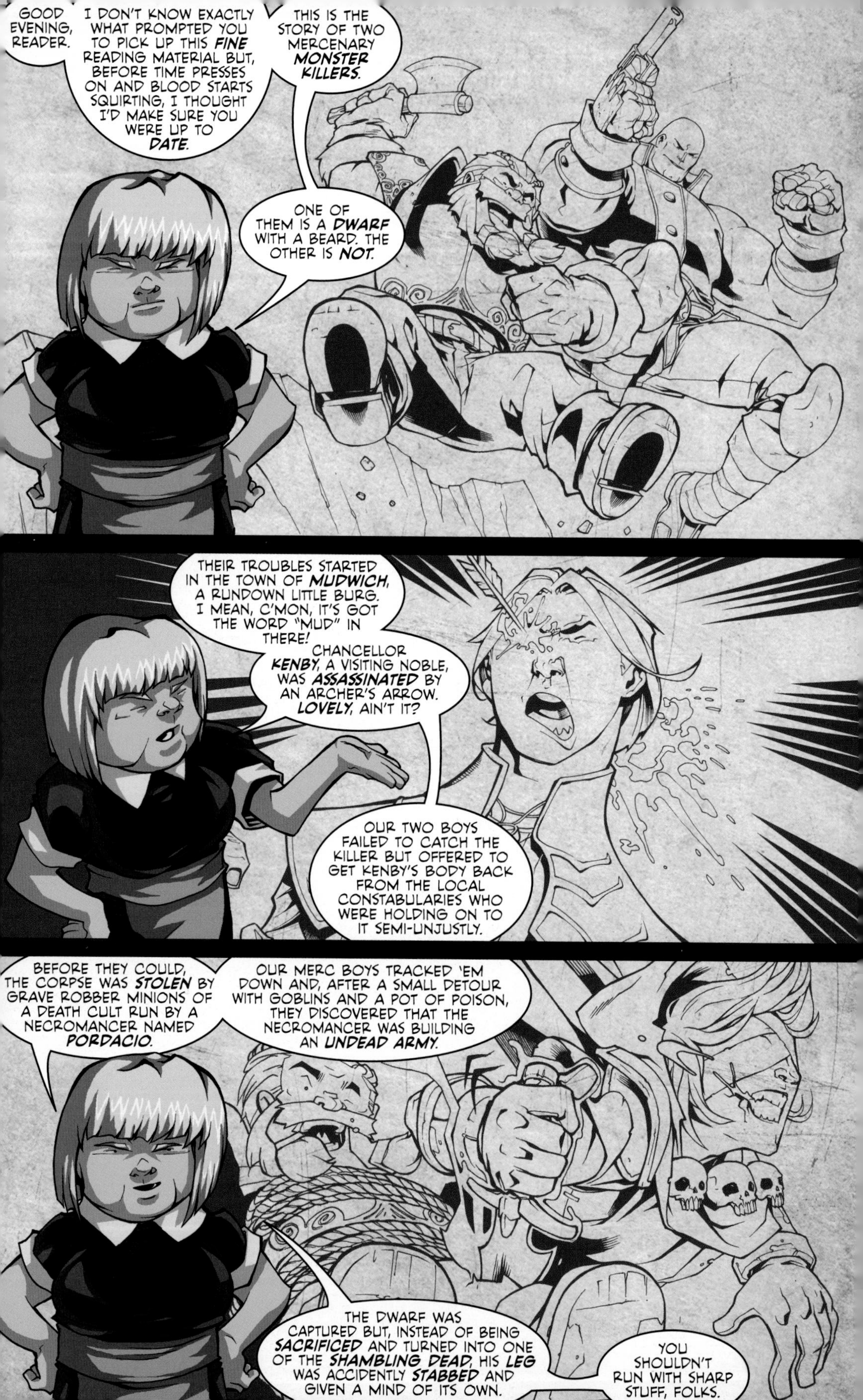
GOOD EVENING, READER.
I DON'T KNOW EXACTLY WHAT PROMPTED YOU TO PICK UP THIS FINE READING MATERIAL BUT, BEFORE TIME PRESSES ON AND BLOOD STARTS SQUIRTING, I THOUGHT I'D MAKE SURE YOU WERE UP TO DATE.
THIS IS THE STORY OF TWO MERCENARY MONSTER KILLERS.
ONE OF THEM IS A DWARF WITH A BEARD. THE OTHER IS NOT.
THEIR TROUBLES STARTED IN THE TOWN OF MUDWICH, A RUNDOWN LITTLE BURG. I MEAN, C'MON, IT'S GOT THE WORD "MUD" IN THERE!
CHANCELLOR KENBY, A VISITING NOBLE, WAS ASSASSINATED BY AN ARCHER'S ARROW. LOVELY, AIN'T IT?
OUR TWO BOYS FAILED TO CATCH THE KILLER BUT OFFERED TO GET KENBY'S BODY BACK FROM THE LOCAL CONSTABULARIES WHO WERE HOLDING ON TO IT SEMI-UNJUSTLY.
BEFORE THEY COULD, THE CORPSE WAS STOLEN BY GRAVE ROBBER MINIONS OF A DEATH CULT RUN BY A NECROMANCER NAMED PORDACIO.
OUR MERC BOYS TRACKED 'EM DOWN AND, AFTER A SMALL DETOUR WITH GOBLINS AND A POT OF POISON, THEY DISCOVERED THAT THE NECROMANCER WAS BUILDING AN UNDEAD ARMY.
THE DWARF WAS CAPTURED BUT, INSTEAD OF BEING SACRIFICED AND TURNED INTO ONE OF THE SHAMBLING DEAD, HIS LEG WAS ACCIDENTLY STABBED AND GIVEN A MIND OF ITS OWN.
YOU SHOULDN'T RUN WITH SHARP STUFF, FOLKS.

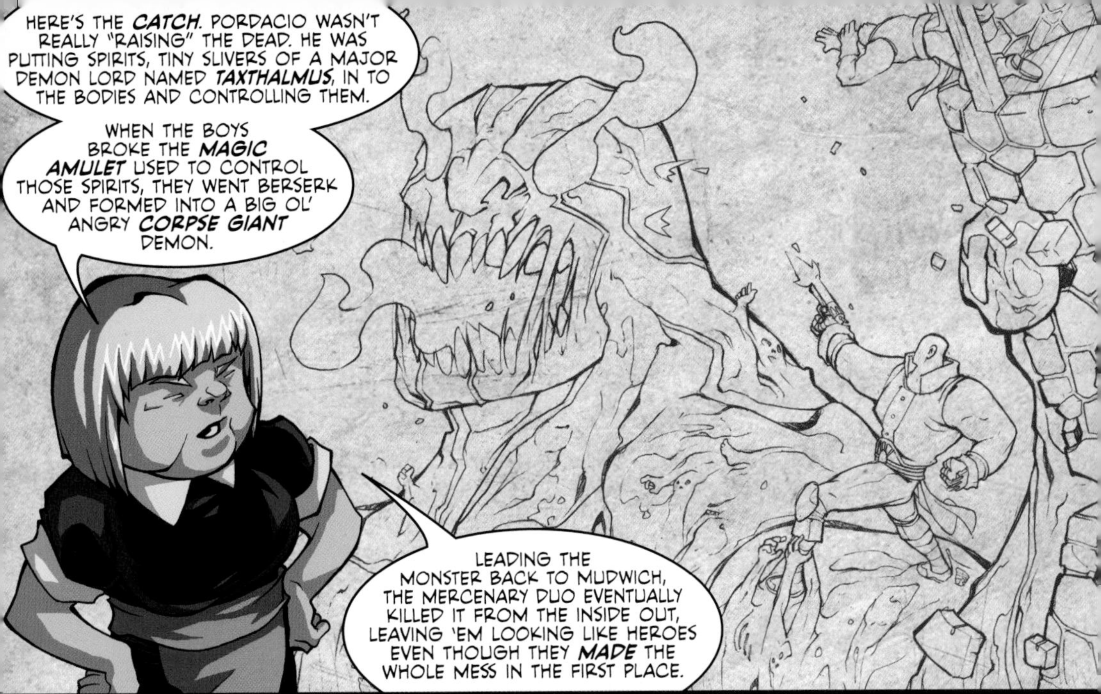
HERE'S THE CATCH. PORDACIO WASN'T REALLY "RAISING" THE DEAD. HE WAS PUTTING SPIRITS, TINY SLIVERS OF A MAJOR DEMON LORD NAMED TAXTHALMUS, IN TO THE BODIES AND CONTROLLING THEM.
WHEN THE BOYS BROKE THE MAGIC AMULET USED TO CONTROL THOSE SPIRITS, THEY WENT BERSERK AND FORMED INTO A BIG OL' ANGRY CORPSE GIANT DEMON.
LEADING THE MONSTER BACK TO MUDWICH, THE MERCENARY DUO EVENTUALLY KILLED IT FROM THE INSIDE OUT, LEAVING 'EM LOOKING LIKE HEROES EVEN THOUGH THEY MADE THE WHOLE MESS IN THE FIRST PLACE.

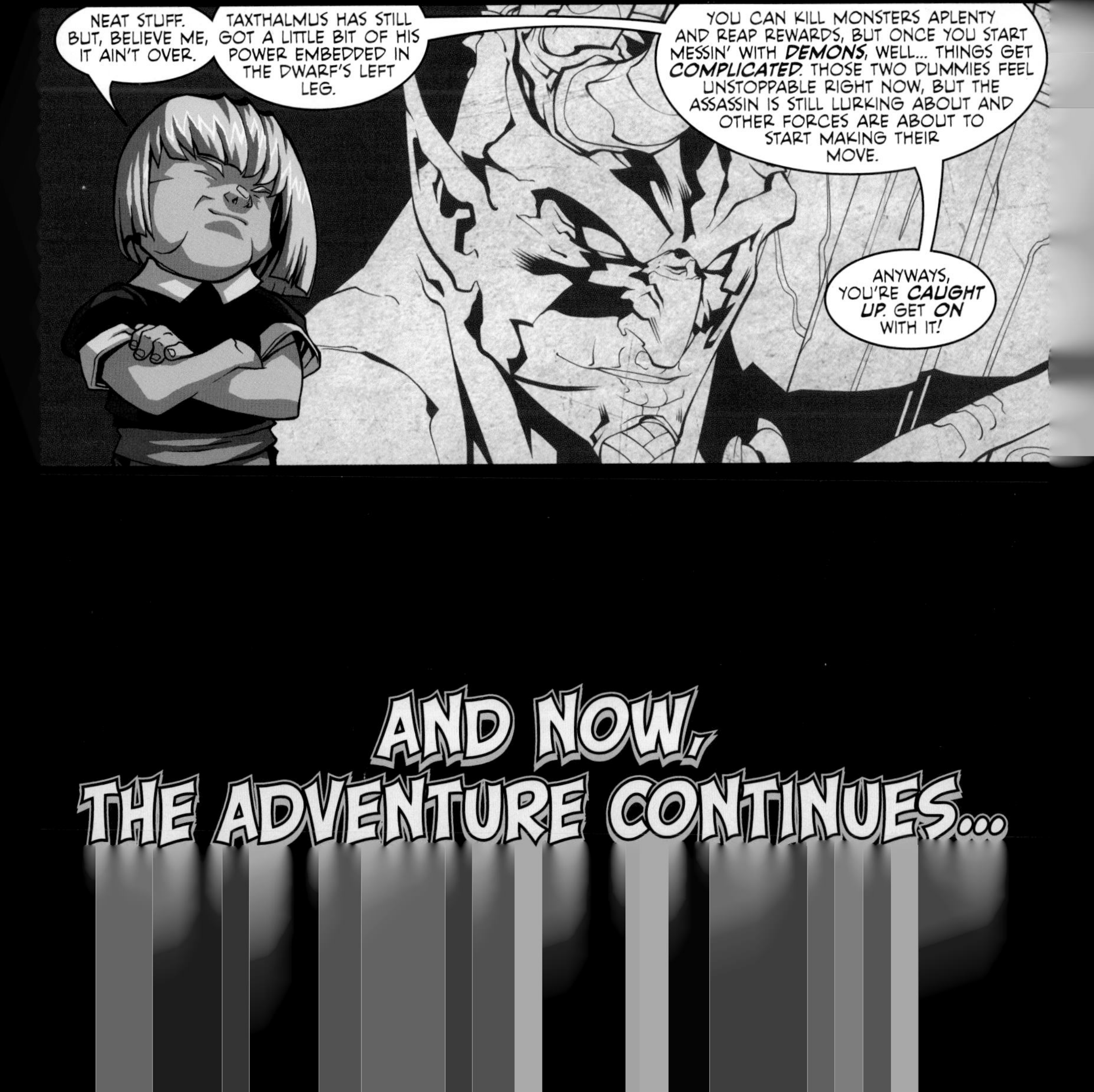
NEAT STUFF. BUT, BELIEVE ME, IT AIN'T OVER.
TAXTHALMUS HAS STILL GOT A LITTLE BIT OF HIS POWER EMBEDDED IN THE DWARF'S LEFT LEG.
YOU CAN KILL MONSTERS APLENTY AND REAP REWARDS, BUT ONCE YOU START MESSIN' WITH DEMONS, WELL... THINGS GET COMPLICATED. THOSE TWO DUMMIES FEEL UNSTOPPABLE RIGHT NOW, BUT THE ASSASSIN IS STILL LURKING ABOUT AND OTHER FORCES ARE ABOUT TO START MAKING THEIR MOVE.
ANYWAYS, YOU'RE CAUGHT UP. GET ON WITH IT!

AND NOW, THE ADVENTURE CONTINUES...

CHAPTER ONE

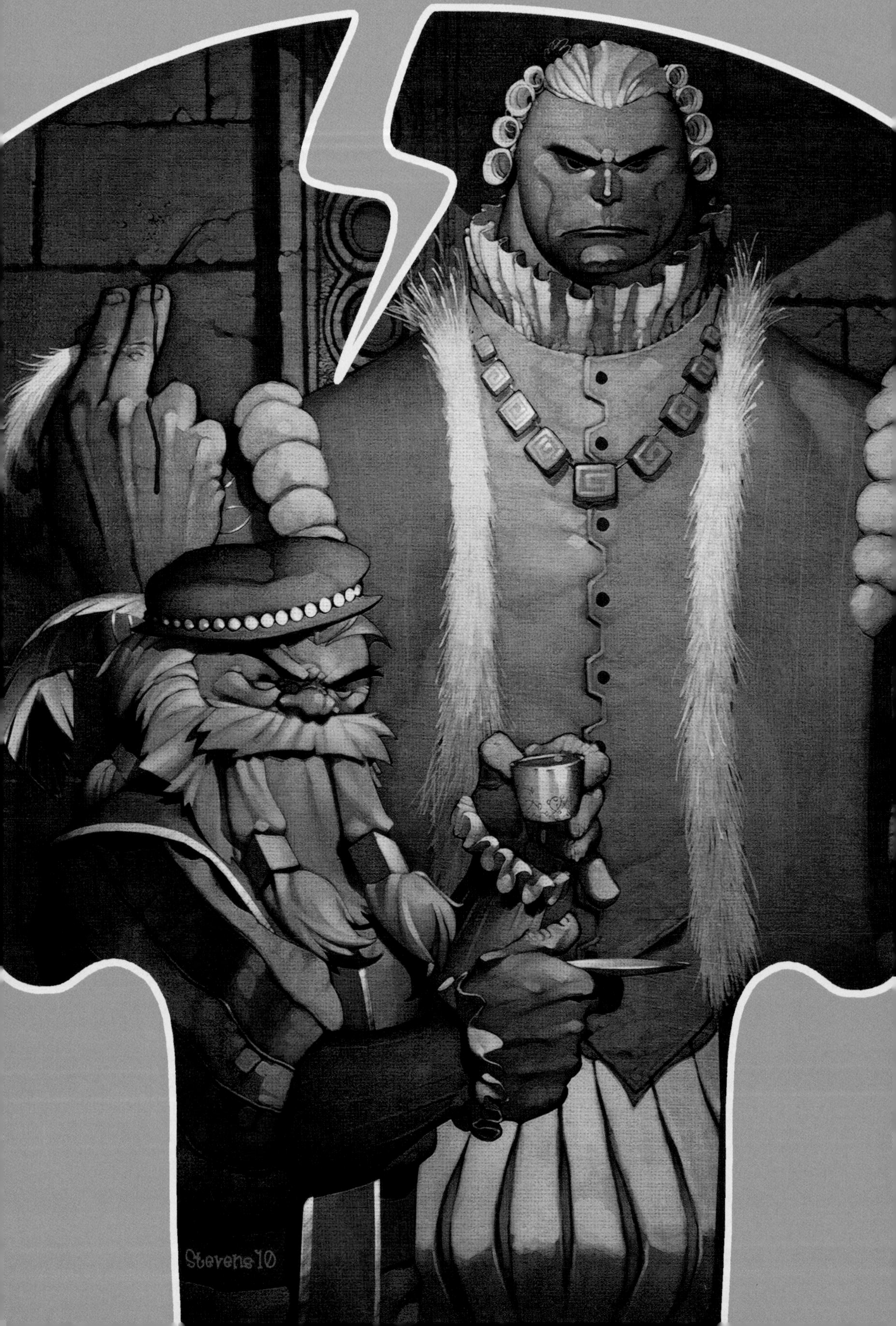
Stevens '10

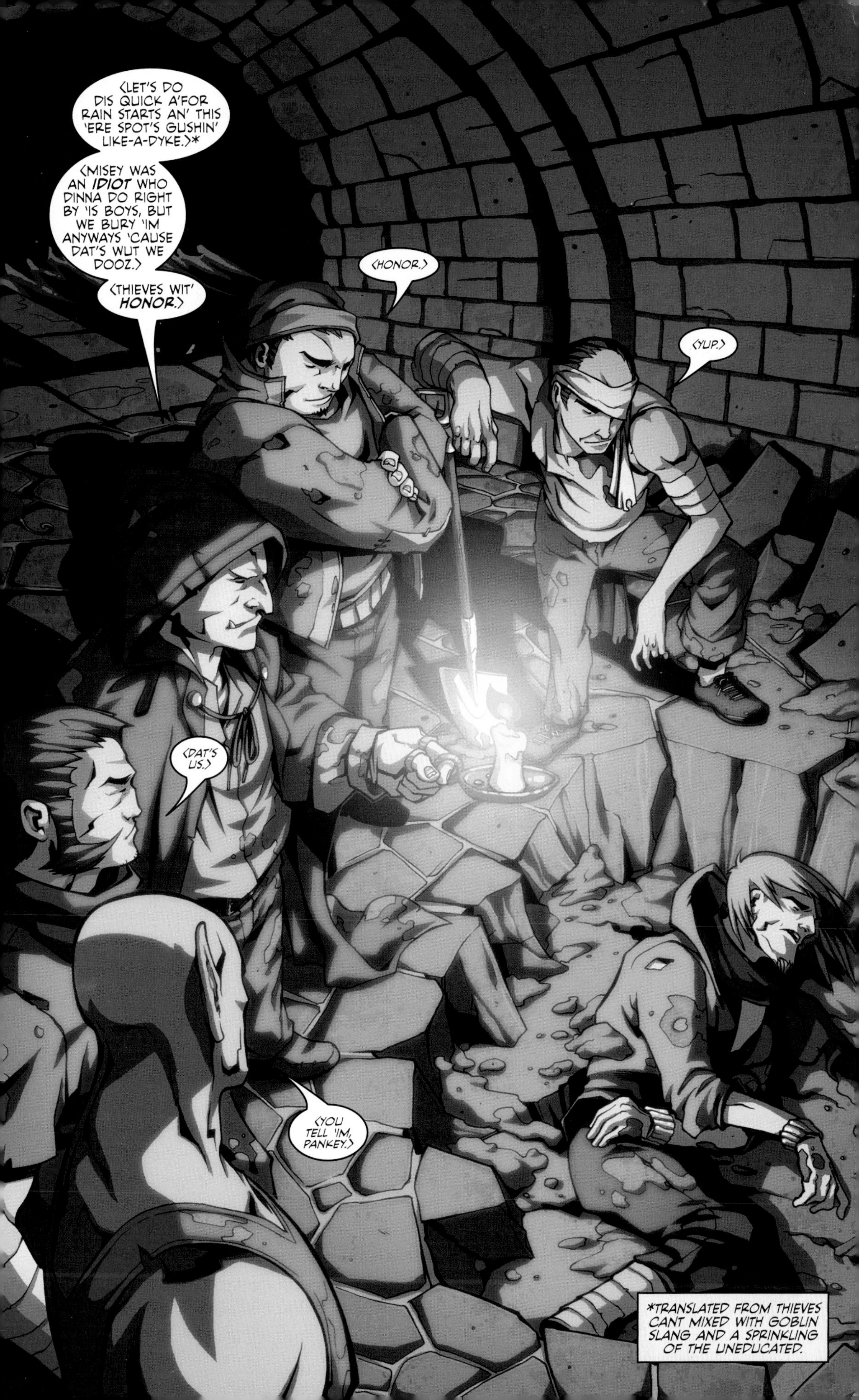
<LET'S DO DIS QUICK A'FOR RAIN STARTS AN' THIS 'ERE SPOT'S GUSHIN' LIKE-A-DYKE.>*
<MISEY WAS AN *IDIOT* WHO DINNA DO RIGHT BY 'IS BOYS, BUT WE BURY 'IM ANYWAYS 'CAUSE DAT'S WUT WE DOOZ.>
<THIEVES WIT' *HONOR*.>
<HONOR.>
<YUP.>
<DAT'S US.>
<YOU TELL 'IM, PANKEY.>
*TRANSLATED FROM THIEVES CANT MIXED WITH GOBLIN SLANG AND A SPRINKLING OF THE UNEDUCATED.

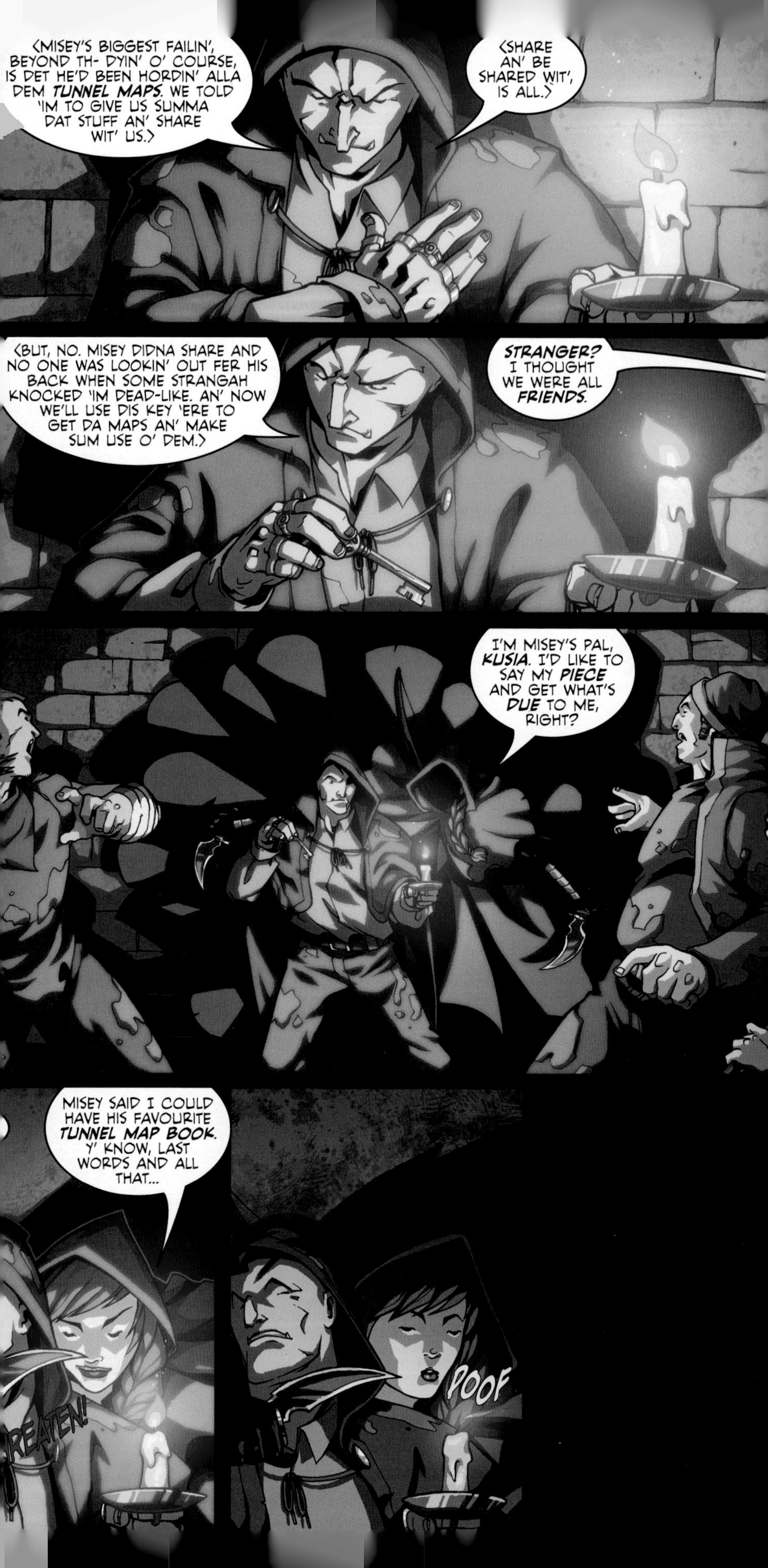
<MISEY'S BIGGEST FAILIN', BEYOND TH- DYIN' O' COURSE, IS DET HE'D BEEN HORDIN' ALLA DEM TUNNEL MAPS. WE TOLD 'IM TO GIVE US SUMMA DAT STUFF AN' SHARE WIT' US.>
<SHARE AN' BE SHARED WIT', IS ALL.>
<BUT, NO. MISEY DIDNA SHARE AND NO ONE WAS LOOKIN' OUT FER HIS BACK WHEN SOME STRANGAH KNOCKED 'IM DEAD-LIKE. AN' NOW WE'LL USE DIS KEY 'ERE TO GET DA MAPS AN' MAKE SUM USE O' DEM.>
STRANGER? I THOUGHT WE WERE ALL FRIENDS.
I'M MISEY'S PAL, KUSIA. I'D LIKE TO SAY MY PIECE AND GET WHAT'S DUE TO ME, RIGHT?
MISEY SAID I COULD HAVE HIS FAVOURITE TUNNEL MAP BOOK. Y' KNOW, LAST WORDS AND ALL THAT...
POOF

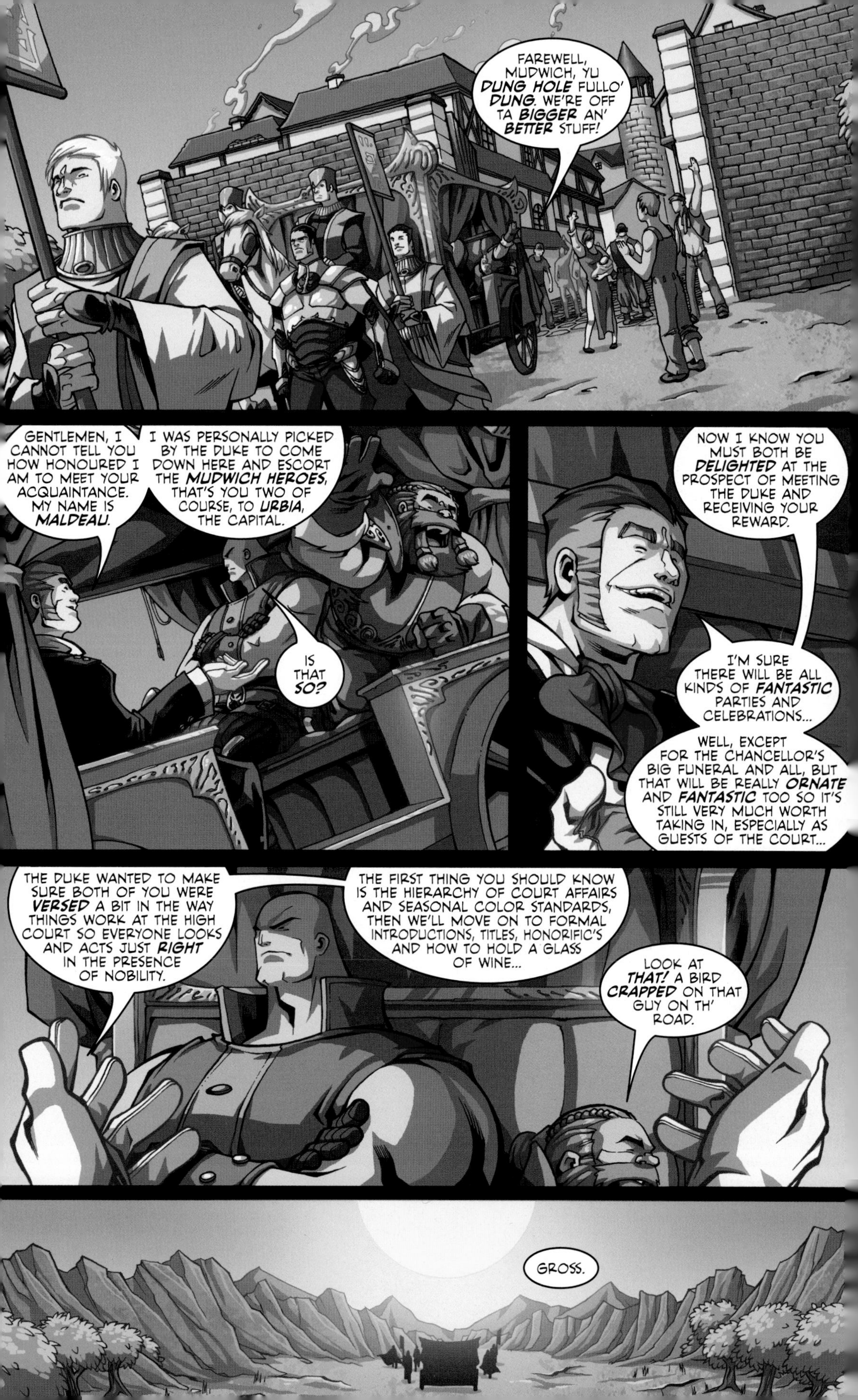
FAREWELL, MUDWICH, YU DUNG HOLE FULLO' DUNG. WE'RE OFF TA BIGGER AN' BETTER STUFF!
GENTLEMEN, I CANNOT TELL YOU HOW HONOURED I AM TO MEET YOUR ACQUAINTANCE. MY NAME IS MALDEAU.
I WAS PERSONALLY PICKED BY THE DUKE TO COME DOWN HERE AND ESCORT THE MUDWICH HEROES, THAT'S YOU TWO OF COURSE, TO URBIA, THE CAPITAL.
IS THAT SO?
NOW I KNOW YOU MUST BOTH BE DELIGHTED AT THE PROSPECT OF MEETING THE DUKE AND RECEIVING YOUR REWARD.
I'M SURE THERE WILL BE ALL KINDS OF FANTASTIC PARTIES AND CELEBRATIONS...
WELL, EXCEPT FOR THE CHANCELLOR'S BIG FUNERAL AND ALL, BUT THAT WILL BE REALLY ORNATE AND FANTASTIC TOO SO IT'S STILL VERY MUCH WORTH TAKING IN, ESPECIALLY AS GUESTS OF THE COURT...
THE DUKE WANTED TO MAKE SURE BOTH OF YOU WERE VERSED A BIT IN THE WAY THINGS WORK AT THE HIGH COURT SO EVERYONE LOOKS AND ACTS JUST RIGHT IN THE PRESENCE OF NOBILITY.
THE FIRST THING YOU SHOULD KNOW IS THE HIERARCHY OF COURT AFFAIRS AND SEASONAL COLOR STANDARDS, THEN WE'LL MOVE ON TO FORMAL INTRODUCTIONS, TITLES, HONORIFIC'S AND HOW TO HOLD A GLASS OF WINE...
LOOK AT THAT! A BIRD CRAPPED ON THAT GUY ON TH' ROAD.
GROSS.

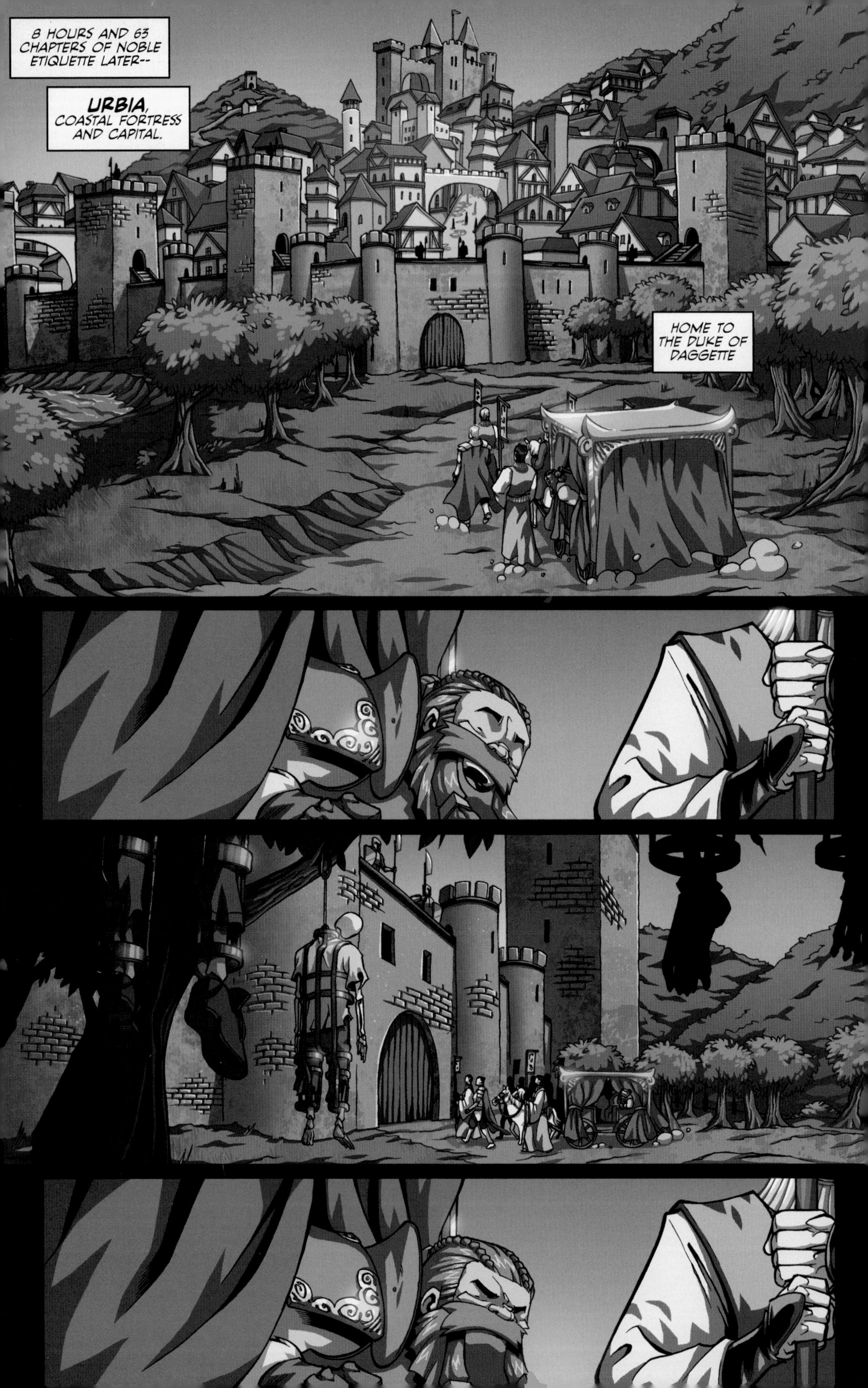
8 HOURS AND 63 CHAPTERS OF NOBLE ETIQUETTE LATER--
URBIA, COASTAL FORTRESS AND CAPITAL.
HOME TO THE DUKE OF DAGGETTE

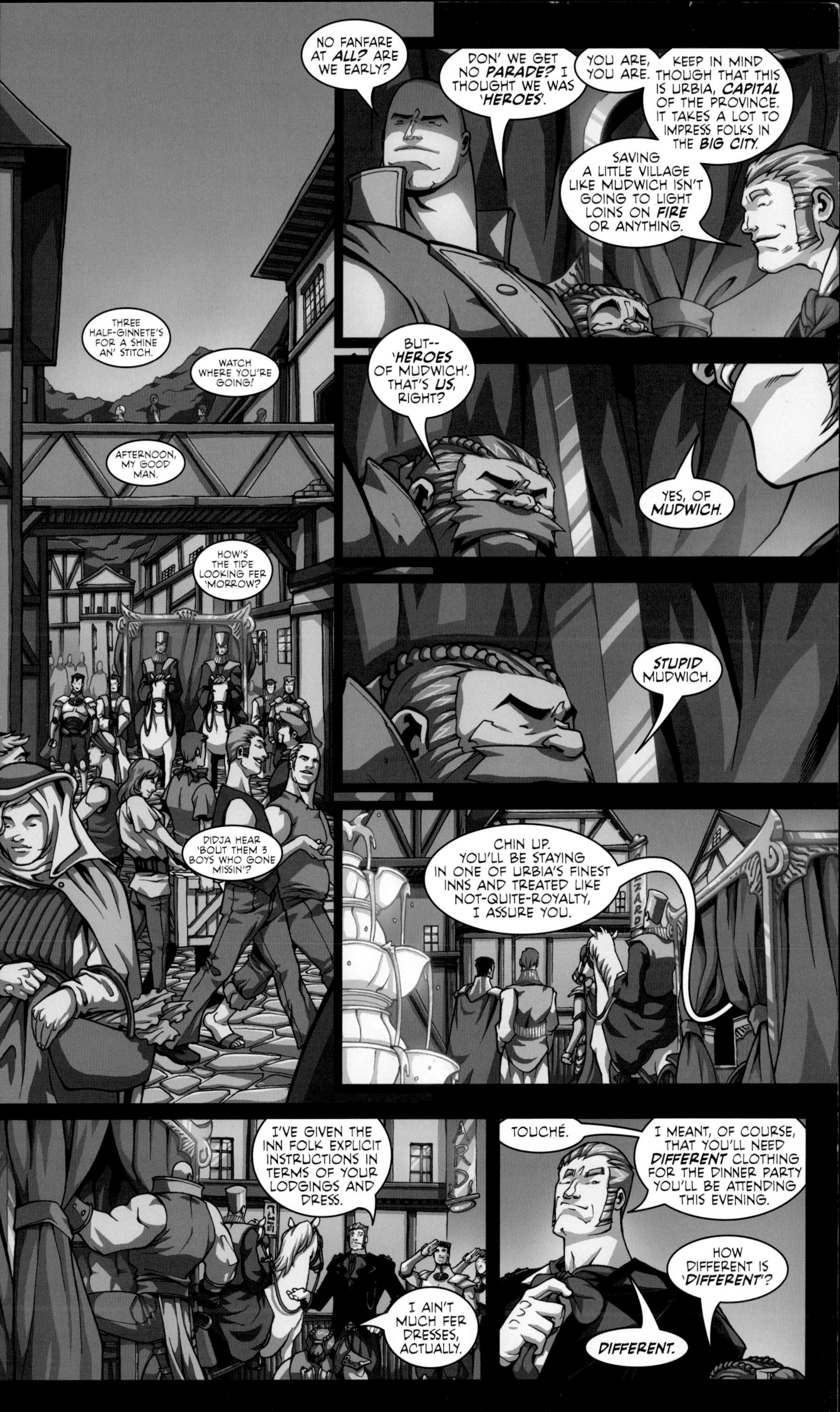
NO FANFARE AT ALL? ARE WE EARLY?
DON' WE GET NO PARADE? I THOUGHT WE WAS 'HEROES'.
YOU ARE, YOU ARE.
KEEP IN MIND THOUGH THAT THIS IS URBIA, CAPITAL OF THE PROVINCE. IT TAKES A LOT TO IMPRESS FOLKS IN THE BIG CITY.
SAVING A LITTLE VILLAGE LIKE MUDWICH ISN'T GOING TO LIGHT LOINS ON FIRE OR ANYTHING.
THREE HALF-GINNETE'S FOR A SHINE AN' STITCH.
WATCH WHERE YOU'RE GOING!
AFTERNOON, MY GOOD MAN.
HOW'S THE TIDE LOOKING FER 'MORROW?
DIDJA HEAR 'BOUT THEM 3 BOYS WHO GONE MISSIN'?
BUT-- 'HEROES OF MUDWICH'. THAT'S US, RIGHT?
YES, OF MUDWICH.
STUPID MUDWICH.
CHIN UP. YOU'LL BE STAYING IN ONE OF URBIA'S FINEST INNS AND TREATED LIKE NOT-QUITE-ROYALTY, I ASSURE YOU.
I'VE GIVEN THE INN FOLK EXPLICIT INSTRUCTIONS IN TERMS OF YOUR LODGINGS AND DRESS.
I AIN'T MUCH FER DRESSES, ACTUALLY.
TOUCHÉ.
I MEANT, OF COURSE, THAT YOU'LL NEED DIFFERENT CLOTHING FOR THE DINNER PARTY YOU'LL BE ATTENDING THIS EVENING.
HOW DIFFERENT IS 'DIFFERENT'?
DIFFERENT.

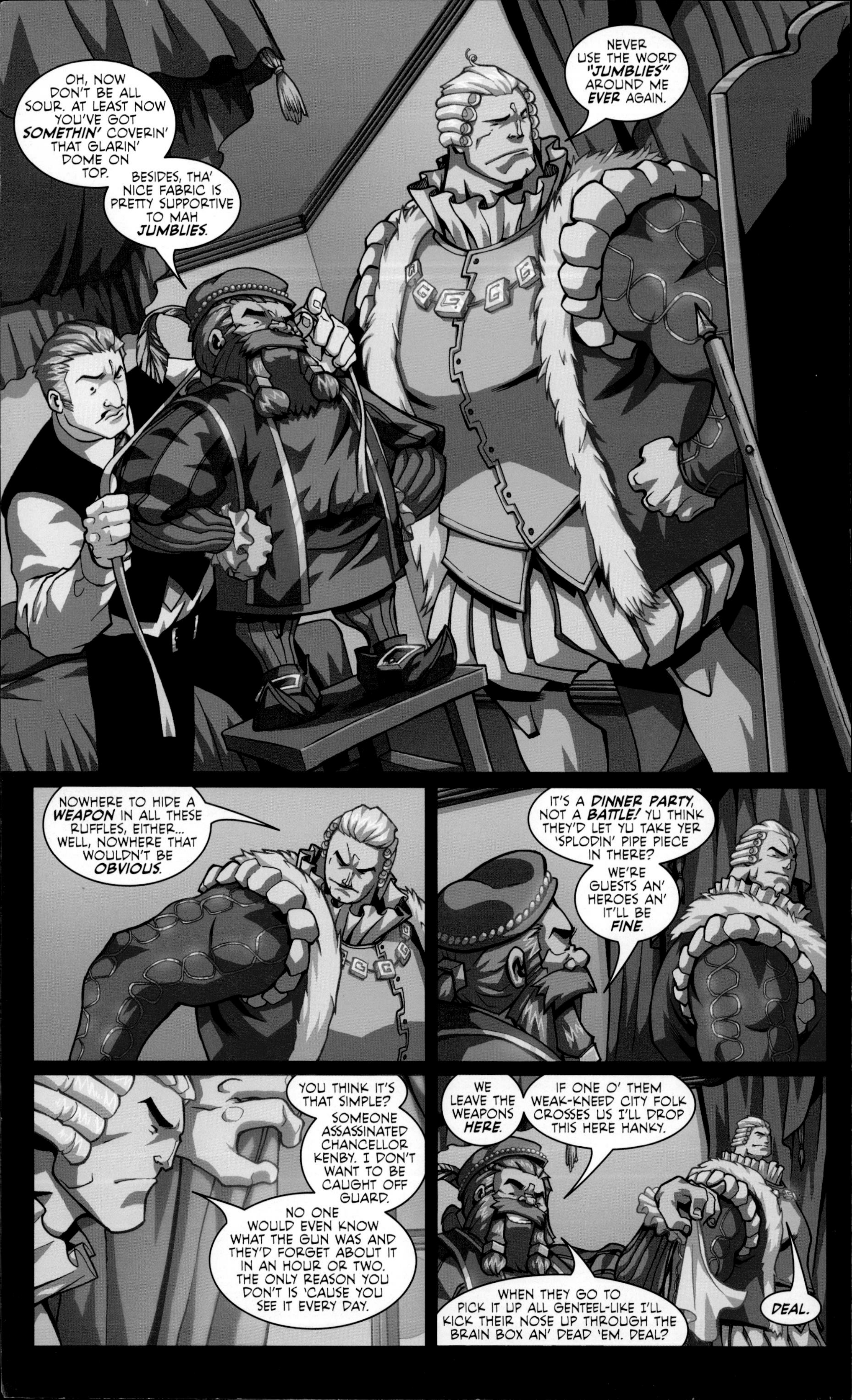

OH, NOW DON'T BE ALL SOUR. AT LEAST NOW YOU'VE GOT SOMETHIN' COVERIN' THAT GLARIN' DOME ON TOP.
BESIDES, THA' NICE FABRIC IS PRETTY SUPPORTIVE TO MAH JUMBLIES.
NEVER USE THE WORD "JUMBLIES" AROUND ME EVER AGAIN.
NOWHERE TO HIDE A WEAPON IN ALL THESE RUFFLES, EITHER... WELL, NOWHERE THAT WOULDN'T BE OBVIOUS.
IT'S A DINNER PARTY, NOT A BATTLE! YU THINK THEY'D LET YU TAKE YER 'SPLODIN' PIPE PIECE IN THERE?
WE'RE GUESTS AN' HEROES AN' IT'LL BE FINE.
YOU THINK IT'S THAT SIMPLE?
SOMEONE ASSASSINATED CHANCELLOR KENBY. I DON'T WANT TO BE CAUGHT OFF GUARD.
NO ONE WOULD EVEN KNOW WHAT THE GUN WAS AND THEY'D FORGET ABOUT IT IN AN HOUR OR TWO. THE ONLY REASON YOU DON'T IS 'CAUSE YOU SEE IT EVERY DAY.
WE LEAVE THE WEAPONS HERE.
IF ONE O' THEM WEAK-KNEED CITY FOLK CROSSES US I'LL DROP THIS HERE HANKY.
WHEN THEY GO TO PICK IT UP ALL GENTEEL-LIKE I'LL KICK THEIR NOSE UP THROUGH THE BRAIN BOX AN' DEAD 'EM. DEAL?
DEAL.

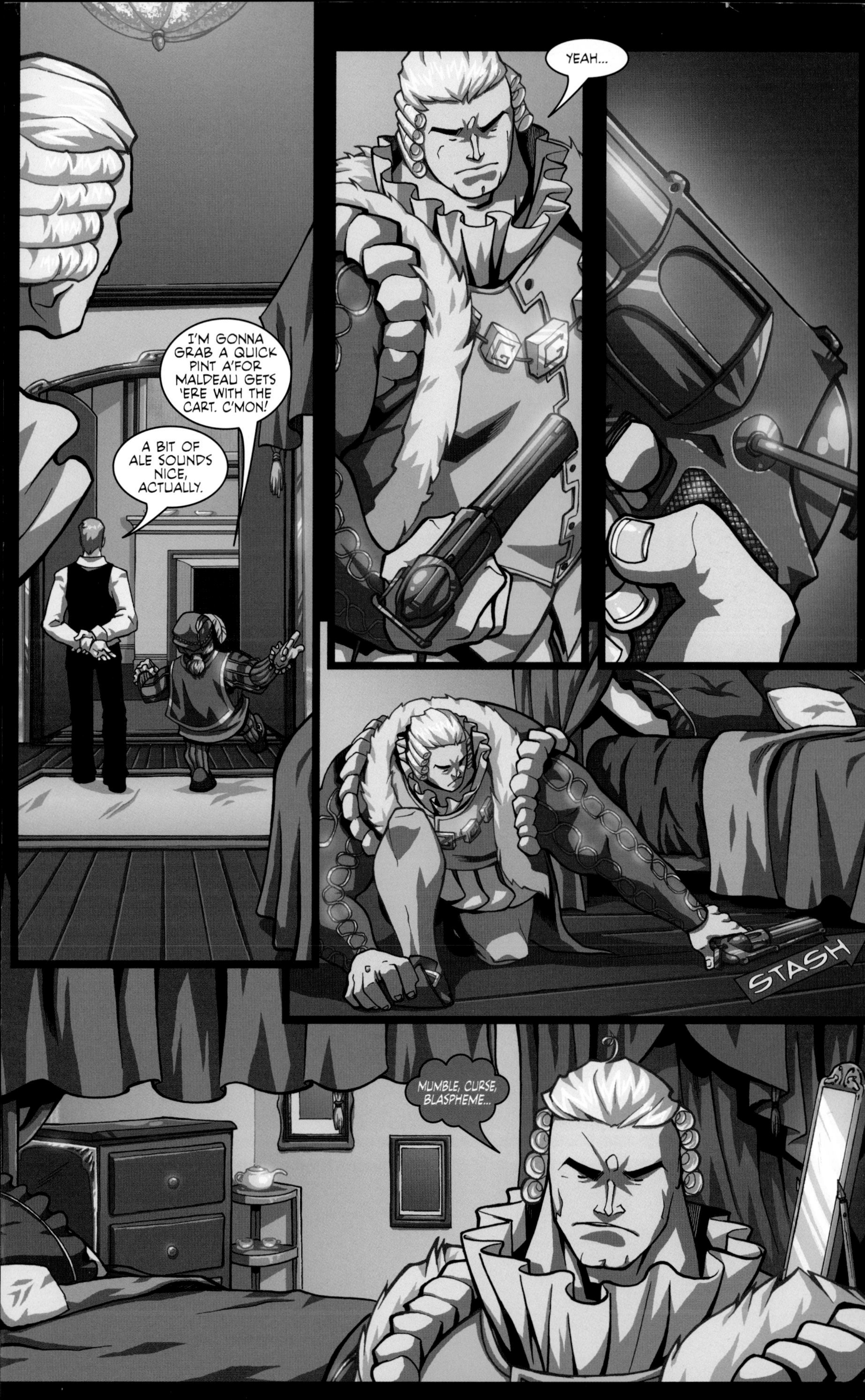

I'M GONNA GRAB A QUICK PINT A'FOR MALDEAU GETS 'ERE WITH THE CART. C'MON!
A BIT OF ALE SOUNDS NICE, ACTUALLY.
YEAH...
STASH
MUMBLE, CURSE, BLASPHEME...

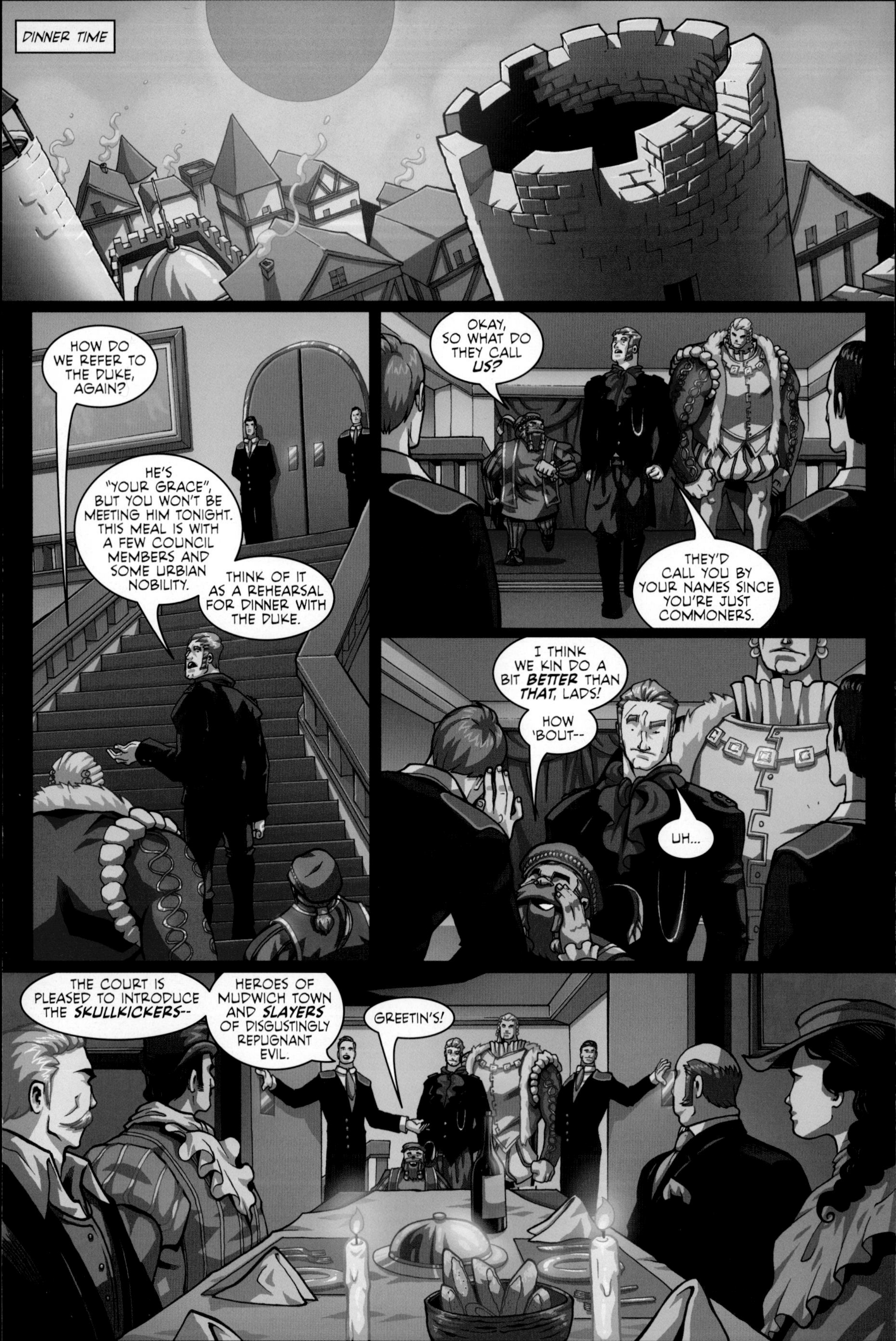
DINNER TIME
HOW DO WE REFER TO THE DUKE, AGAIN?
HE'S "YOUR GRACE", BUT YOU WON'T BE MEETING HIM TONIGHT. THIS MEAL IS WITH A FEW COUNCIL MEMBERS AND SOME URBIAN NOBILITY.
THINK OF IT AS A REHEARSAL FOR DINNER WITH THE DUKE.
OKAY, SO WHAT DO THEY CALL US?
THEY'D CALL YOU BY YOUR NAMES SINCE YOU'RE JUST COMMONERS.
I THINK WE KIN DO A BIT BETTER THAN THAT, LADS!
HOW 'BOUT--
UH...
THE COURT IS PLEASED TO INTRODUCE THE SKULLKICKERS--
HEROES OF MUDWICH TOWN AND SLAYERS OF DISGUSTINGLY REPUGNANT EVIL.
GREETIN'S!

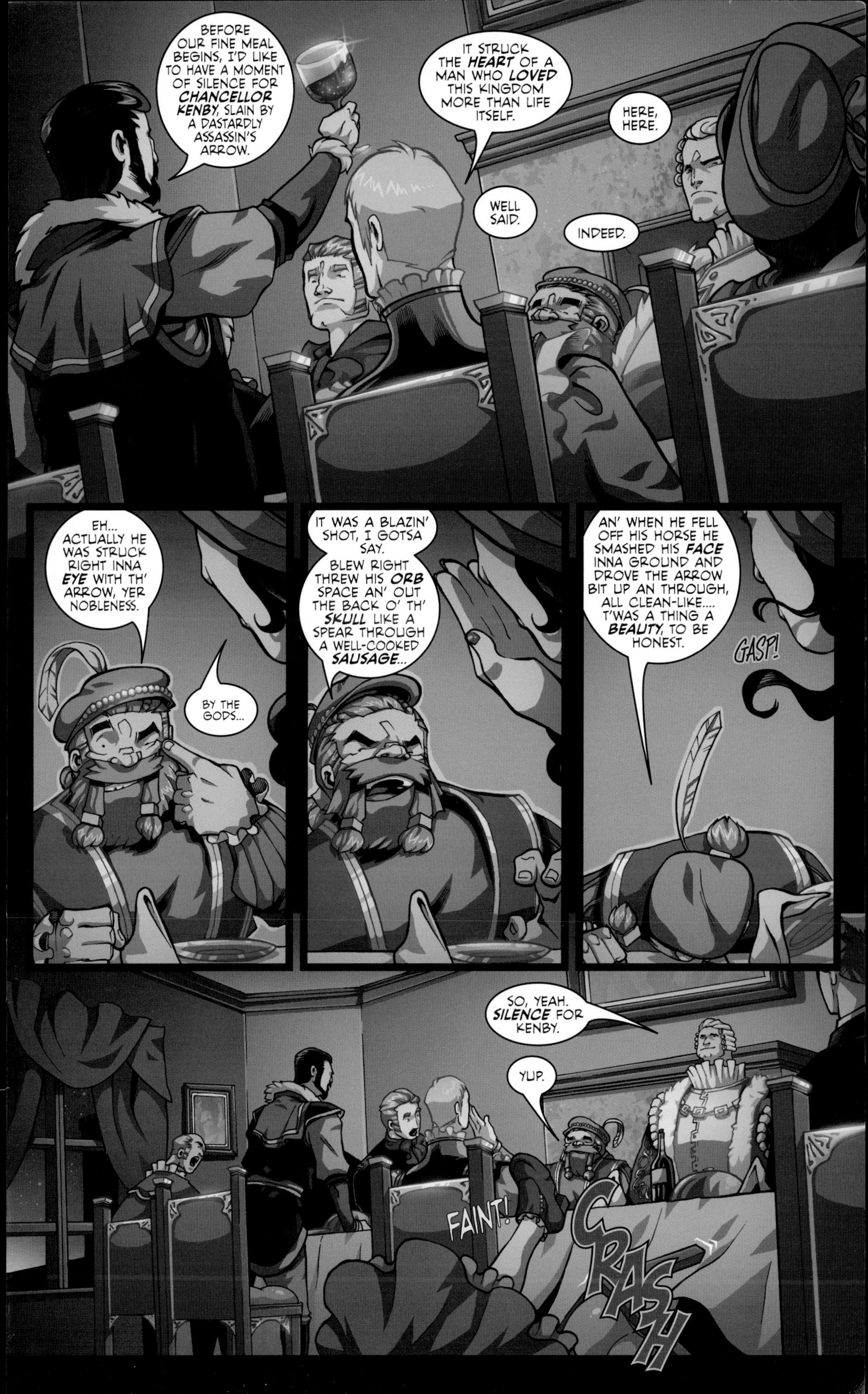
BEFORE OUR FINE MEAL BEGINS, I'D LIKE TO HAVE A MOMENT OF SILENCE FOR CHANCELLOR KENBY, SLAIN BY A DASTARDLY ASSASSIN'S ARROW.
IT STRUCK THE HEART OF A MAN WHO LOVED THIS KINGDOM MORE THAN LIFE ITSELF.
HERE, HERE.
WELL SAID.
INDEED.
EH... ACTUALLY HE WAS STRUCK RIGHT INNA EYE WITH TH' ARROW, YER NOBLENESS.
BY THE GODS...
IT WAS A BLAZIN' SHOT, I GOTSA SAY.
BLEW RIGHT THREW HIS ORB SPACE AN' OUT THE BACK O' TH' SKULL LIKE A SPEAR THROUGH A WELL-COOKED SAUSAGE...
AN' WHEN HE FELL OFF HIS HORSE HE SMASHED HIS FACE INNA GROUND AND DROVE THE ARROW BIT UP AN THROUGH, ALL CLEAN-LIKE.... T'WAS A THING A BEAUTY, TO BE HONEST.
GASP!
SO, YEAH. SILENCE FOR KENBY.
YUP.
FAINT!
CRASH

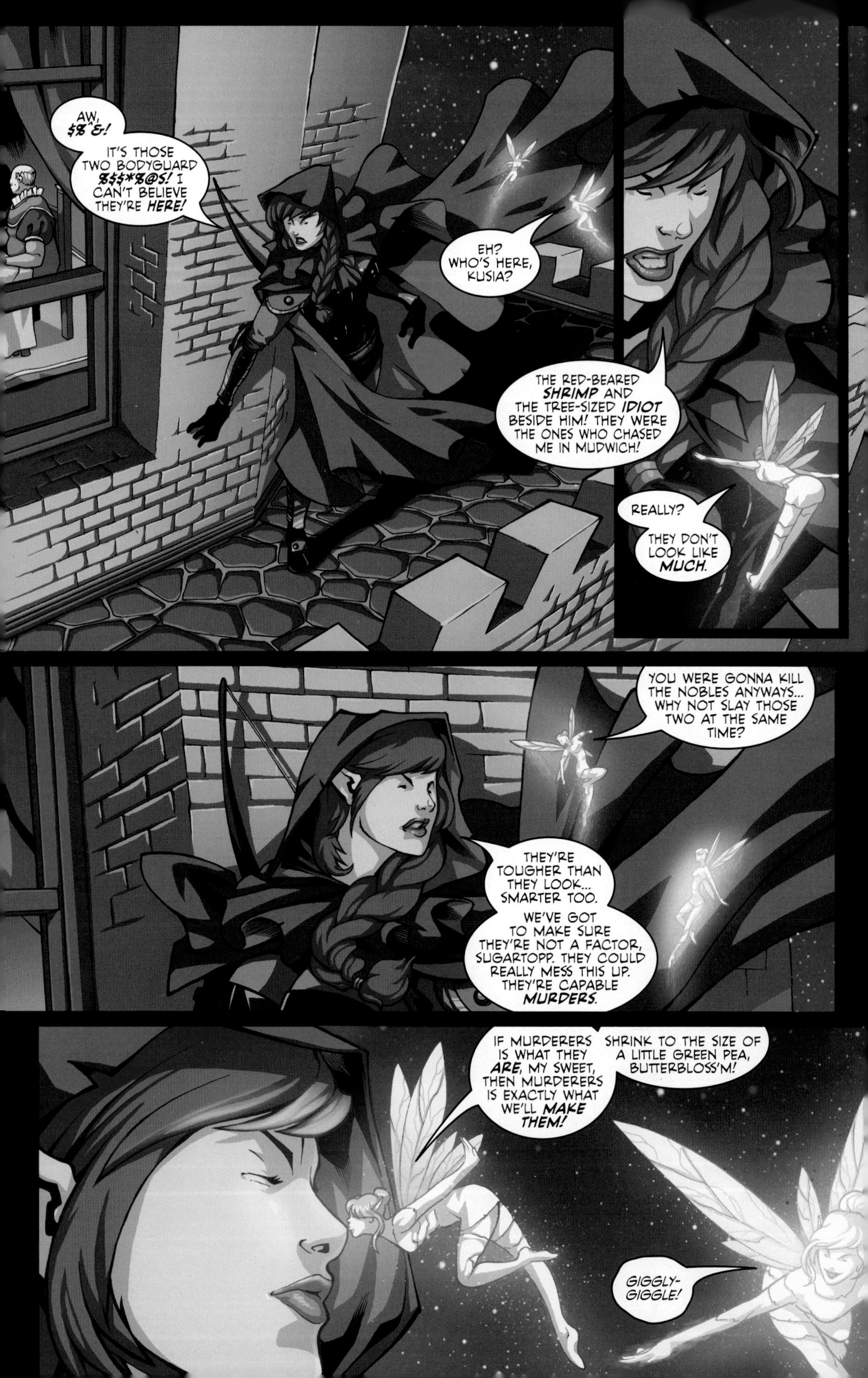

AW, $%^&!
IT'S THOSE TWO BODYGUARD %$$*%@S! I CAN'T BELIEVE THEY'RE HERE!
EH? WHO'S HERE, KUSIA?
THE RED-BEARED SHRIMP AND THE TREE-SIZED IDIOT BESIDE HIM! THEY WERE THE ONES WHO CHASED ME IN MUDWICH!
REALLY?
THEY DON'T LOOK LIKE MUCH.
YOU WERE GONNA KILL THE NOBLES ANYWAYS... WHY NOT SLAY THOSE TWO AT THE SAME TIME?
THEY'RE TOUGHER THAN THEY LOOK... SMARTER TOO.
WE'VE GOT TO MAKE SURE THEY'RE NOT A FACTOR, SUGARTOPP. THEY COULD REALLY MESS THIS UP. THEY'RE CAPABLE MURDERS.
IF MURDERERS IS WHAT THEY ARE, MY SWEET, THEN MURDERERS IS EXACTLY WHAT WE'LL MAKE THEM!
SHRINK TO THE SIZE OF A LITTLE GREEN PEA, BUTTERBLOSS'M!
GIGGLY-GIGGLE!

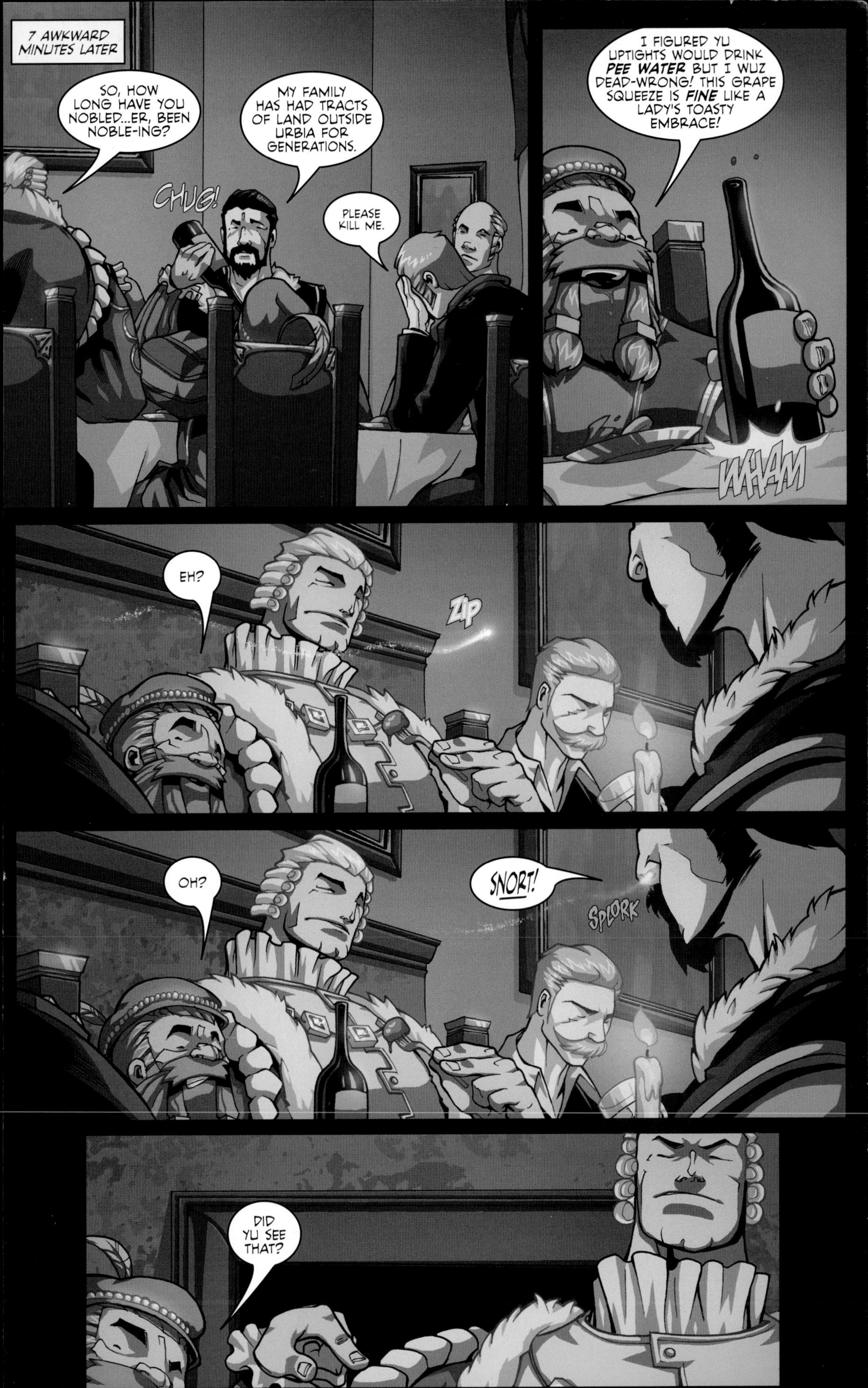
7 AWKWARD MINUTES LATER
SO, HOW LONG HAVE YOU NOBLED...ER, BEEN NOBLE-ING?
CHUG!
MY FAMILY HAS HAD TRACTS OF LAND OUTSIDE URBIA FOR GENERATIONS.
PLEASE KILL ME.
I FIGURED YU UPTIGHTS WOULD DRINK PEE WATER BUT I WUZ DEAD-WRONG! THIS GRAPE SQUEEZE IS FINE LIKE A LADY'S TOASTY EMBRACE!
WHAM
EH?
ZIP
OH?
SNORT!
SPLORK
DID YU SEE THAT?

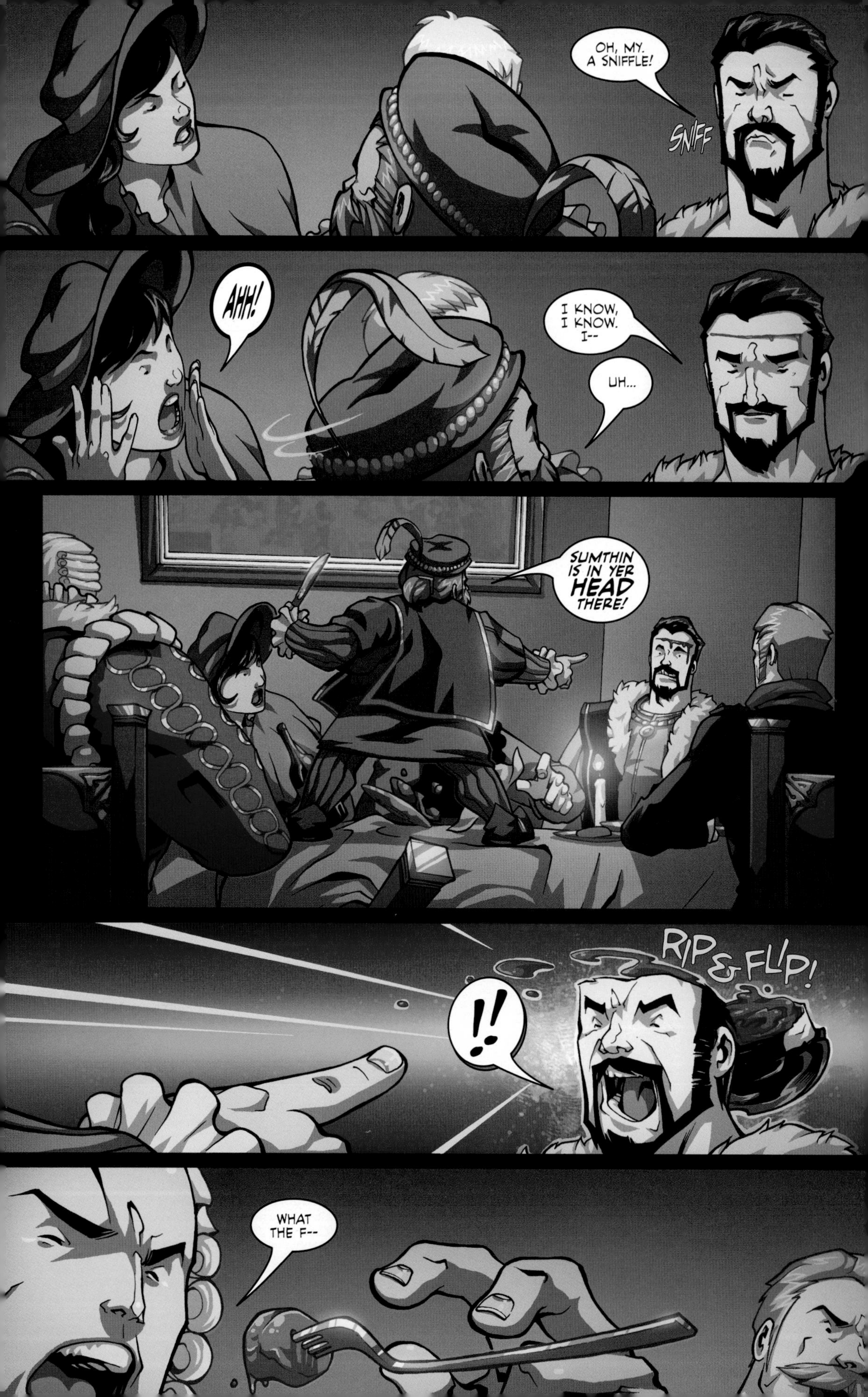
OH, MY. A SNIFFLE!
SNIFF
AHH!
I KNOW, I KNOW. I--
UH...
SUMTHIN IS IN YER HEAD THERE!
RIP & FLIP!
!!
WHAT THE F--

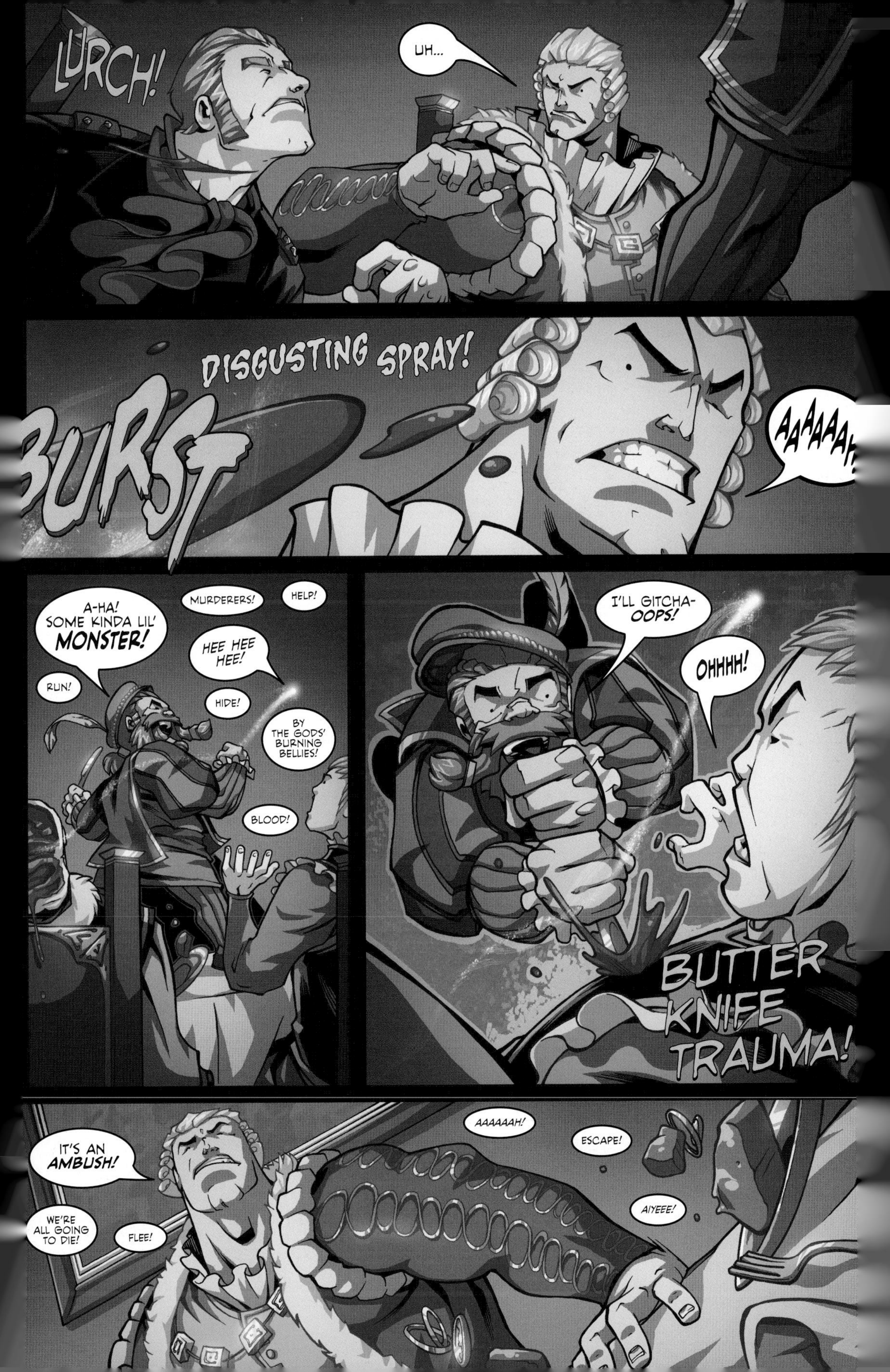
LURCH!
UH...
DISGUSTING SPRAY!
BURST
AAAAAAH!
A-HA! SOME KINDA LIL' MONSTER!
MURDERERS!
HELP!
HEE HEE HEE!
RUN!
HIDE!
BY THE GODS' BURNING BELLIES!
BLOOD!
I'LL GITCHA- OOPS!
OHHHH!
BUTTER KNIFE TRAUMA!
IT'S AN AMBUSH!
AAAAAAH!
ESCAPE!
AIYEEE!
WE'RE ALL GOING TO DIE!
FLEE!

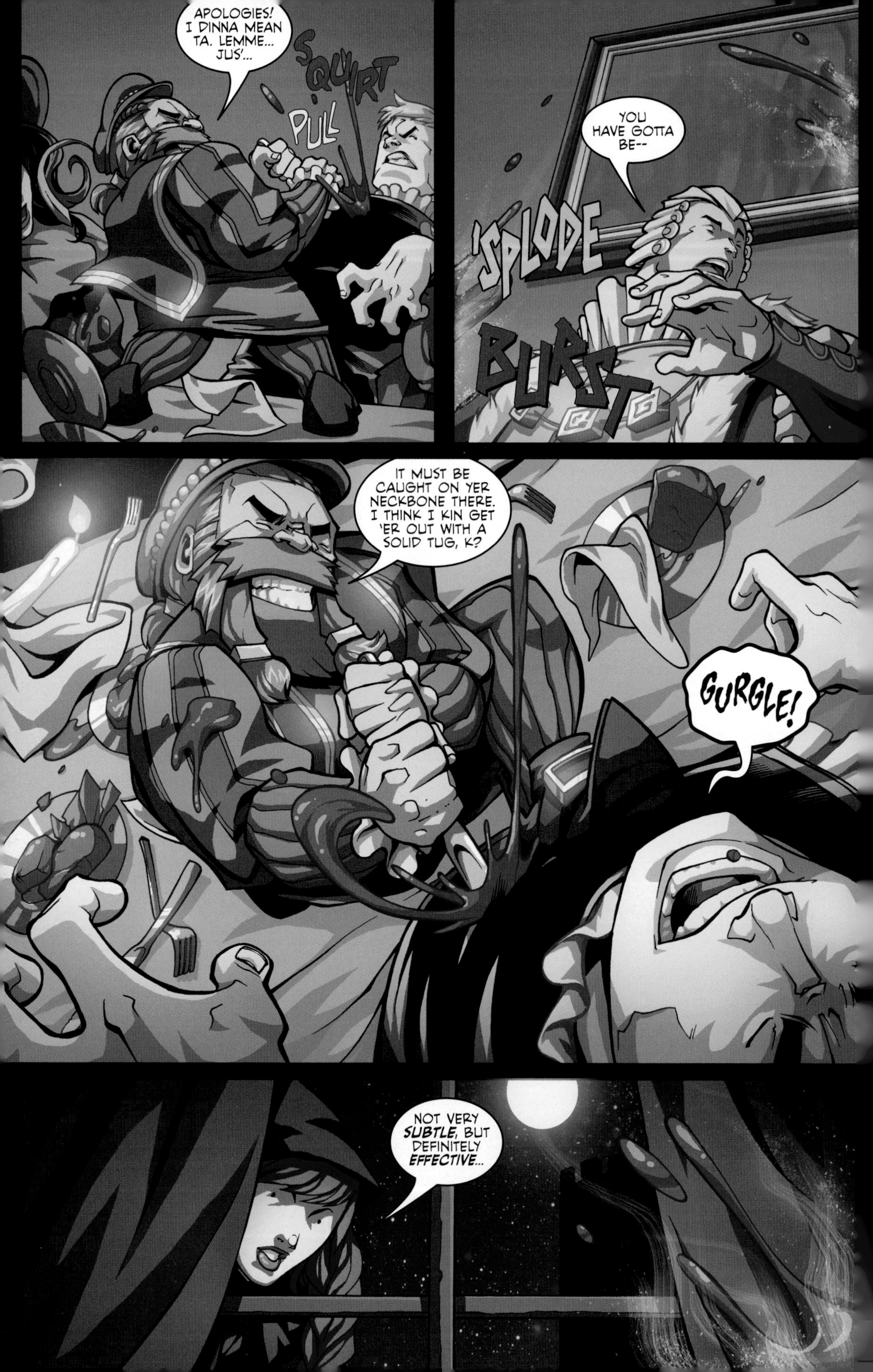
APOLOGIES! I DINNA MEAN TA. LEMME... JUS'...
SQUIRT
PULL
YOU HAVE GOTTA BE--
'SPLODE
BURST
IT MUST BE CAUGHT ON YER NECKBONE THERE. I THINK I KIN GET 'ER OUT WITH A SOLID TUG, K?
GURGLE!
NOT VERY *SUBTLE*, BUT DEFINITELY *EFFECTIVE*...

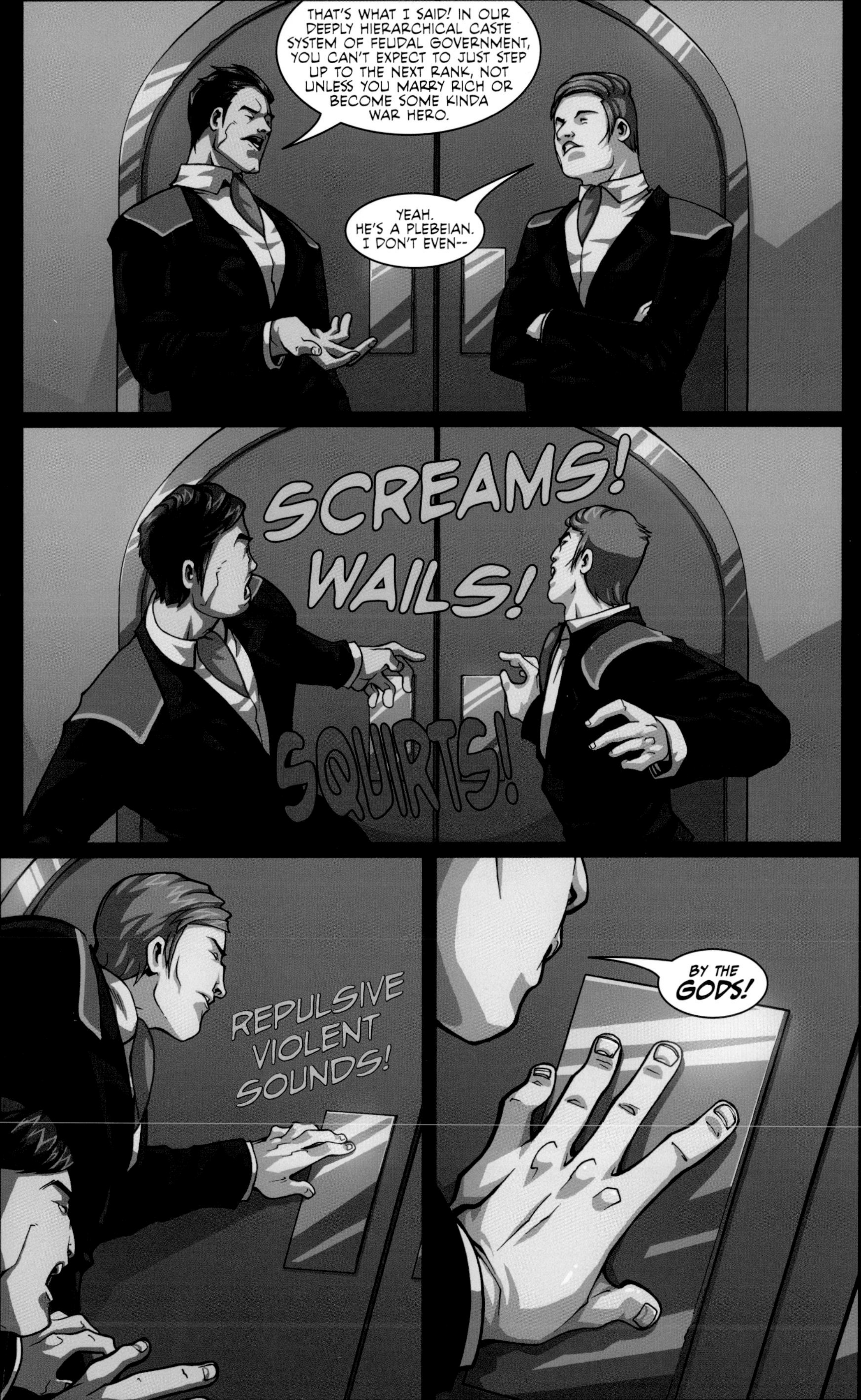
THAT'S WHAT I SAID! IN OUR DEEPLY HIERARCHICAL CASTE SYSTEM OF FEUDAL GOVERNMENT, YOU CAN'T EXPECT TO JUST STEP UP TO THE NEXT RANK, NOT UNLESS YOU MARRY RICH OR BECOME SOME KINDA WAR HERO.
YEAH. HE'S A PLEBEIAN. I DON'T EVEN--
SCREAMS!
WAILS!
SQUIRTS!
REPULSIVE VIOLENT SOUNDS!
BY THE GODS!

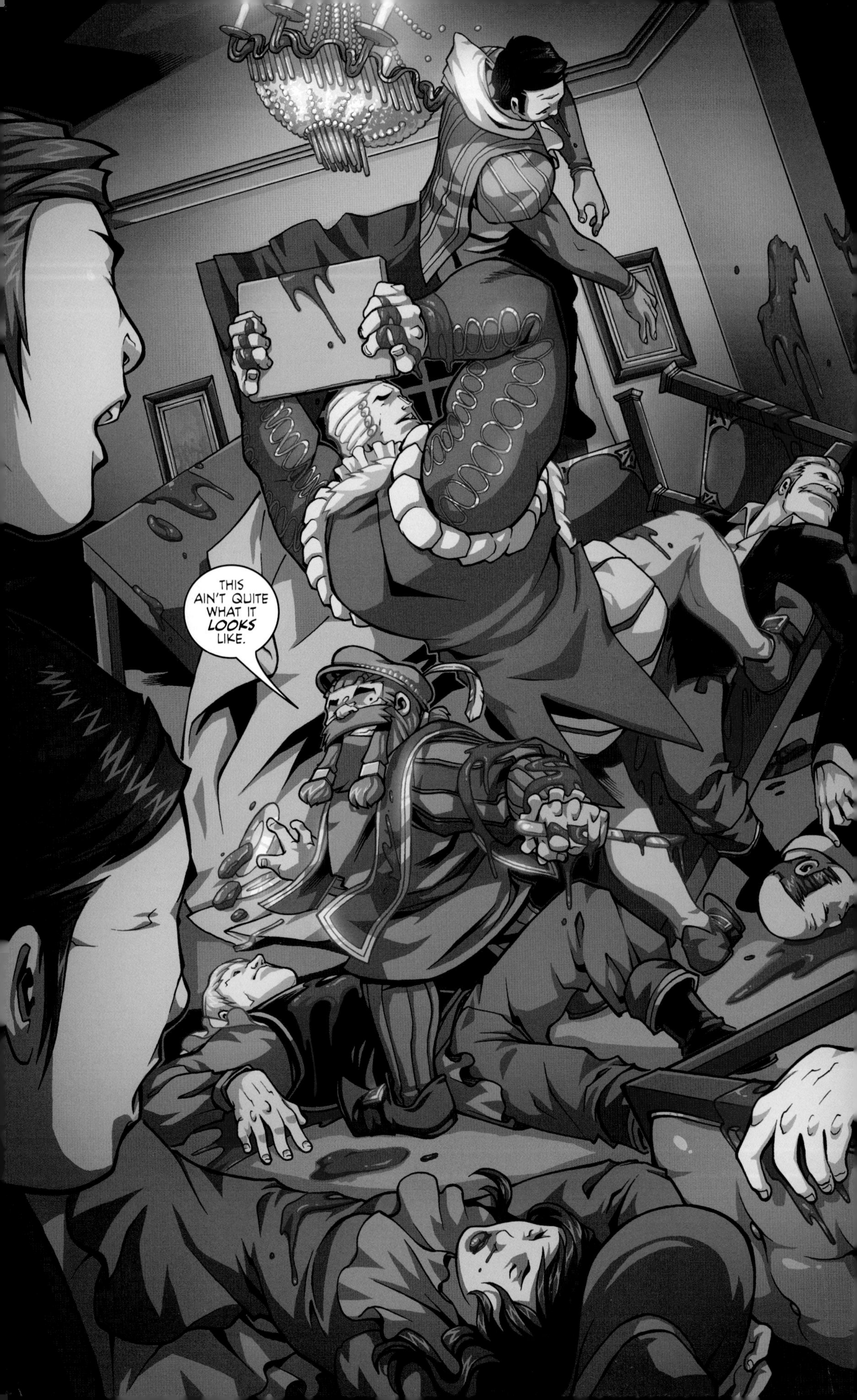
THIS AIN'T QUITE WHAT IT *LOOKS* LIKE.

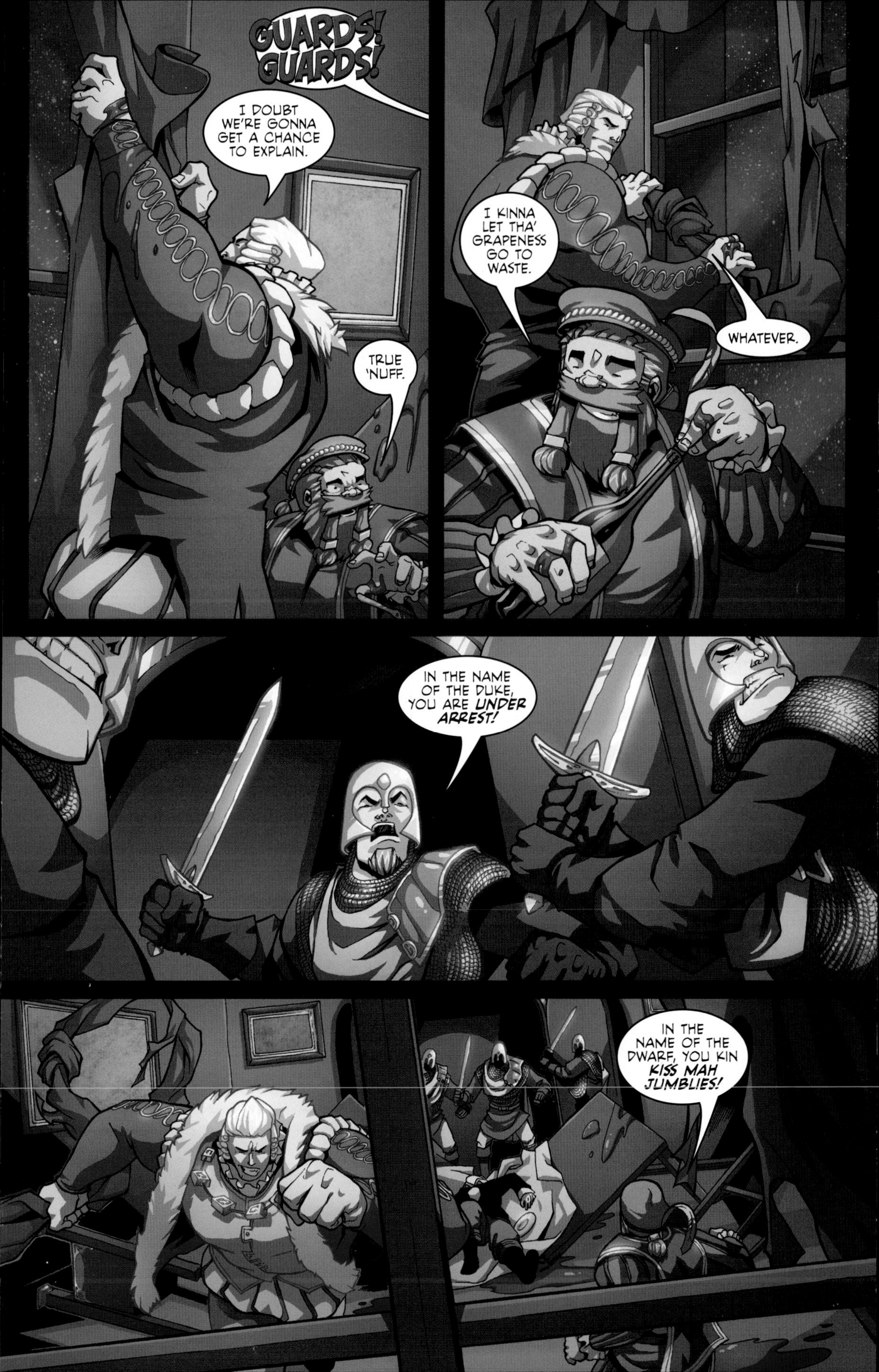
GUARDS! GUARDS!
I DOUBT WE'RE GONNA GET A CHANCE TO EXPLAIN.
TRUE 'NUFF.
I KINNA LET THA' GRAPENESS GO TO WASTE.
WHATEVER.
IN THE NAME OF THE DUKE, YOU ARE *UNDER ARREST!*
IN THE NAME OF THE DWARF, YOU KIN *KISS MAH JUMBLIES!*

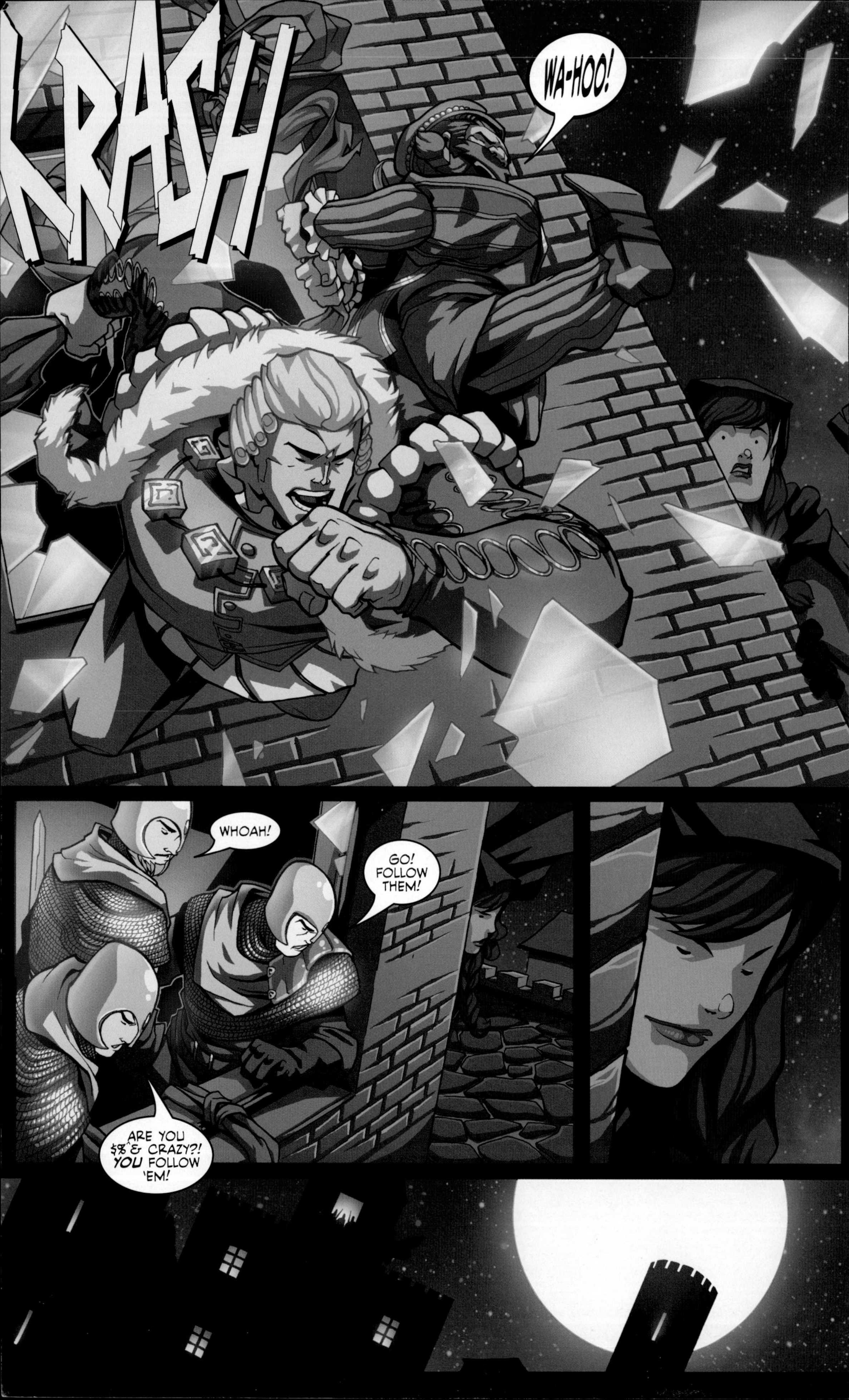
KRASH
WA-HOO!
WHOAH!
GO! FOLLOW THEM!
ARE YOU $%^& CRAZY?! YOU FOLLOW 'EM!

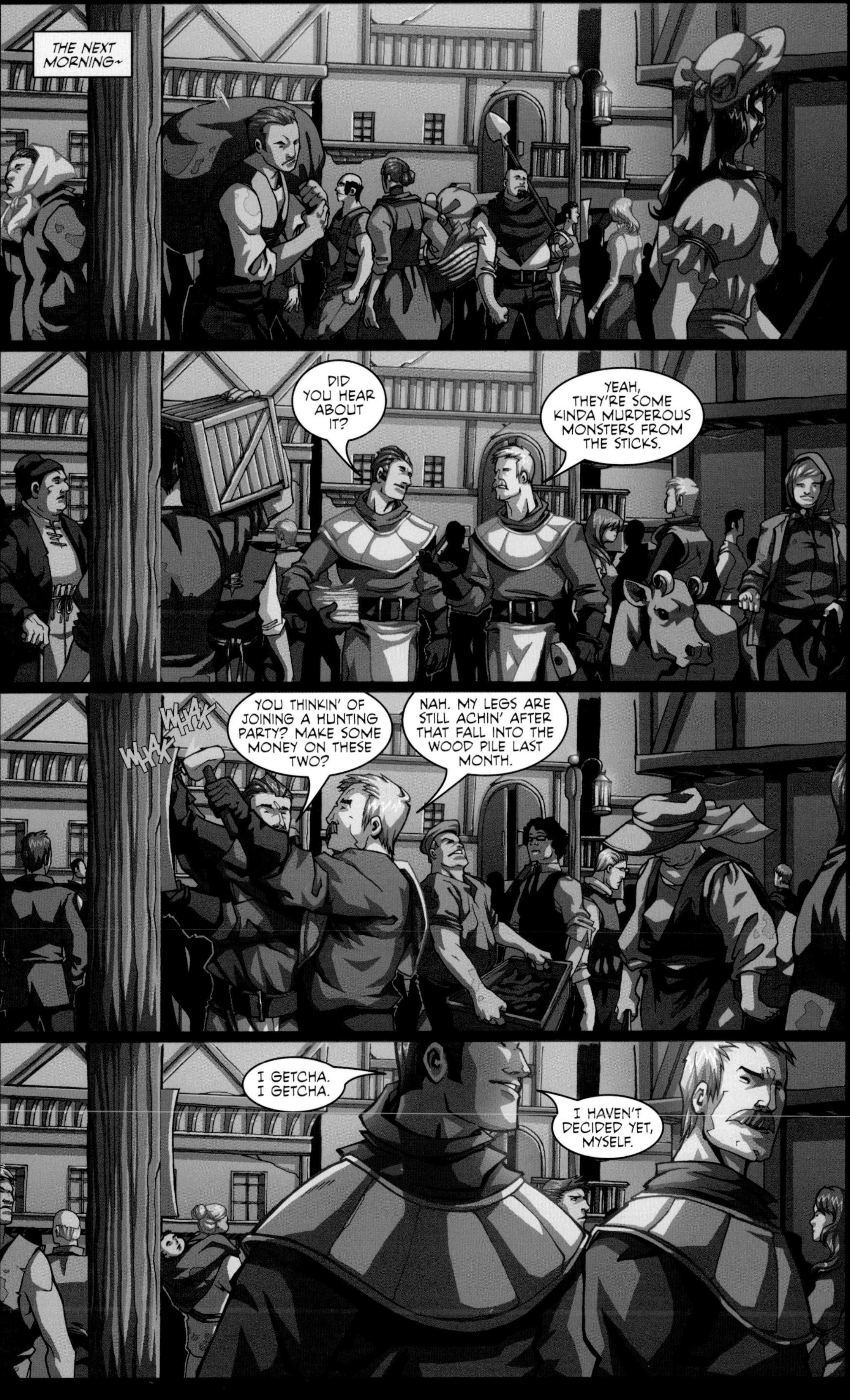
THE NEXT MORNING~
DID YOU HEAR ABOUT IT?
YEAH, THEY'RE SOME KINDA MURDEROUS MONSTERS FROM THE STICKS.
WHAK WHAK WHAK
YOU THINKIN' OF JOINING A HUNTING PARTY? MAKE SOME MONEY ON THESE TWO?
NAH. MY LEGS ARE STILL ACHIN' AFTER THAT FALL INTO THE WOOD PILE LAST MONTH.
I GETCHA. I GETCHA.
I HAVEN'T DECIDED YET, MYSELF.

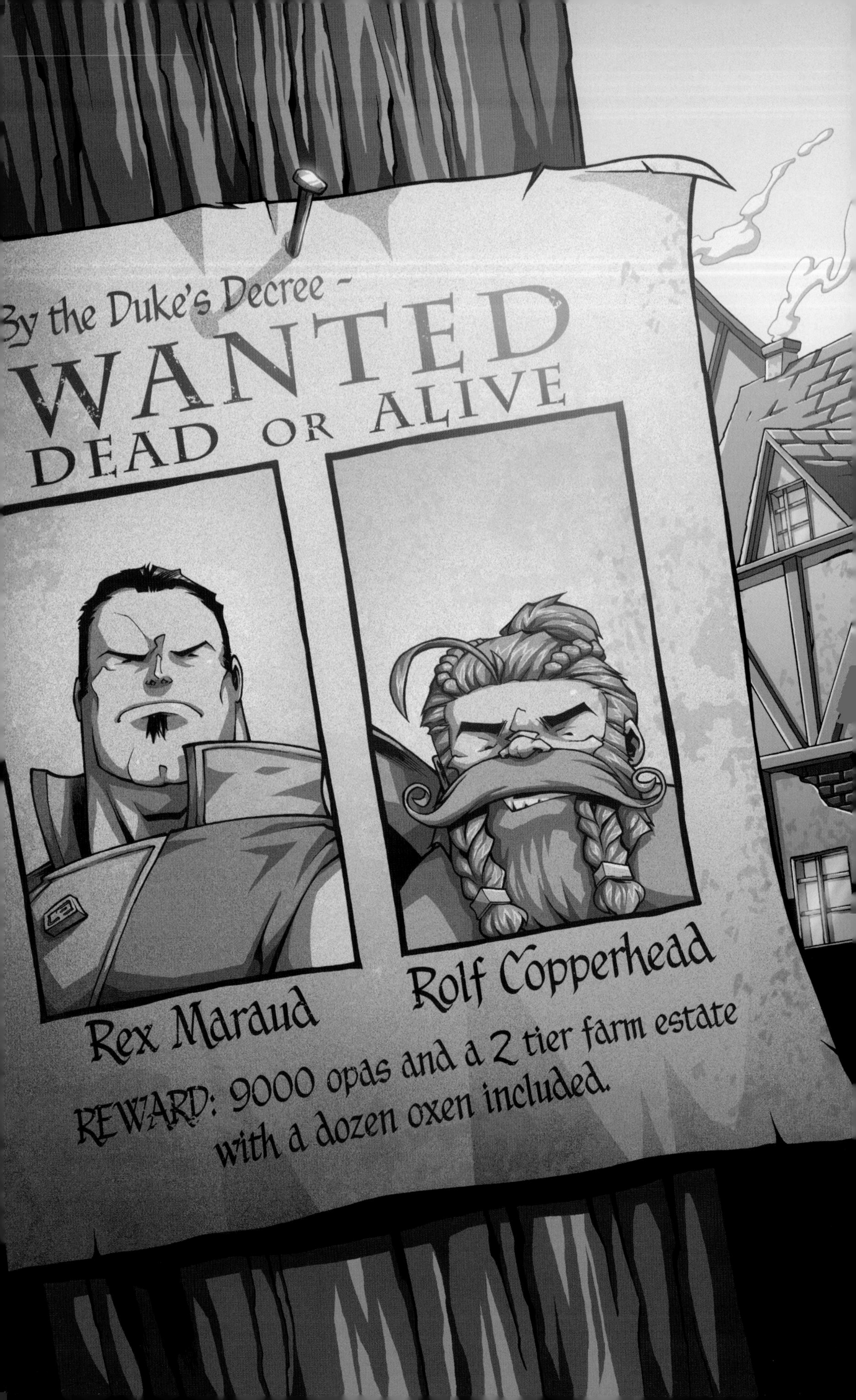

By the Duke's Decree -
WANTED
DEAD OR ALIVE
Rex Maraud
Rolf Copperhead
REWARD: 9000 opas and a 2 tier farm estate with a dozen oxen included.

CHAPTER TWO

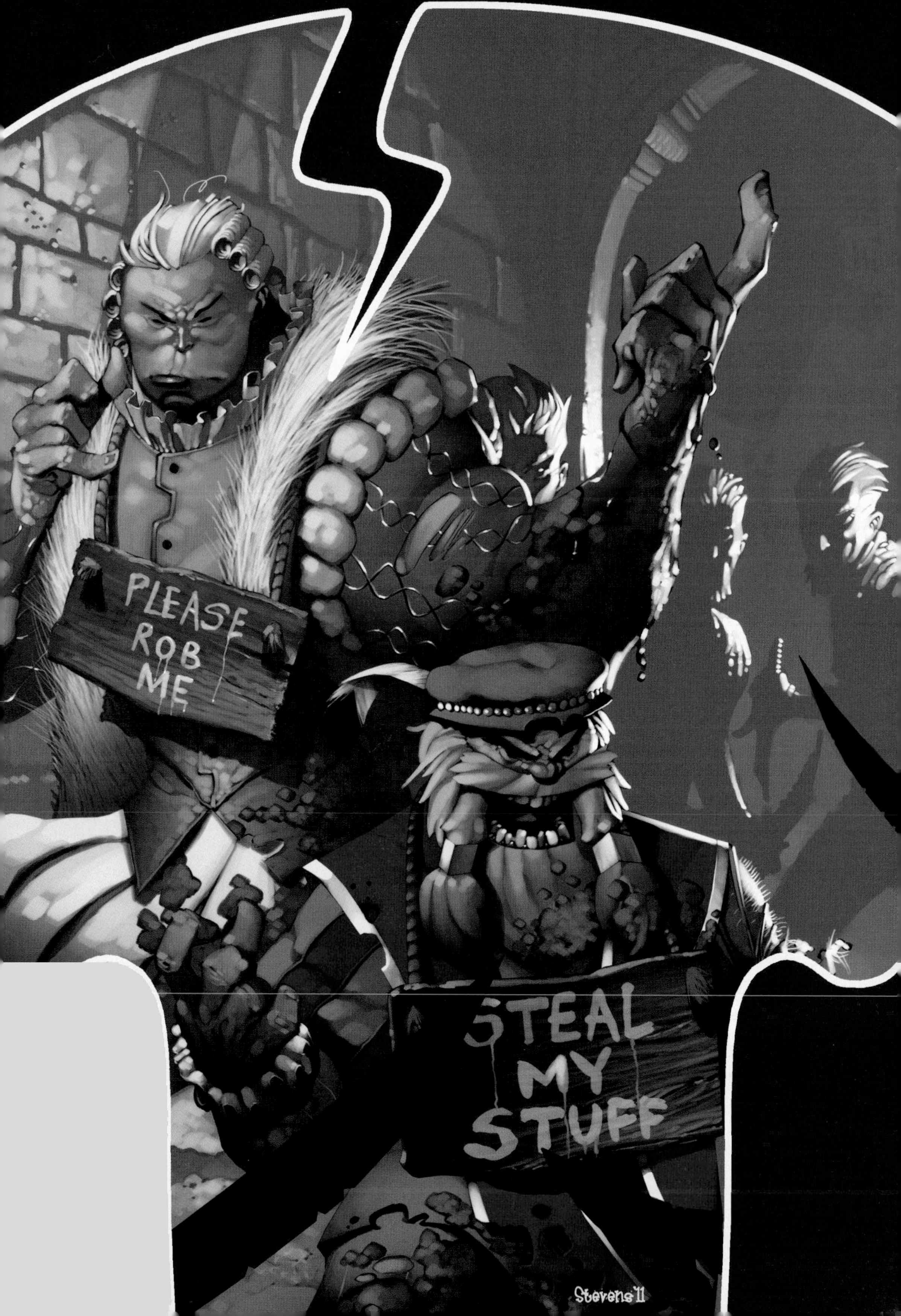
PLEASE ROB ME
STEAL MY STUFF
Stevens'11

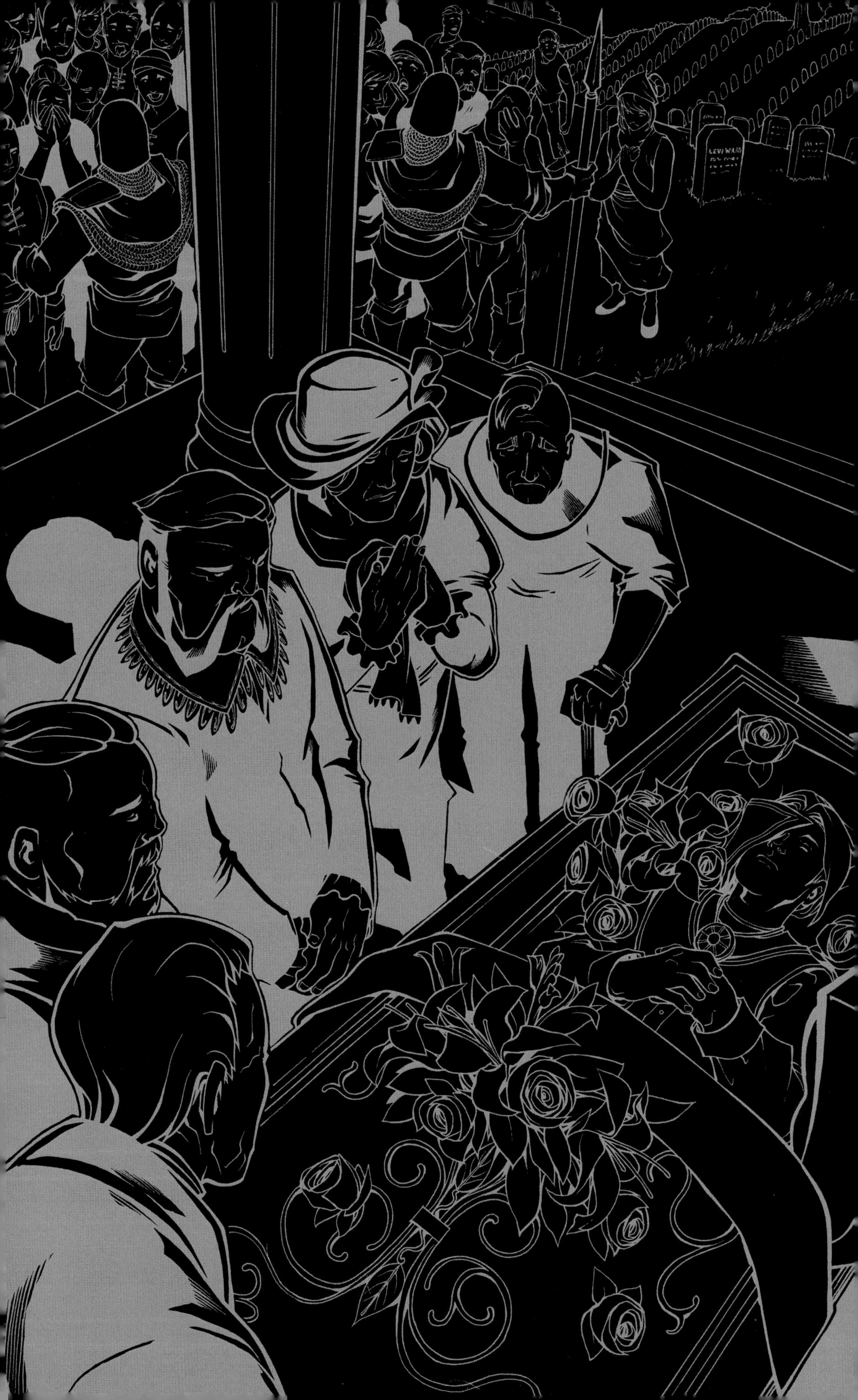
LEVI WARD

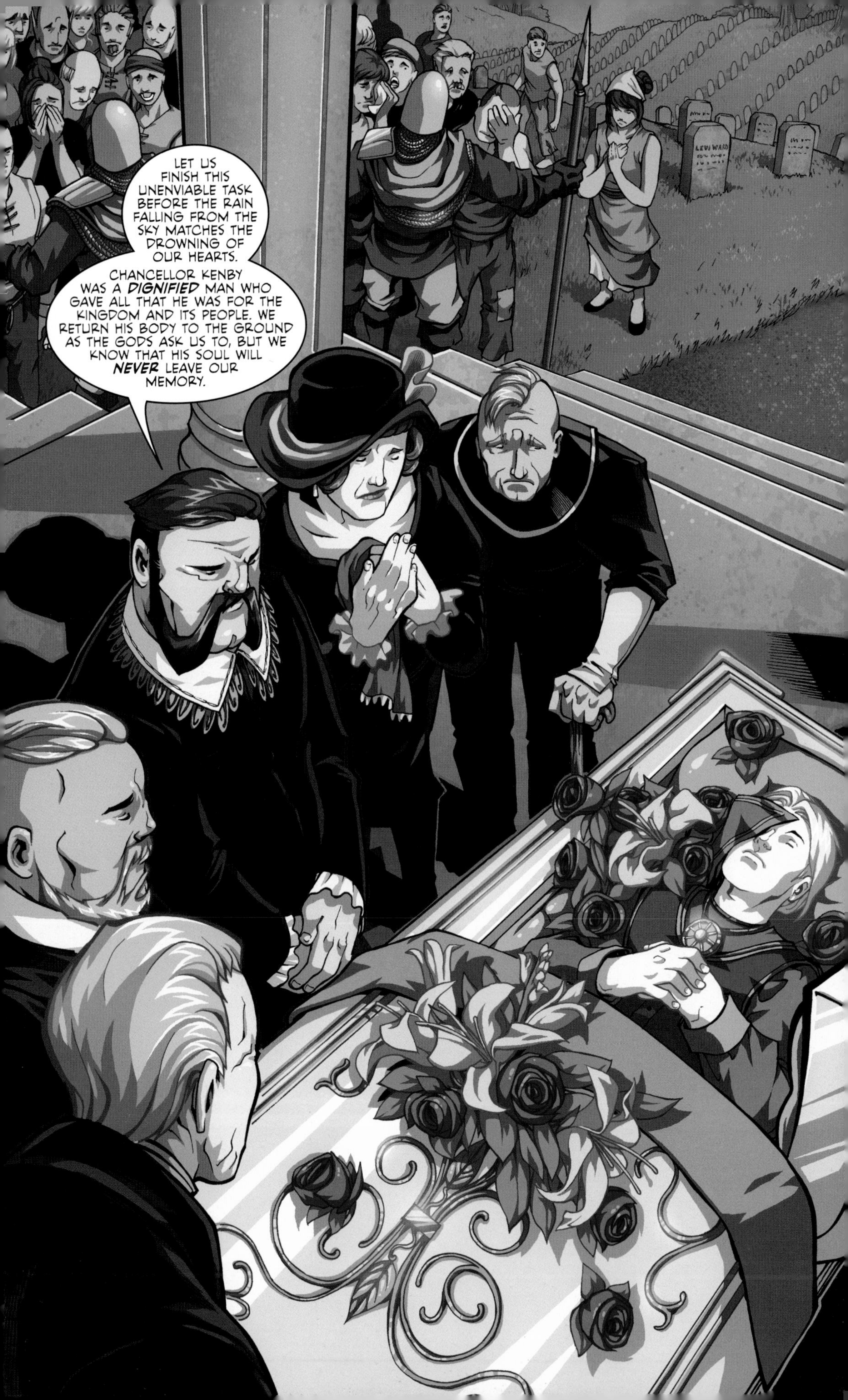
LET US FINISH THIS UNENVIABLE TASK BEFORE THE RAIN FALLING FROM THE SKY MATCHES THE DROWNING OF OUR HEARTS.
CHANCELLOR KENBY WAS A DIGNIFIED MAN WHO GAVE ALL THAT HE WAS FOR THE KINGDOM AND ITS PEOPLE. WE RETURN HIS BODY TO THE GROUND AS THE GODS ASK US TO, BUT WE KNOW THAT HIS SOUL WILL NEVER LEAVE OUR MEMORY.

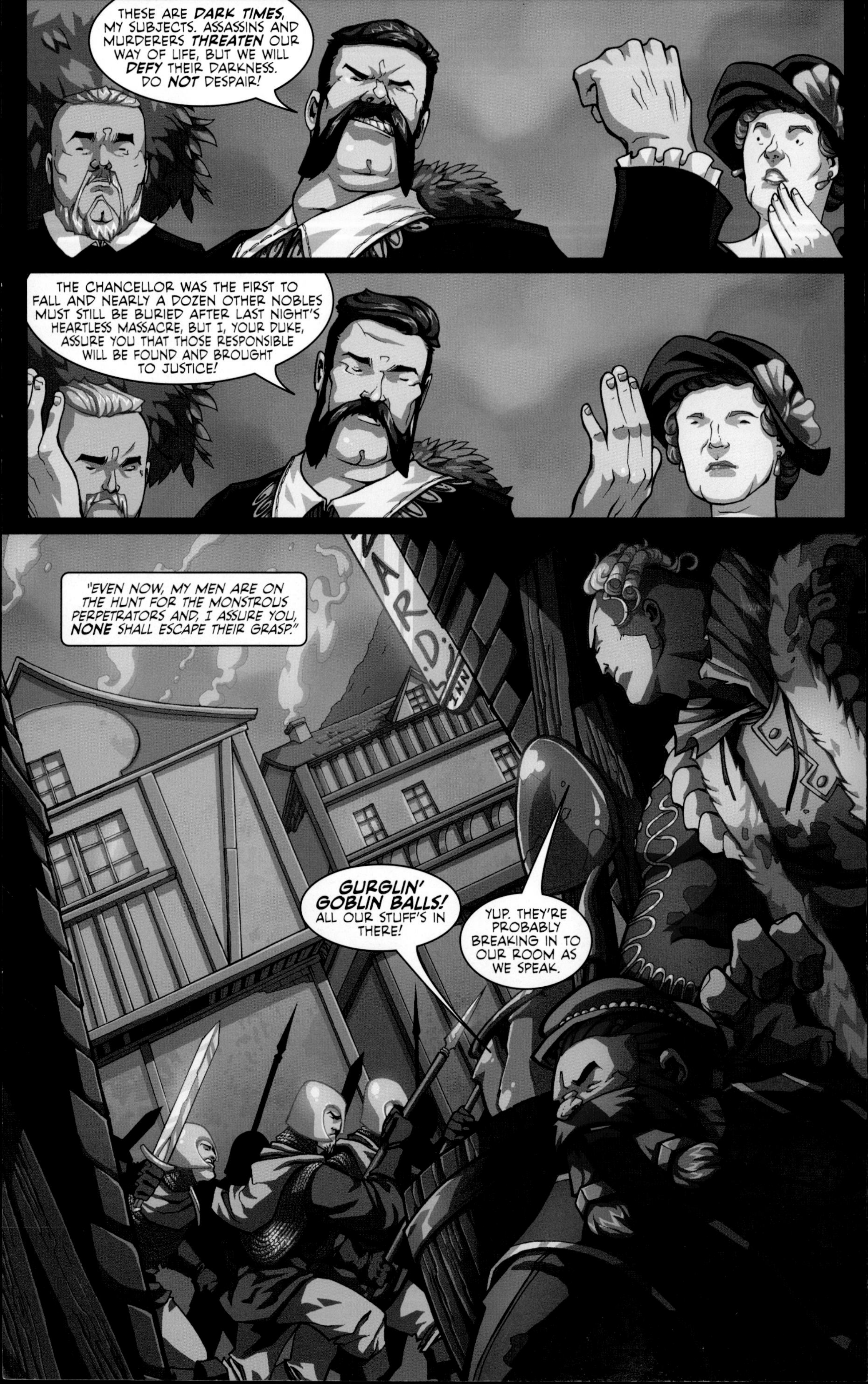
THESE ARE **DARK TIMES**, MY SUBJECTS. ASSASSINS AND MURDERERS **THREATEN** OUR WAY OF LIFE, BUT WE WILL **DEFY** THEIR DARKNESS. DO **NOT** DESPAIR!
THE CHANCELLOR WAS THE FIRST TO FALL AND NEARLY A DOZEN OTHER NOBLES MUST STILL BE BURIED AFTER LAST NIGHT'S HEARTLESS MASSACRE, BUT I, YOUR DUKE, ASSURE YOU THAT THOSE RESPONSIBLE WILL BE FOUND AND BROUGHT TO JUSTICE!
*"EVEN NOW, MY MEN ARE ON THE HUNT FOR THE MONSTROUS PERPETRATORS AND, I ASSURE YOU, **NONE** SHALL ESCAPE THEIR GRASP."*
GURGLIN' GOBLIN BALLS! ALL OUR STUFF'S IN THERE!
YUP. THEY'RE PROBABLY BREAKING IN TO OUR ROOM AS WE SPEAK.

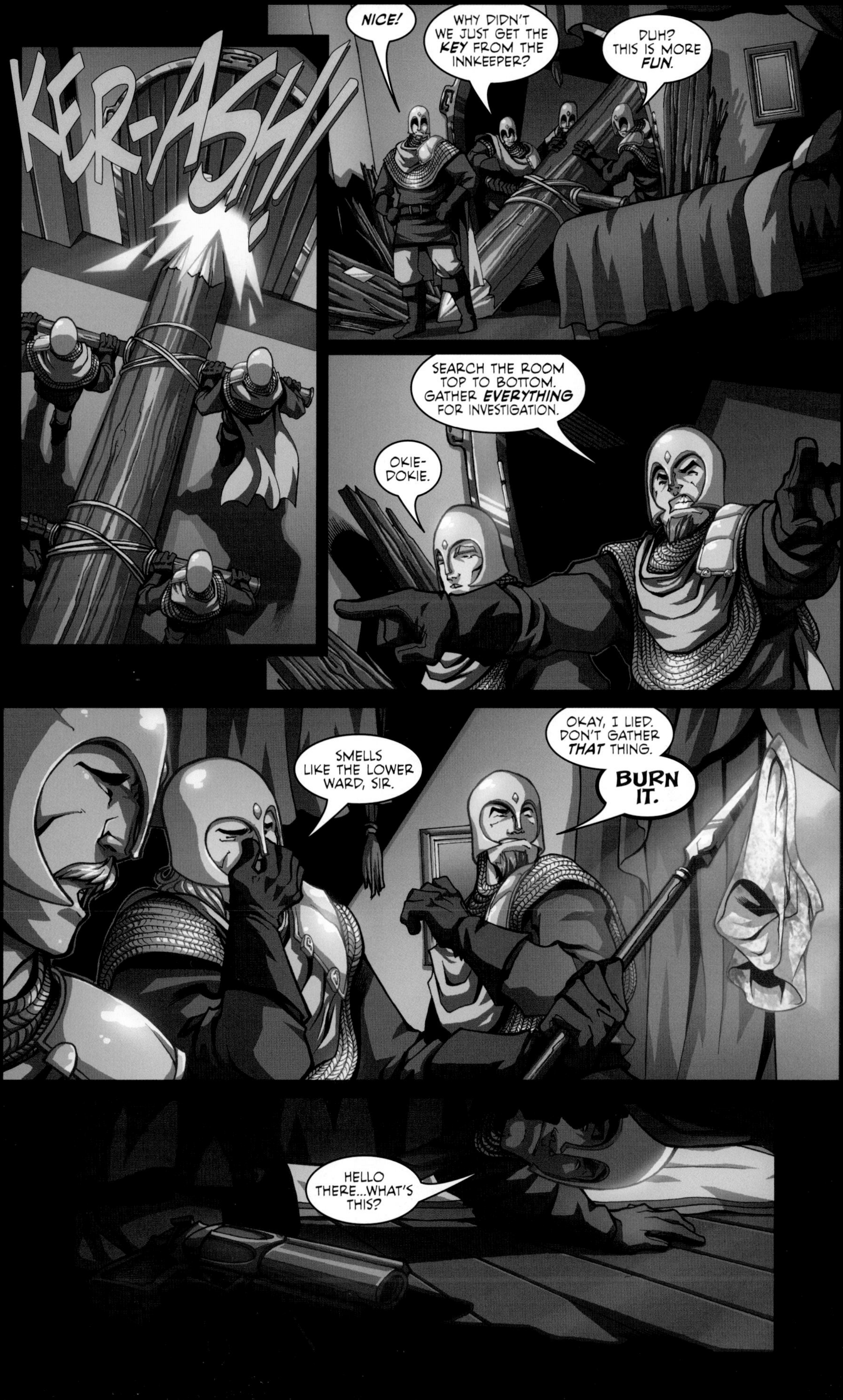
KER-ASH!
NICE!
WHY DIDN'T WE JUST GET THE KEY FROM THE INNKEEPER?
DUH? THIS IS MORE FUN.
SEARCH THE ROOM TOP TO BOTTOM. GATHER EVERYTHING FOR INVESTIGATION.
OKIE-DOKIE.
SMELLS LIKE THE LOWER WARD, SIR.
OKAY, I LIED. DON'T GATHER THAT THING.
BURN IT.
HELLO THERE...WHAT'S THIS?

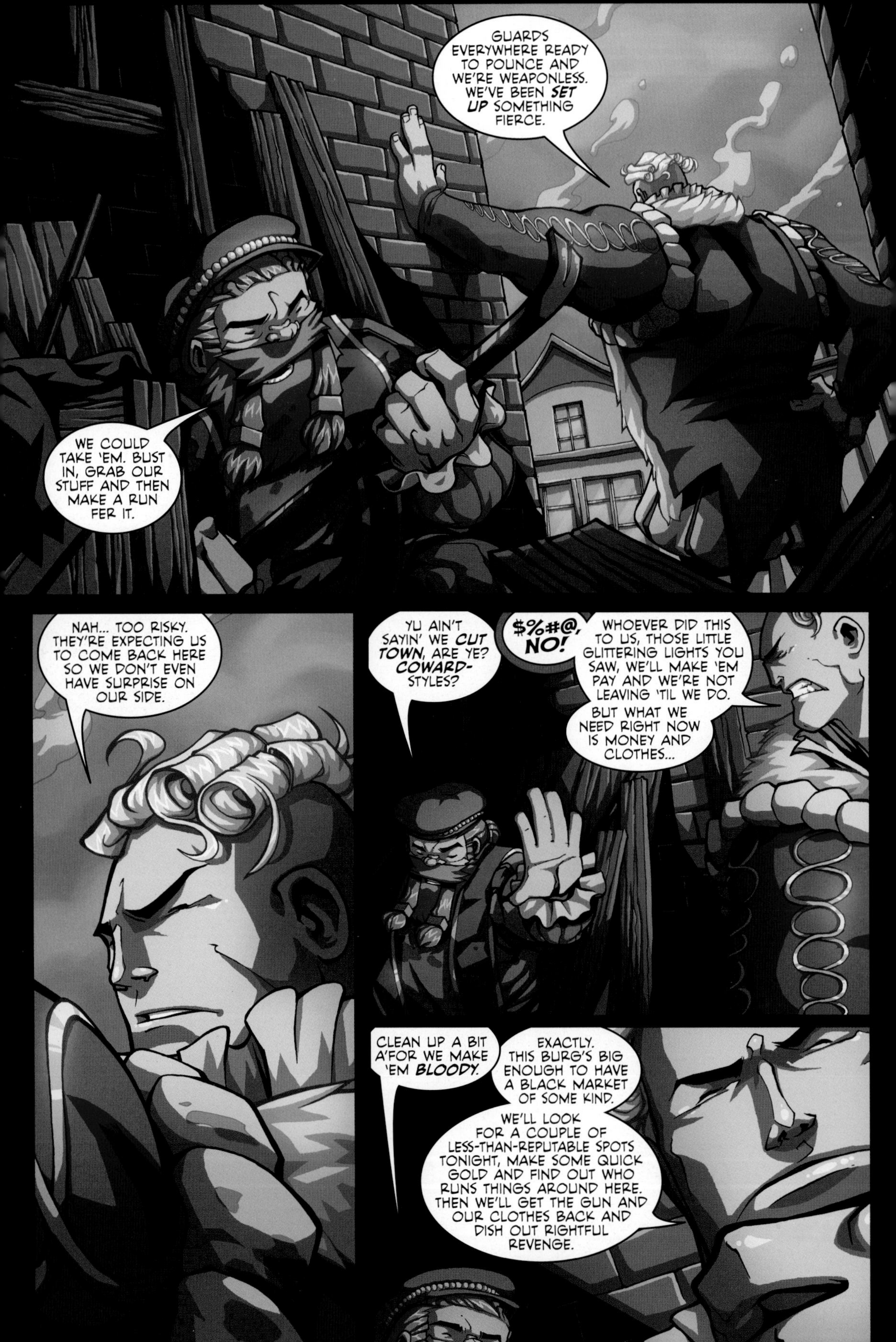
GUARDS EVERYWHERE READY TO POUNCE AND WE'RE WEAPONLESS. WE'VE BEEN SET UP SOMETHING FIERCE.
WE COULD TAKE 'EM. BUST IN, GRAB OUR STUFF AND THEN MAKE A RUN FER IT.
NAH... TOO RISKY. THEY'RE EXPECTING US TO COME BACK HERE SO WE DON'T EVEN HAVE SURPRISE ON OUR SIDE.
YU AIN'T SAYIN' WE CUT TOWN, ARE YE? COWARD-STYLES?
$%#@, NO!
WHOEVER DID THIS TO US, THOSE LITTLE GLITTERING LIGHTS YOU SAW, WE'LL MAKE 'EM PAY AND WE'RE NOT LEAVING 'TIL WE DO.
BUT WHAT WE NEED RIGHT NOW IS MONEY AND CLOTHES...
CLEAN UP A BIT A'FOR WE MAKE 'EM BLOODY.
EXACTLY. THIS BURG'S BIG ENOUGH TO HAVE A BLACK MARKET OF SOME KIND.
WE'LL LOOK FOR A COUPLE OF LESS-THAN-REPUTABLE SPOTS TONIGHT, MAKE SOME QUICK GOLD AND FIND OUT WHO RUNS THINGS AROUND HERE. THEN WE'LL GET THE GUN AND OUR CLOTHES BACK AND DISH OUT RIGHTFUL REVENGE.

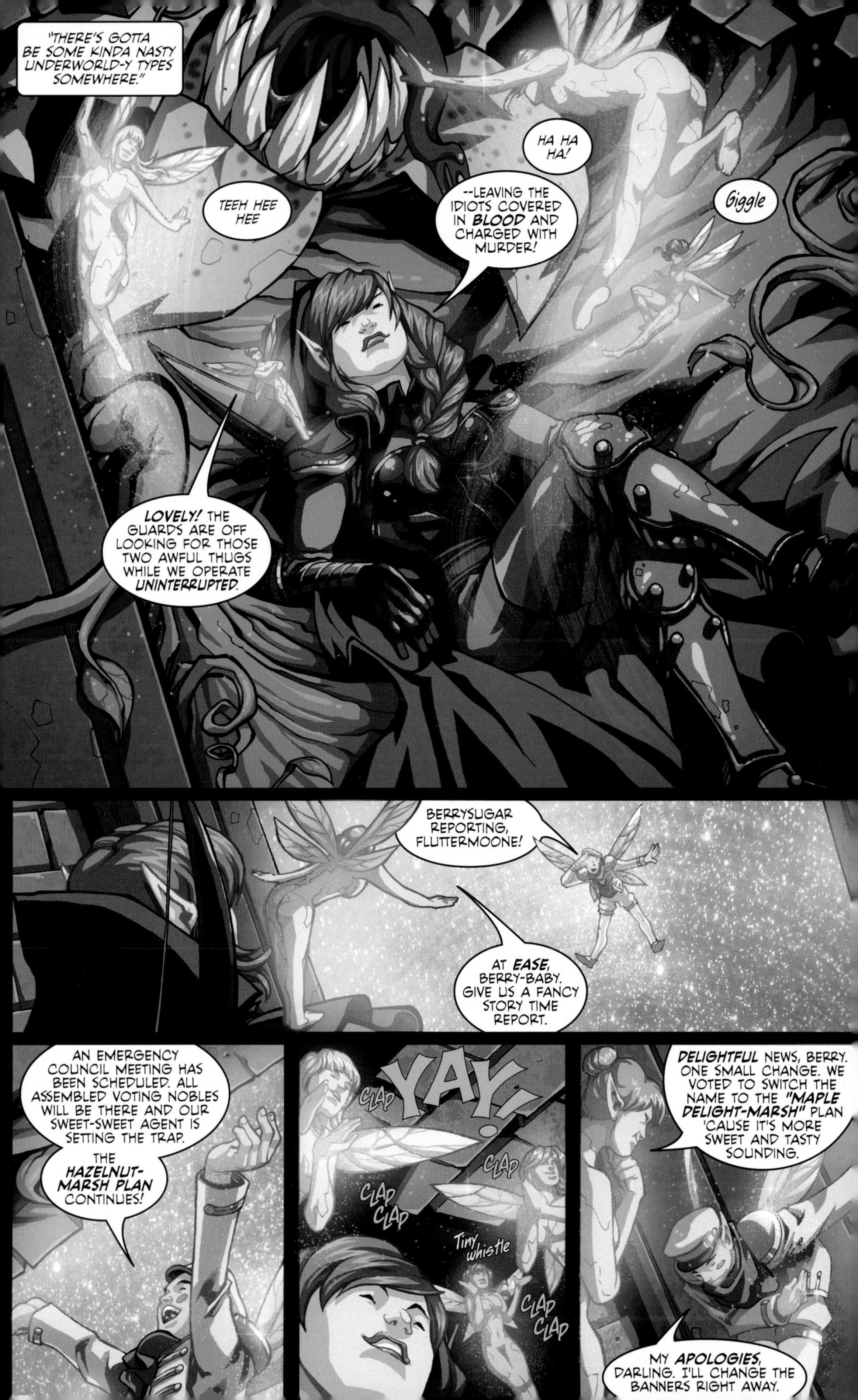
"THERE'S GOTTA BE SOME KINDA NASTY UNDERWORLD-Y TYPES SOMEWHERE."
TEEH HEE HEE
HA HA HA!
--LEAVING THE IDIOTS COVERED IN BLOOD AND CHARGED WITH MURDER!
Giggle
LOVELY! THE GUARDS ARE OFF LOOKING FOR THOSE TWO AWFUL THUGS WHILE WE OPERATE UNINTERRUPTED.
BERRYSUGAR REPORTING, FLUTTERMOONE!
AT EASE, BERRY-BABY. GIVE US A FANCY STORY TIME REPORT.
AN EMERGENCY COUNCIL MEETING HAS BEEN SCHEDULED. ALL ASSEMBLED VOTING NOBLES WILL BE THERE AND OUR SWEET-SWEET AGENT IS SETTING THE TRAP.
THE HAZELNUT-MARSH PLAN CONTINUES!
CLAP
YAY!
CLAP
CLAP CLAP
Tiny whistle
CLAP CLAP
DELIGHTFUL NEWS, BERRY. ONE SMALL CHANGE. WE VOTED TO SWITCH THE NAME TO THE "MAPLE DELIGHT-MARSH" PLAN 'CAUSE IT'S MORE SWEET AND TASTY SOUNDING.
MY APOLOGIES, DARLING. I'LL CHANGE THE BANNERS RIGHT AWAY.

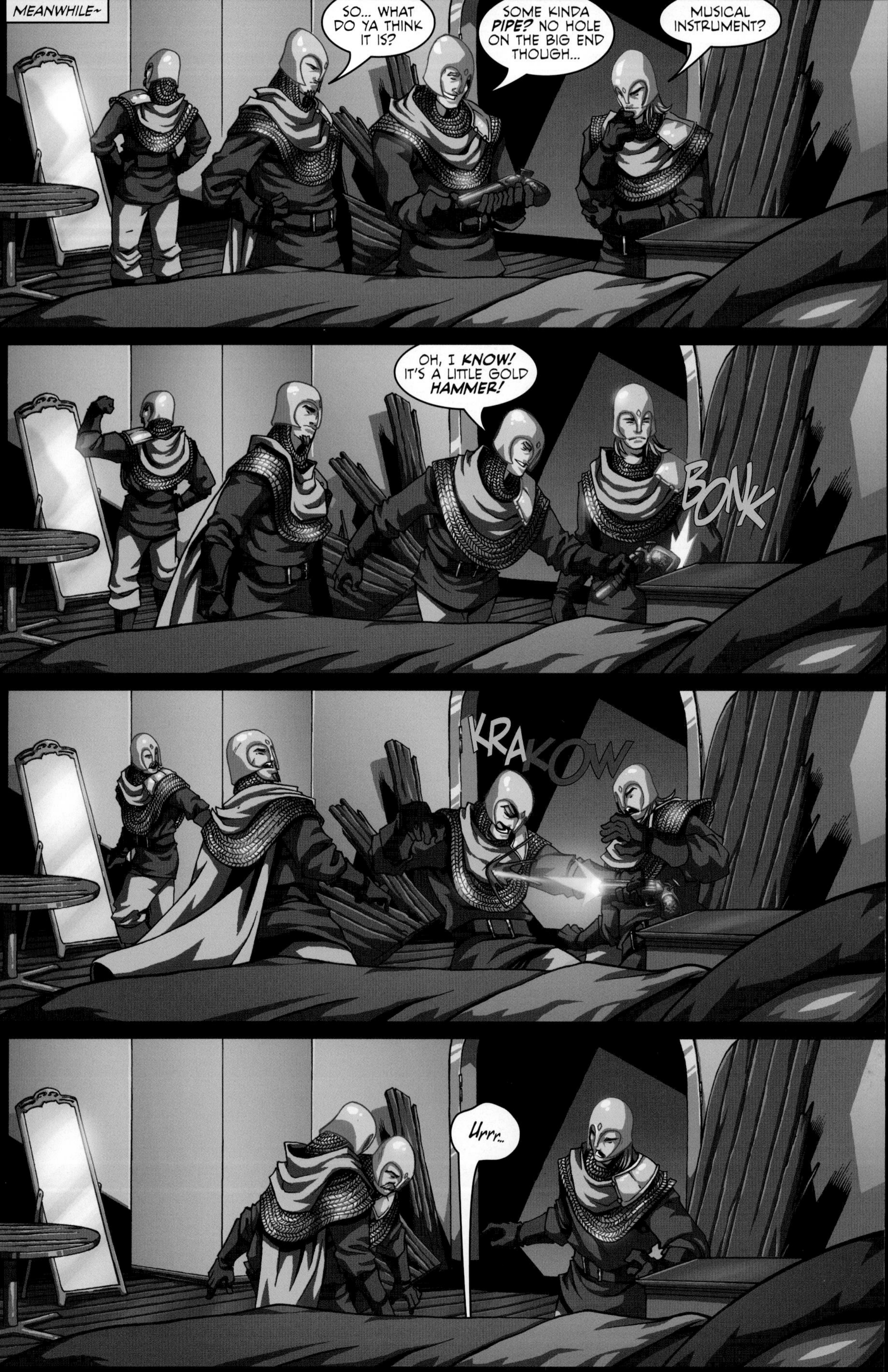

MEANWHILE~
SO... WHAT DO YA THINK IT IS?
SOME KINDA *PIPE?* NO HOLE ON THE BIG END THOUGH...
MUSICAL INSTRUMENT?
OH, I **KNOW!** IT'S A LITTLE GOLD **HAMMER!**
BONK
KRAKOW
Urrr...

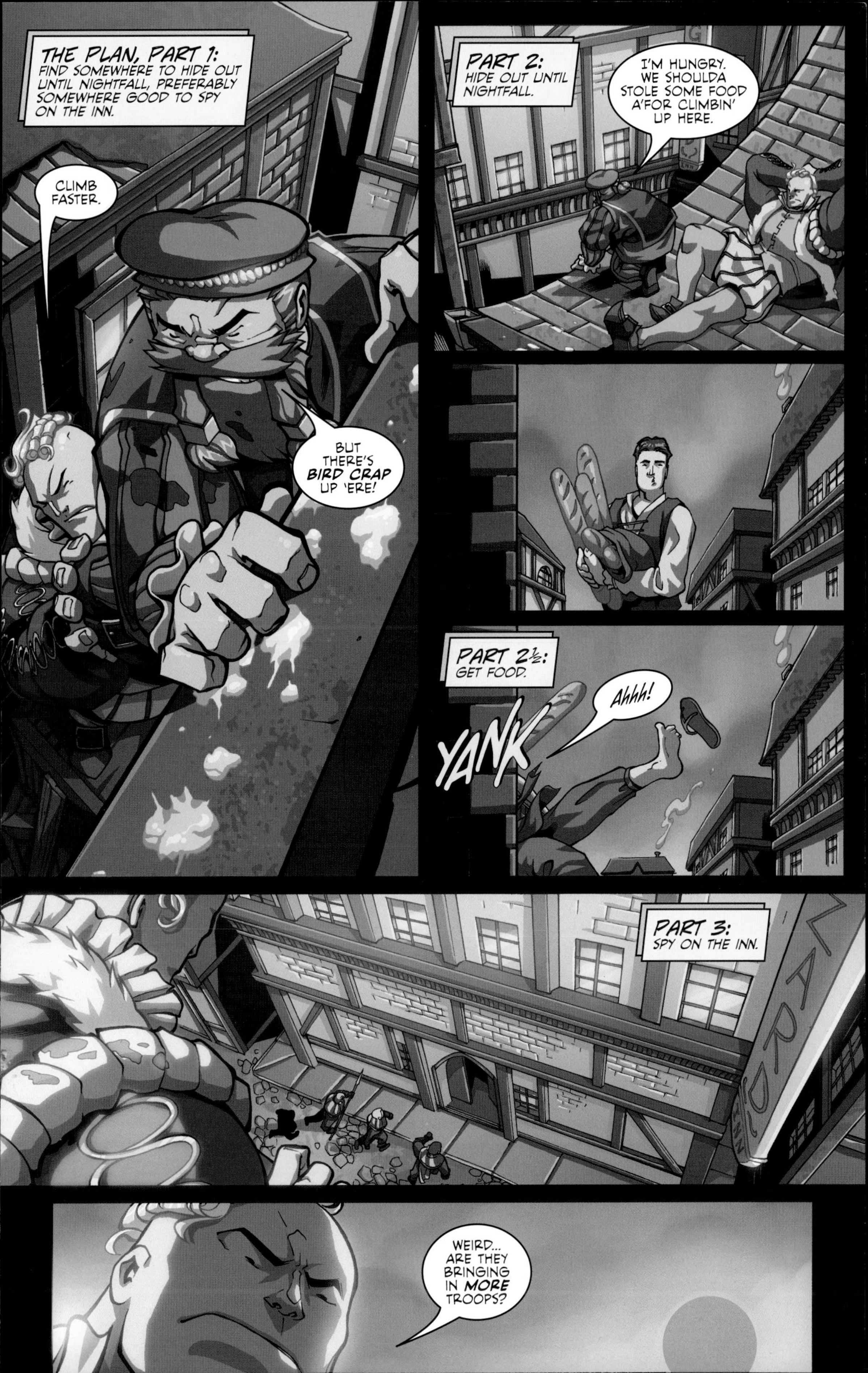
THE PLAN, PART 1:
FIND SOMEWHERE TO HIDE OUT UNTIL NIGHTFALL, PREFERABLY SOMEWHERE GOOD TO SPY ON THE INN.
CLIMB FASTER.
BUT THERE'S BIRD CRAP UP 'ERE!
PART 2:
HIDE OUT UNTIL NIGHTFALL.
I'M HUNGRY. WE SHOULDA STOLE SOME FOOD A'FOR CLIMBIN' UP HERE.
PART 2½:
GET FOOD.
YANK
Ahhh!
PART 3:
SPY ON THE INN.
WEIRD... ARE THEY BRINGING IN MORE TROOPS?

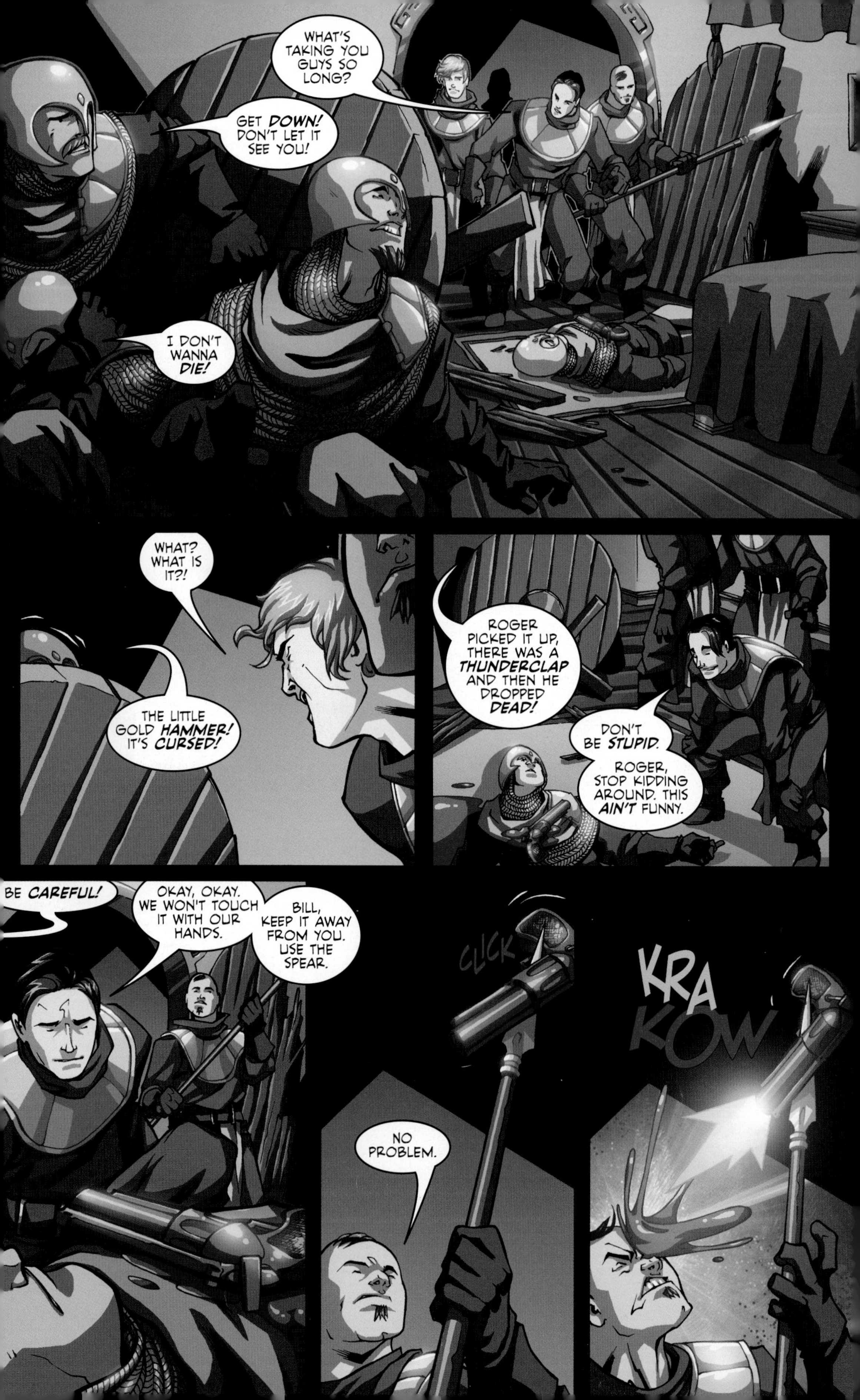
WHAT'S TAKING YOU GUYS SO LONG?
GET DOWN! DON'T LET IT SEE YOU!
I DON'T WANNA DIE!
WHAT? WHAT IS IT?!
THE LITTLE GOLD HAMMER! IT'S CURSED!
ROGER PICKED IT UP, THERE WAS A THUNDERCLAP AND THEN HE DROPPED DEAD!
DON'T BE STUPID.
ROGER, STOP KIDDING AROUND. THIS AIN'T FUNNY.
BE CAREFUL!
OKAY, OKAY. WE WON'T TOUCH IT WITH OUR HANDS.
BILL, KEEP IT AWAY FROM YOU. USE THE SPEAR.
CLICK
NO PROBLEM.
KRA KOW

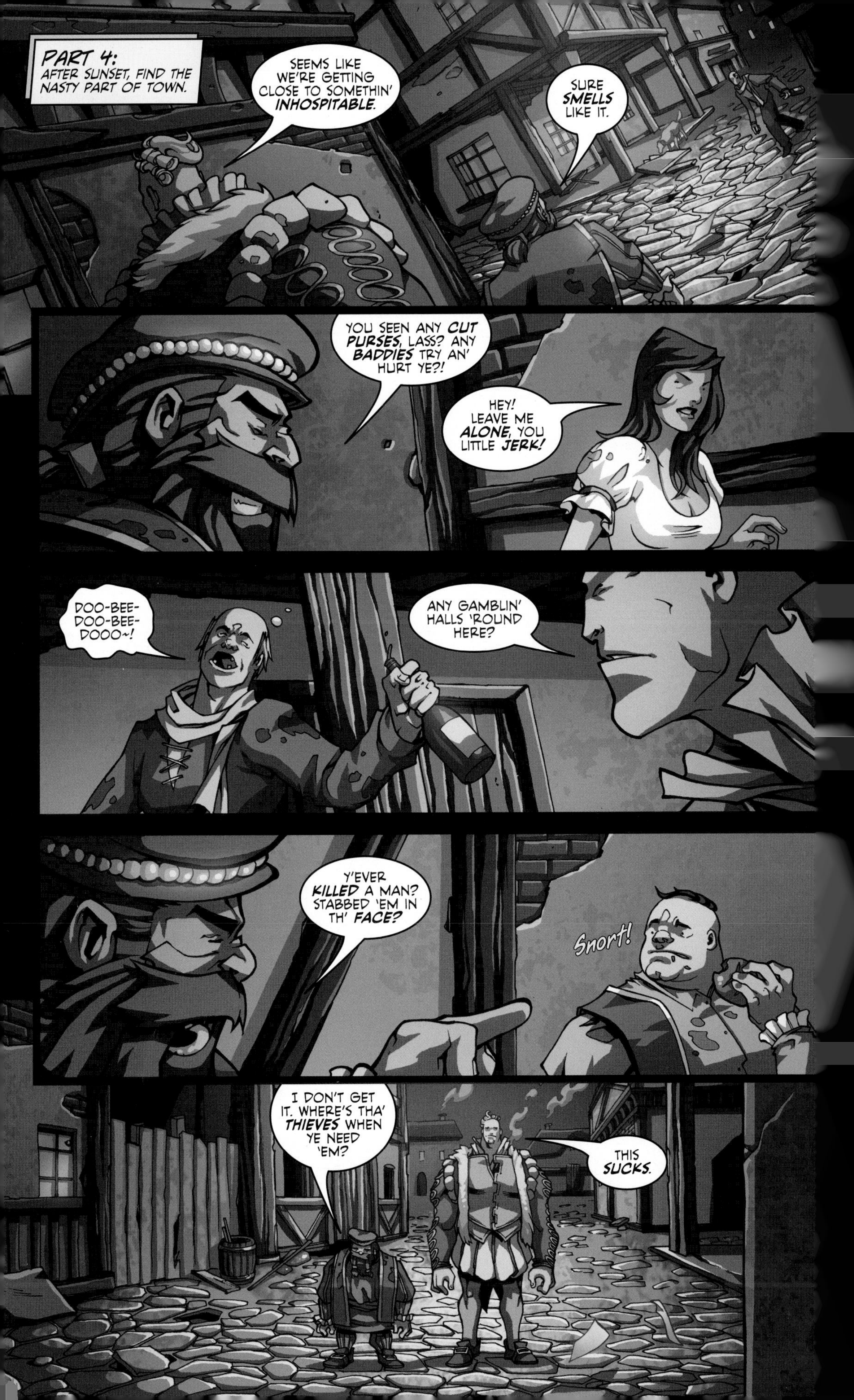
PART 4:
AFTER SUNSET, FIND THE NASTY PART OF TOWN.
SEEMS LIKE WE'RE GETTING CLOSE TO SOMETHIN' INHOSPITABLE.
SURE SMELLS LIKE IT.
YOU SEEN ANY CUT PURSES, LASS? ANY BADDIES TRY AN' HURT YE?!
HEY! LEAVE ME ALONE, YOU LITTLE JERK!
DOO-BEE-DOO-BEE-DOOO~!
ANY GAMBLIN' HALLS 'ROUND HERE?
Y'EVER KILLED A MAN? STABBED 'EM IN TH' FACE?
Snort!
I DON'T GET IT. WHERE'S THA' THIEVES WHEN YE NEED 'EM?
THIS SUCKS.

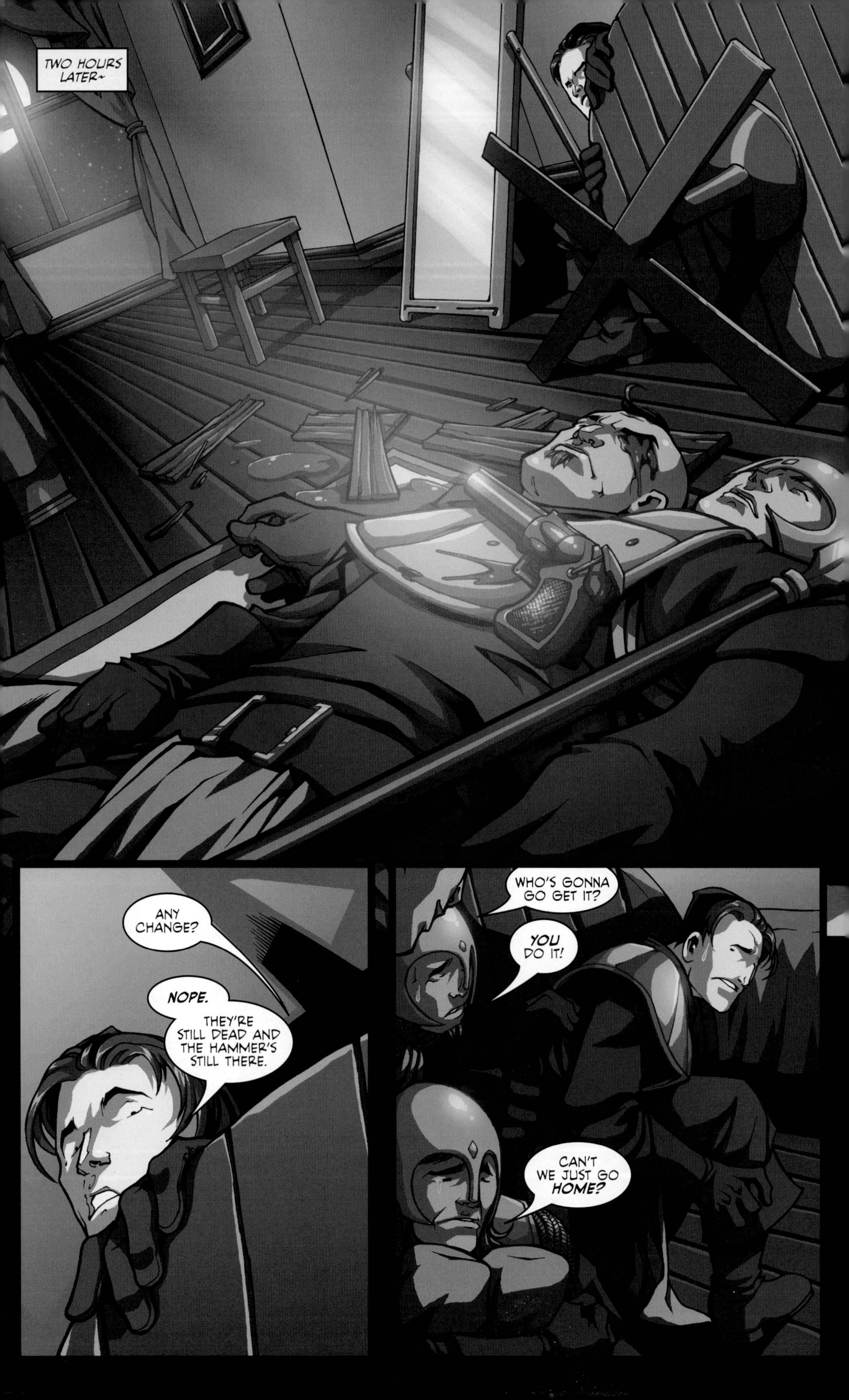

TWO HOURS LATER~
ANY CHANGE?
NOPE.
THEY'RE STILL DEAD AND THE HAMMER'S STILL THERE.
WHO'S GONNA GO GET IT?
YOU DO IT!
CAN'T WE JUST GO HOME?

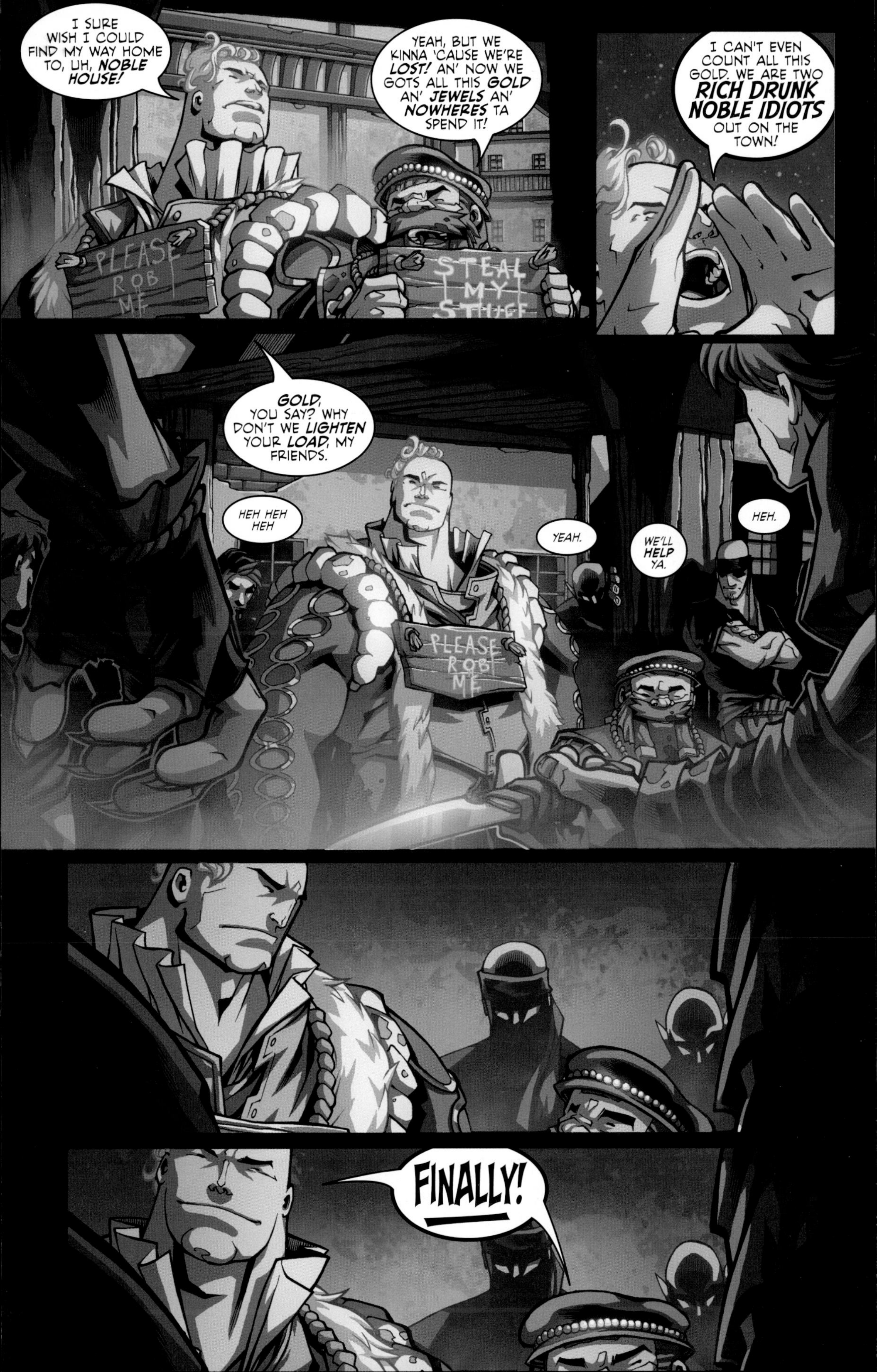
I SURE WISH I COULD FIND MY WAY HOME TO, UH, NOBLE HOUSE!
YEAH, BUT WE KINNA 'CAUSE WE'RE LOST! AN' NOW WE GOTS ALL THIS GOLD AN' JEWELS AN' NOWHERES TA SPEND IT!
PLEASE ROB ME
STEAL MY STUFF
I CAN'T EVEN COUNT ALL THIS GOLD. WE ARE TWO RICH DRUNK NOBLE IDIOTS OUT ON THE TOWN!
GOLD, YOU SAY? WHY DON'T WE LIGHTEN YOUR LOAD, MY FRIENDS.
HEH HEH HEH
YEAH.
WE'LL HELP YA.
HEH.
PLEASE ROB ME
FINALLY!

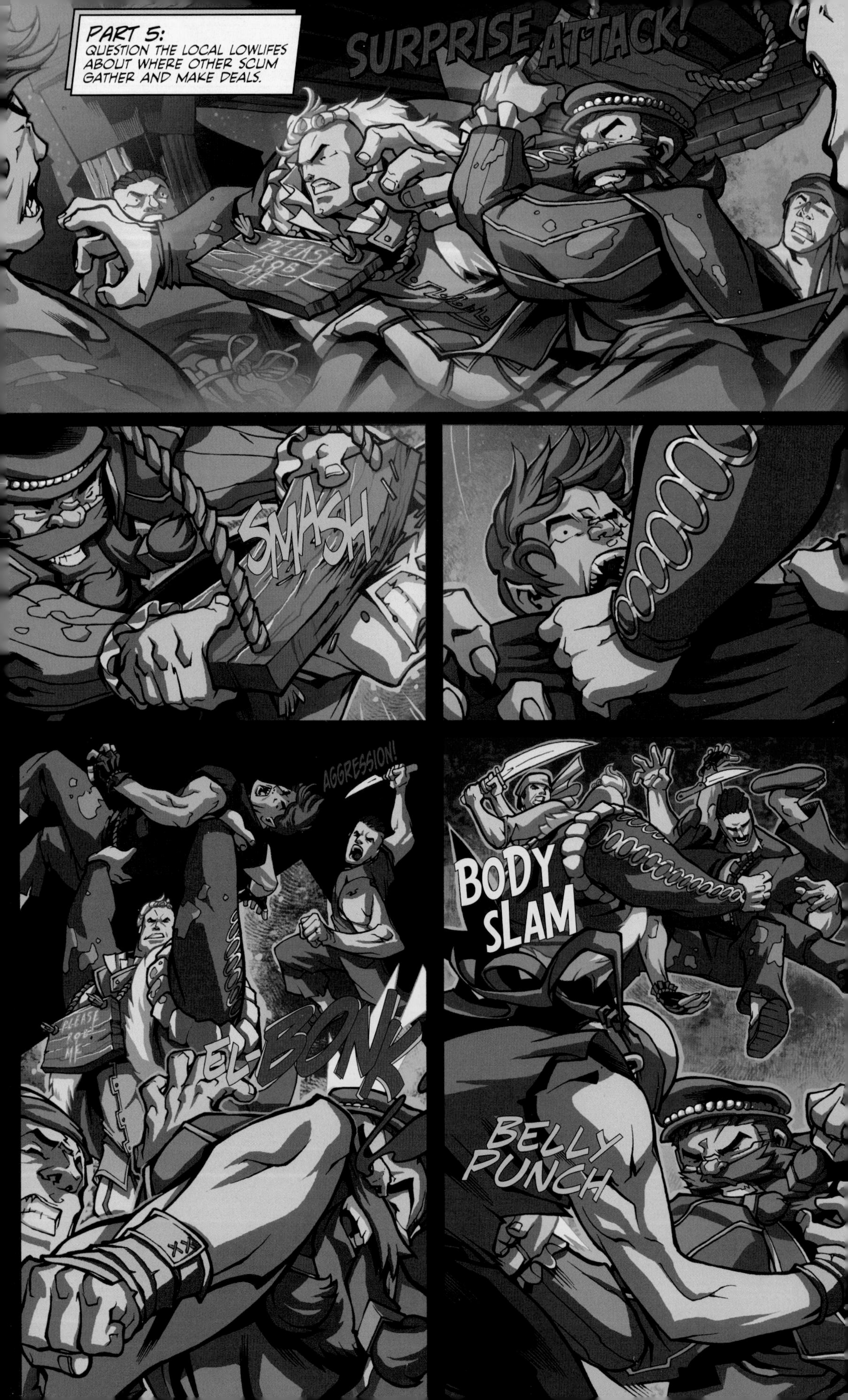
PART 5:
QUESTION THE LOCAL LOWLIFES ABOUT WHERE OTHER SCUM GATHER AND MAKE DEALS.
SURPRISE ATTACK!
PLEASE ROB ME
SMASH
AGGRESSION!
PLEASE ROB ME
EL-BONK
BODY SLAM
BELLY PUNCH

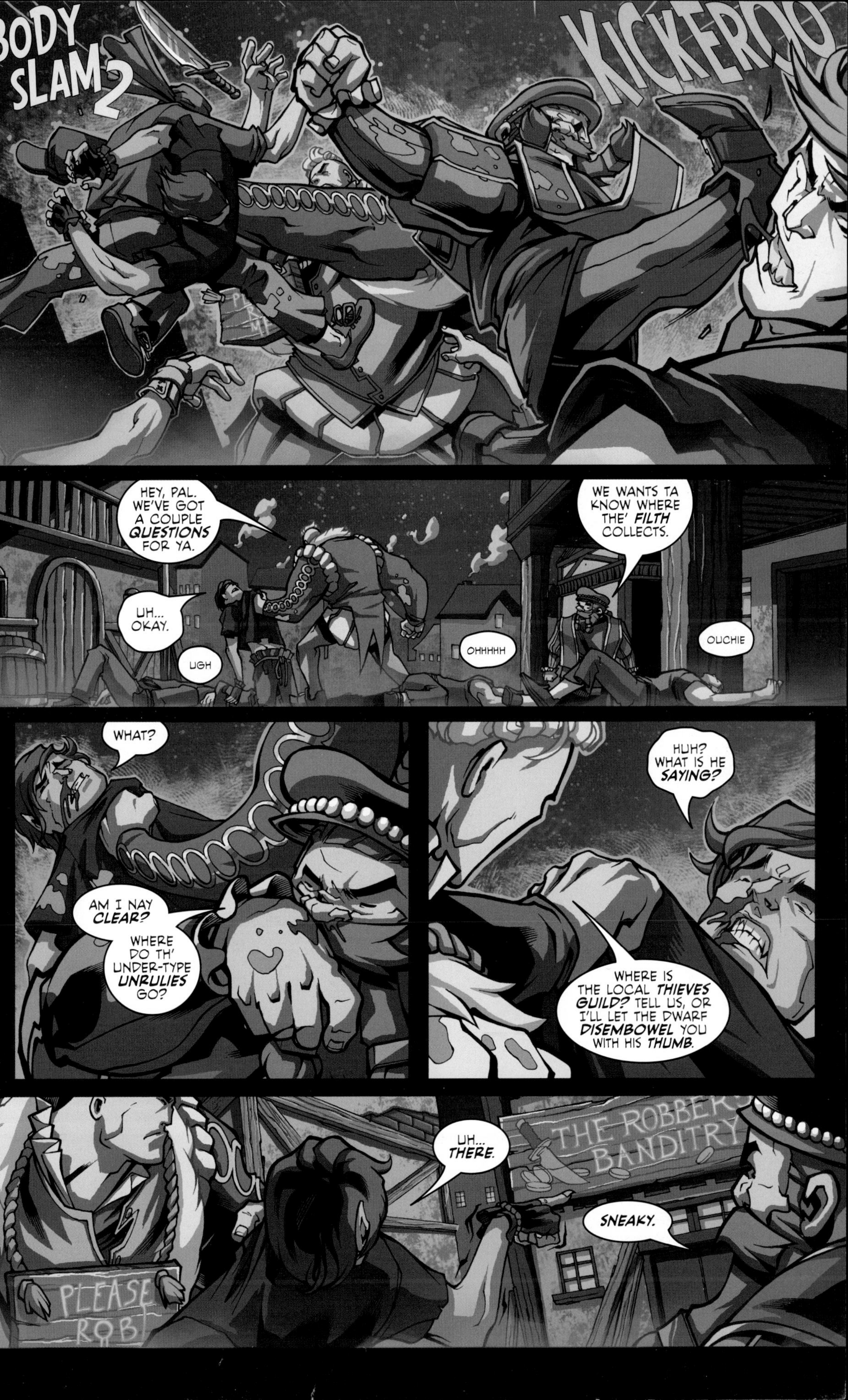
BODY SLAM 2
KICKEROO
HEY, PAL. WE'VE GOT A COUPLE QUESTIONS FOR YA.
WE WANTS TA KNOW WHERE THE' FILTH COLLECTS.
UH... OKAY.
UGH
OHHHHH
OUCHIE
WHAT?
AM I NAY CLEAR?
WHERE DO TH' UNDER-TYPE UNRULIES GO?
HUH? WHAT IS HE SAYING?
WHERE IS THE LOCAL THIEVES GUILD? TELL US, OR I'LL LET THE DWARF DISEMBOWEL YOU WITH HIS THUMB.
UH... THERE.
THE ROBBERS BANDITRY
SNEAKY.
PLEASE ROB

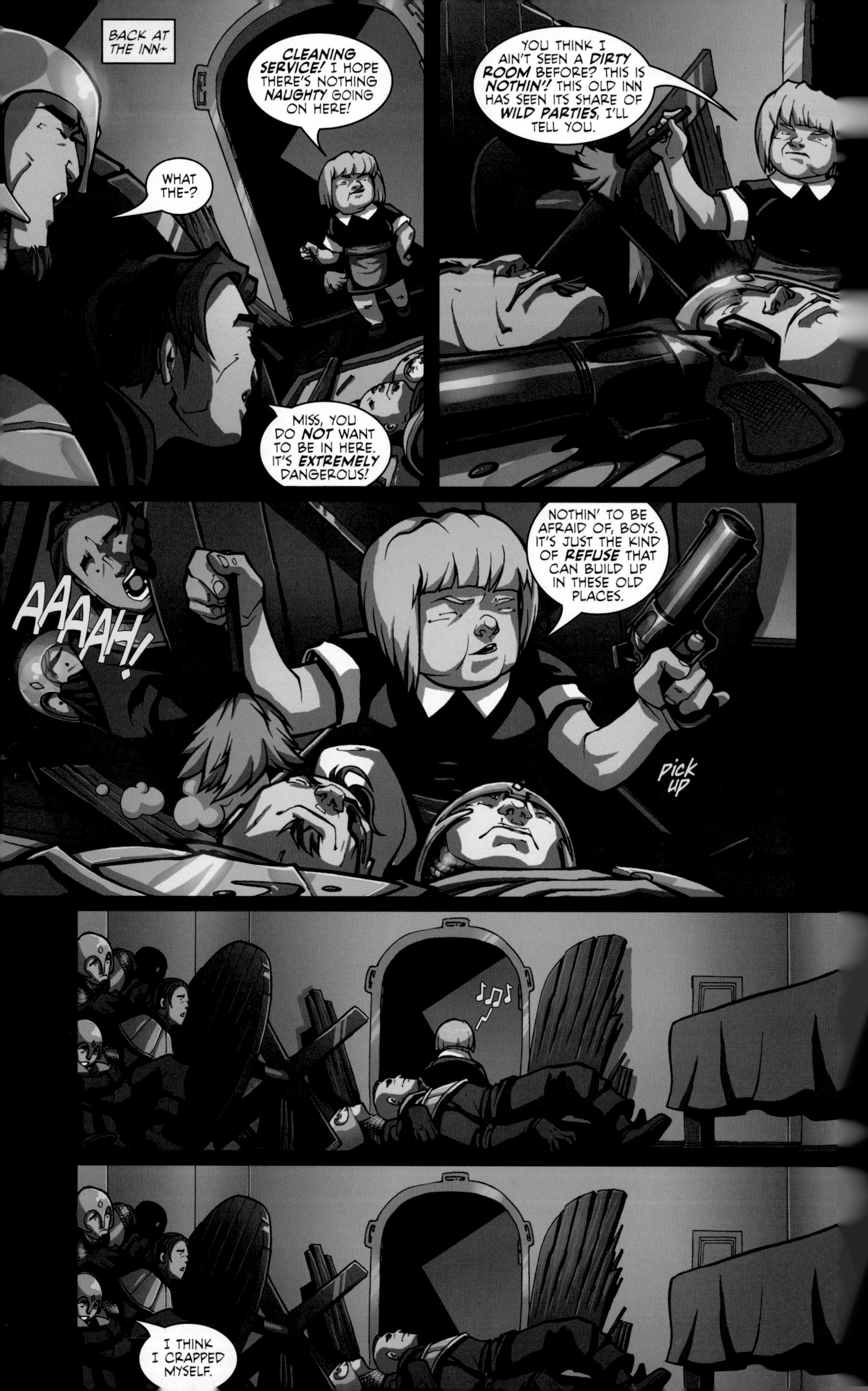
BACK AT THE INN~
CLEANING SERVICE! I HOPE THERE'S NOTHING NAUGHTY GOING ON HERE!
WHAT THE-?
MISS, YOU DO NOT WANT TO BE IN HERE. IT'S EXTREMELY DANGEROUS!
YOU THINK I AIN'T SEEN A DIRTY ROOM BEFORE? THIS IS NOTHIN'! THIS OLD INN HAS SEEN ITS SHARE OF WILD PARTIES, I'LL TELL YOU.
AAAAH!
NOTHIN' TO BE AFRAID OF, BOYS. IT'S JUST THE KIND OF REFUSE THAT CAN BUILD UP IN THESE OLD PLACES.
PICK UP
I THINK I CRAPPED MYSELF.

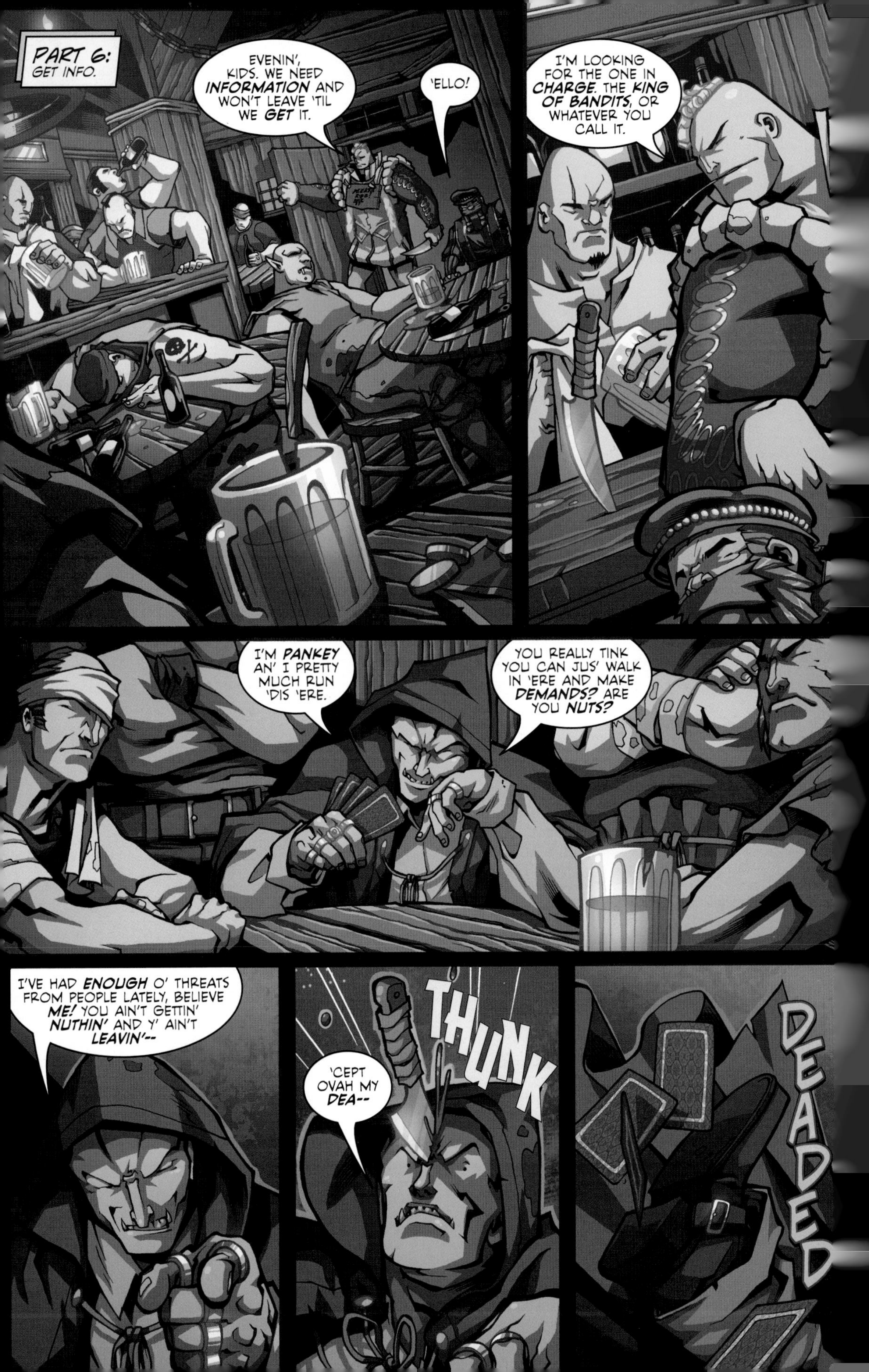
PART 6:
GET INFO.
EVENIN', KIDS. WE NEED INFORMATION AND WON'T LEAVE 'TIL WE GET IT.
'ELLO!
I'M LOOKING FOR THE ONE IN CHARGE. THE KING OF BANDITS, OR WHATEVER YOU CALL IT.
I'M PANKEY AN' I PRETTY MUCH RUN 'DIS 'ERE.
YOU REALLY TINK YOU CAN JUS' WALK IN 'ERE AND MAKE DEMANDS? ARE YOU NUTS?
I'VE HAD ENOUGH O' THREATS FROM PEOPLE LATELY, BELIEVE ME! YOU AIN'T GETTIN' NUTHIN' AND Y' AIN'T LEAVIN'--
'CEPT OVAH MY DEA--
THUNK
DEADED

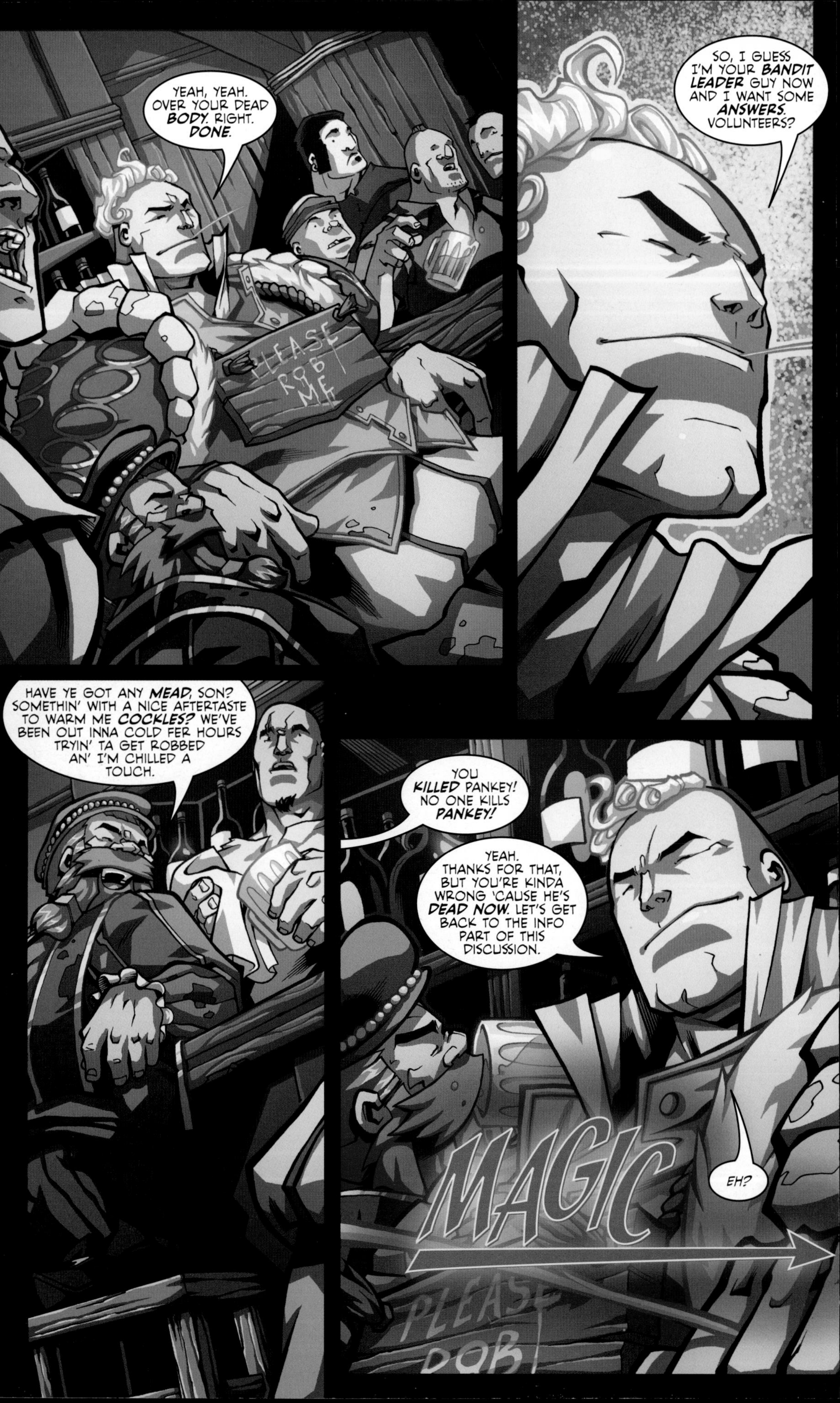

YEAH, YEAH. OVER YOUR DEAD BODY. RIGHT. DONE.
PLEASE ROB ME
SO, I GUESS I'M YOUR BANDIT LEADER GUY NOW AND I WANT SOME ANSWERS. VOLUNTEERS?
HAVE YE GOT ANY MEAD, SON? SOMETHIN' WITH A NICE AFTERTASTE TO WARM ME COCKLES? WE'VE BEEN OUT INNA COLD FER HOURS TRYIN' TA GET ROBBED AN' I'M CHILLED A TOUCH.
YOU KILLED PANKEY! NO ONE KILLS PANKEY!
YEAH. THANKS FOR THAT, BUT YOU'RE KINDA WRONG 'CAUSE HE'S DEAD NOW. LET'S GET BACK TO THE INFO PART OF THIS DISCUSSION.
MAGIC
EH?
PLEASE ROB

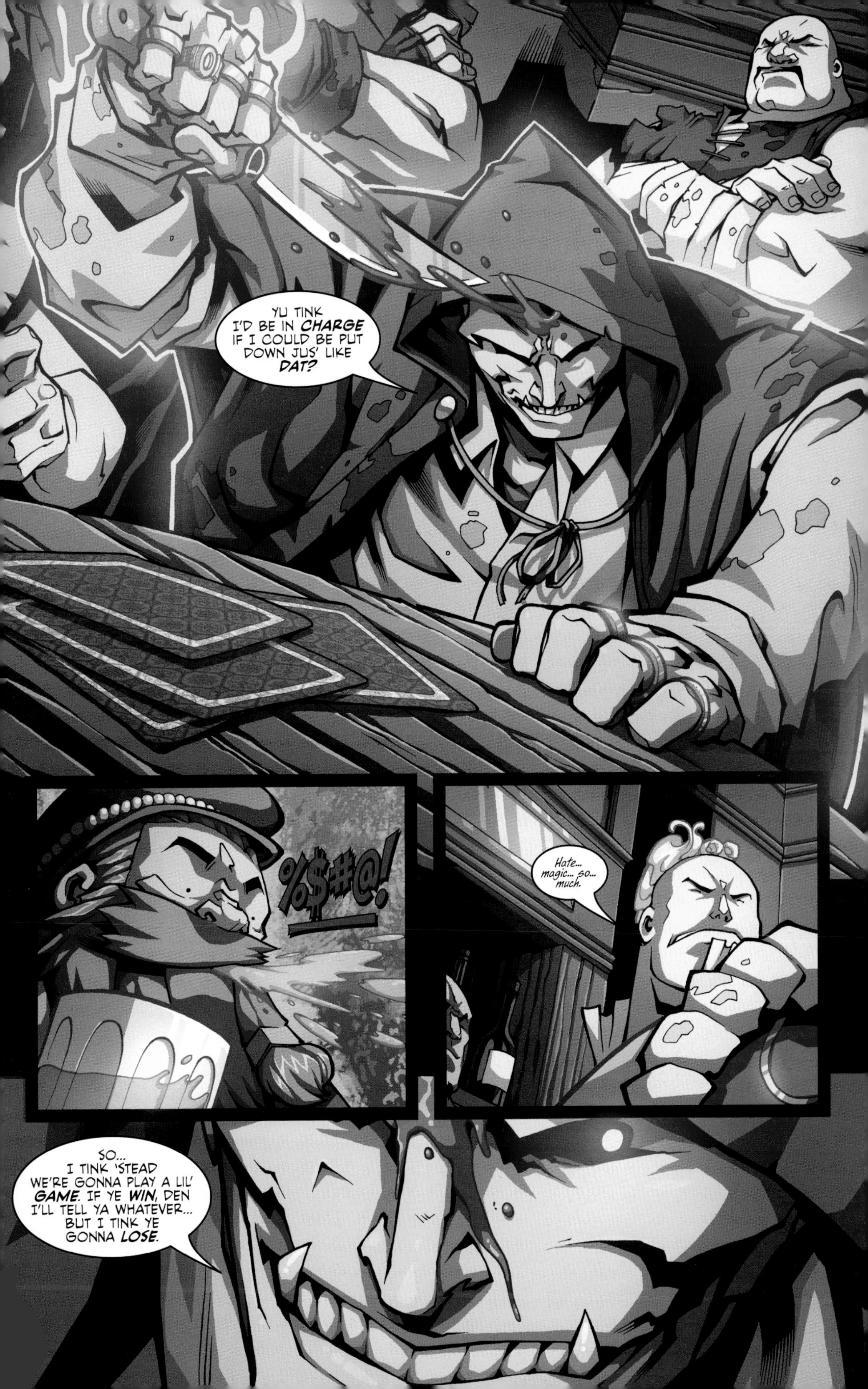
YU TINK I'D BE IN CHARGE IF I COULD BE PUT DOWN JUS' LIKE DAT?
%$#@!
Hate... magic... so... much.
SO... I TINK 'STEAD WE'RE GONNA PLAY A LIL' GAME. IF YE WIN, DEN I'LL TELL YA WHATEVER... BUT I TINK YE GONNA LOSE.

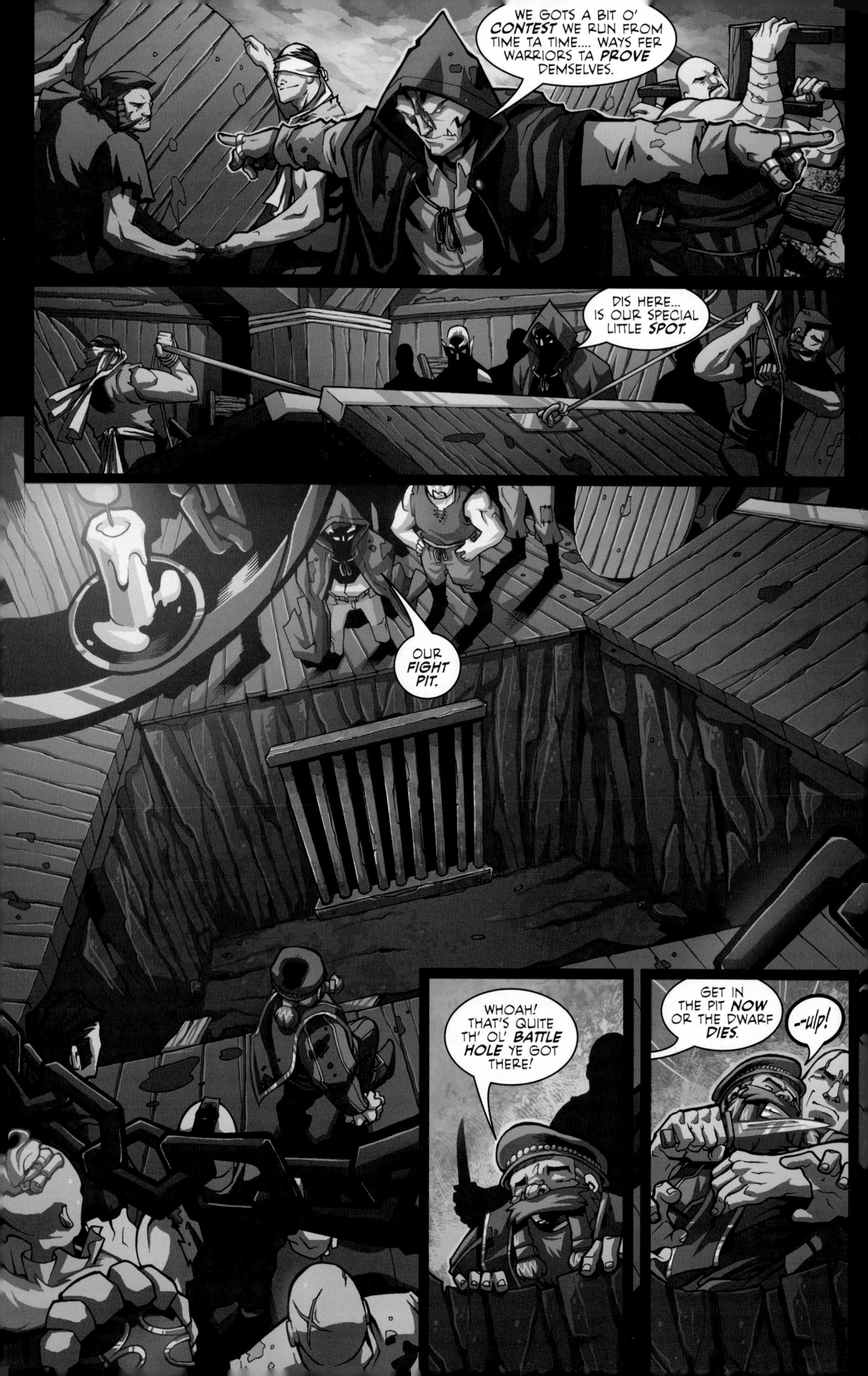
WE GOTS A BIT O' CONTEST WE RUN FROM TIME TA TIME.... WAYS FER WARRIORS TA PROVE DEMSELVES.
DIS HERE... IS OUR SPECIAL LITTLE SPOT.
OUR FIGHT PIT.
WHOAH! THAT'S QUITE TH' OL' BATTLE HOLE YE GOT THERE!
GET IN THE PIT NOW OR THE DWARF DIES.
--ulp!

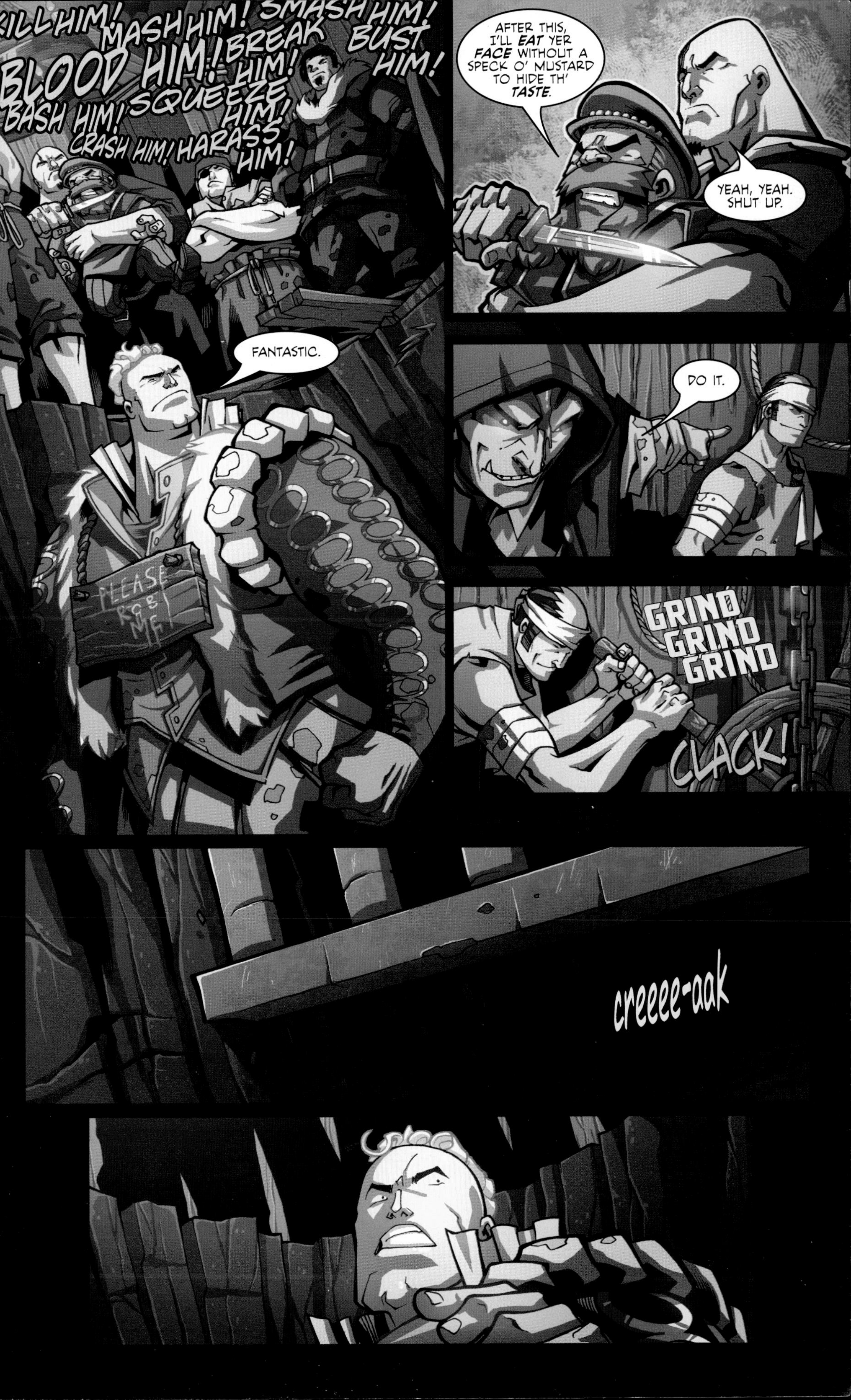
KILL HIM! MASH HIM! SMASH HIM!
BLOOD HIM! BREAK HIM! BUST HIM!
BASH HIM! SQUEEZE HIM!
CRASH HIM! HARASS HIM!
FANTASTIC.
PLEASE ROB ME
AFTER THIS, I'LL **EAT** YER **FACE** WITHOUT A SPECK O' MUSTARD TO HIDE TH' **TASTE**.
YEAH, YEAH. SHUT UP.
DO IT.
GRIND GRIND GRIND
CLACK!
creeee-aak

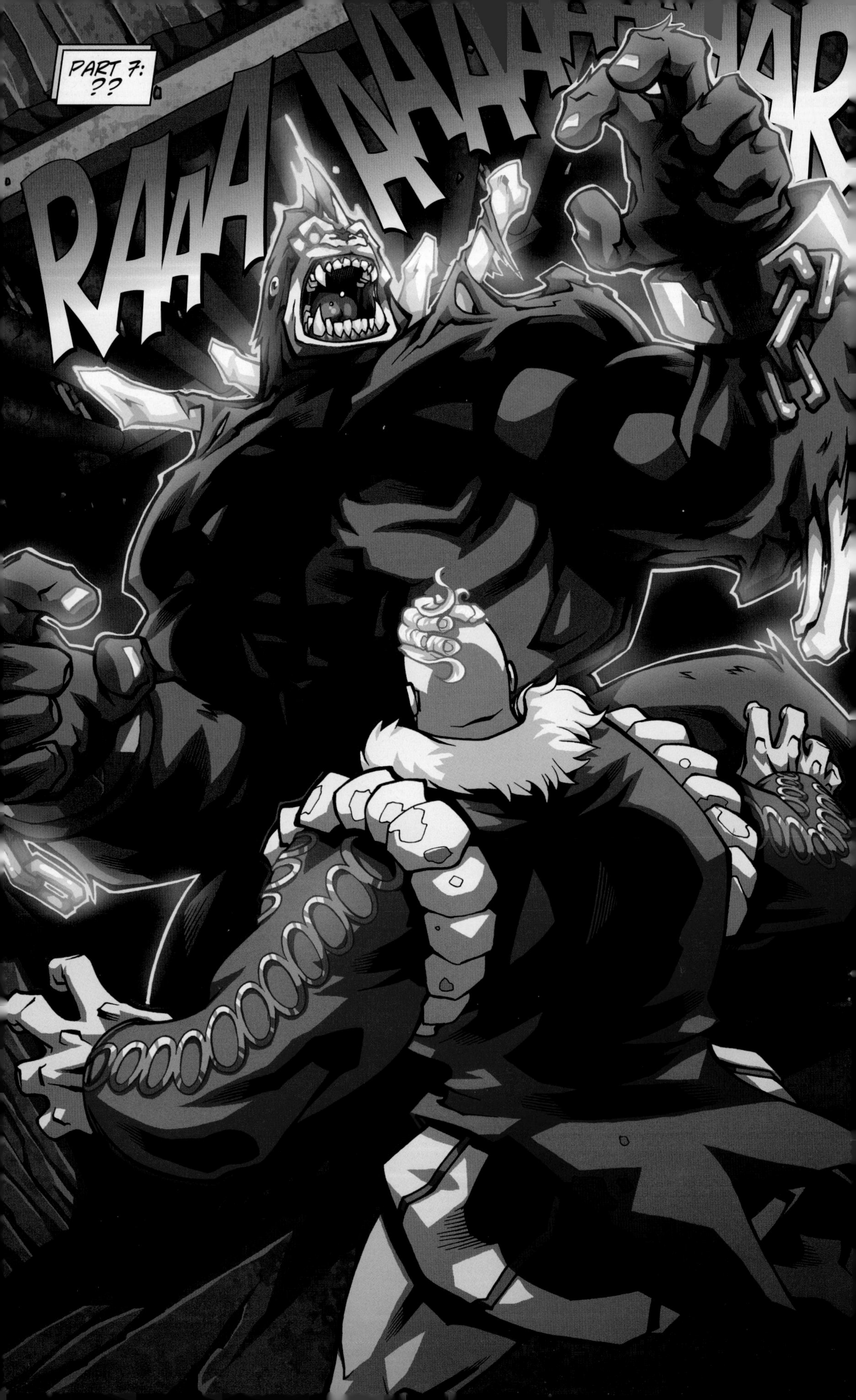
PART 7:
??

CHAPTER THREE

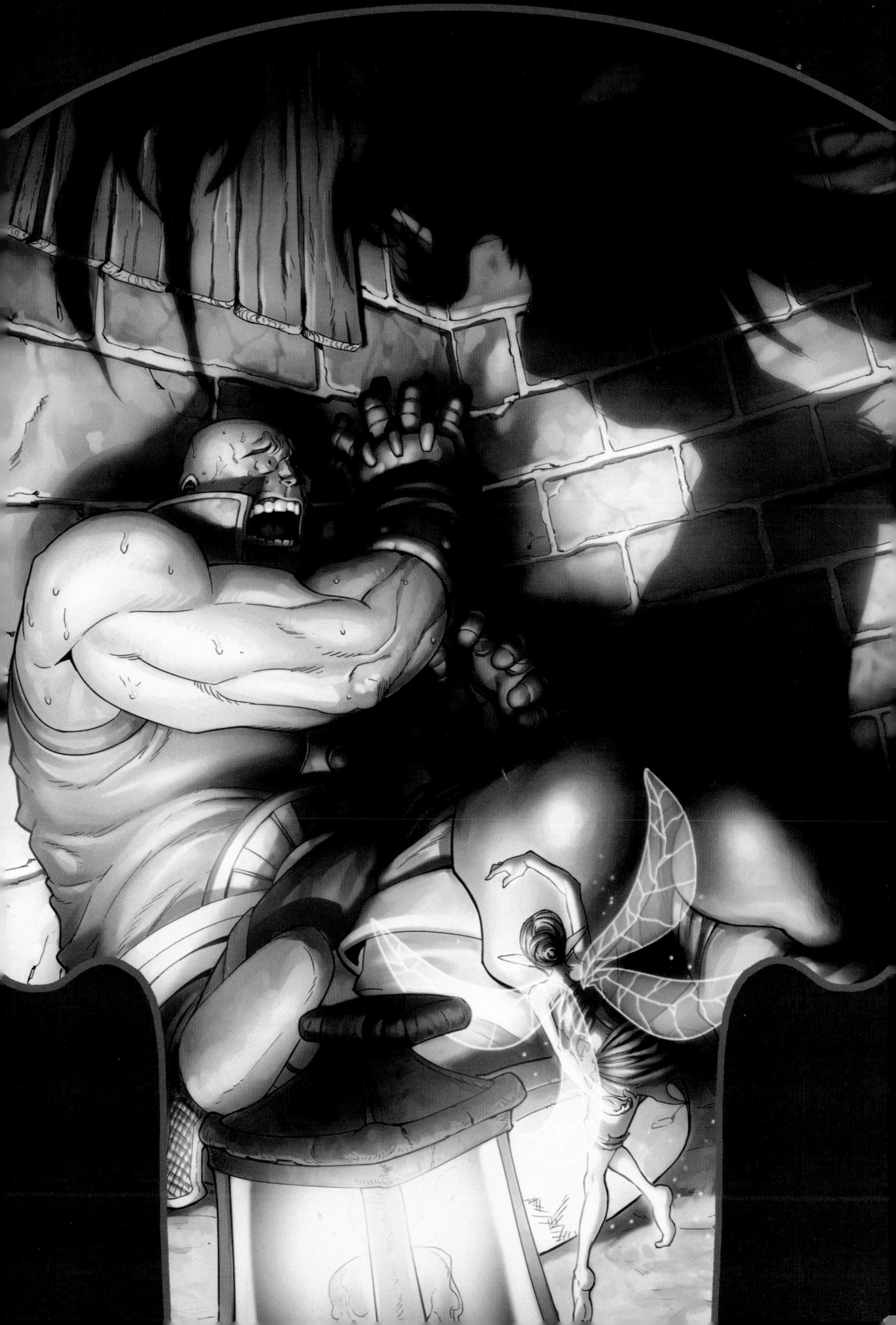

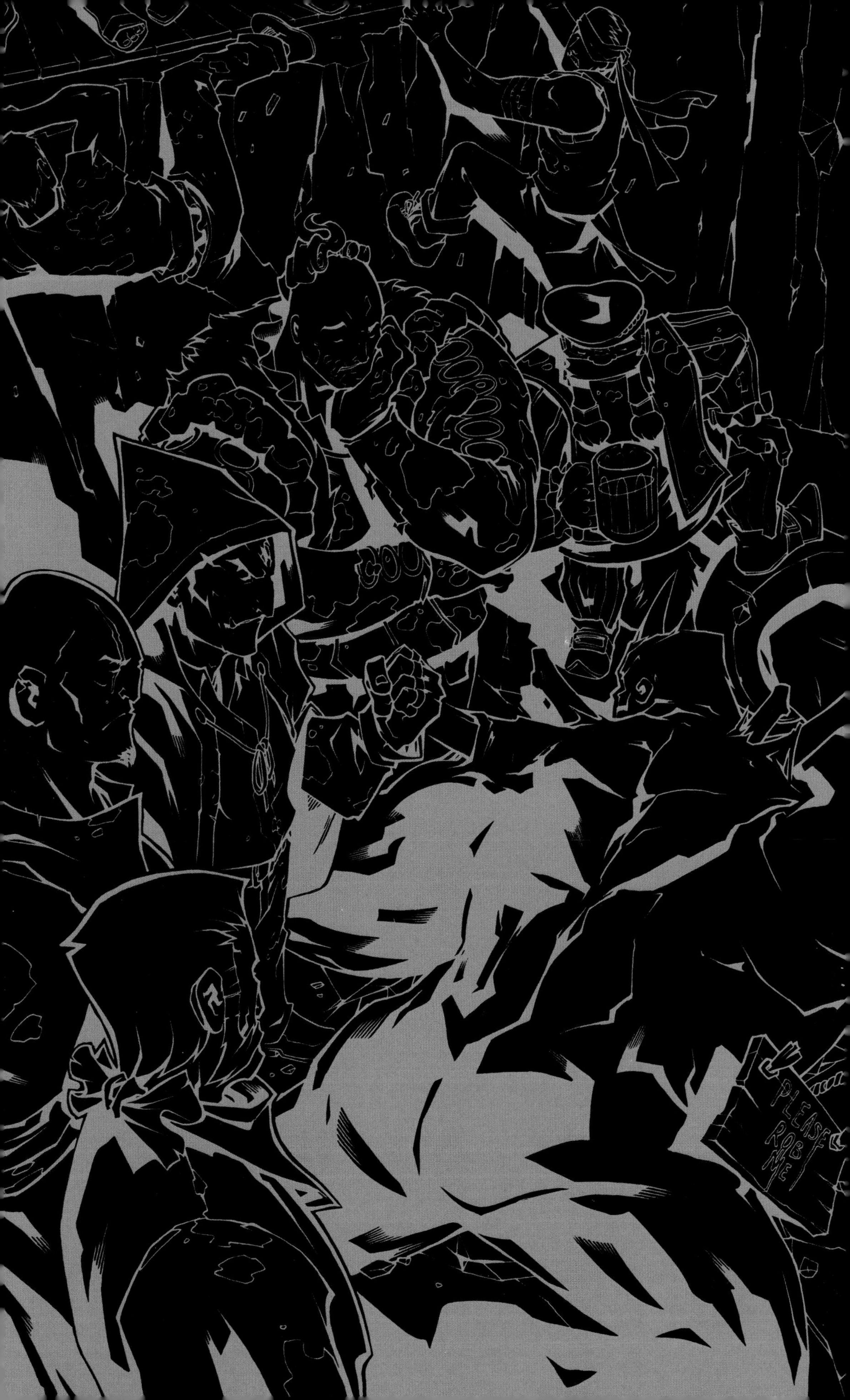
PLEASE ROB ME

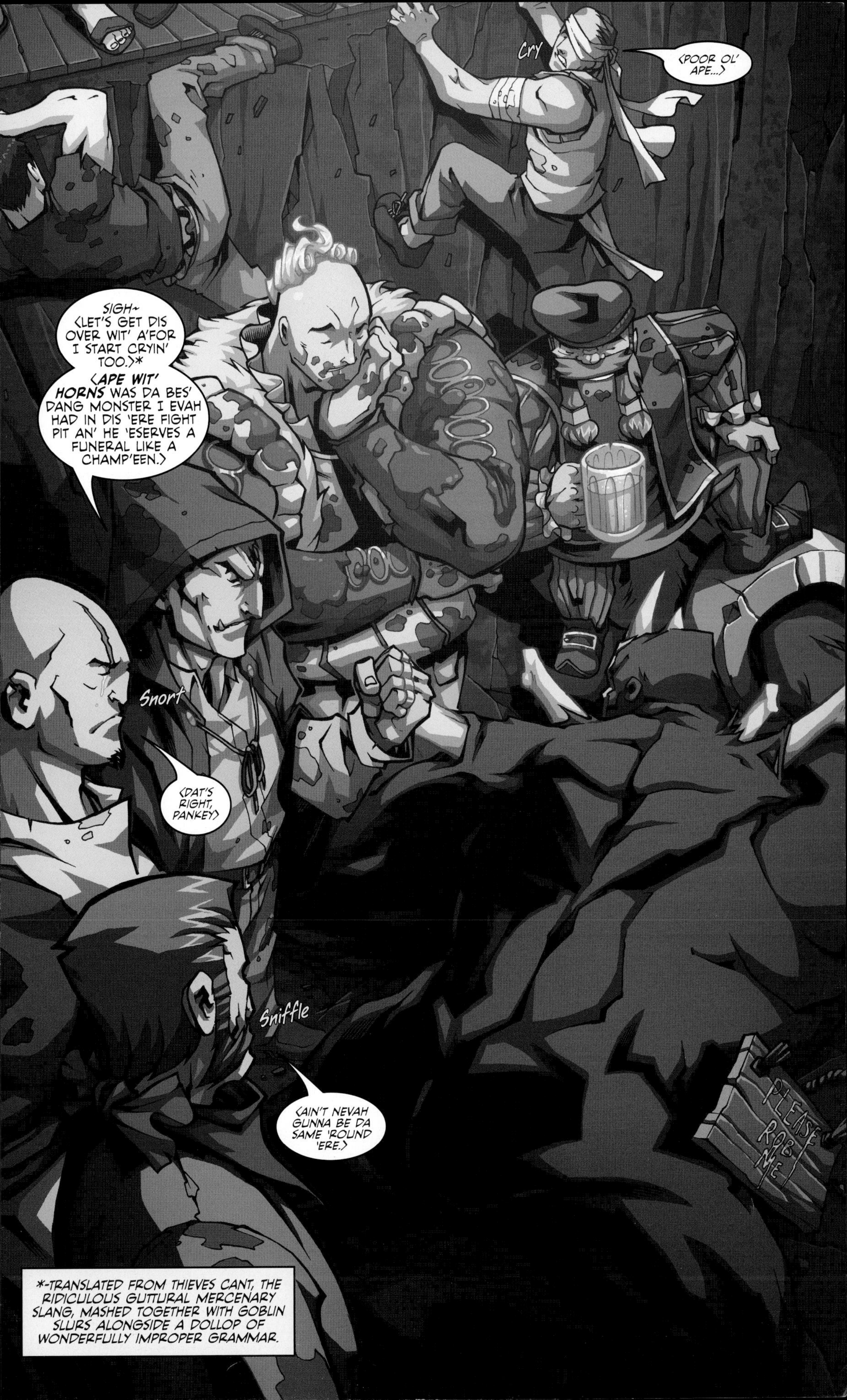
Cry
<POOR OL' APE...>
SIGH~ <LET'S GET DIS OVER WIT' A'FOR I START CRYIN' TOO.>*
<**APE WIT' HORNS** WAS DA BES' DANG MONSTER I EVAH HAD IN DIS 'ERE FIGHT PIT AN' HE 'ESERVES A FUNERAL LIKE A CHAMP'EEN.>
Snort
<DAT'S RIGHT, PANKEY>
Sniffle
<AIN'T NEVAH GUNNA BE DA SAME 'ROUND 'ERE.>
PLEASE ROB ME
*-TRANSLATED FROM THIEVES CANT, THE RIDICULOUS GUTTURAL MERCENARY SLANG, MASHED TOGETHER WITH GOBLIN SLURS ALONGSIDE A DOLLOP OF WONDERFULLY IMPROPER GRAMMAR.

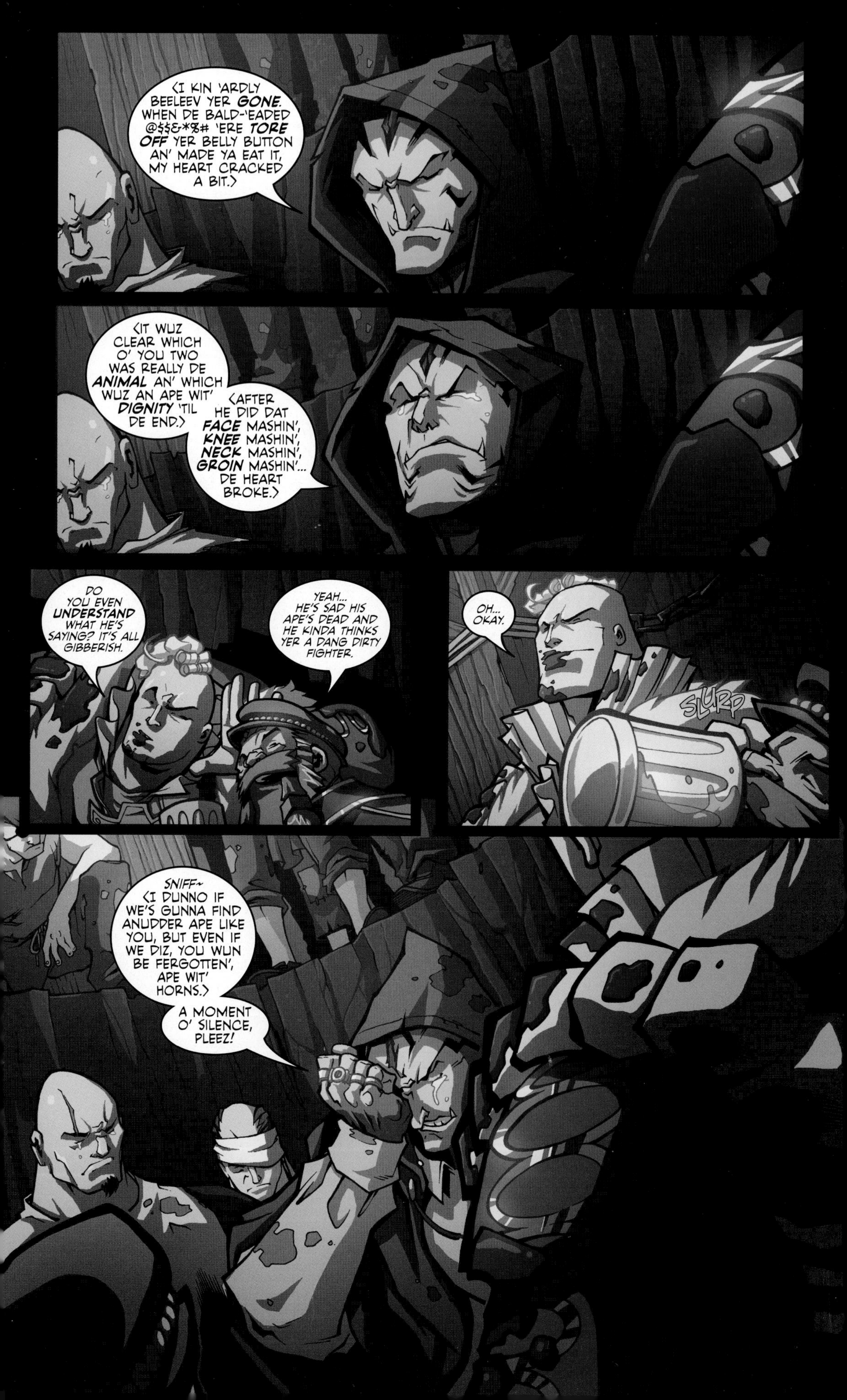
<I KIN 'ARDLY BEELEEV YER GONE. WHEN DE BALD-'EADED @$$&*%# 'ERE TORE OFF YER BELLY BUTTON AN' MADE YA EAT IT, MY HEART CRACKED A BIT.>
<IT WUZ CLEAR WHICH O' YOU TWO WAS REALLY DE ANIMAL AN' WHICH WUZ AN APE WIT' DIGNITY 'TIL DE END.>
<AFTER HE DID DAT FACE MASHIN', KNEE MASHIN', NECK MASHIN', GROIN MASHIN'... DE HEART BROKE.>
DO YOU EVEN UNDERSTAND WHAT HE'S SAYING? IT'S ALL GIBBERISH.
YEAH... HE'S SAD HIS APE'S DEAD AND HE KINDA THINKS YER A DANG DIRTY FIGHTER.
OH... OKAY.
SLURP
SNIFF~ <I DUNNO IF WE'S GUNNA FIND ANUDDER APE LIKE YOU, BUT EVEN IF WE DIZ, YOU WUN BE FERGOTTEN', APE WIT' HORNS.>
A MOMENT O' SILENCE, PLEEZ!

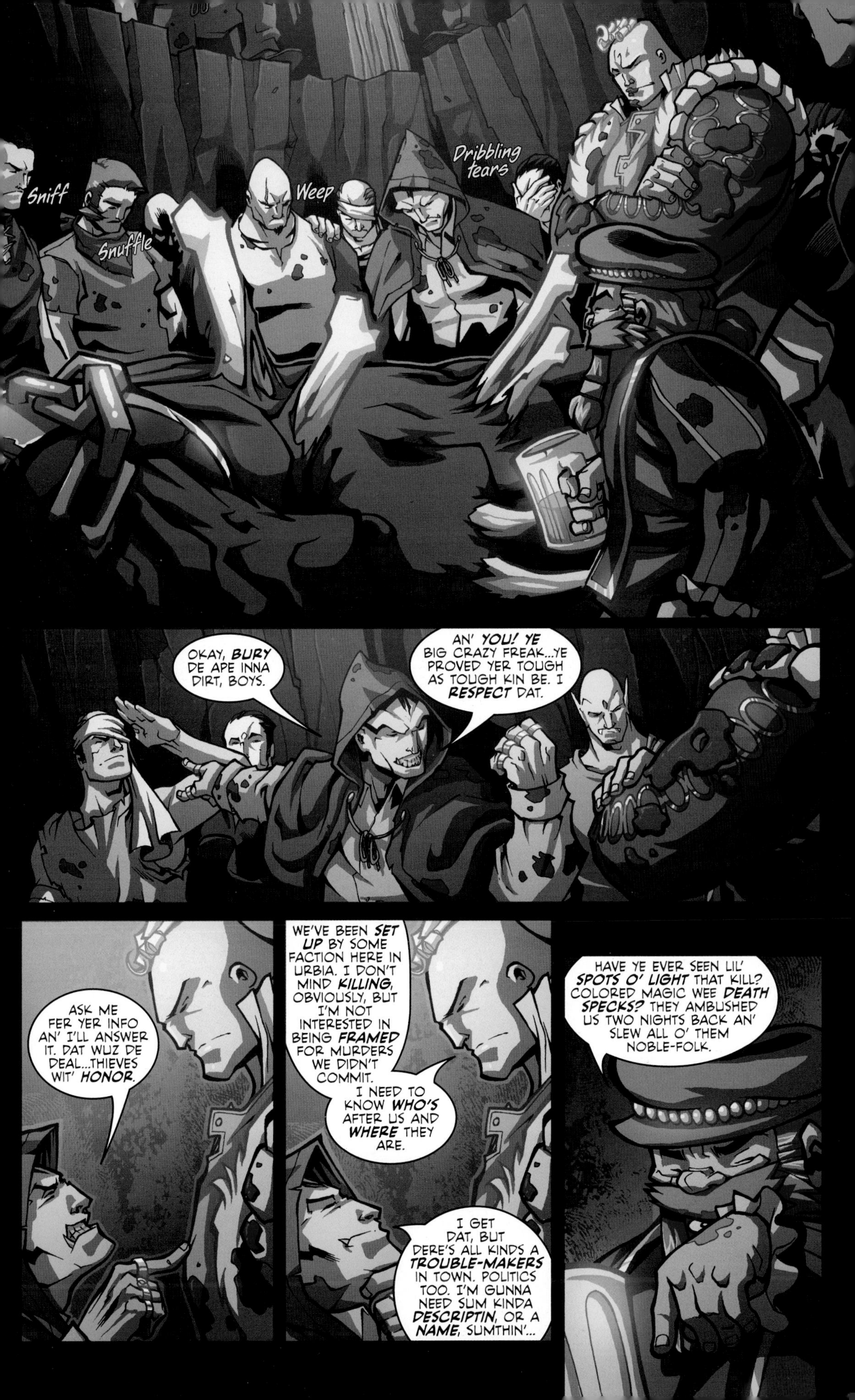
Sniff
Snuffle
Weep
Dribbling tears
OKAY, BURY DE APE INNA DIRT, BOYS.
AN' YOU! YE BIG CRAZY FREAK...YE PROVED YER TOUGH AS TOUGH KIN BE. I RESPECT DAT.
ASK ME FER YER INFO AN' I'LL ANSWER IT. DAT WUZ DE DEAL...THIEVES WIT' HONOR.
WE'VE BEEN SET UP BY SOME FACTION HERE IN URBIA. I DON'T MIND KILLING, OBVIOUSLY, BUT I'M NOT INTERESTED IN BEING FRAMED FOR MURDERS WE DIDN'T COMMIT.
I NEED TO KNOW WHO'S AFTER US AND WHERE THEY ARE.
I GET DAT, BUT DERE'S ALL KINDS A TROUBLE-MAKERS IN TOWN. POLITICS TOO. I'M GUNNA NEED SUM KINDA DESCRIPTIN, OR A NAME, SUMTHIN'...
HAVE YE EVER SEEN LIL' SPOTS O' LIGHT THAT KILL? COLORED MAGIC WEE DEATH SPECKS? THEY AMBUSHED US TWO NIGHTS BACK AN' SLEW ALL O' THEM NOBLE-FOLK.

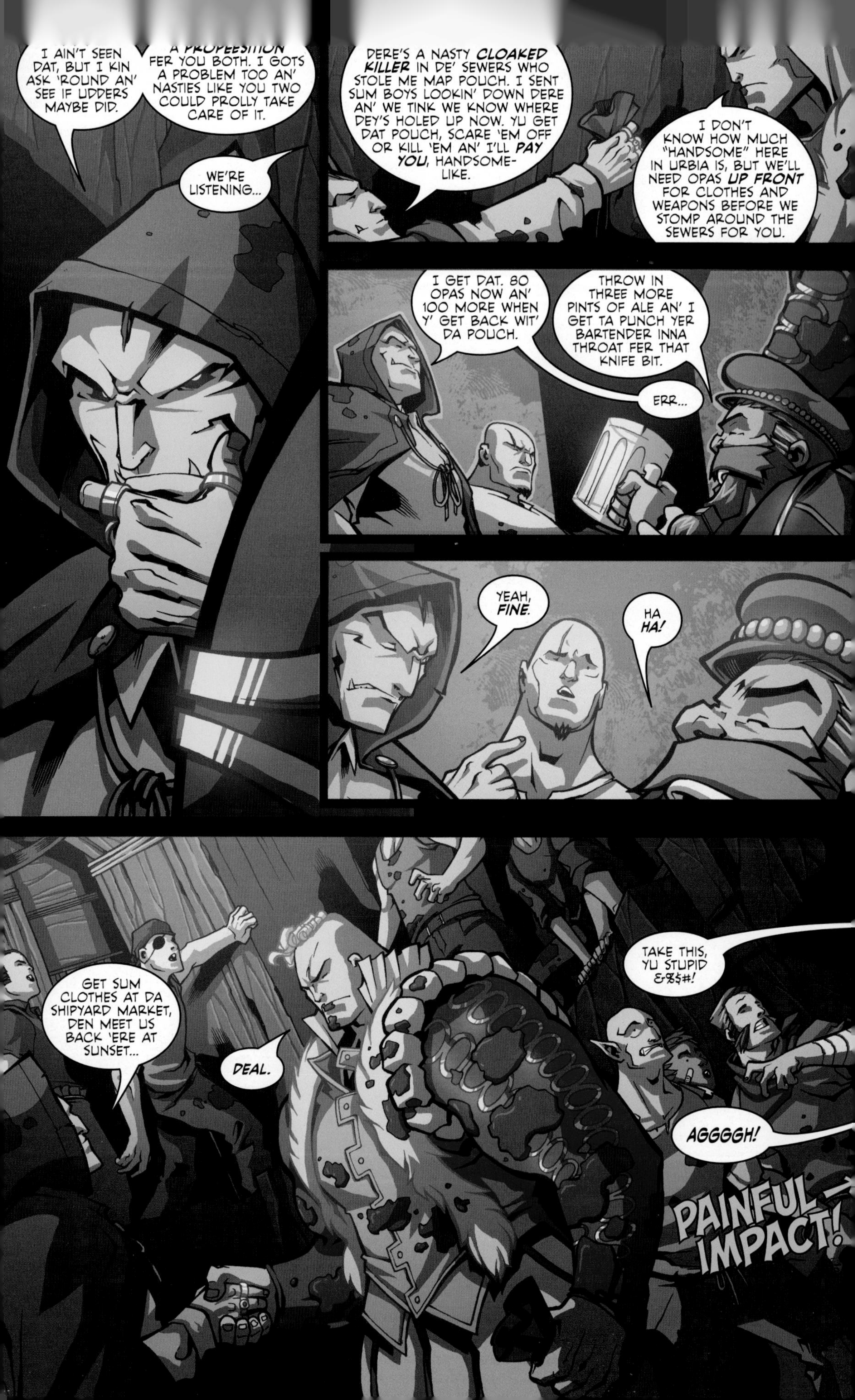
I AIN'T SEEN DAT, BUT I KIN ASK 'ROUND AN' SEE IF UDDERS MAYBE DID.
A PROPEESITION FER YOU BOTH. I GOTS A PROBLEM TOO AN' NASTIES LIKE YOU TWO COULD PROLLY TAKE CARE OF IT.
WE'RE LISTENING...
DERE'S A NASTY CLOAKED KILLER IN DE' SEWERS WHO STOLE ME MAP POUCH. I SENT SUM BOYS LOOKIN' DOWN DERE AN' WE TINK WE KNOW WHERE DEY'S HOLED UP NOW. YU GET DAT POUCH, SCARE 'EM OFF OR KILL 'EM AN' I'LL PAY YOU, HANDSOME-LIKE.
I DON'T KNOW HOW MUCH "HANDSOME" HERE IN URBIA IS, BUT WE'LL NEED OPAS UP FRONT FOR CLOTHES AND WEAPONS BEFORE WE STOMP AROUND THE SEWERS FOR YOU.
I GET DAT. 80 OPAS NOW AN' 100 MORE WHEN Y' GET BACK WIT' DA POUCH.
THROW IN THREE MORE PINTS OF ALE AN' I GET TA PUNCH YER BARTENDER INNA THROAT FER THAT KNIFE BIT.
ERR...
YEAH, FINE.
HA HA!
GET SUM CLOTHES AT DA SHIPYARD MARKET, DEN MEET US BACK 'ERE AT SUNSET...
DEAL.
TAKE THIS, YU STUPID &%$#!
AGGGGH!
PAINFUL IMPACT!

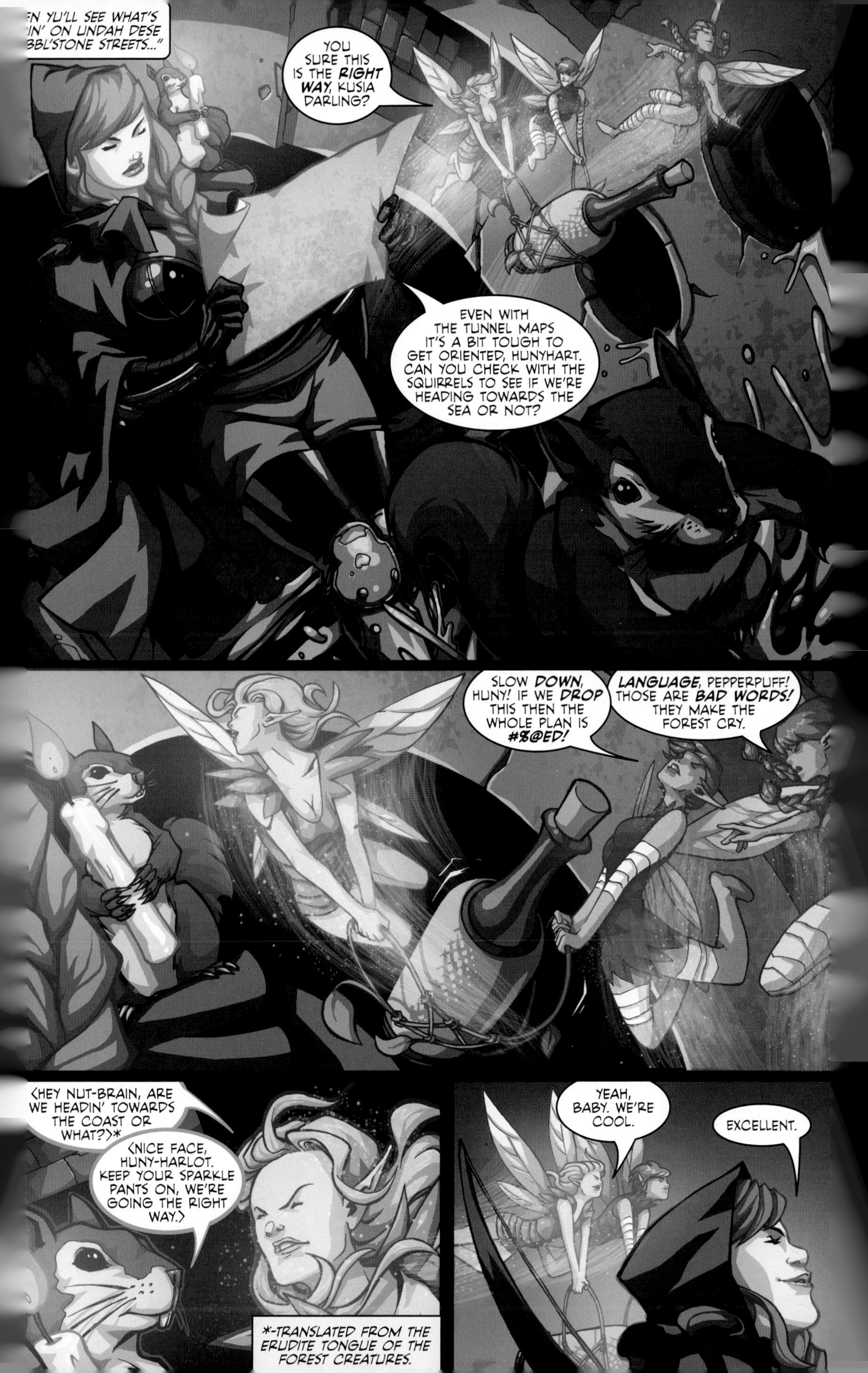

EN YU'LL SEE WHAT'S
IN' ON UNDAH DESE
BBL'STONE STREETS..."
YOU SURE THIS IS THE RIGHT WAY, KUSIA DARLING?
EVEN WITH THE TUNNEL MAPS IT'S A BIT TOUGH TO GET ORIENTED, HUNYHART. CAN YOU CHECK WITH THE SQUIRRELS TO SEE IF WE'RE HEADING TOWARDS THE SEA OR NOT?
SLOW DOWN, HUNY! IF WE DROP THIS THEN THE WHOLE PLAN IS #%@ED!
LANGUAGE, PEPPERPUFF! THOSE ARE BAD WORDS! THEY MAKE THE FOREST CRY.
<HEY NUT-BRAIN, ARE WE HEADIN' TOWARDS THE COAST OR WHAT?>*
<NICE FACE, HUNY-HARLOT. KEEP YOUR SPARKLE PANTS ON, WE'RE GOING THE RIGHT WAY.>
*-TRANSLATED FROM THE ERUDITE TONGUE OF THE FOREST CREATURES.
YEAH, BABY. WE'RE COOL.
EXCELLENT.

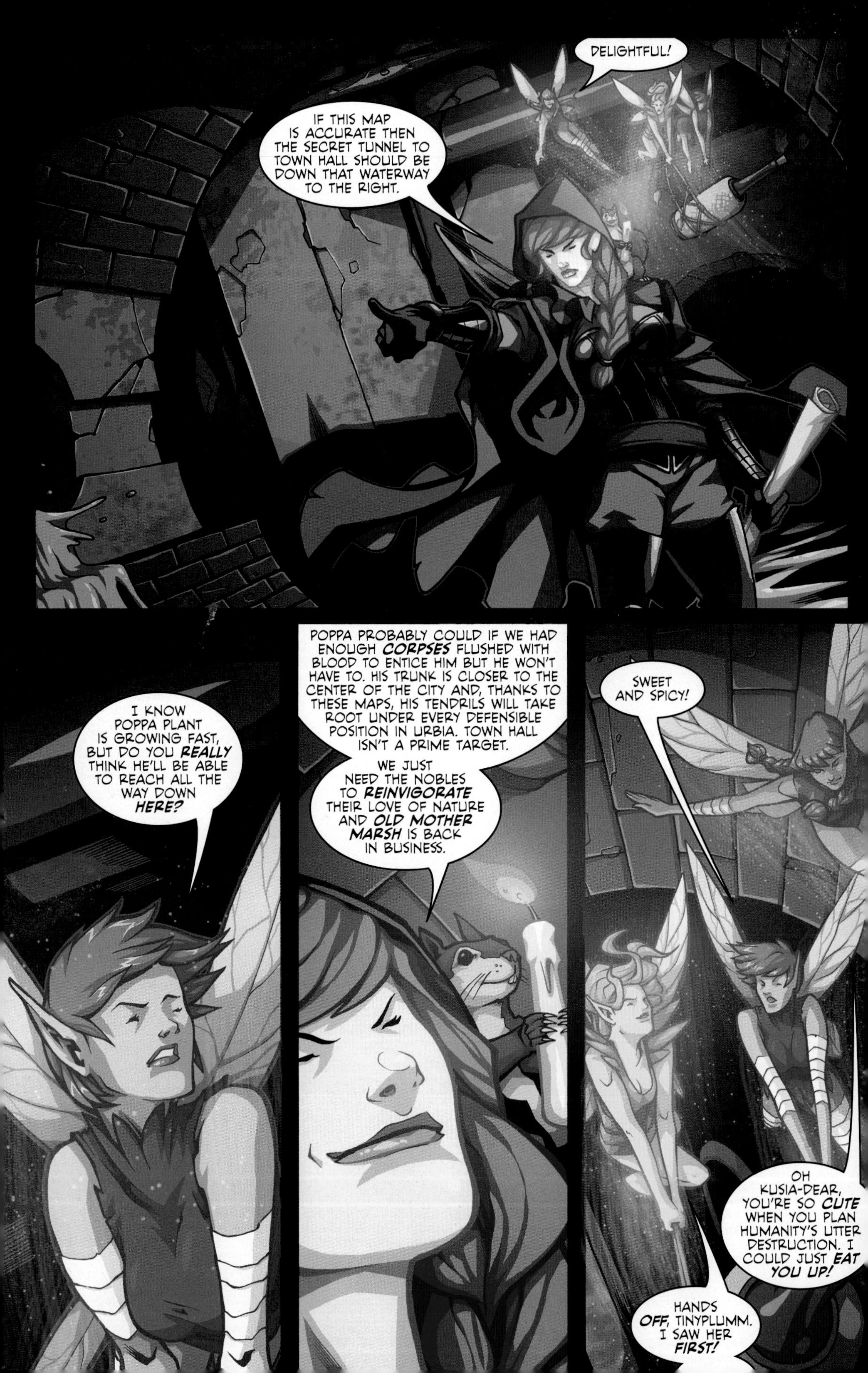
DELIGHTFUL!
IF THIS MAP IS ACCURATE THEN THE SECRET TUNNEL TO TOWN HALL SHOULD BE DOWN THAT WATERWAY TO THE RIGHT.
I KNOW POPPA PLANT IS GROWING FAST, BUT DO YOU REALLY THINK HE'LL BE ABLE TO REACH ALL THE WAY DOWN HERE?
POPPA PROBABLY COULD IF WE HAD ENOUGH CORPSES FLUSHED WITH BLOOD TO ENTICE HIM BUT HE WON'T HAVE TO. HIS TRUNK IS CLOSER TO THE CENTER OF THE CITY AND, THANKS TO THESE MAPS, HIS TENDRILS WILL TAKE ROOT UNDER EVERY DEFENSIBLE POSITION IN URBIA. TOWN HALL ISN'T A PRIME TARGET.
WE JUST NEED THE NOBLES TO REINVIGORATE THEIR LOVE OF NATURE AND OLD MOTHER MARSH IS BACK IN BUSINESS.
SWEET AND SPICY!
OH KUSIA-DEAR, YOU'RE SO CUTE WHEN YOU PLAN HUMANITY'S UTTER DESTRUCTION. I COULD JUST EAT YOU UP!
HANDS OFF, TINYPLUMM. I SAW HER FIRST!

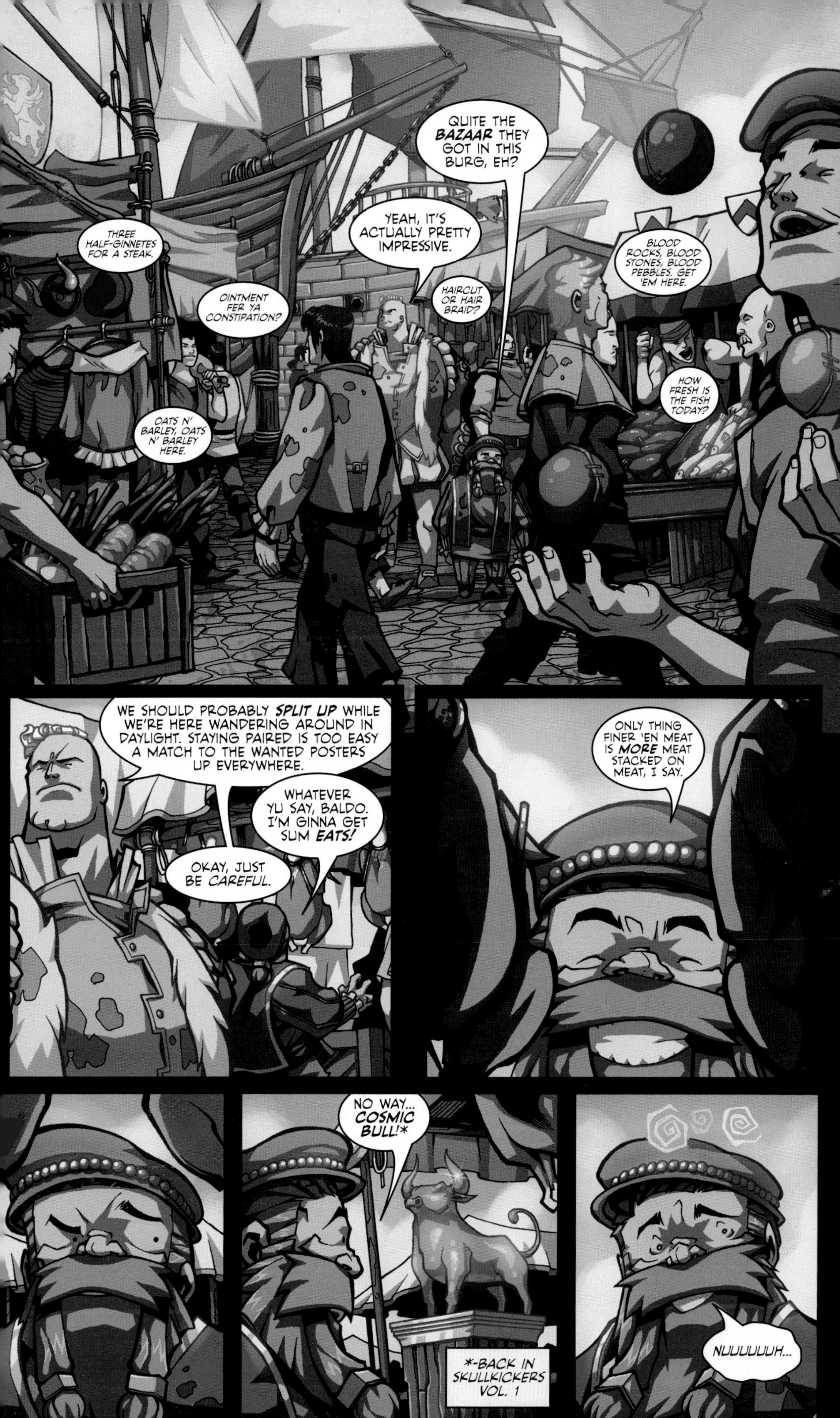
THREE HALF-GINNETES FOR A STEAK.
OINTMENT FER YA CONSTIPATION?
QUITE THE BAZAAR THEY GOT IN THIS BURG, EH?
YEAH, IT'S ACTUALLY PRETTY IMPRESSIVE.
HAIRCUT OR HAIR BRAID?
BLOOD ROCKS, BLOOD STONES, BLOOD PEBBLES. GET 'EM HERE.
OATS N' BARLEY, OATS N' BARLEY HERE.
HOW FRESH IS THE FISH TODAY?
WE SHOULD PROBABLY SPLIT UP WHILE WE'RE HERE WANDERING AROUND IN DAYLIGHT. STAYING PAIRED IS TOO EASY A MATCH TO THE WANTED POSTERS UP EVERYWHERE.
WHATEVER YU SAY, BALDO. I'M GINNA GET SUM EATS!
OKAY, JUST BE CAREFUL.
ONLY THING FINER 'EN MEAT IS MORE MEAT STACKED ON MEAT, I SAY.
NO WAY... COSMIC BULL!*
*-BACK IN SKULLKICKERS VOL. 1
NUUUUUUH...

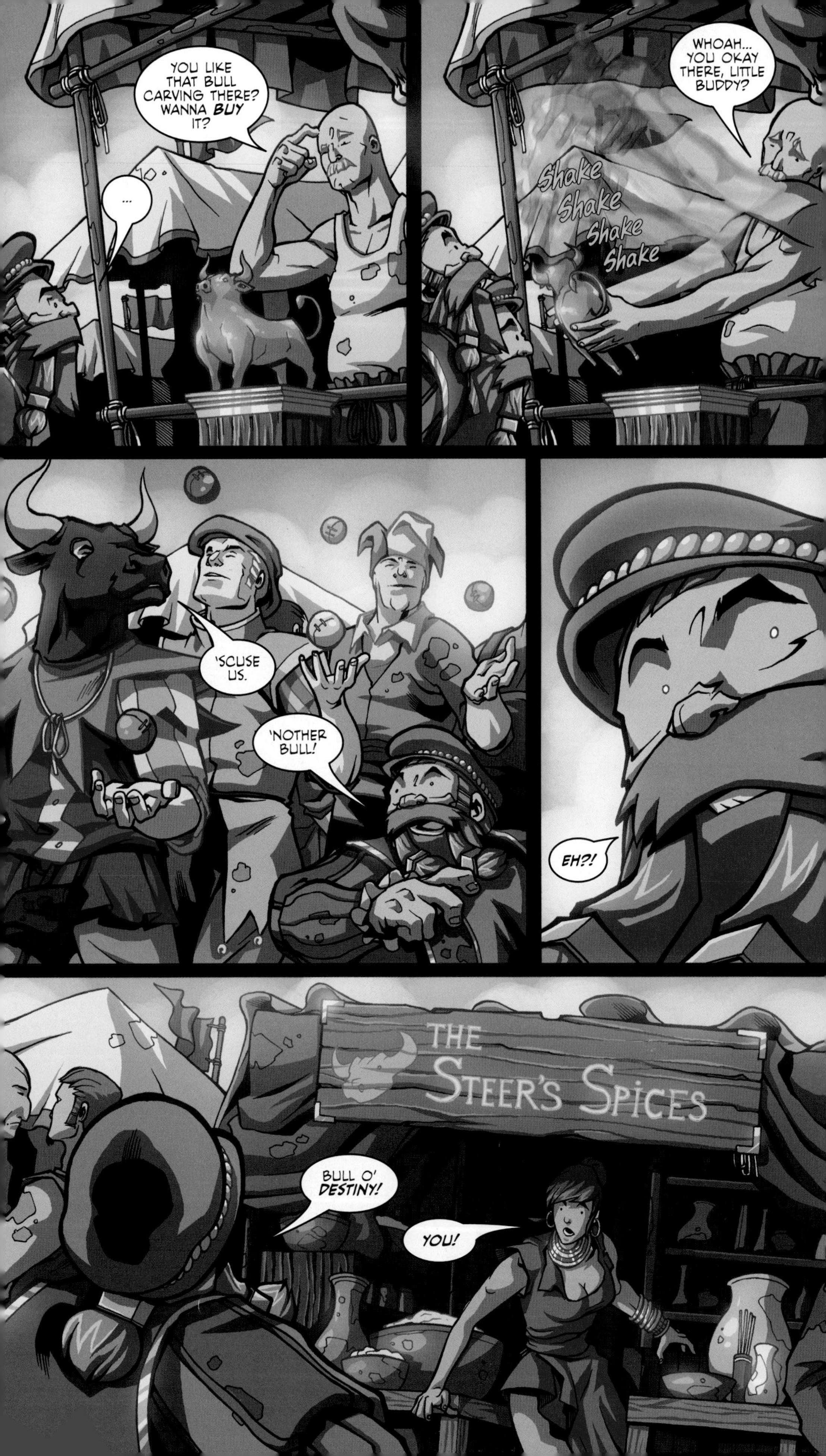
YOU LIKE THAT BULL CARVING THERE? WANNA BUY IT?
...
WHOAH... YOU OKAY THERE, LITTLE BUDDY?
Shake Shake Shake Shake
'SCUSE US.
'NOTHER BULL!
EH?!
THE STEER'S SPICES
BULL O' DESTINY!
YOU!

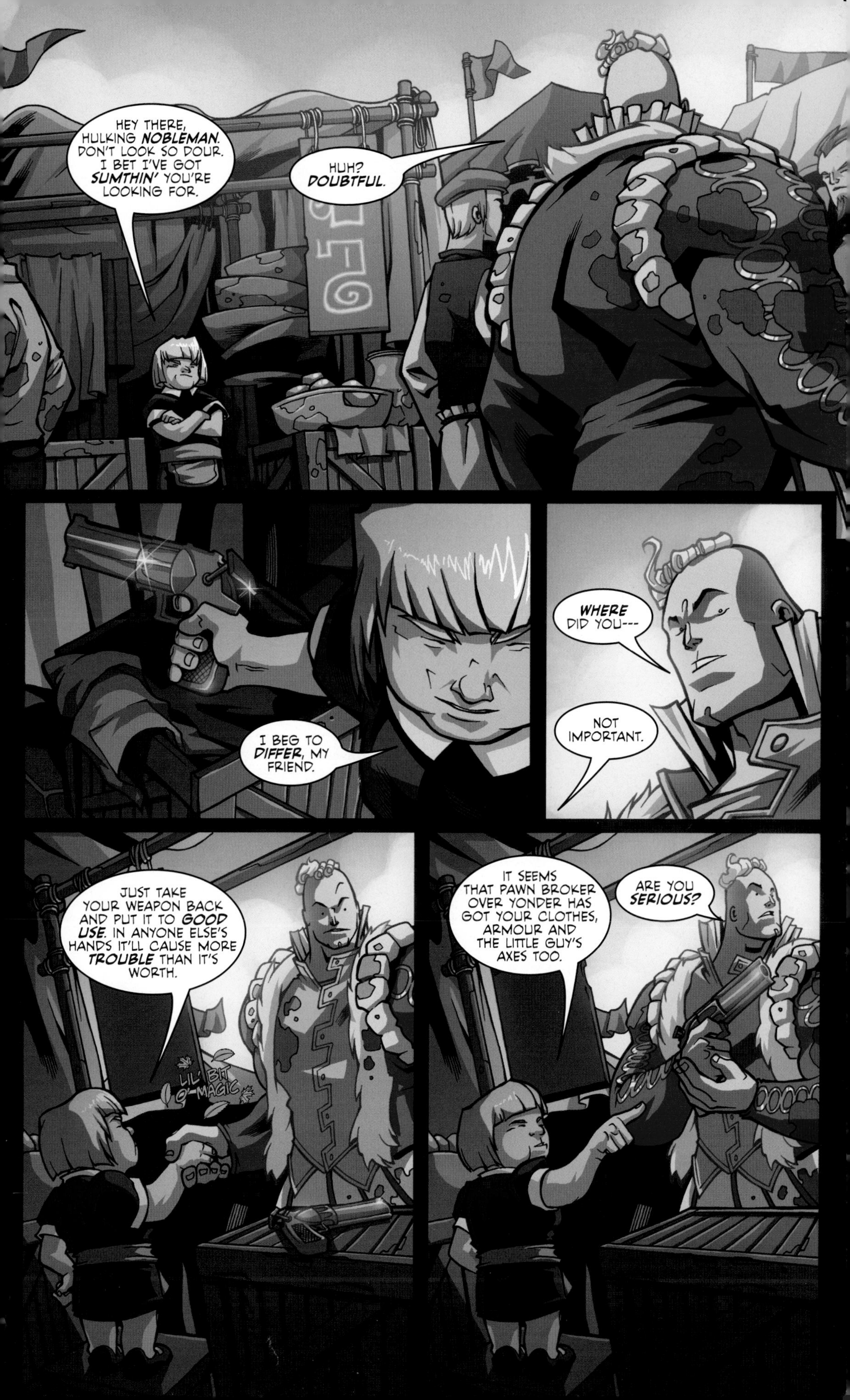
HEY THERE, HULKING NOBLEMAN. DON'T LOOK SO DOUR. I BET I'VE GOT SUMTHIN' YOU'RE LOOKING FOR.
HUH? DOUBTFUL.
I BEG TO DIFFER, MY FRIEND.
WHERE DID YOU---
NOT IMPORTANT.
JUST TAKE YOUR WEAPON BACK AND PUT IT TO GOOD USE. IN ANYONE ELSE'S HANDS IT'LL CAUSE MORE TROUBLE THAN IT'S WORTH.
LIL' BIT O' MAGIC
IT SEEMS THAT PAWN BROKER OVER YONDER HAS GOT YOUR CLOTHES, ARMOUR AND THE LITTLE GUY'S AXES TOO.
ARE YOU SERIOUS?

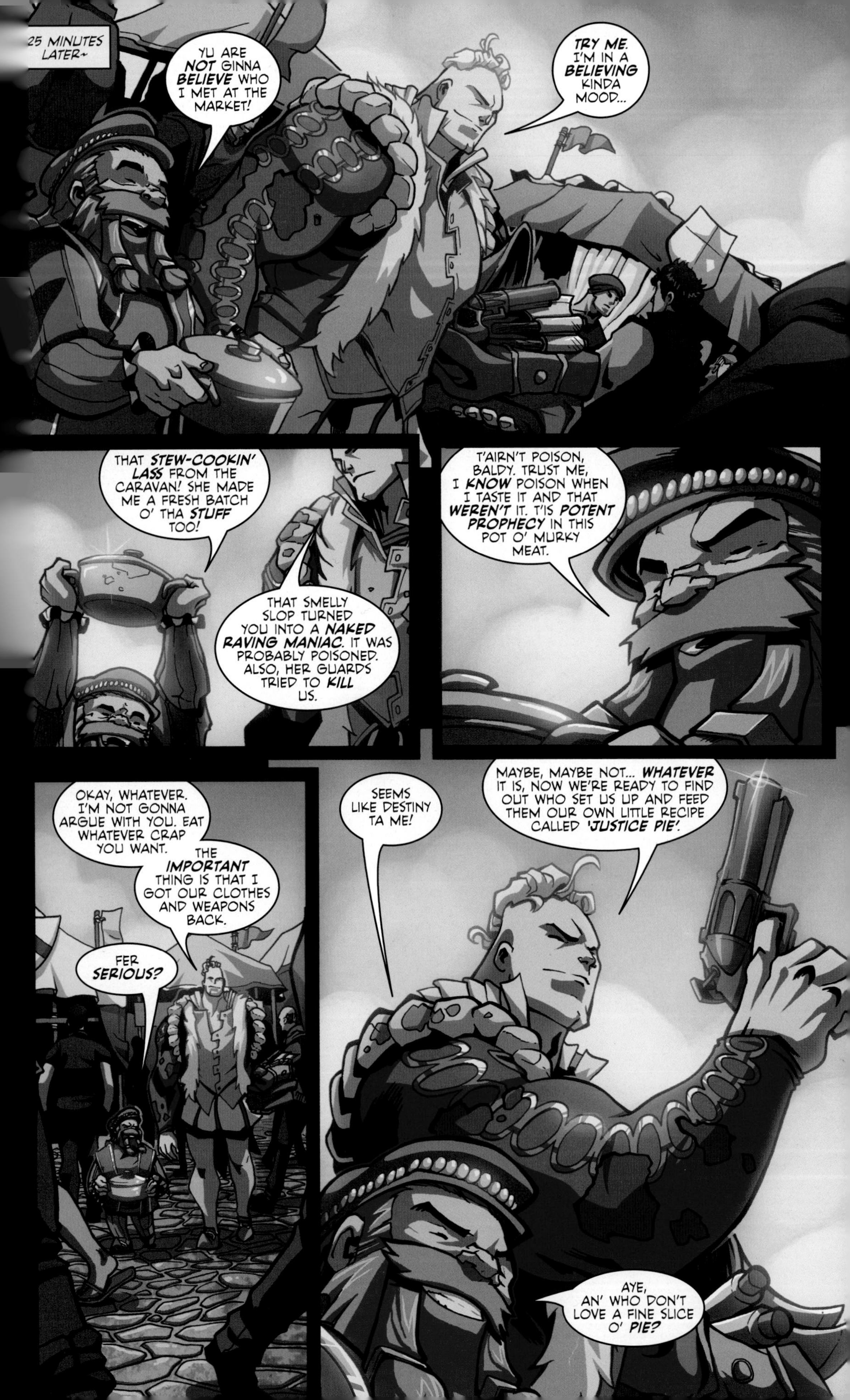
25 MINUTES LATER~
YU ARE NOT GINNA BELIEVE WHO I MET AT THE MARKET!
TRY ME. I'M IN A BELIEVING KINDA MOOD...
THAT STEW-COOKIN' LASS FROM THE CARAVAN! SHE MADE ME A FRESH BATCH O' THA STUFF TOO!
THAT SMELLY SLOP TURNED YOU INTO A NAKED RAVING MANIAC. IT WAS PROBABLY POISONED. ALSO, HER GUARDS TRIED TO KILL US.
T'AIRN'T POISON, BALDY. TRUST ME, I KNOW POISON WHEN I TASTE IT AND THAT WEREN'T IT. T'IS POTENT PROPHECY IN THIS POT O' MURKY MEAT.
OKAY, WHATEVER. I'M NOT GONNA ARGUE WITH YOU. EAT WHATEVER CRAP YOU WANT.
THE IMPORTANT THING IS THAT I GOT OUR CLOTHES AND WEAPONS BACK.
FER SERIOUS?
SEEMS LIKE DESTINY TA ME!
MAYBE, MAYBE NOT... WHATEVER IT IS, NOW WE'RE READY TO FIND OUT WHO SET US UP AND FEED THEM OUR OWN LITTLE RECIPE CALLED 'JUSTICE PIE'.
AYE, AN' WHO DON'T LOVE A FINE SLICE O' PIE?

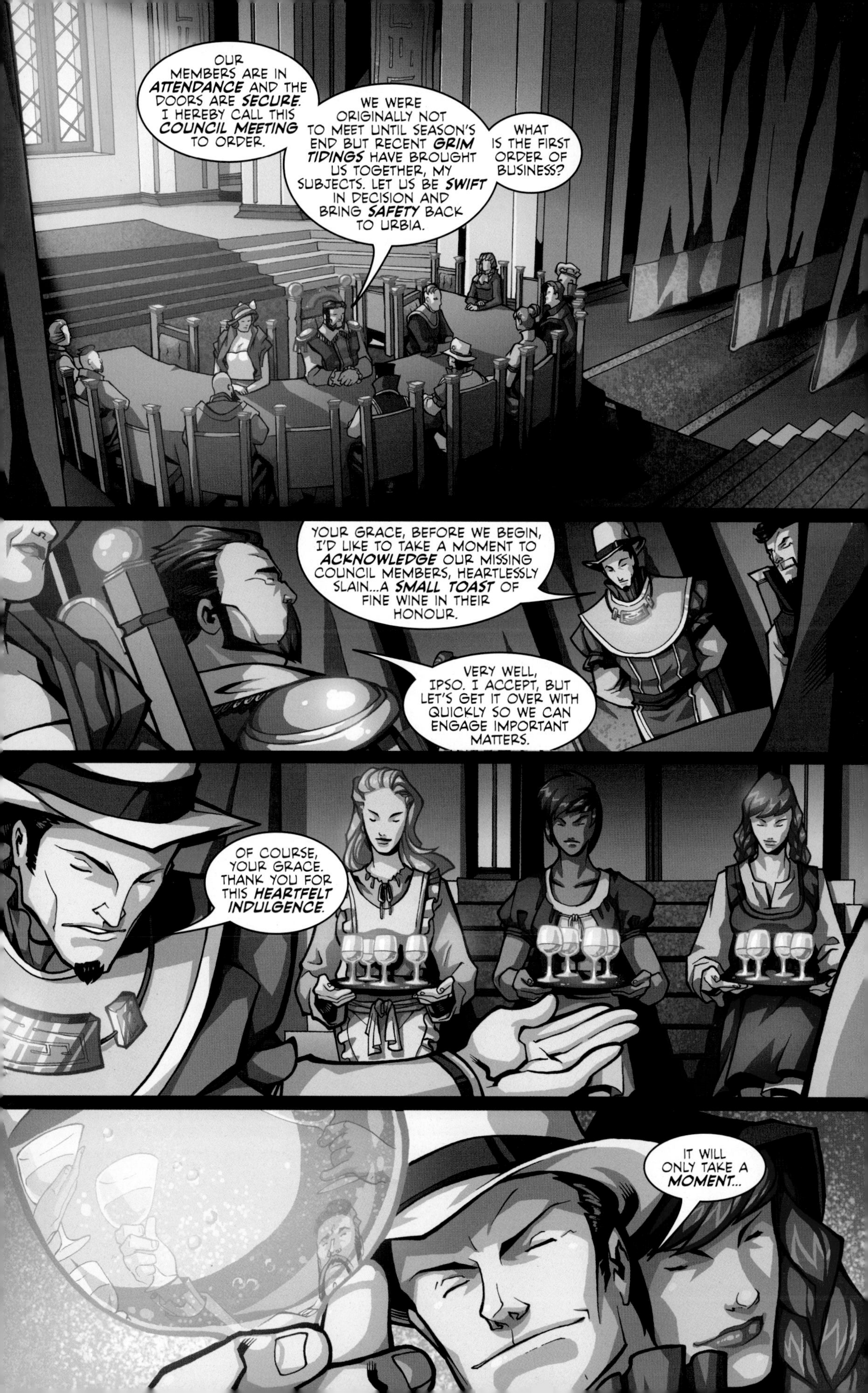
OUR MEMBERS ARE IN ATTENDANCE AND THE DOORS ARE SECURE. I HEREBY CALL THIS COUNCIL MEETING TO ORDER.
WE WERE ORIGINALLY NOT TO MEET UNTIL SEASON'S END BUT RECENT GRIM TIDINGS HAVE BROUGHT US TOGETHER, MY SUBJECTS. LET US BE SWIFT IN DECISION AND BRING SAFETY BACK TO URBIA.
WHAT IS THE FIRST ORDER OF BUSINESS?
YOUR GRACE, BEFORE WE BEGIN, I'D LIKE TO TAKE A MOMENT TO ACKNOWLEDGE OUR MISSING COUNCIL MEMBERS, HEARTLESSLY SLAIN...A SMALL TOAST OF FINE WINE IN THEIR HONOUR.
VERY WELL, IPSO. I ACCEPT, BUT LET'S GET IT OVER WITH QUICKLY SO WE CAN ENGAGE IMPORTANT MATTERS.
OF COURSE, YOUR GRACE. THANK YOU FOR THIS HEARTFELT INDULGENCE.
IT WILL ONLY TAKE A MOMENT...

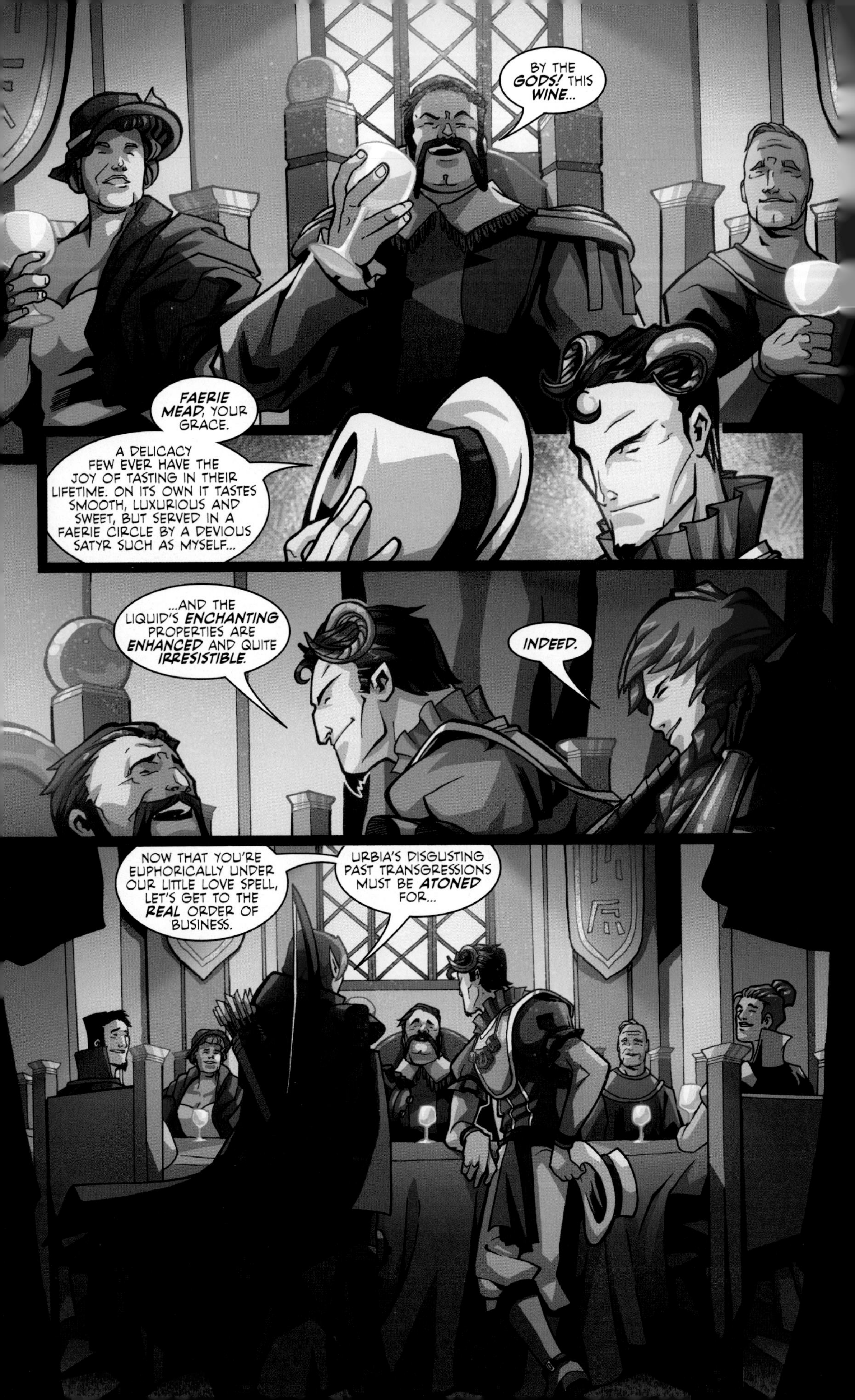
BY THE GODS! THIS WINE...
FAERIE MEAD, YOUR GRACE.
A DELICACY FEW EVER HAVE THE JOY OF TASTING IN THEIR LIFETIME. ON ITS OWN IT TASTES SMOOTH, LUXURIOUS AND SWEET, BUT SERVED IN A FAERIE CIRCLE BY A DEVIOUS SATYR SUCH AS MYSELF...
...AND THE LIQUID'S ENCHANTING PROPERTIES ARE ENHANCED AND QUITE IRRESISTIBLE.
INDEED.
NOW THAT YOU'RE EUPHORICALLY UNDER OUR LITTLE LOVE SPELL, LET'S GET TO THE REAL ORDER OF BUSINESS.
URBIA'S DISGUSTING PAST TRANSGRESSIONS MUST BE ATONED FOR...

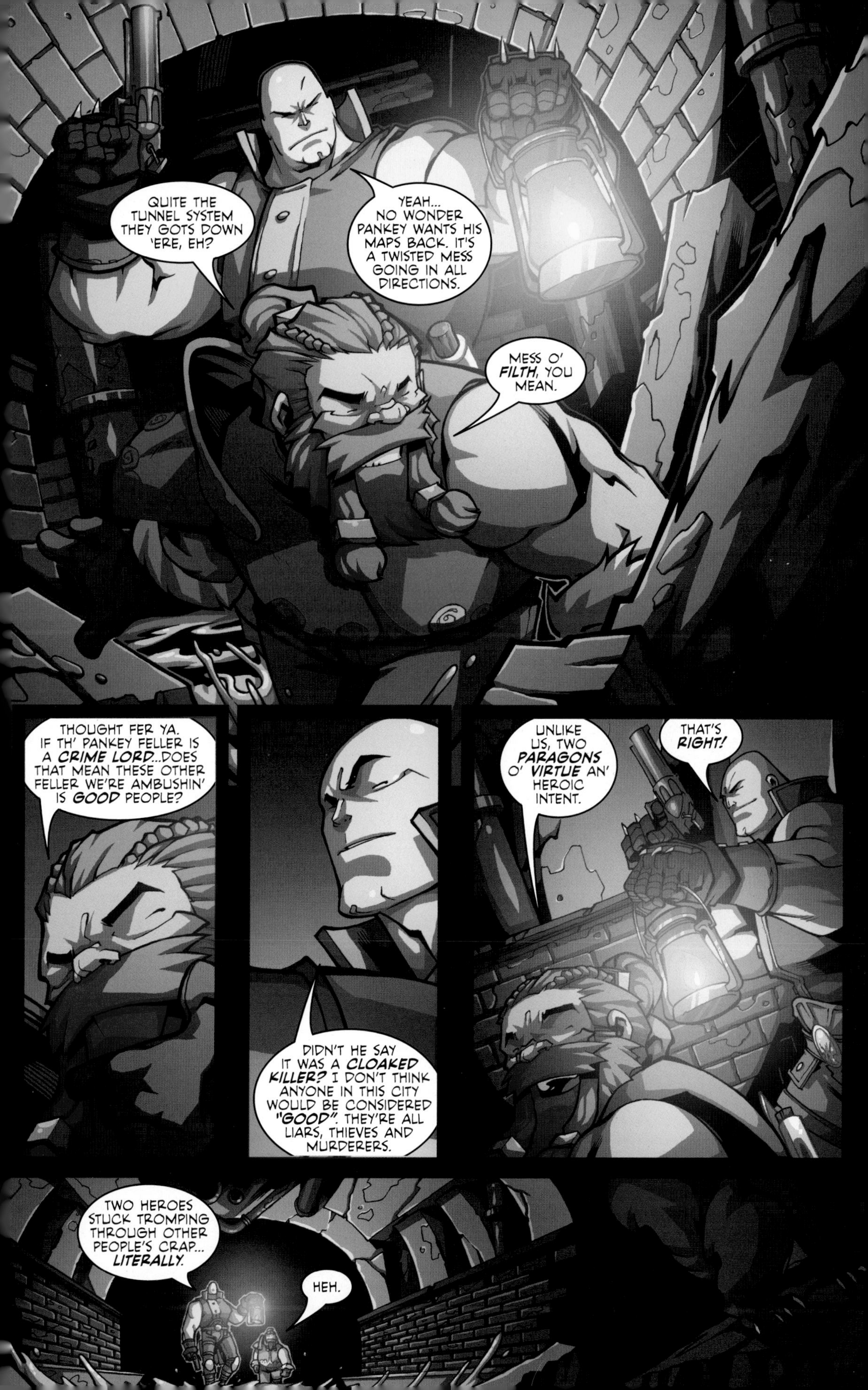
QUITE THE TUNNEL SYSTEM THEY GOTS DOWN 'ERE, EH?
YEAH... NO WONDER PANKEY WANTS HIS MAPS BACK. IT'S A TWISTED MESS GOING IN ALL DIRECTIONS.
MESS O' FILTH, YOU MEAN.
THOUGHT FER YA. IF TH' PANKEY FELLER IS A CRIME LORD...DOES THAT MEAN THESE OTHER FELLER WE'RE AMBUSHIN' IS GOOD PEOPLE?
DIDN'T HE SAY IT WAS A CLOAKED KILLER? I DON'T THINK ANYONE IN THIS CITY WOULD BE CONSIDERED "GOOD". THEY'RE ALL LIARS, THIEVES AND MURDERERS.
UNLIKE US, TWO PARAGONS O' VIRTUE AN' HEROIC INTENT.
THAT'S RIGHT!
TWO HEROES STUCK TROMPING THROUGH OTHER PEOPLE'S CRAP... LITERALLY.
HEH.

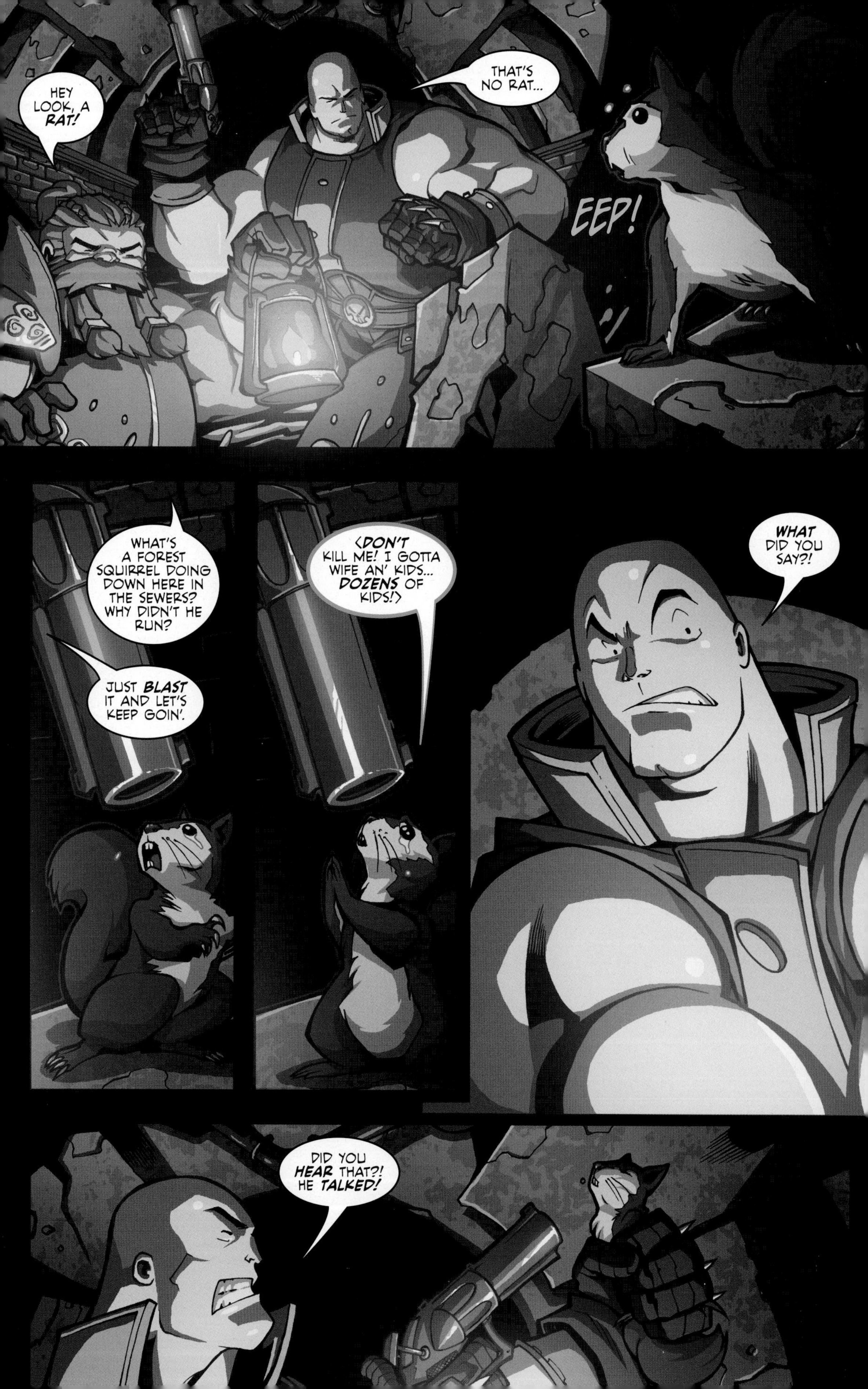
HEY LOOK, A RAT!
THAT'S NO RAT...
EEP!
WHAT'S A FOREST SQUIRREL DOING DOWN HERE IN THE SEWERS? WHY DIDN'T HE RUN?
JUST BLAST IT AND LET'S KEEP GOIN'.
<DON'T KILL ME! I GOTTA WIFE AN' KIDS... DOZENS OF KIDS!>
WHAT DID YOU SAY?!
DID YOU HEAR THAT?! HE TALKED!

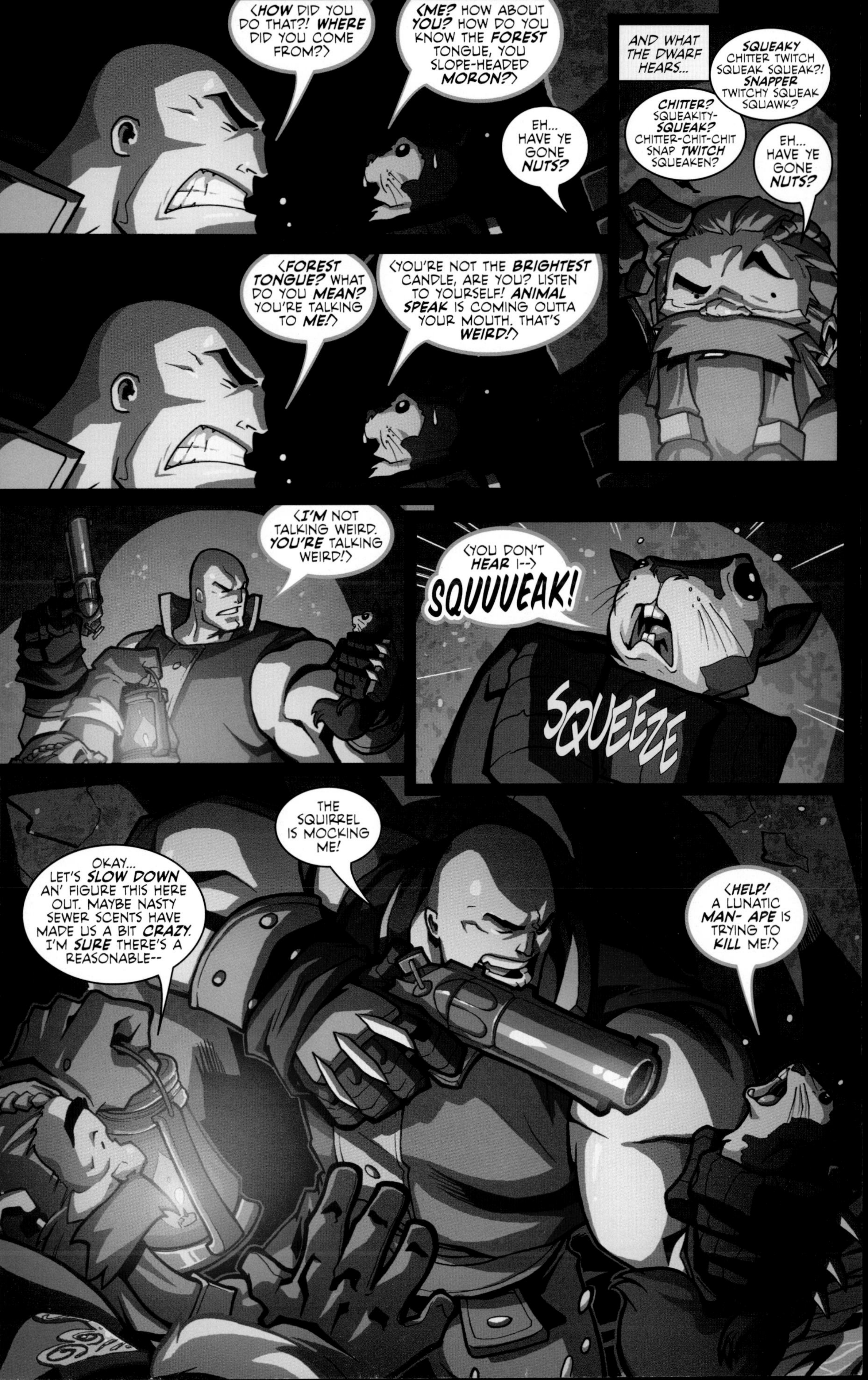

<HOW DID YOU DO THAT?! WHERE DID YOU COME FROM?>
<ME? HOW ABOUT YOU? HOW DO YOU KNOW THE FOREST TONGUE, YOU SLOPE-HEADED MORON?>
EH... HAVE YE GONE NUTS?
AND WHAT THE DWARF HEARS...
SQUEAKY CHITTER TWITCH SQUEAK SQUEAK?! SNAPPER TWITCHY SQUEAK SQUAWK?
CHITTER? SQUEAKITY-SQUEAK? CHITTER-CHIT-CHIT SNAP TWITCH SQUEAKEN?
EH... HAVE YE GONE NUTS?
<FOREST TONGUE? WHAT DO YOU MEAN? YOU'RE TALKING TO ME!>
<YOU'RE NOT THE BRIGHTEST CANDLE, ARE YOU? LISTEN TO YOURSELF! ANIMAL SPEAK IS COMING OUTTA YOUR MOUTH. THAT'S WEIRD!>
<I'M NOT TALKING WEIRD. YOU'RE TALKING WEIRD!>
<YOU DON'T HEAR I-->
SQUUUEAK!
SQUEEZE
THE SQUIRREL IS MOCKING ME!
OKAY... LET'S SLOW DOWN AN' FIGURE THIS HERE OUT. MAYBE NASTY SEWER SCENTS HAVE MADE US A BIT CRAZY. I'M SURE THERE'S A REASONABLE--
<HELP! A LUNATIC MAN- APE IS TRYING TO KILL ME!>

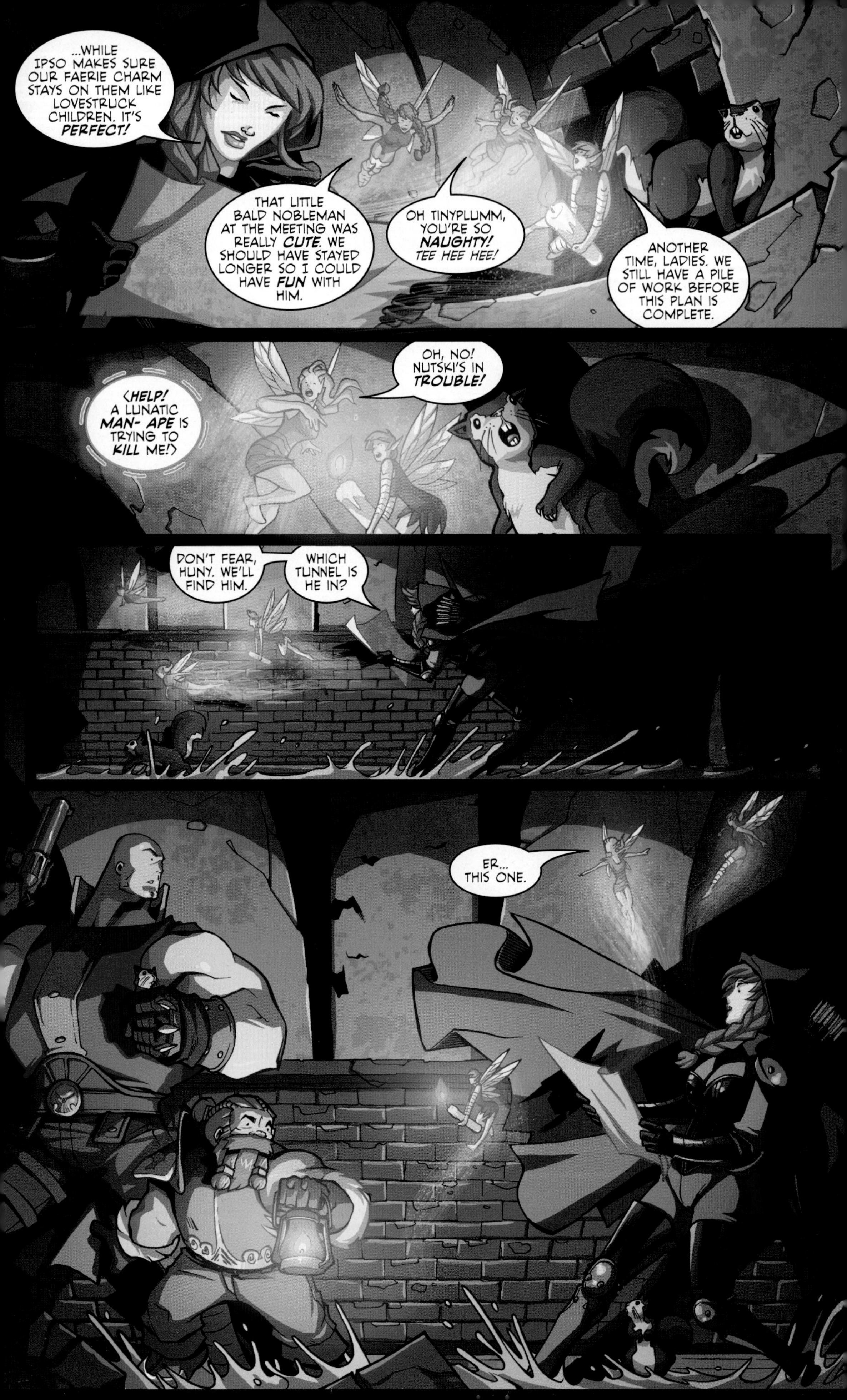
...WHILE IPSO MAKES SURE OUR FAERIE CHARM STAYS ON THEM LIKE LOVESTRUCK CHILDREN. IT'S *PERFECT!*
THAT LITTLE BALD NOBLEMAN AT THE MEETING WAS REALLY *CUTE*. WE SHOULD HAVE STAYED LONGER SO I COULD HAVE *FUN* WITH HIM.
OH TINYPLUMM, YOU'RE SO *NAUGHTY!* *TEE HEE HEE!*
ANOTHER TIME, LADIES. WE STILL HAVE A PILE OF WORK BEFORE THIS PLAN IS COMPLETE.
<*HELP!* A LUNATIC *MAN- APE* IS TRYING TO *KILL* ME!>
OH, NO! NUTSKI'S IN *TROUBLE!*
DON'T FEAR, HUNY. WE'LL FIND HIM.
WHICH TUNNEL IS HE IN?
ER... THIS ONE.

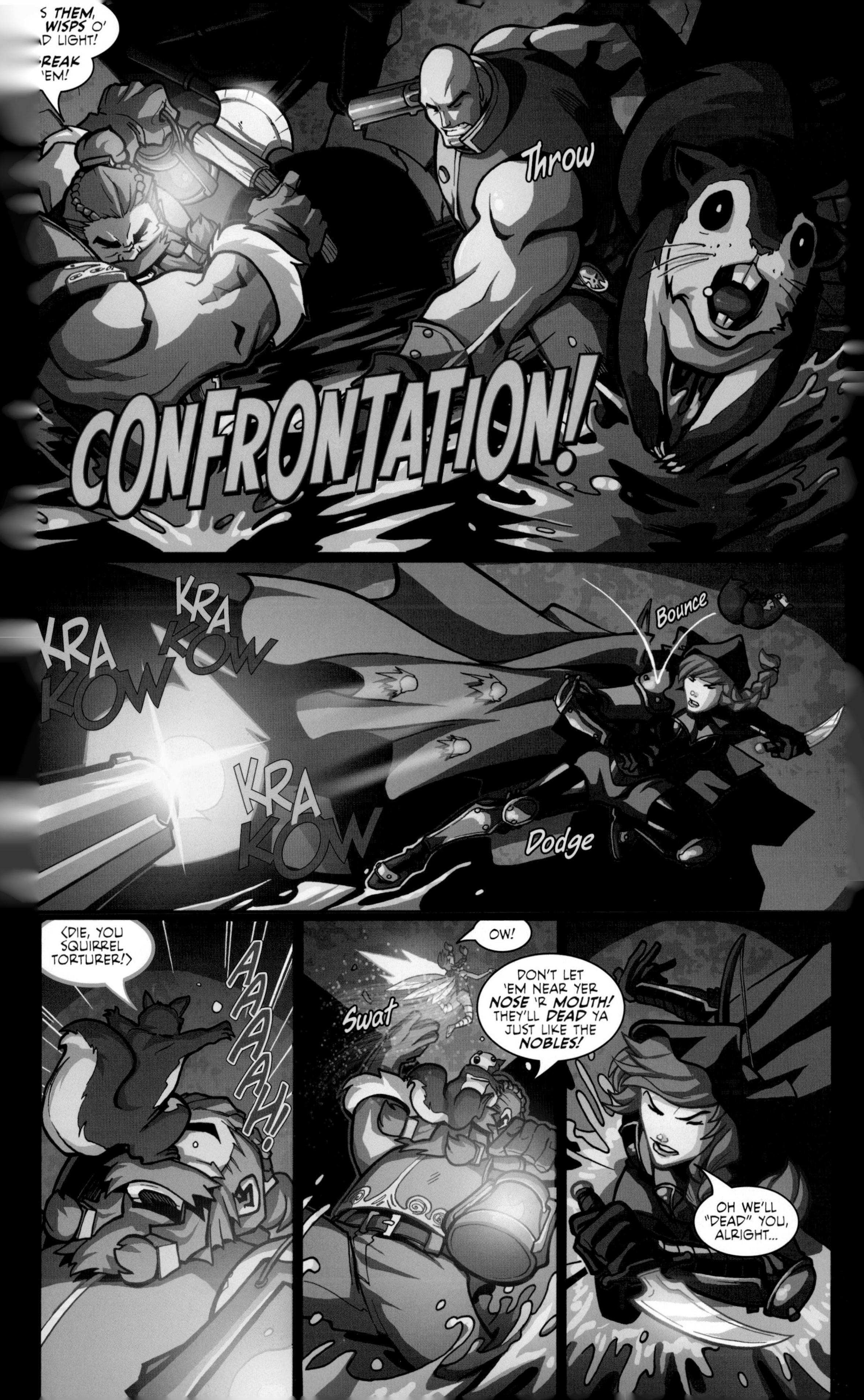
S THEM, WISPS O' D LIGHT! REAK 'EM!
Throw
CONFRONTATION!
KRA KOW
KRA KOW
KRA KOW
Bounce
Dodge
<DIE, YOU SQUIRREL TORTURER!>
AAAAAH!
OW!
Swat
DON'T LET 'EM NEAR YER NOSE 'R MOUTH! THEY'LL DEAD YA JUST LIKE THE NOBLES!
OH WE'LL "DEAD" YOU, ALRIGHT...

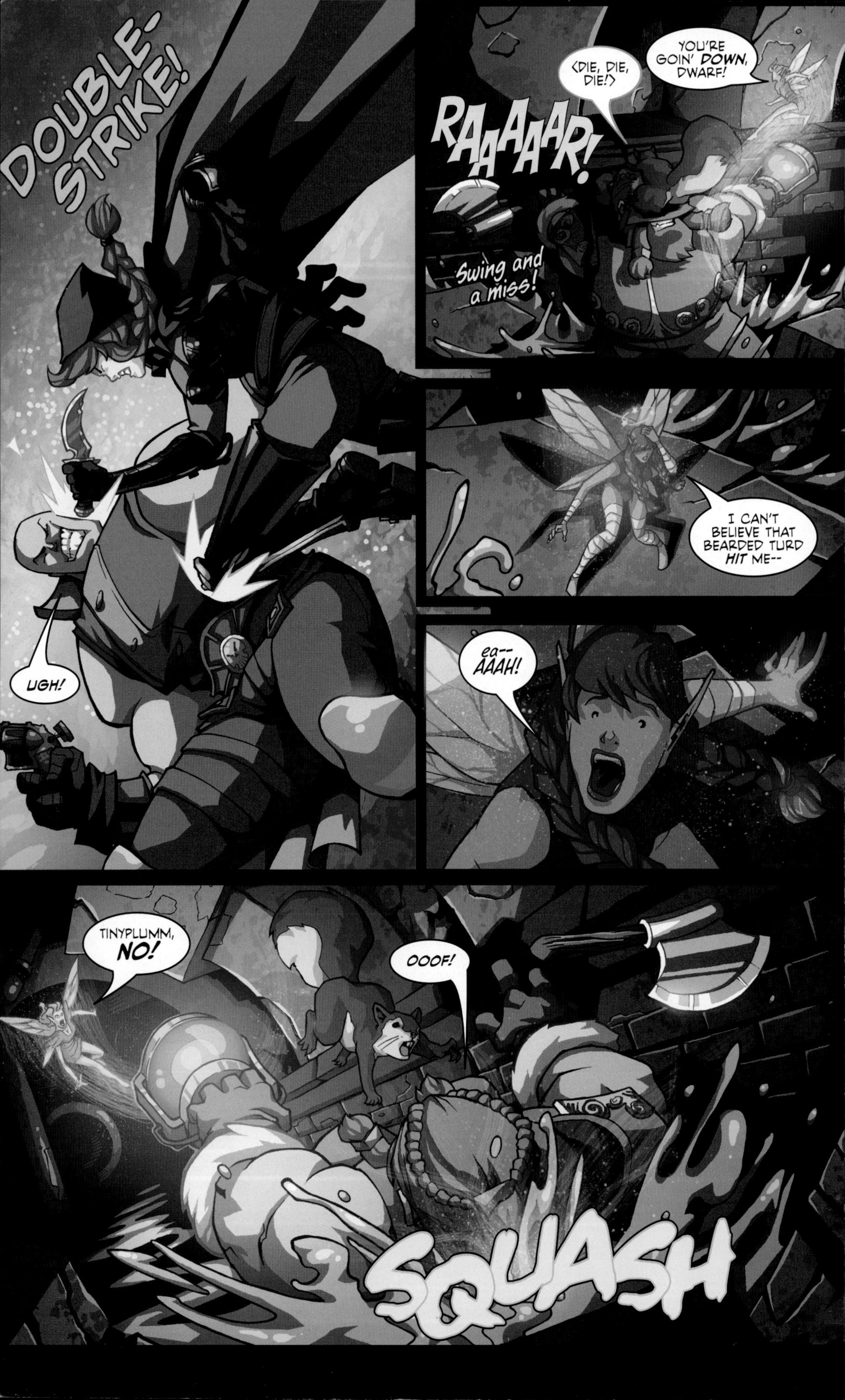
DOUBLE-STRIKE!
UGH!
RAAAAAR!
<DIE, DIE, DIE!>
YOU'RE GOIN' DOWN, DWARF!
Swing and a miss!
I CAN'T BELIEVE THAT BEARDED TURD HIT ME--
ea-- AAAH!
TINYPLUMM, NO!
OOOF!
SQUASH

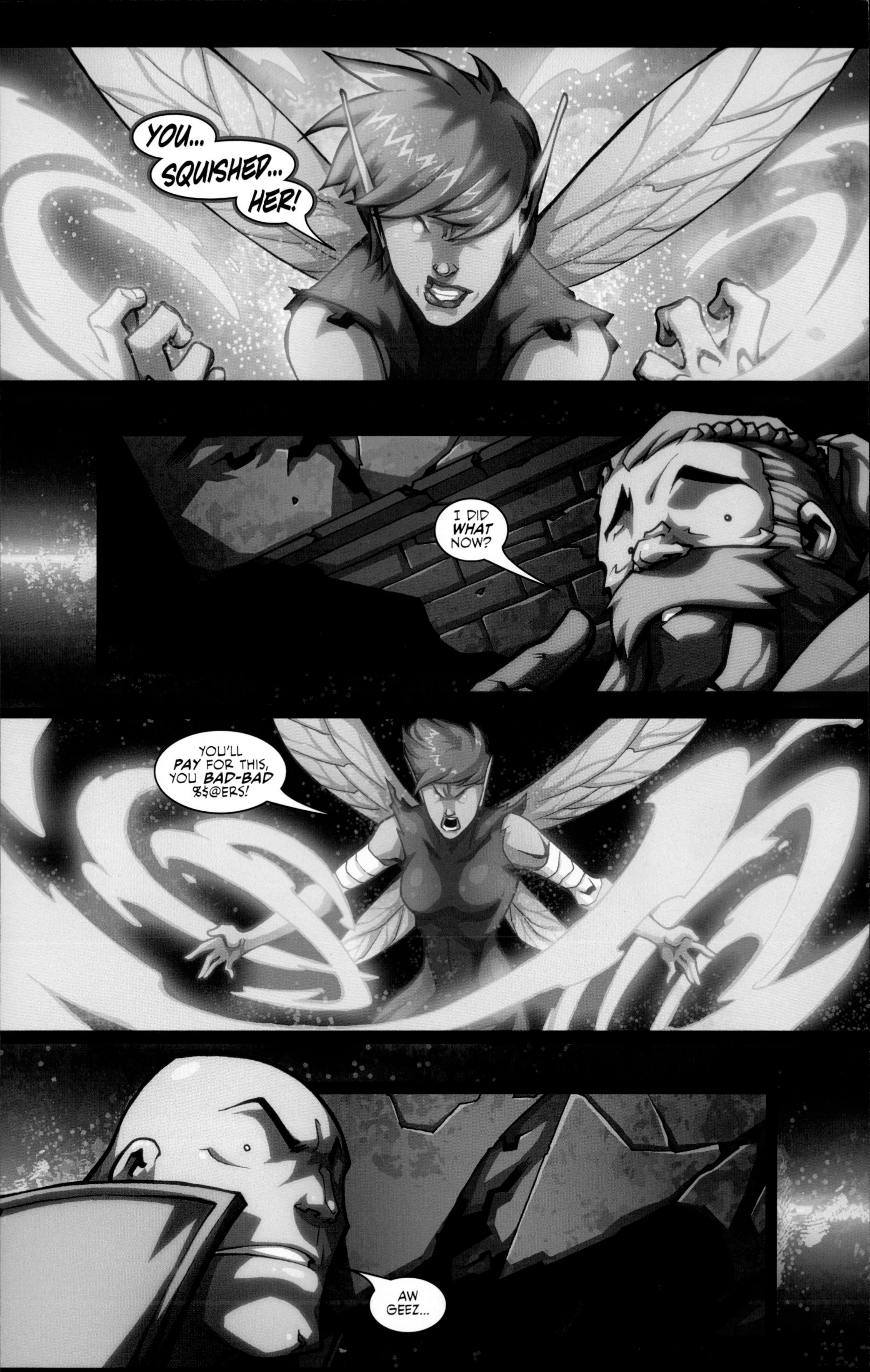
YOU... SQUISHED... HER!
I DID WHAT NOW?
YOU'LL PAY FOR THIS, YOU BAD-BAD %$@ERS!
AW GEEZ...

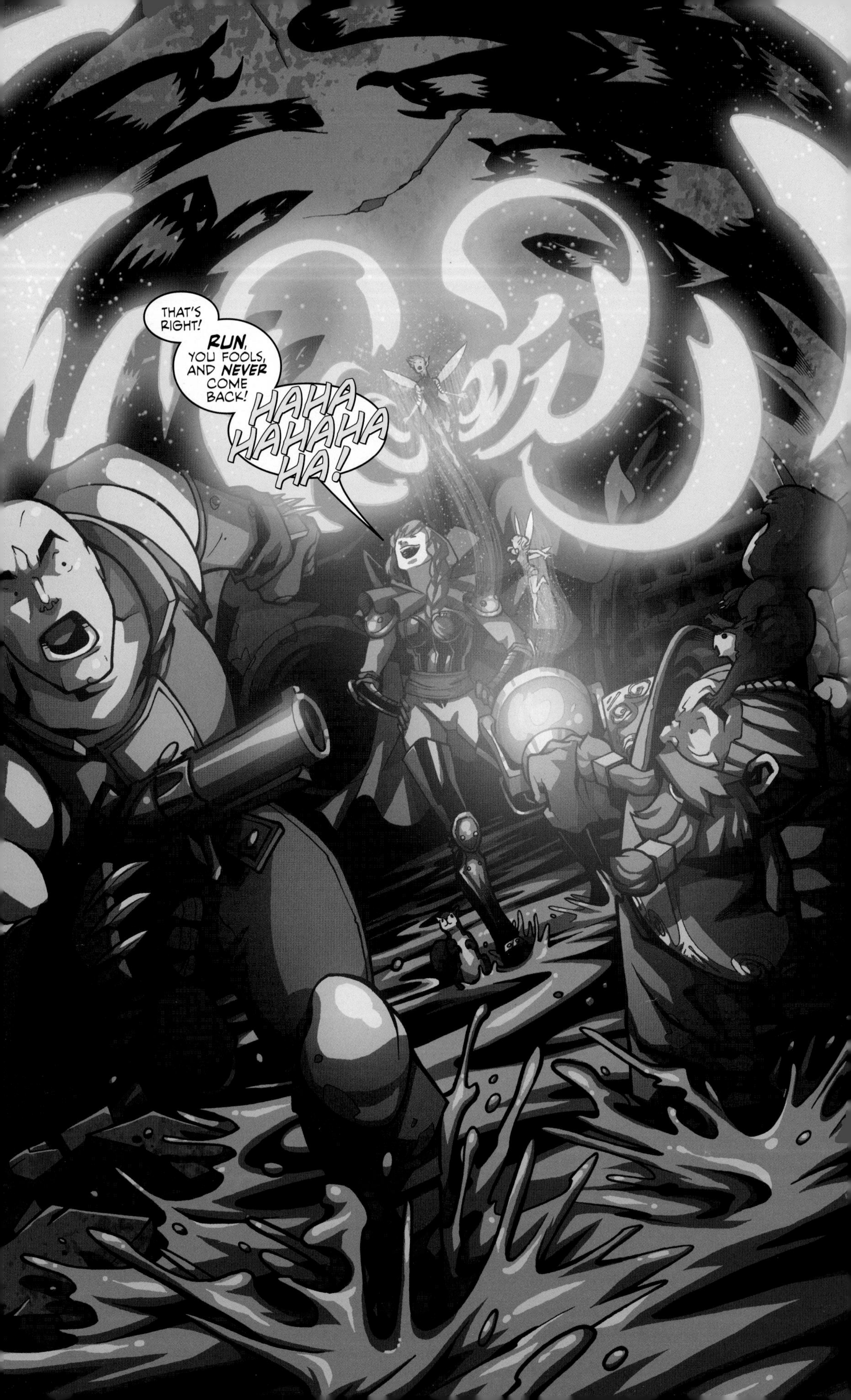
THAT'S RIGHT! **RUN**, YOU FOOLS, AND **NEVER** COME BACK!
HAHA HAHAHA HA!

CHAPTER FOUR

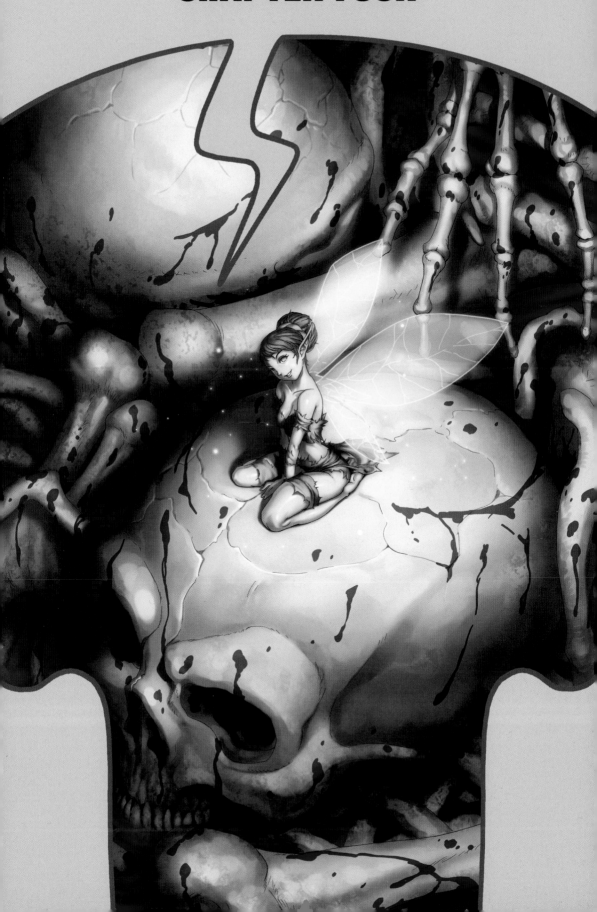

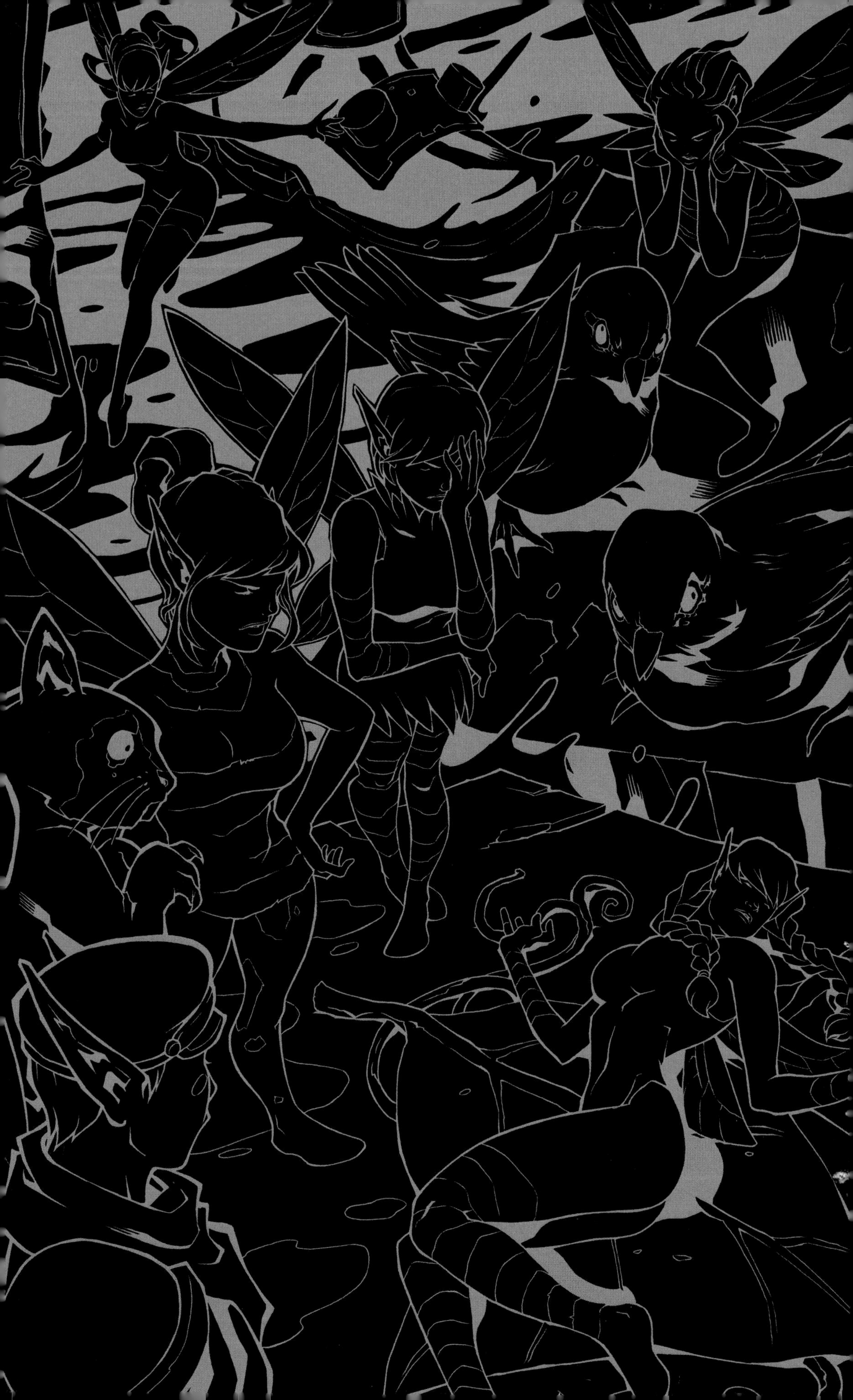

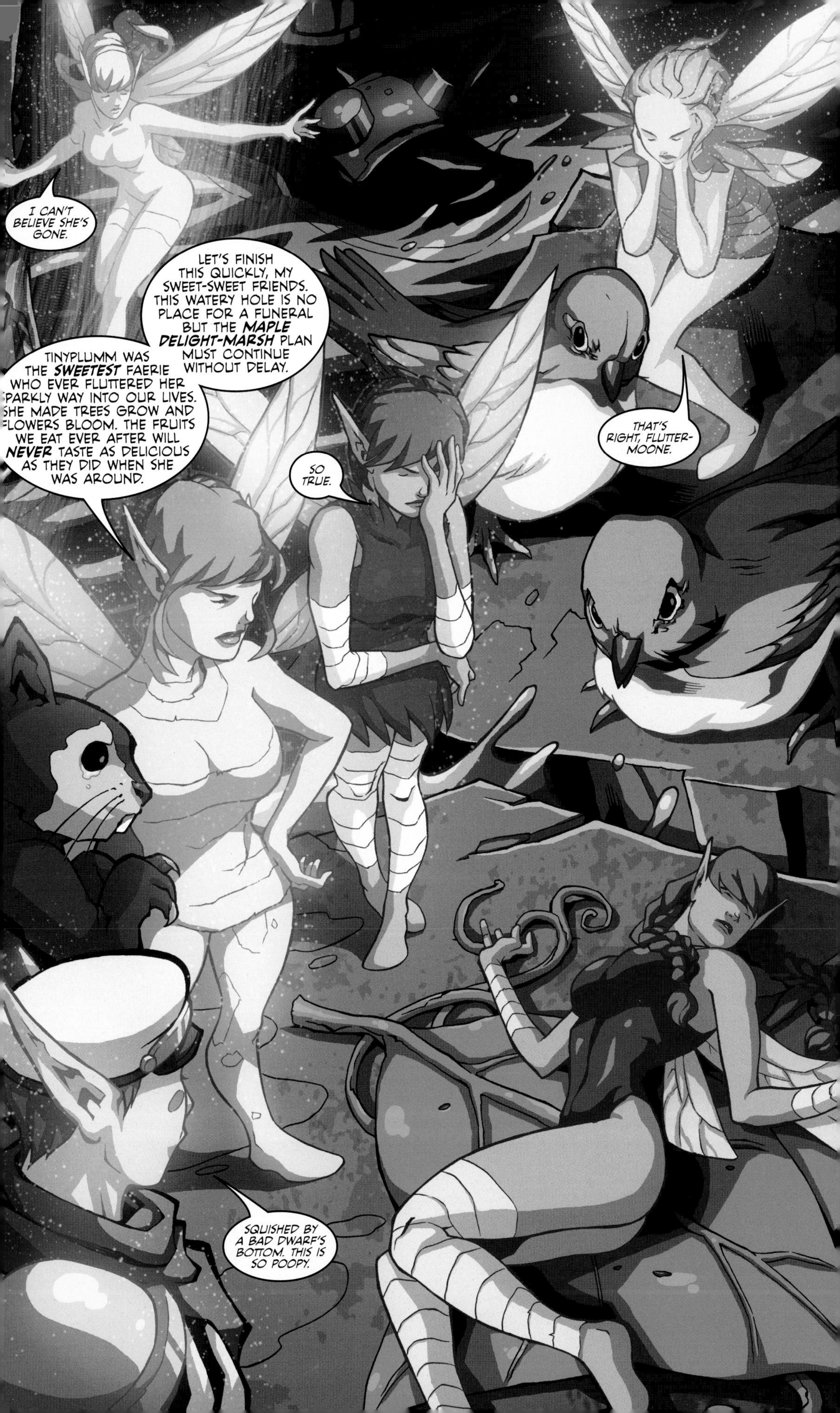
I CAN'T BELIEVE SHE'S GONE.
LET'S FINISH THIS QUICKLY, MY SWEET-SWEET FRIENDS. THIS WATERY HOLE IS NO PLACE FOR A FUNERAL BUT THE MAPLE DELIGHT-MARSH PLAN MUST CONTINUE WITHOUT DELAY.
TINYPLUMM WAS THE SWEETEST FAERIE WHO EVER FLUTTERED HER SPARKLY WAY INTO OUR LIVES. SHE MADE TREES GROW AND FLOWERS BLOOM. THE FRUITS WE EAT EVER AFTER WILL NEVER TASTE AS DELICIOUS AS THEY DID WHEN SHE WAS AROUND.
SO TRUE.
THAT'S RIGHT, FLUTTER-MOONE.
SQUISHED BY A BAD DWARF'S BOTTOM. THIS IS SO POOPY.

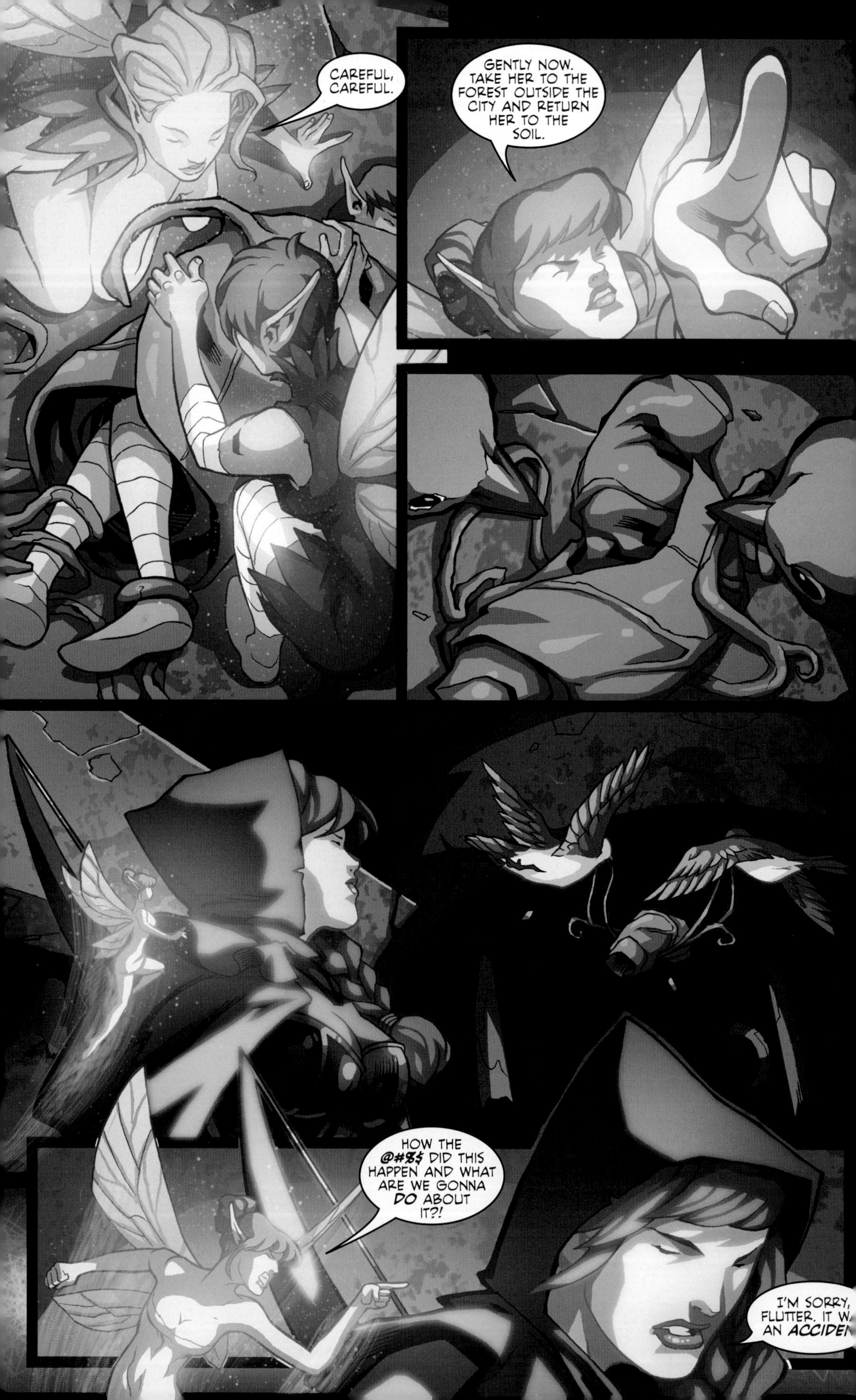
CAREFUL, CAREFUL.
GENTLY NOW. TAKE HER TO THE FOREST OUTSIDE THE CITY AND RETURN HER TO THE SOIL.
HOW THE @#$$ DID THIS HAPPEN AND WHAT ARE WE GONNA DO ABOUT IT?!
I'M SORRY, FLUTTER. IT WA AN ACCIDE

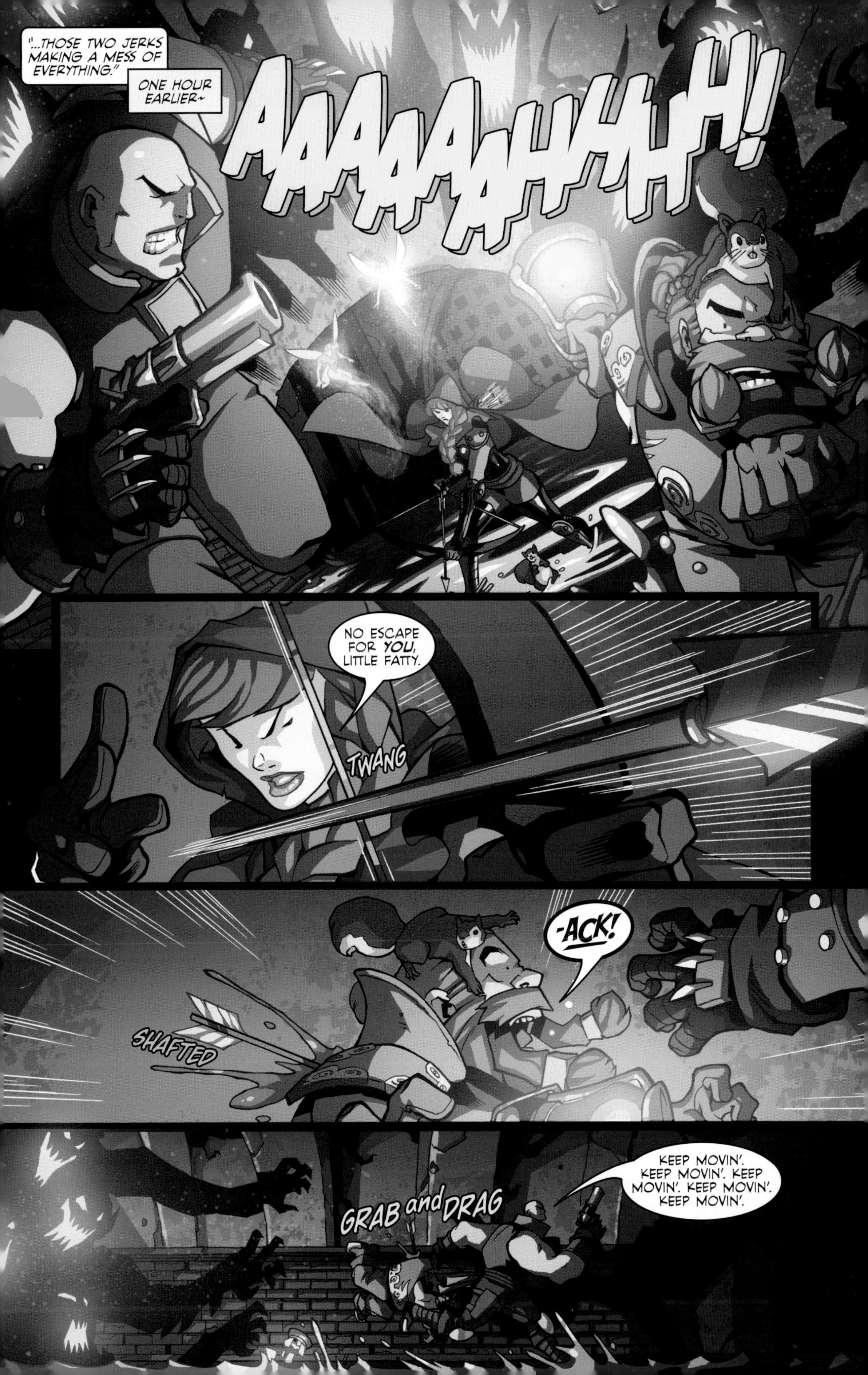
"...THOSE TWO JERKS MAKING A MESS OF EVERYTHING."
ONE HOUR EARLIER--
AAAAAAHHHHH!
NO ESCAPE FOR *YOU*, LITTLE FATTY.
TWANG
-ACK!
SHAFTED
KEEP MOVIN'. KEEP MOVIN'. KEEP MOVIN'. KEEP MOVIN'. KEEP MOVIN'.
GRAB and DRAG

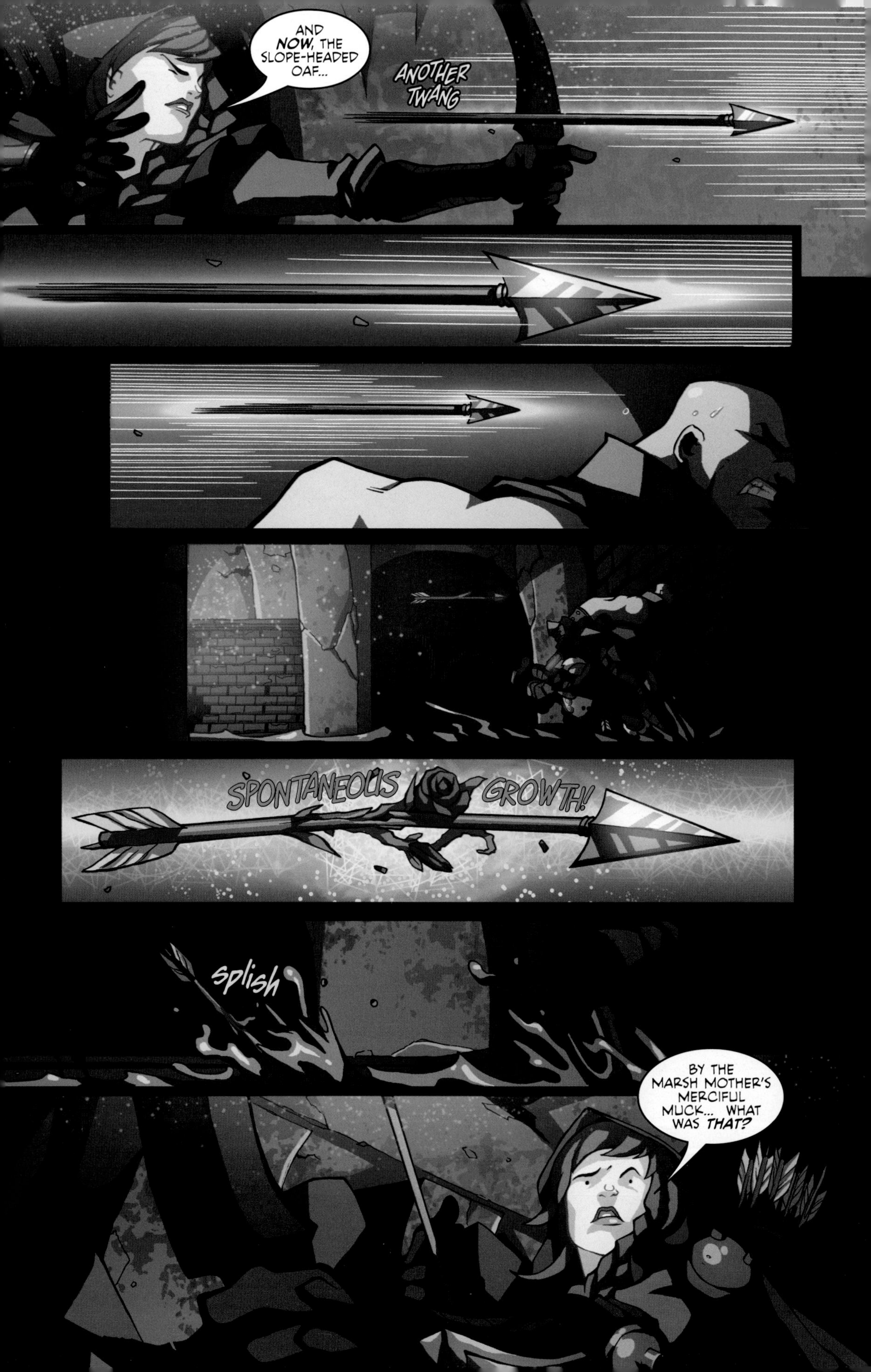
AND NOW, THE SLOPE-HEADED OAF...
ANOTHER TWANG
SPONTANEOUS GROWTH!
splish
BY THE MARSH MOTHER'S MERCIFUL MUCK... WHAT WAS THAT?

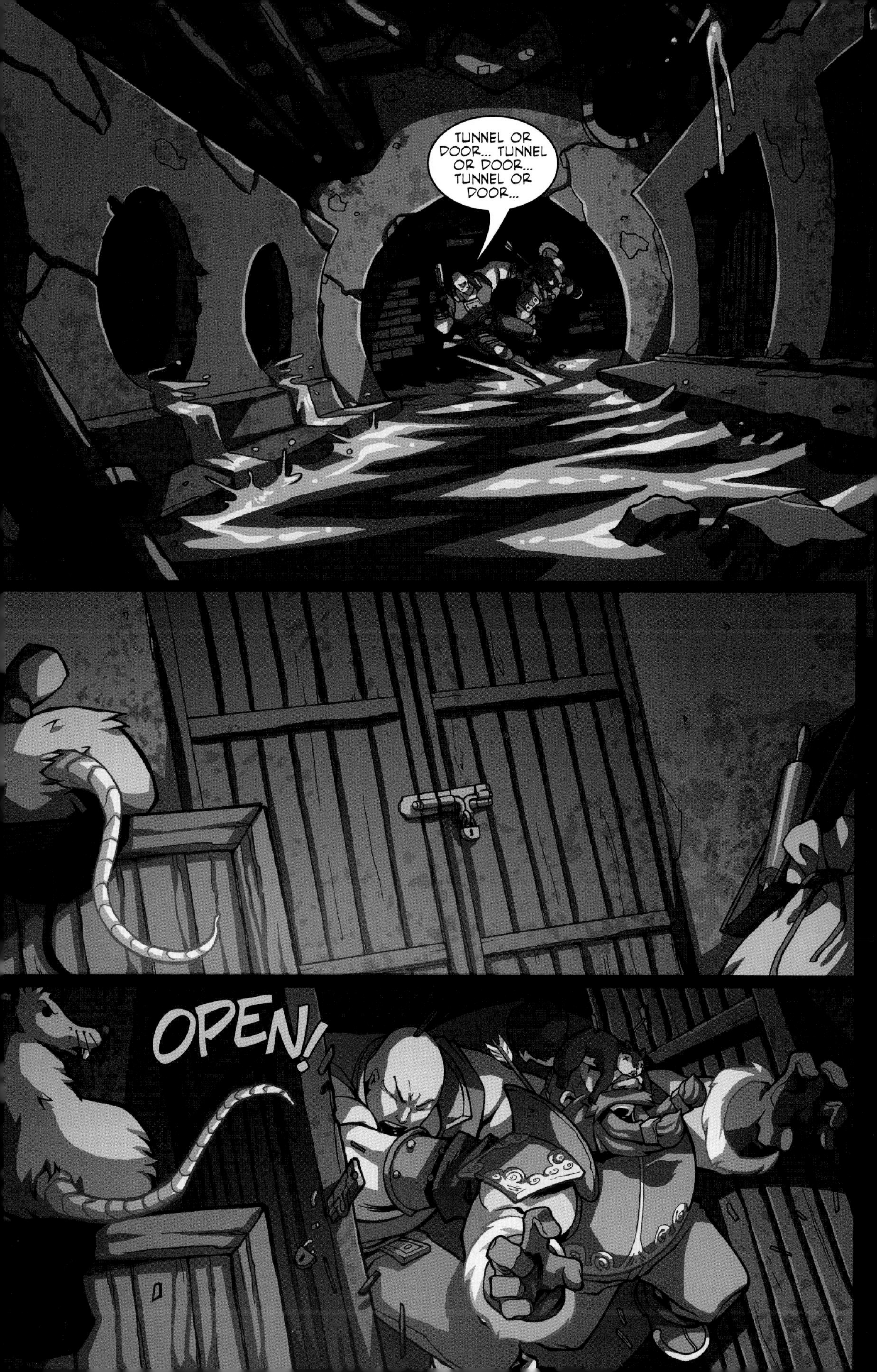
TUNNEL OR DOOR... TUNNEL OR DOOR... TUNNEL OR DOOR...
OPEN!

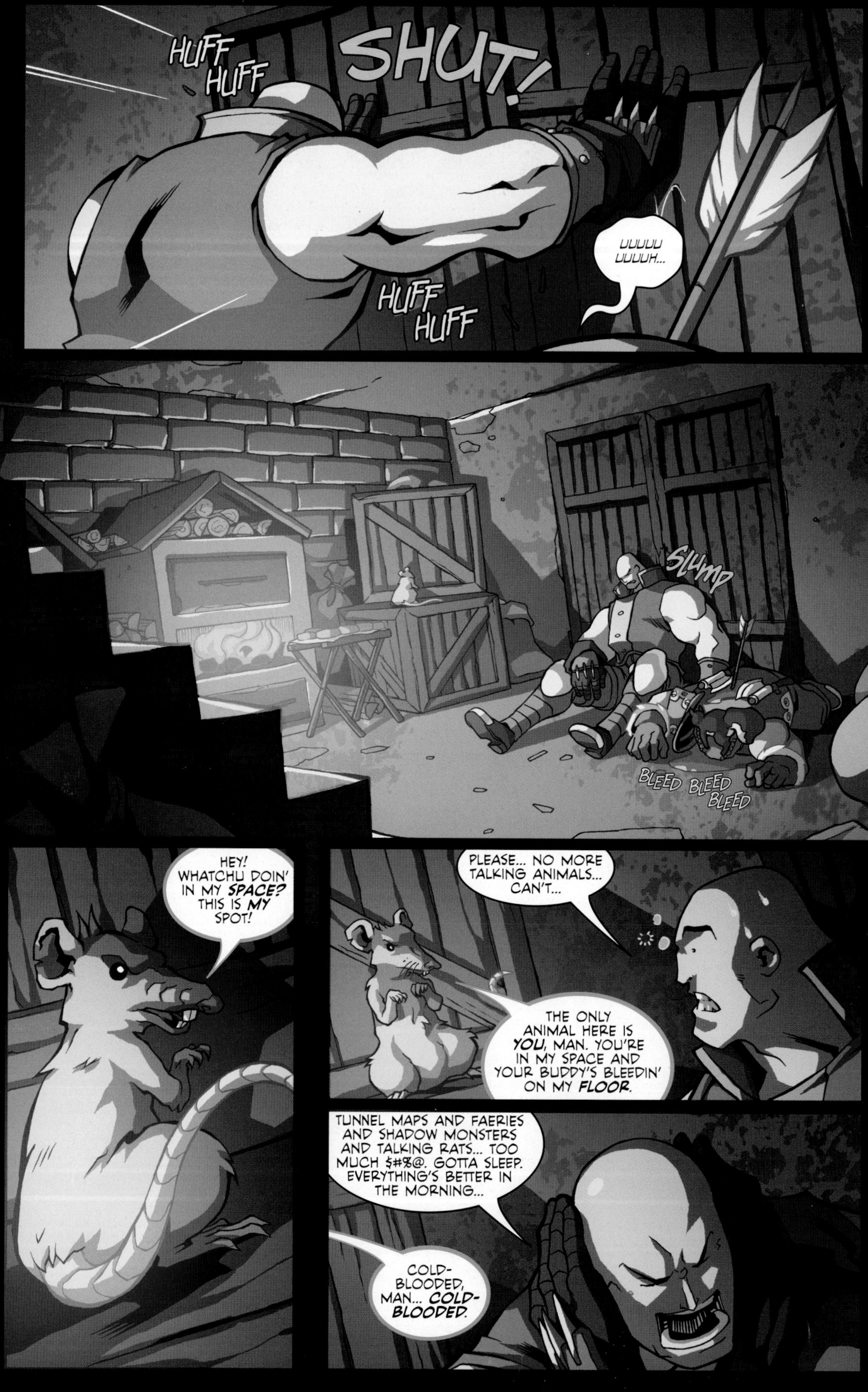
HUFF HUFF
SHUT!
UUUUU UUUUH...
HUFF HUFF
SLUMP
BLEED BLEED BLEED
HEY! WHATCHU DOIN' IN MY SPACE? THIS IS MY SPOT!
PLEASE... NO MORE TALKING ANIMALS... CAN'T...
THE ONLY ANIMAL HERE IS YOU, MAN. YOU'RE IN MY SPACE AND YOUR BUDDY'S BLEEDIN' ON MY FLOOR.
TUNNEL MAPS AND FAERIES AND SHADOW MONSTERS AND TALKING RATS... TOO MUCH $#%@. GOTTA SLEEP. EVERYTHING'S BETTER IN THE MORNING...
COLD-BLOODED, MAN... COLD-BLOODED.

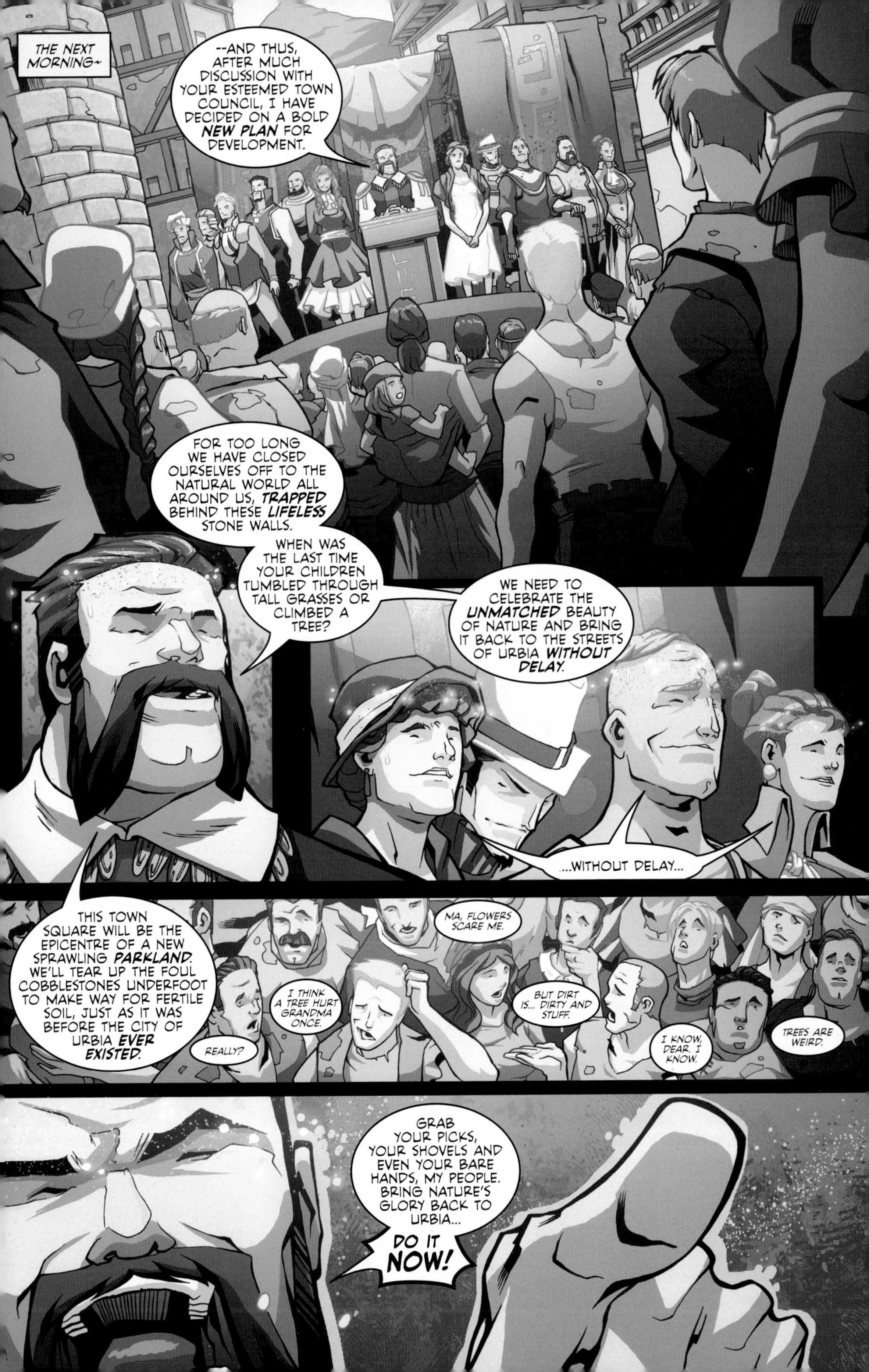
THE NEXT MORNING~
--AND THUS, AFTER MUCH DISCUSSION WITH YOUR ESTEEMED TOWN COUNCIL, I HAVE DECIDED ON A BOLD NEW PLAN FOR DEVELOPMENT.
FOR TOO LONG WE HAVE CLOSED OURSELVES OFF TO THE NATURAL WORLD ALL AROUND US, TRAPPED BEHIND THESE LIFELESS STONE WALLS.
WHEN WAS THE LAST TIME YOUR CHILDREN TUMBLED THROUGH TALL GRASSES OR CLIMBED A TREE?
WE NEED TO CELEBRATE THE UNMATCHED BEAUTY OF NATURE AND BRING IT BACK TO THE STREETS OF URBIA WITHOUT DELAY.
...WITHOUT DELAY...
THIS TOWN SQUARE WILL BE THE EPICENTRE OF A NEW SPRAWLING PARKLAND. WE'LL TEAR UP THE FOUL COBBLESTONES UNDERFOOT TO MAKE WAY FOR FERTILE SOIL, JUST AS IT WAS BEFORE THE CITY OF URBIA EVER EXISTED.
REALLY?
I THINK A TREE HURT GRANDMA ONCE.
MA, FLOWERS SCARE ME.
BUT DIRT IS... DIRTY AND STUFF.
I KNOW, DEAR. I KNOW.
TREES ARE WEIRD.
GRAB YOUR PICKS, YOUR SHOVELS AND EVEN YOUR BARE HANDS, MY PEOPLE. BRING NATURE'S GLORY BACK TO URBIA...
DO IT NOW!

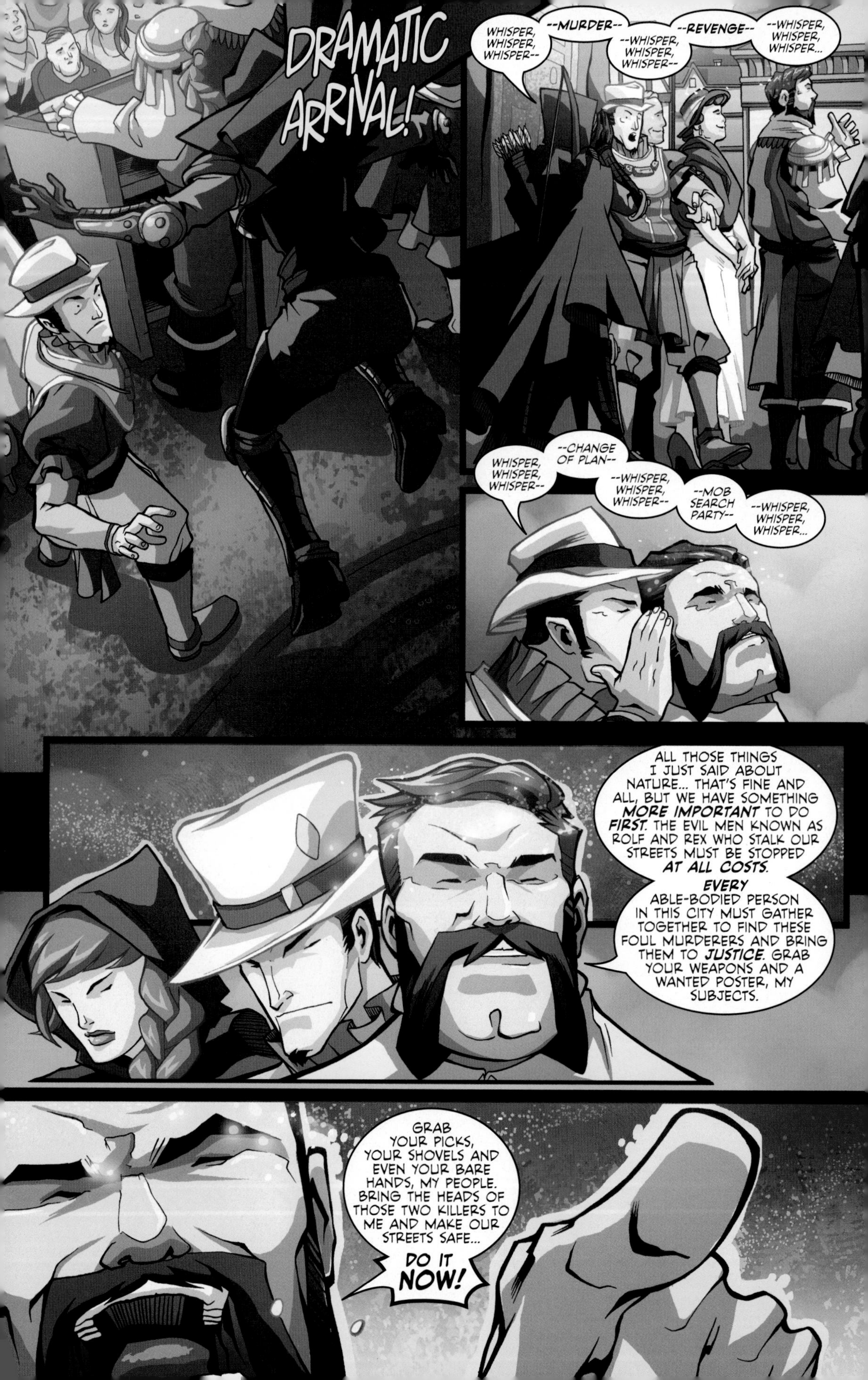
DRAMATIC ARRIVAL!
WHISPER, WHISPER, WHISPER--
--MURDER--
--WHISPER, WHISPER, WHISPER--
--REVENGE--
--WHISPER, WHISPER, WHISPER...
WHISPER, WHISPER, WHISPER--
--CHANGE OF PLAN--
--WHISPER, WHISPER, WHISPER--
--MOB SEARCH PARTY--
--WHISPER, WHISPER, WHISPER...
ALL THOSE THINGS I JUST SAID ABOUT NATURE... THAT'S FINE AND ALL, BUT WE HAVE SOMETHING MORE IMPORTANT TO DO FIRST. THE EVIL MEN KNOWN AS ROLF AND REX WHO STALK OUR STREETS MUST BE STOPPED AT ALL COSTS. EVERY ABLE-BODIED PERSON IN THIS CITY MUST GATHER TOGETHER TO FIND THESE FOUL MURDERERS AND BRING THEM TO JUSTICE. GRAB YOUR WEAPONS AND A WANTED POSTER, MY SUBJECTS.
GRAB YOUR PICKS, YOUR SHOVELS AND EVEN YOUR BARE HANDS, MY PEOPLE. BRING THE HEADS OF THOSE TWO KILLERS TO ME AND MAKE OUR STREETS SAFE...
DO IT NOW!

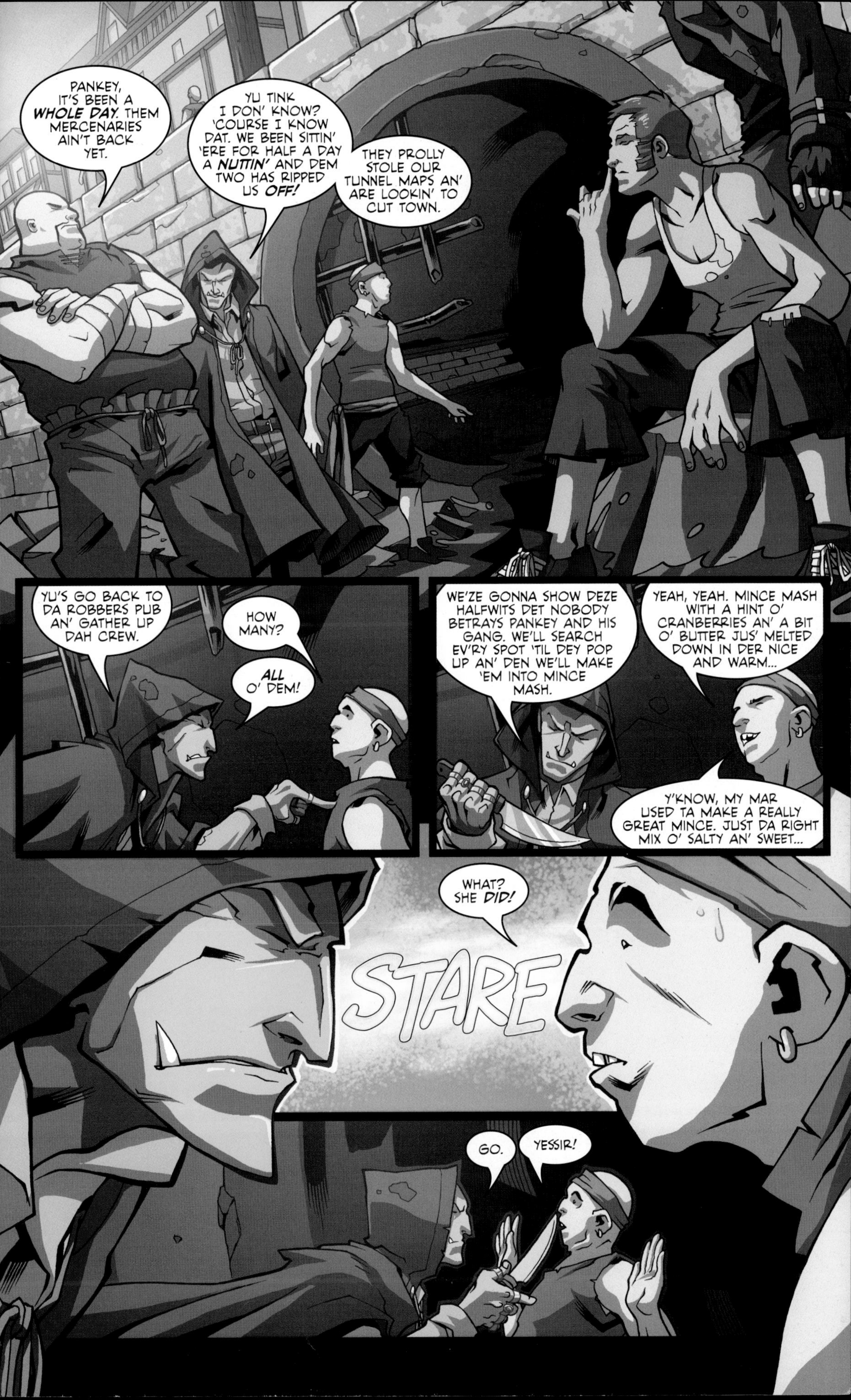
PANKEY, IT'S BEEN A WHOLE DAY. THEM MERCENARIES AIN'T BACK YET.
YU TINK I DON' KNOW? 'COURSE I KNOW DAT. WE BEEN SITTIN' 'ERE FOR HALF A DAY A NUTTIN' AND DEM TWO HAS RIPPED US OFF!
THEY PROLLY STOLE OUR TUNNEL MAPS AN' ARE LOOKIN' TO CUT TOWN.
YU'S GO BACK TO DA ROBBERS PUB AN' GATHER UP DAH CREW.
HOW MANY?
ALL O' DEM!
WE'ZE GONNA SHOW DEZE HALFWITS DET NOBODY BETRAYS PANKEY AND HIS GANG. WE'LL SEARCH EV'RY SPOT 'TIL DEY POP UP AN' DEN WE'LL MAKE 'EM INTO MINCE MASH.
YEAH, YEAH. MINCE MASH WITH A HINT O' CRANBERRIES AN' A BIT O' BUTTER JUS' MELTED DOWN IN DER NICE AND WARM...
Y'KNOW, MY MAR USED TA MAKE A REALLY GREAT MINCE. JUST DA RIGHT MIX O' SALTY AN' SWEET...
WHAT? SHE DID!
STARE
GO.
YESSIR!

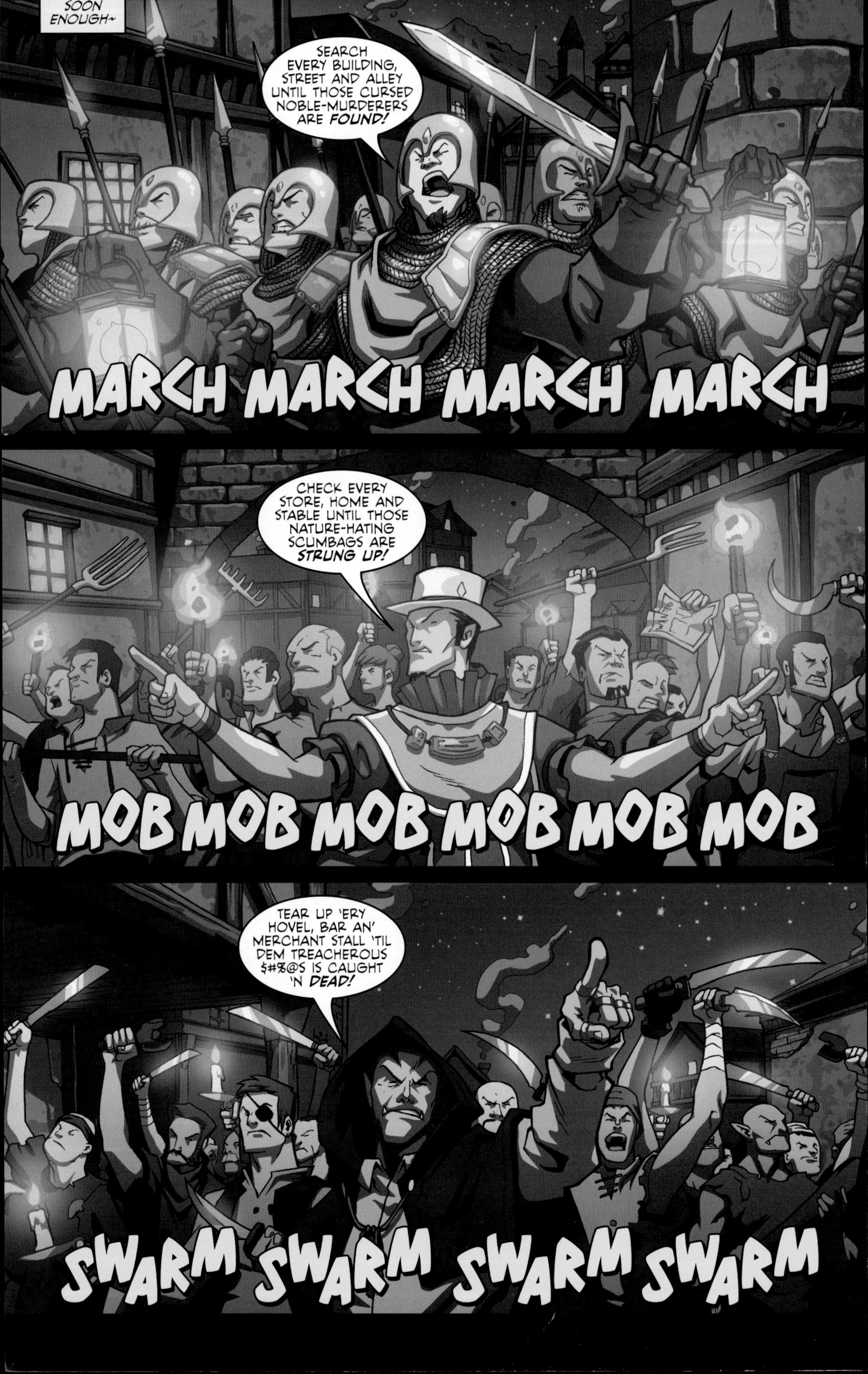
SOON ENOUGH~
SEARCH EVERY BUILDING, STREET AND ALLEY UNTIL THOSE CURSED NOBLE-MURDERERS ARE FOUND!
MARCH MARCH MARCH MARCH
CHECK EVERY STORE, HOME AND STABLE UNTIL THOSE NATURE-HATING SCUMBAGS ARE STRUNG UP!
MOB MOB MOB MOB MOB MOB
TEAR UP 'ERY HOVEL, BAR AN' MERCHANT STALL 'TIL DEM TREACHEROUS $#%@S IS CAUGHT 'N DEAD!
SWARM SWARM SWARM SWARM

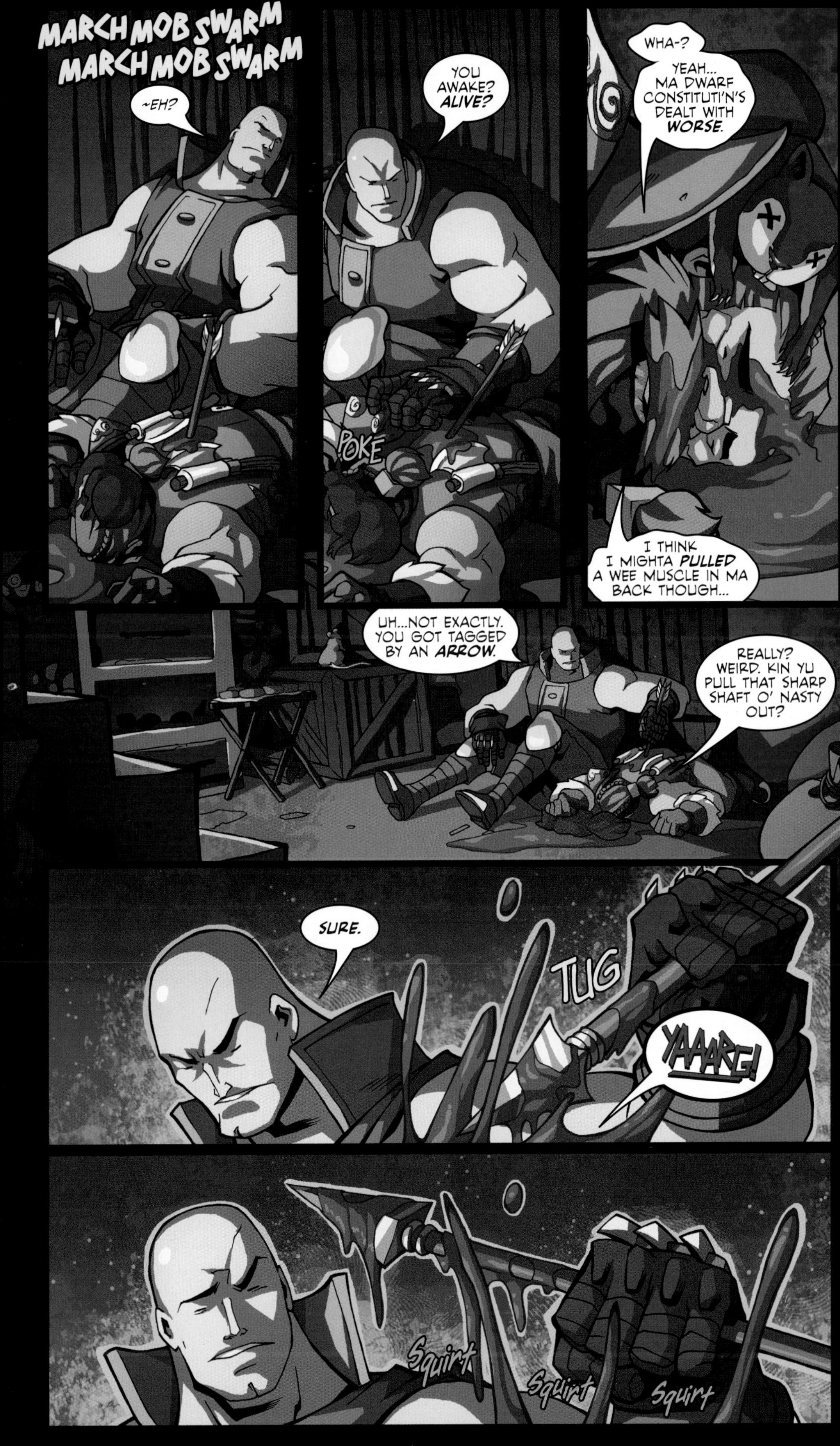
MARCH MOB SWARM
MARCH MOB SWARM
~EH?
YOU AWAKE? ALIVE?
POKE
WHA-?
YEAH... MA DWARF CONSTITUTI'N'S DEALT WITH WORSE.
I THINK I MIGHTA PULLED A WEE MUSCLE IN MA BACK THOUGH...
UH...NOT EXACTLY. YOU GOT TAGGED BY AN ARROW.
REALLY? WEIRD. KIN YU PULL THAT SHARP SHAFT O' NASTY OUT?
SURE.
TUG
YAAARG!
Squirt
Squirt
Squirt

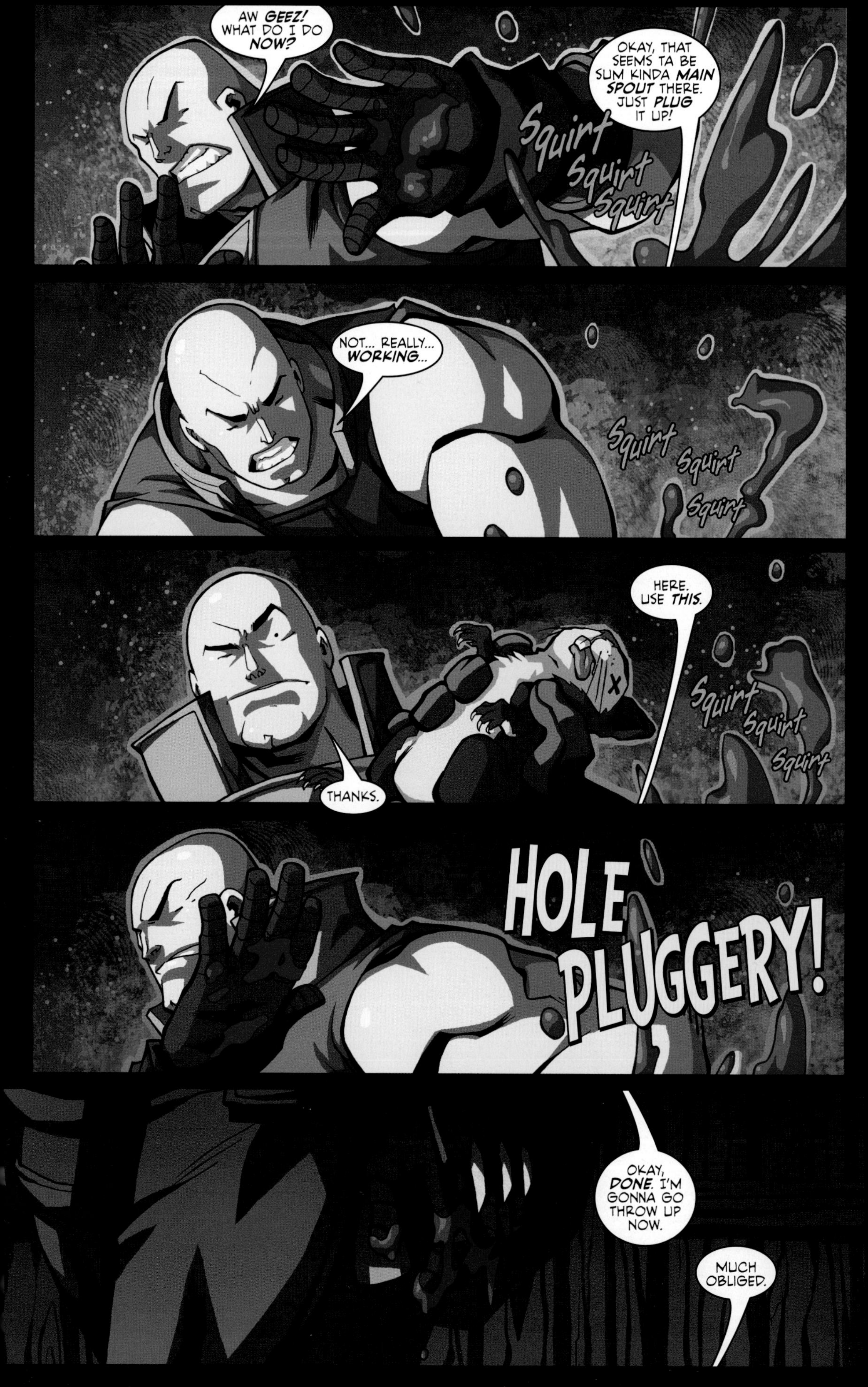
AW GEEZ! WHAT DO I DO NOW?
OKAY, THAT SEEMS TA BE SUM KINDA MAIN SPOUT THERE. JUST PLUG IT UP!
Squirt Squirt Squirt
NOT... REALLY... WORKING...
Squirt Squirt Squirt
HERE. USE THIS.
Squirt Squirt Squirt
THANKS.
HOLE PLUGGERY!
OKAY, DONE. I'M GONNA GO THROW UP NOW.
MUCH OBLIGED.

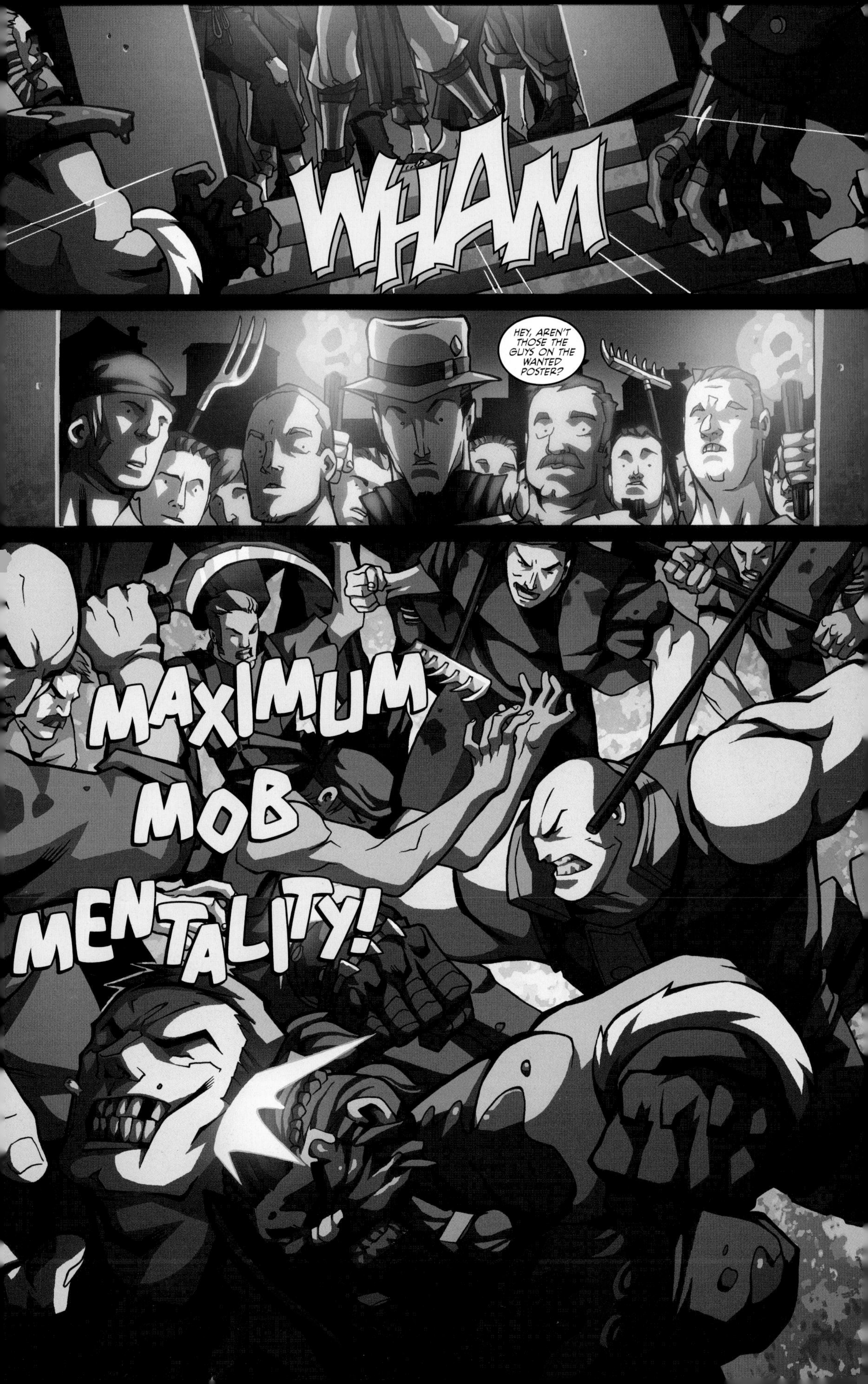
WHAM
HEY, AREN'T THOSE THE GUYS ON THE WANTED POSTER?
MAXIMUM MOB MENTALITY!

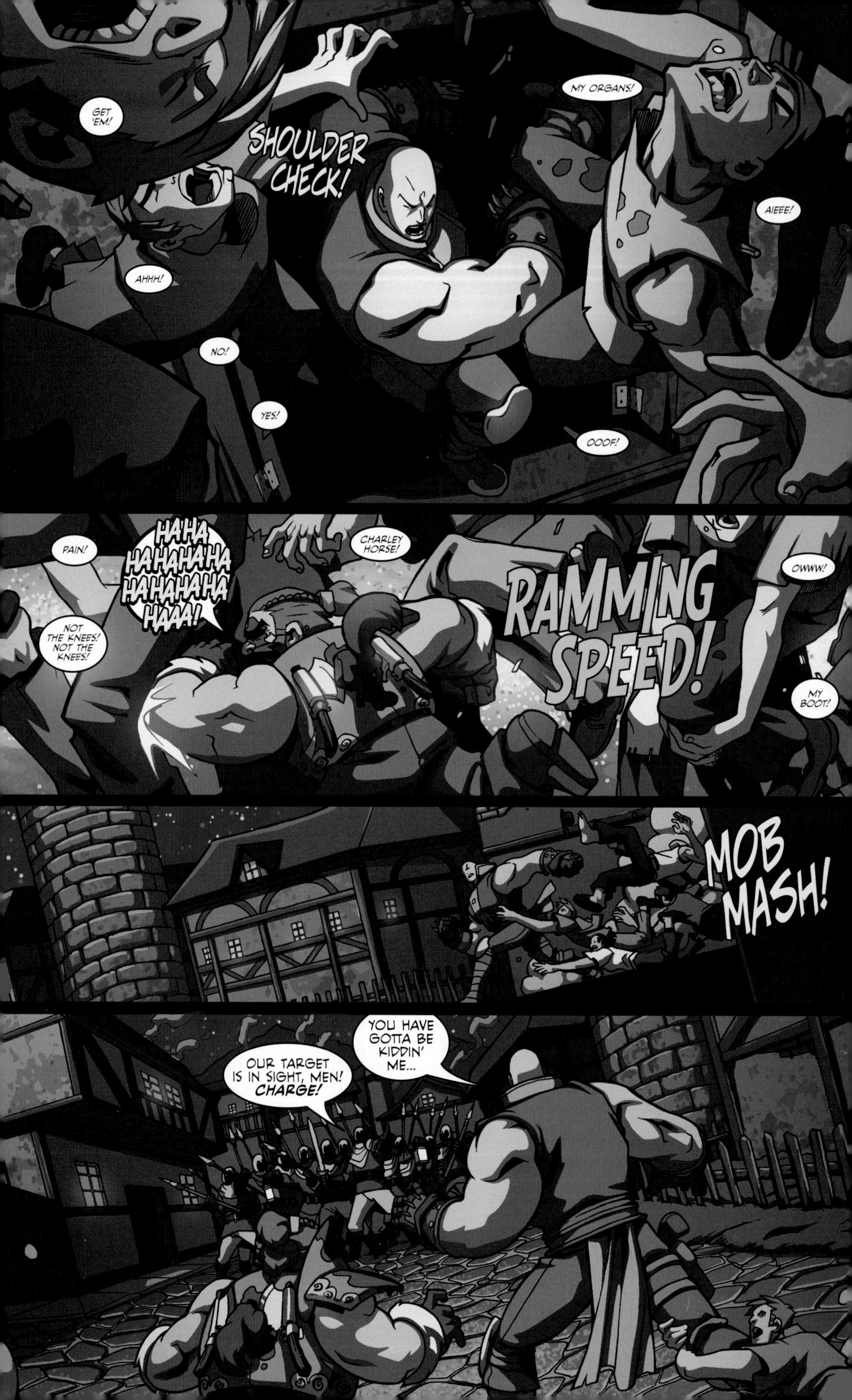
GET 'EM!
SHOULDER CHECK!
MY ORGANS!
AIEEE!
AHHH!
NO!
YES!
OOOF!
PAIN!
HA HA HA HA HA HA HA HA HA HA HA HAAA!
CHARLEY HORSE!
NOT THE KNEES! NOT THE KNEES!
RAMMING SPEED!
OWWW!
MY BOOT!
MOB MASH!
YOU HAVE GOTTA BE KIDDIN' ME...
OUR TARGET IS IN SIGHT, MEN! CHARGE!

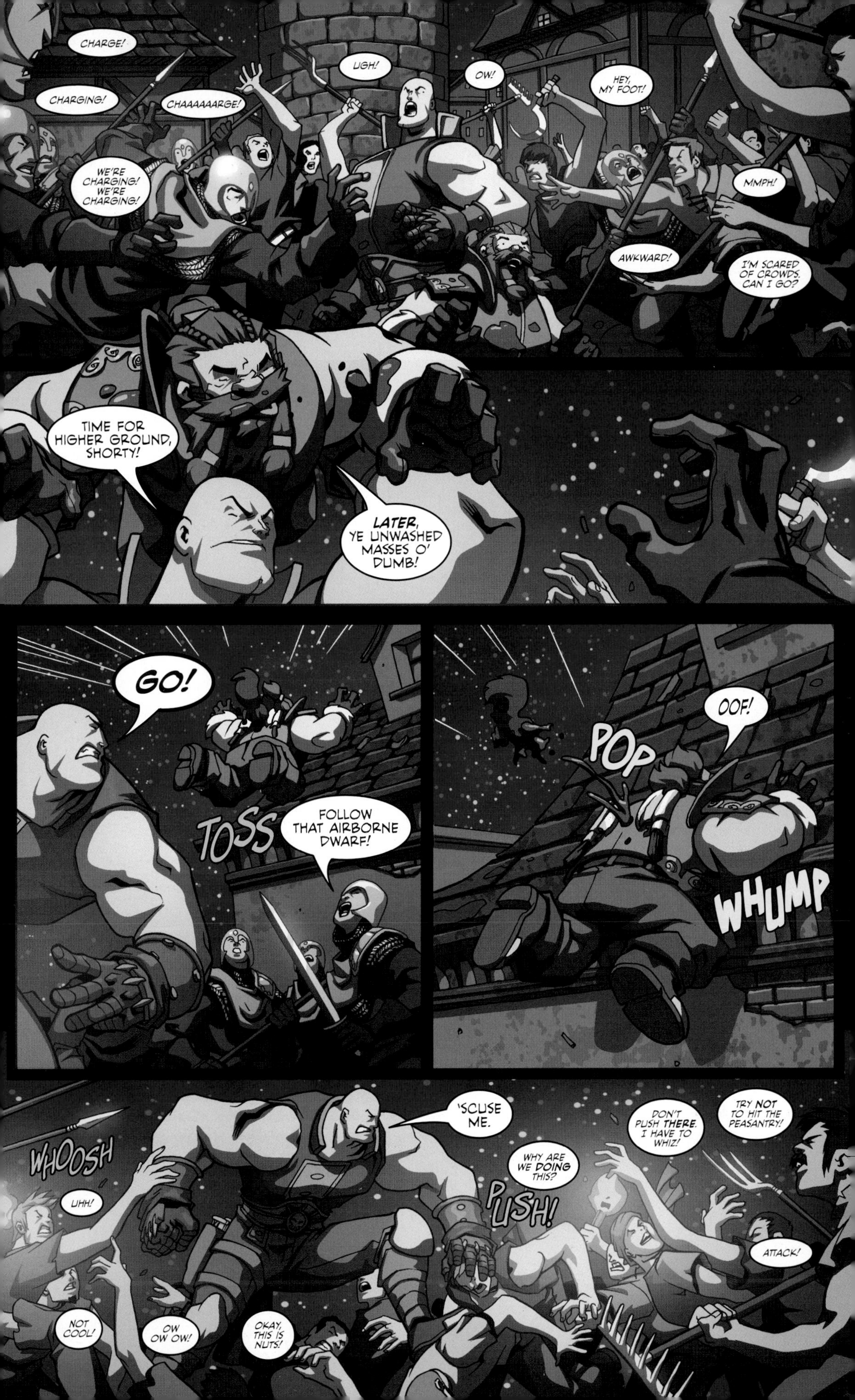
CHARGE!
CHARGING!
CHAAAAAARGE!
WE'RE CHARGING! WE'RE CHARGING!
UGH!
OW!
HEY, MY FOOT!
MMPH!
AWKWARD!
I'M SCARED OF CROWDS. CAN I GO?
TIME FOR HIGHER GROUND, SHORTY!
LATER, YE UNWASHED MASSES O' DUMB!
GO!
TOSS
FOLLOW THAT AIRBORNE DWARF!
OOF!
POP
WHUMP
WHOOSH
UHH!
'SCUSE ME.
WHY ARE WE DOING THIS?
PUSH!
DON'T PUSH THERE. I HAVE TO WHIZ!
TRY NOT TO HIT THE PEASANTRY!
ATTACK!
NOT COOL!
OW OW OW!
OKAY, THIS IS NUTS!

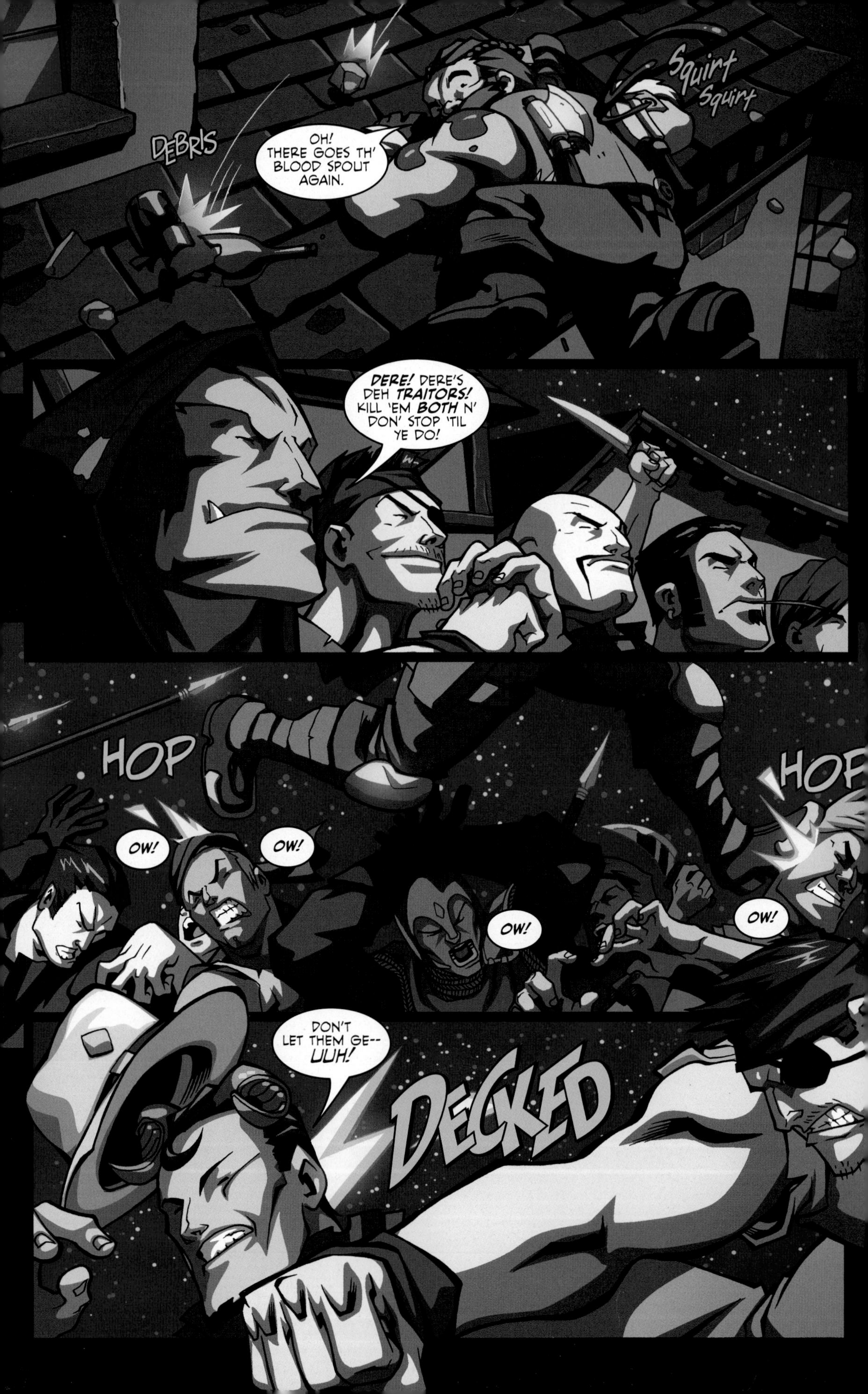
Squirt Squirt
DEBRIS
OH! THERE GOES TH' BLOOD SPOUT AGAIN.
DERE! DERE'S DEH TRAITORS! KILL 'EM BOTH N' DON' STOP 'TIL YE DO!
HOP
HOP
OW!
OW!
OW!
OW!
DON'T LET THEM GE-- UUH!
DECKED

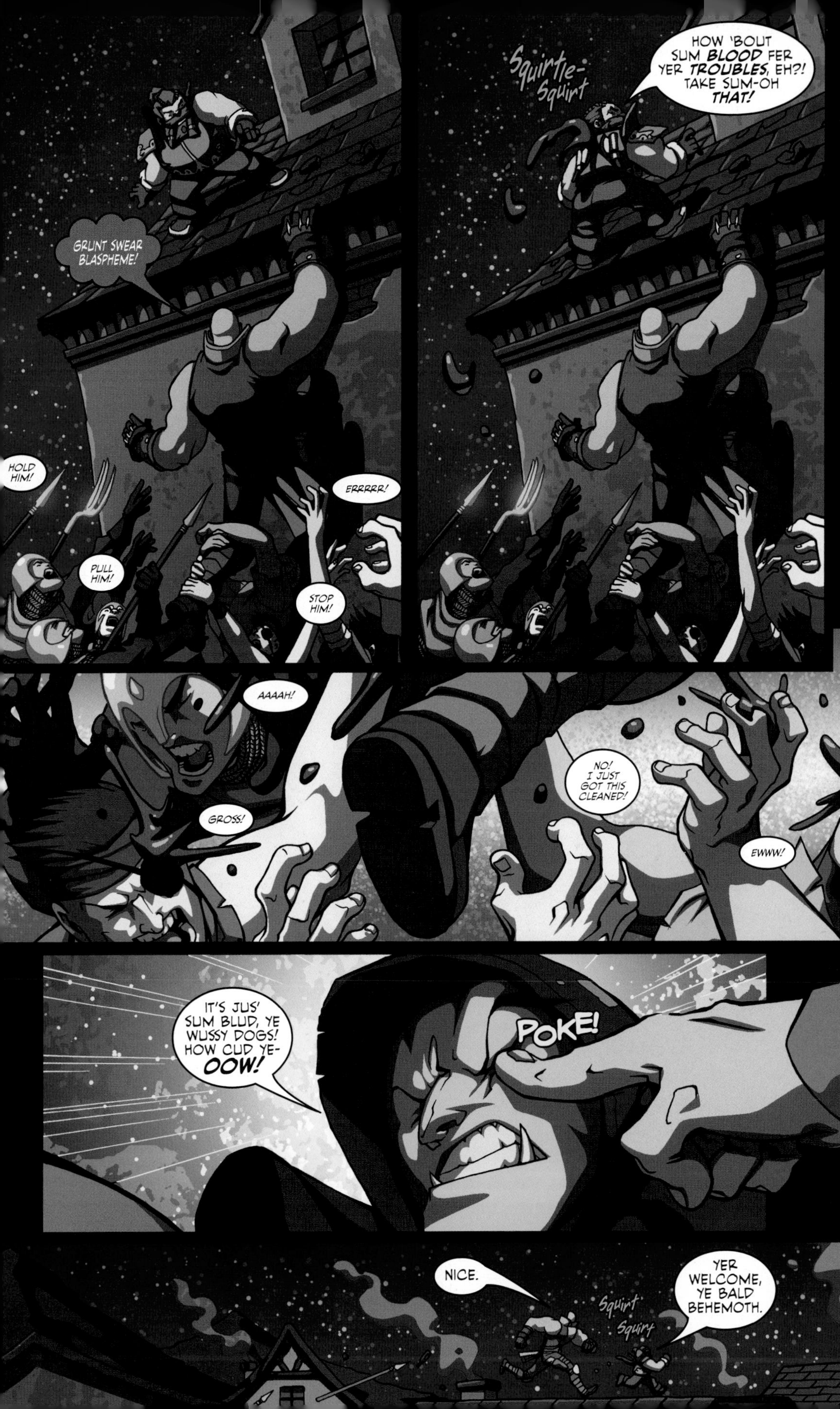
GRUNT SWEAR BLASPHEME!
HOLD HIM!
PULL HIM!
ERRRRR!
STOP HIM!
Squirtle-Squirt
HOW 'BOUT SUM BLOOD FER YER TROUBLES, EH?! TAKE SUM-OH THAT!
AAAAH!
GROSS!
NO! I JUST GOT THIS CLEANED!
EWWW!
IT'S JUS' SUM BLUD, YE WUSSY DOGS! HOW CUD YE-OOW!
POKE!
NICE.
Squirt Squirt
YER WELCOME, YE BALD BEHEMOTH.

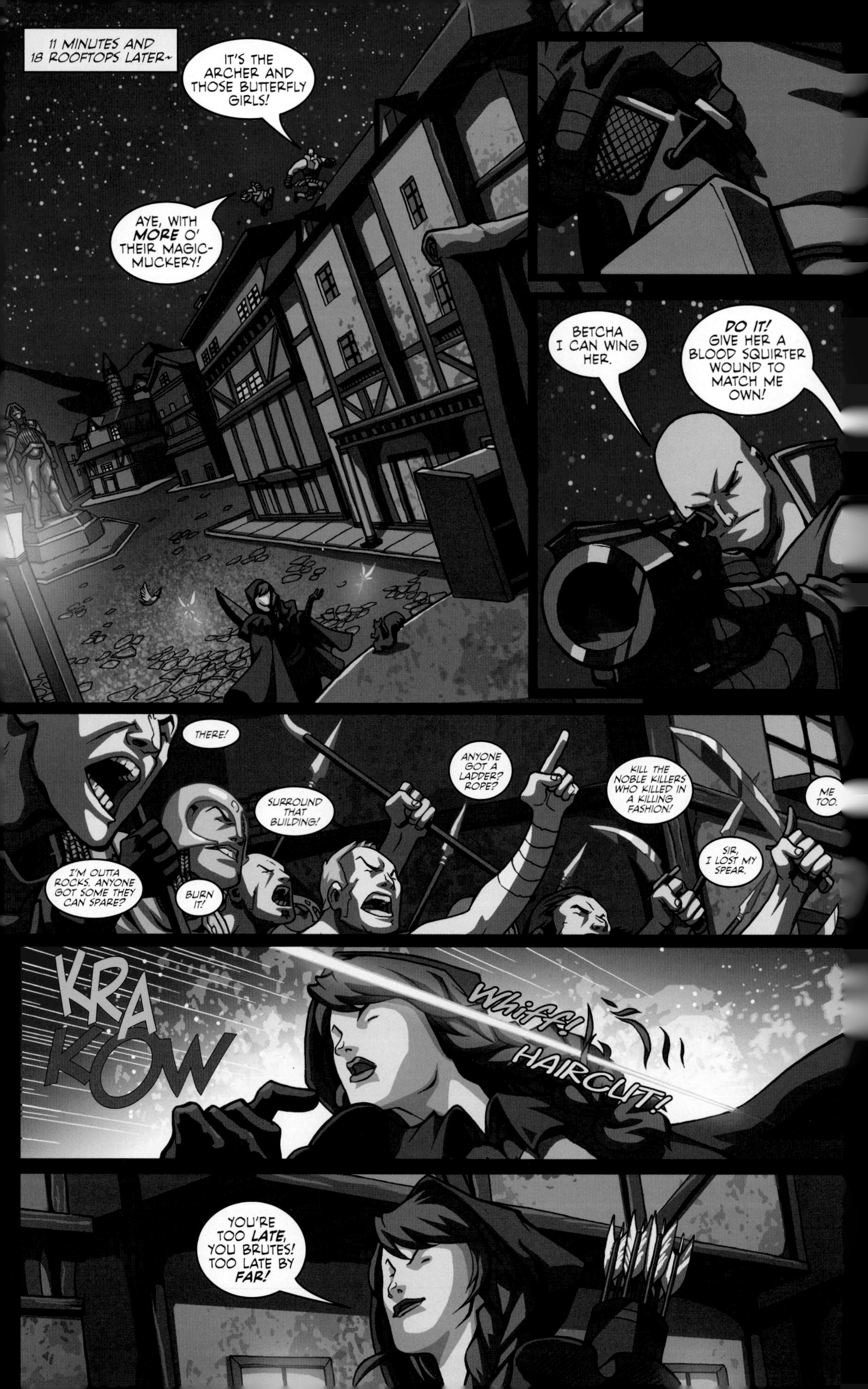

11 MINUTES AND 18 ROOFTOPS LATER~
IT'S THE ARCHER AND THOSE BUTTERFLY GIRLS!
AYE, WITH MORE O' THEIR MAGIC-MUCKERY!
BETCHA I CAN WING HER.
DO IT! GIVE HER A BLOOD SQUIRTER WOUND TO MATCH ME OWN!
THERE!
SURROUND THAT BUILDING!
ANYONE GOT A LADDER? ROPE?
KILL THE NOBLE KILLERS WHO KILLED IN A KILLING FASHION!
ME TOO.
I'M OUTTA ROCKS. ANYONE GOT SOME THEY CAN SPARE?
BURN IT!
SIR, I LOST MY SPEAR.
KRA KOW
Whiff!
HAIRCUT!
YOU'RE TOO LATE, YOU BRUTES! TOO LATE BY FAR!

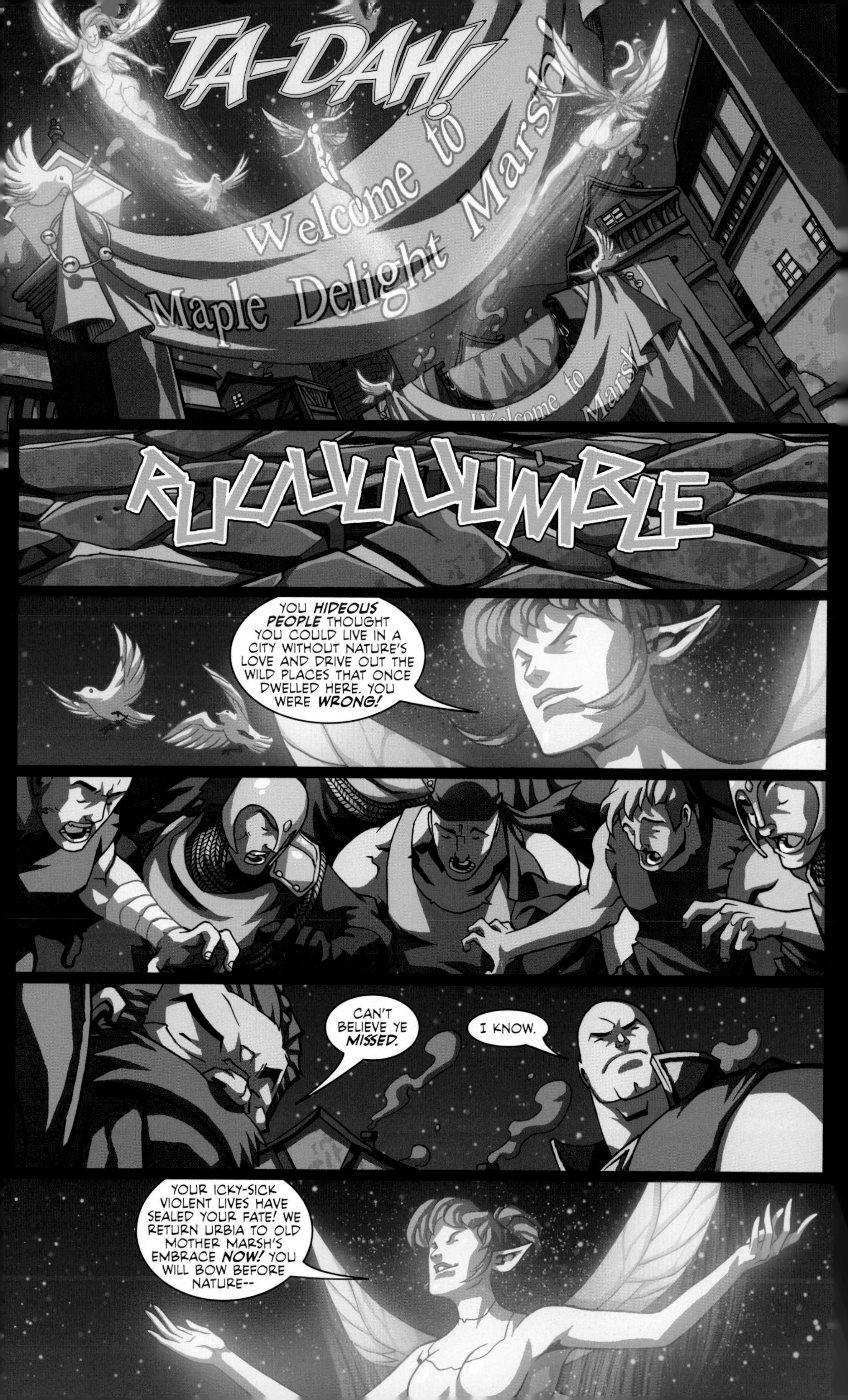
TA-DAH!
Welcome to Maple Delight Marsh
Welcome to Marsh
RUKUUUUUUMBLE
YOU HIDEOUS PEOPLE THOUGHT YOU COULD LIVE IN A CITY WITHOUT NATURE'S LOVE AND DRIVE OUT THE WILD PLACES THAT ONCE DWELLED HERE. YOU WERE WRONG!
CAN'T BELIEVE YE MISSED.
I KNOW.
YOUR ICKY-SICK VIOLENT LIVES HAVE SEALED YOUR FATE! WE RETURN URBIA TO OLD MOTHER MARSH'S EMBRACE NOW! YOU WILL BOW BEFORE NATURE--

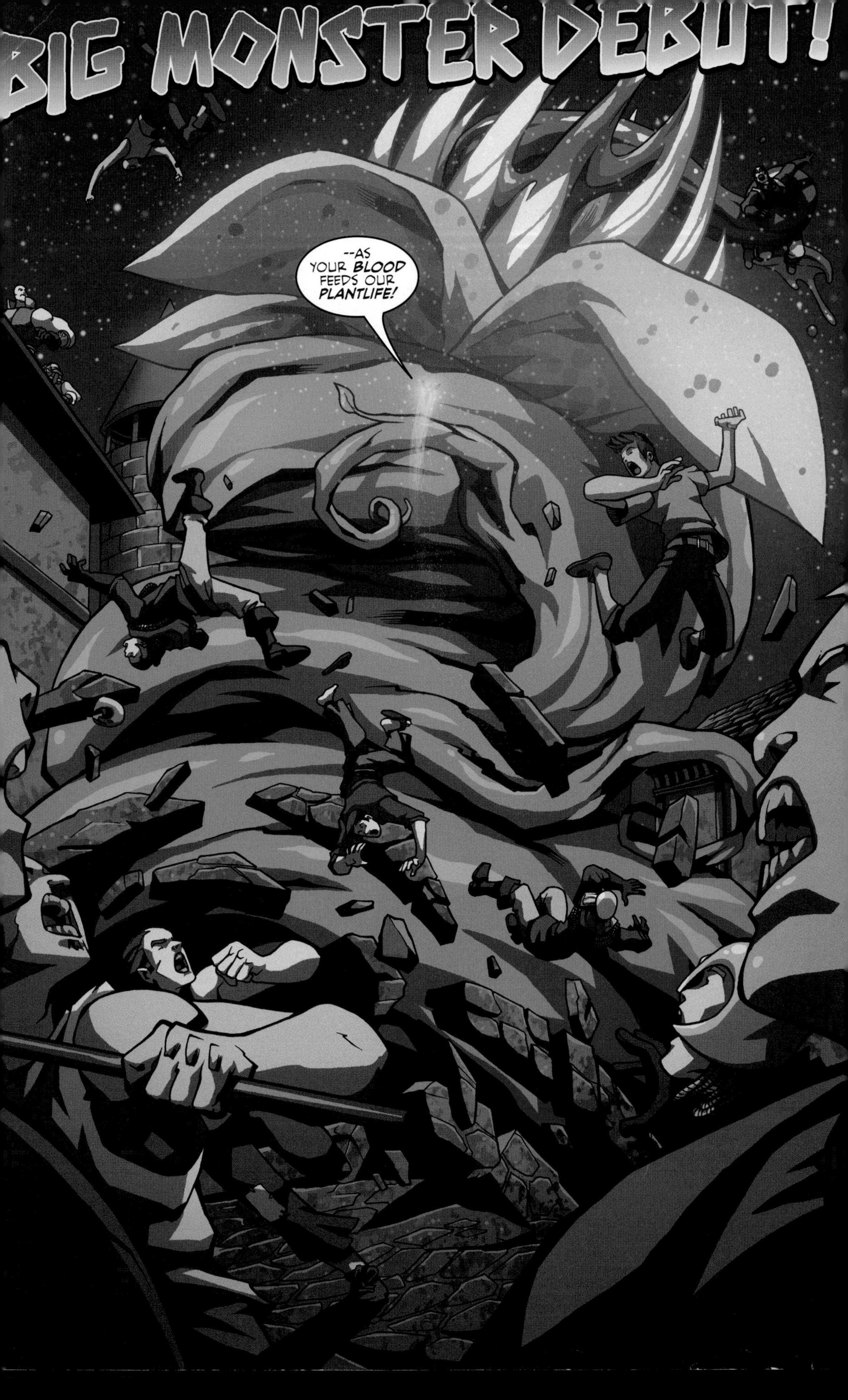
BIG MONSTER DEBUT!
--AS YOUR BLOOD FEEDS OUR PLANTLIFE!

CHAPTER FIVE

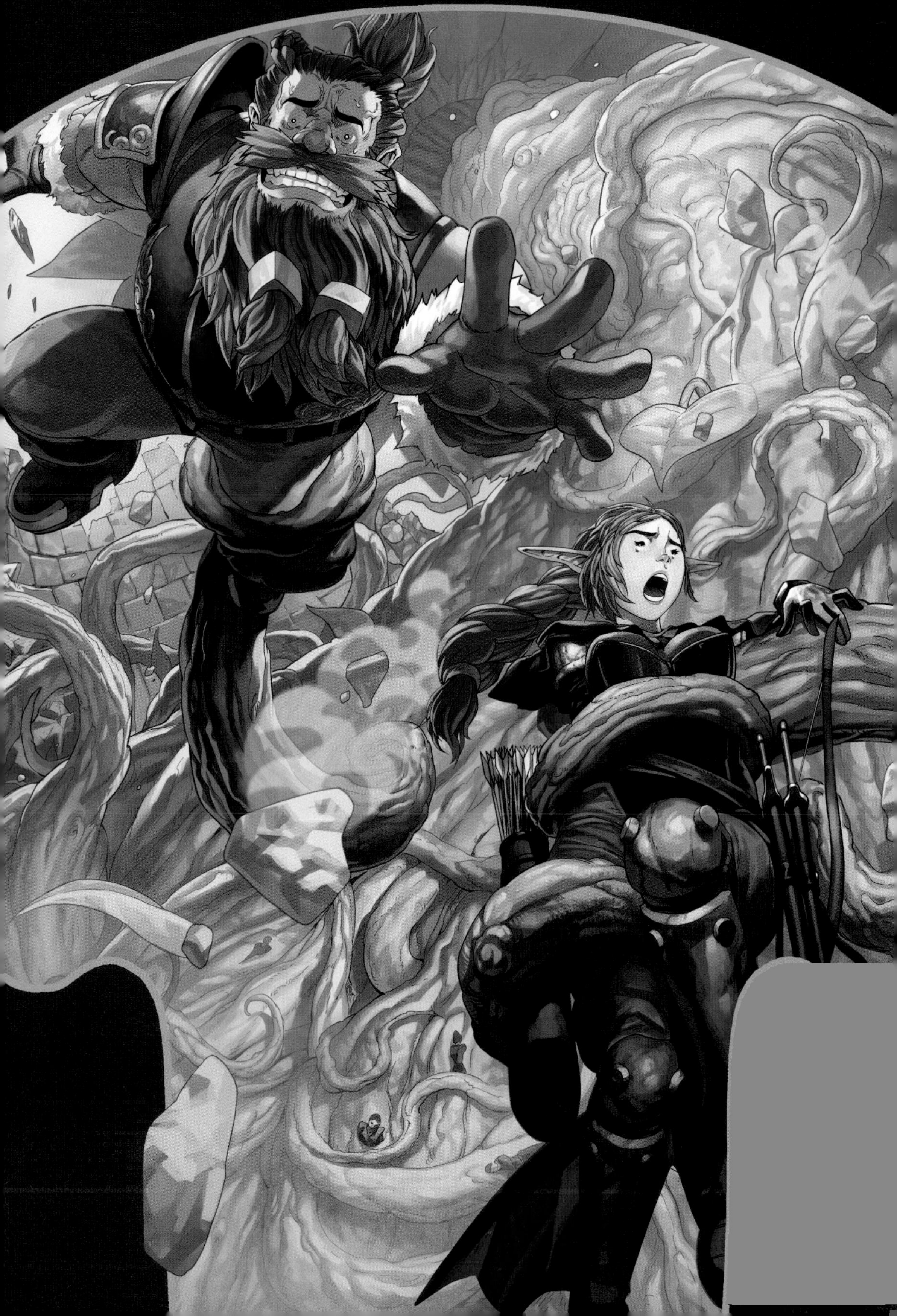

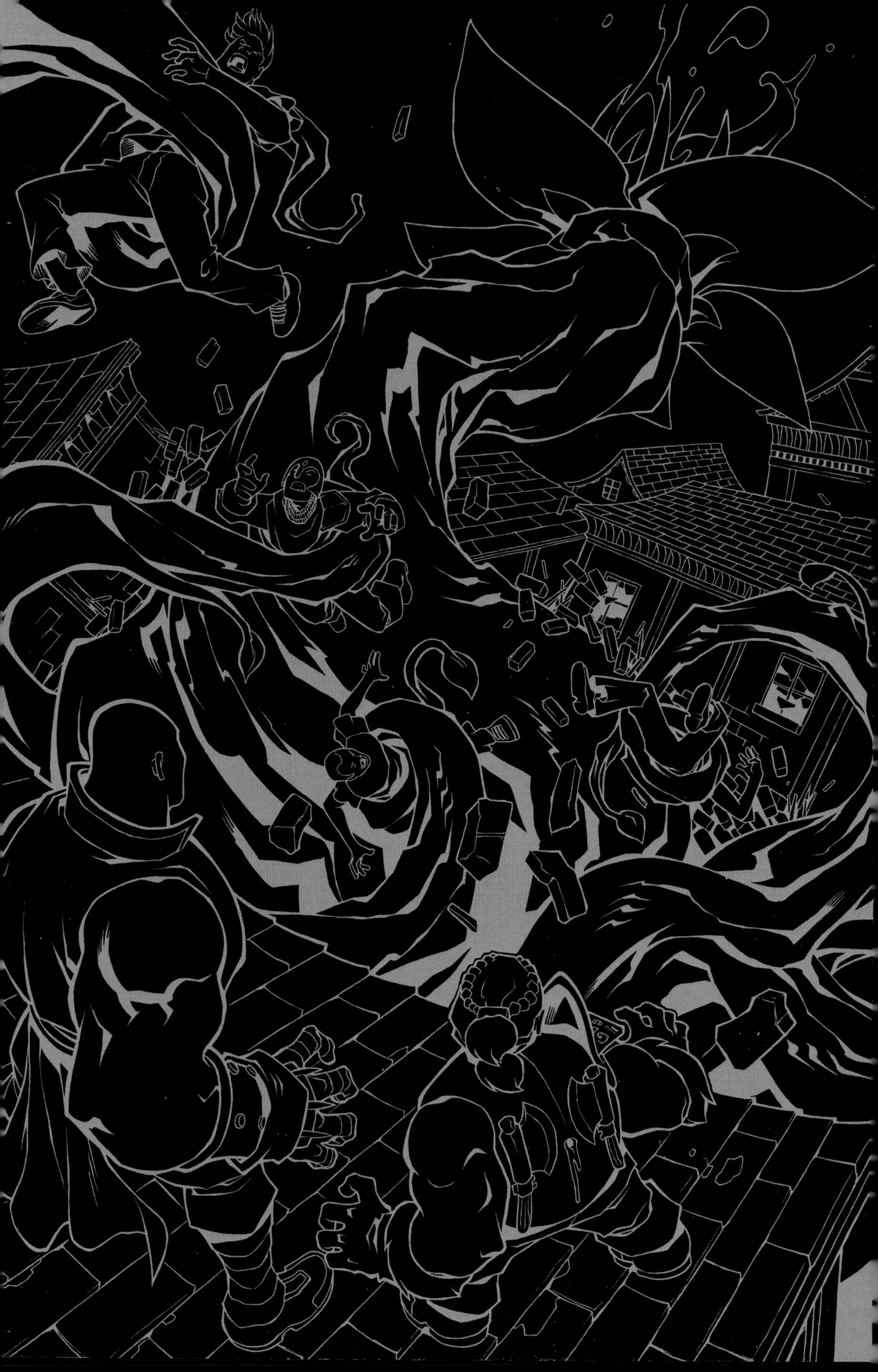

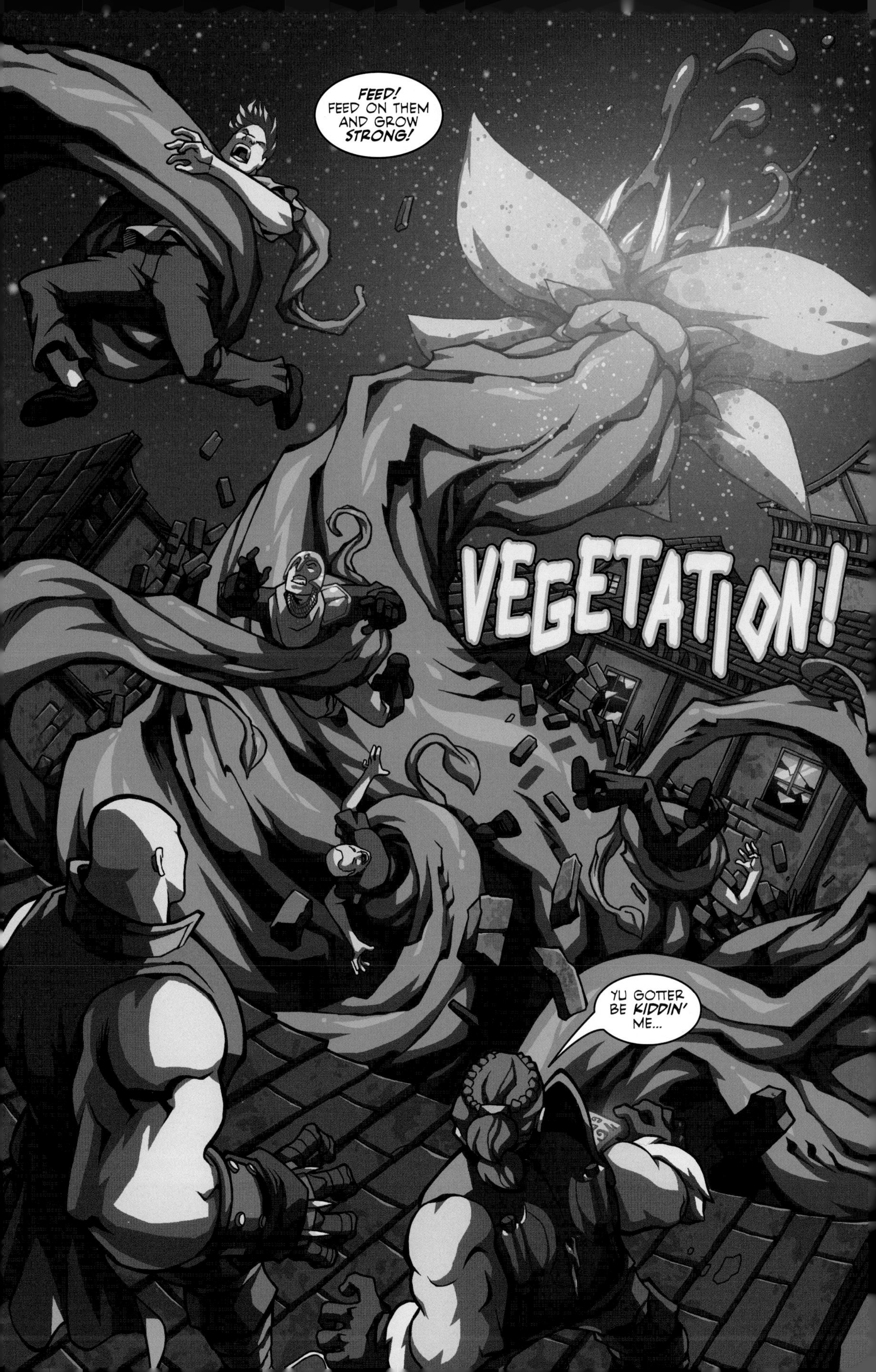
FEED! FEED ON THEM AND GROW STRONG!
VEGETATION!
YU GOTTER BE KIDDIN' ME...

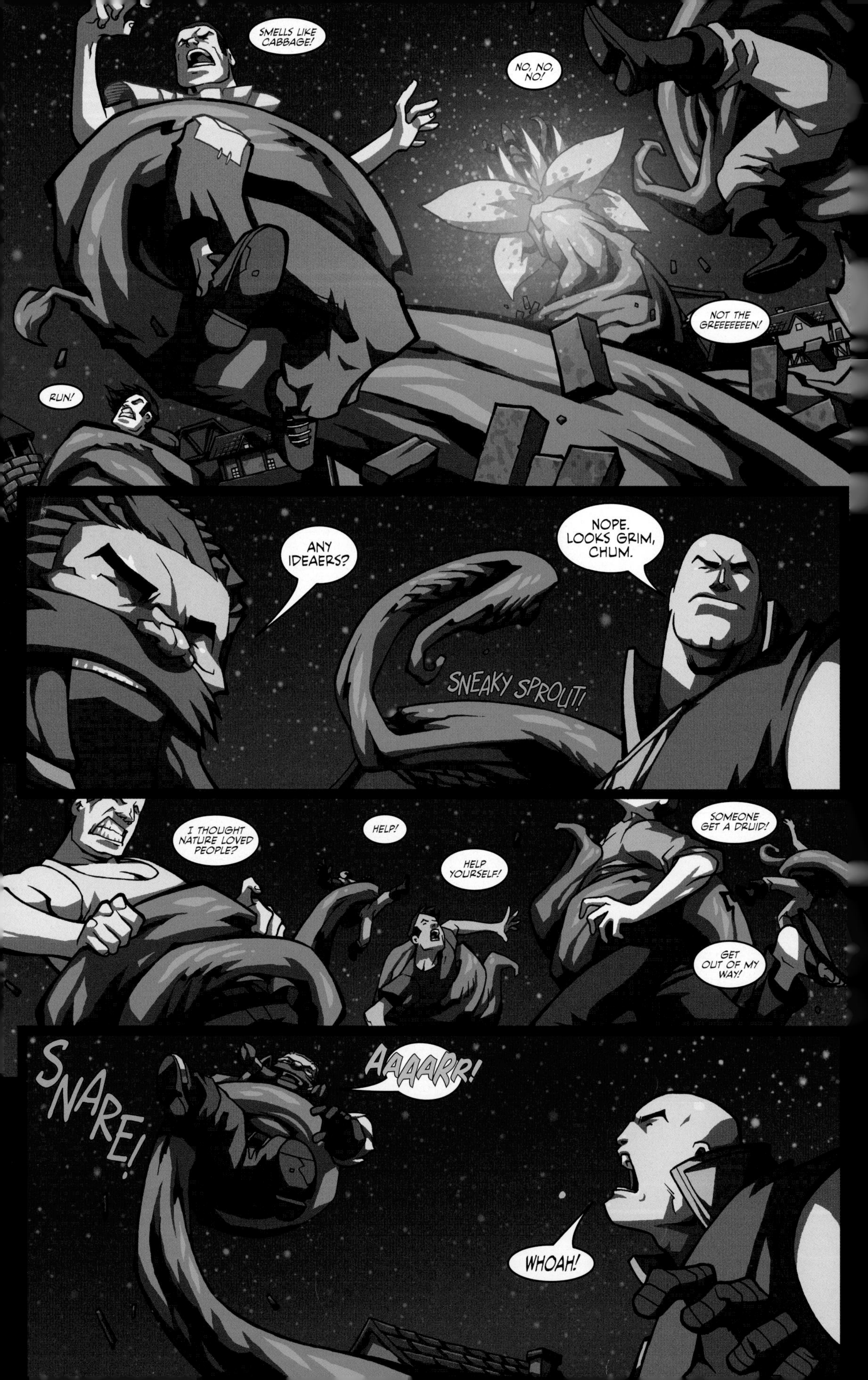
SMELLS LIKE CABBAGE!
NO, NO, NO!
NOT THE GREEEEEEEN!
RUN!
ANY IDEAERS?
NOPE. LOOKS GRIM, CHUM.
SNEAKY SPROUT!
I THOUGHT NATURE LOVED PEOPLE?
HELP!
HELP YOURSELF!
SOMEONE GET A DRUID!
GET OUT OF MY WAY!
SNARE!
AAAARR!
WHOAH!

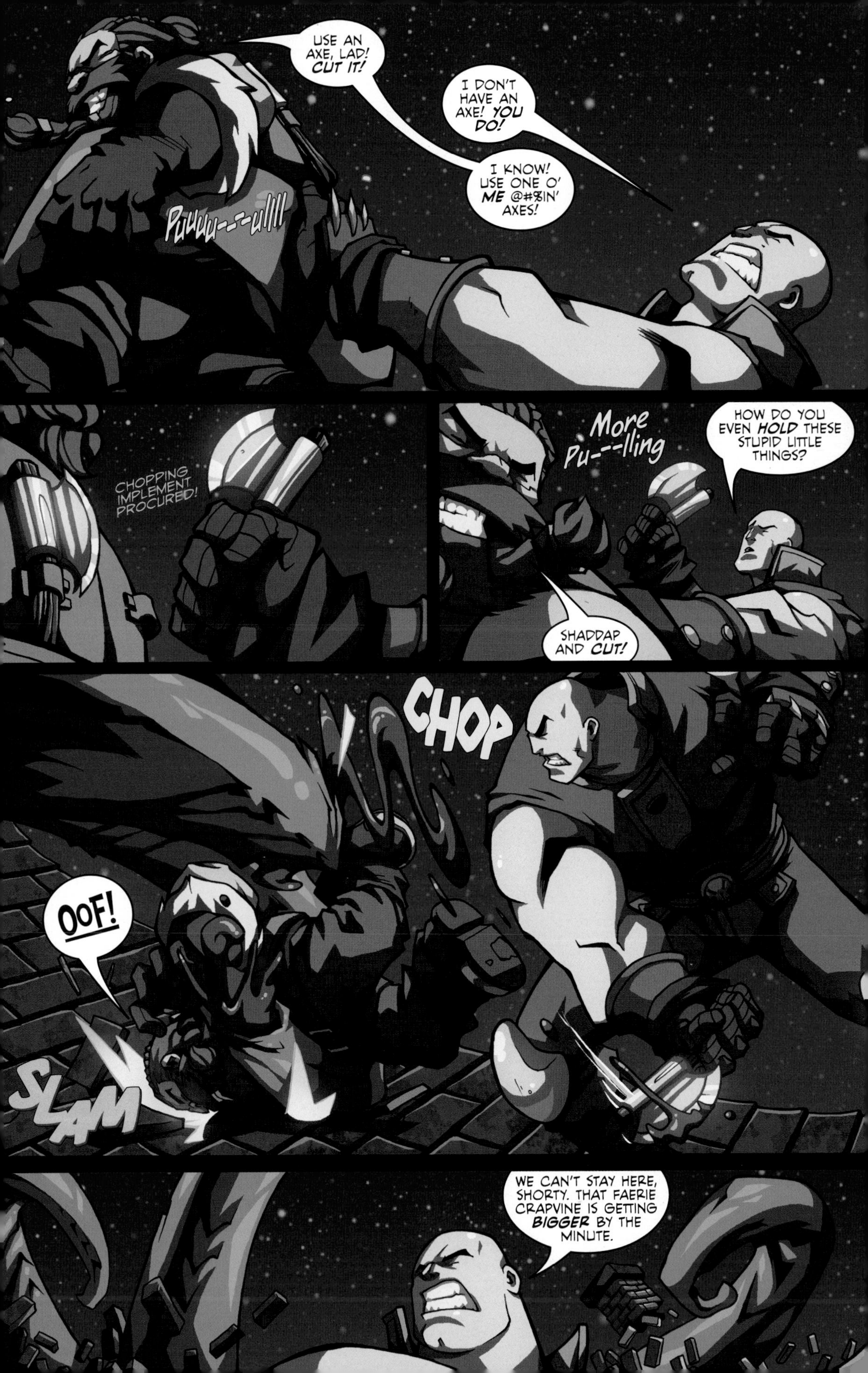

USE AN AXE, LAD! **CUT IT!**
I DON'T HAVE AN AXE! ***YOU DO!***
I KNOW! USE ONE O' ***ME*** @#%IN' AXES!
Puuuu---ulll
CHOPPING IMPLEMENT PROCURED!
More Pu---lling
HOW DO YOU EVEN ***HOLD*** THESE STUPID LITTLE THINGS?
SHADDAP AND ***CUT!***
CHOP
OOF!
SLAM
WE CAN'T STAY HERE, SHORTY. THAT FAERIE CRAPVINE IS GETTING ***BIGGER*** BY THE MINUTE.

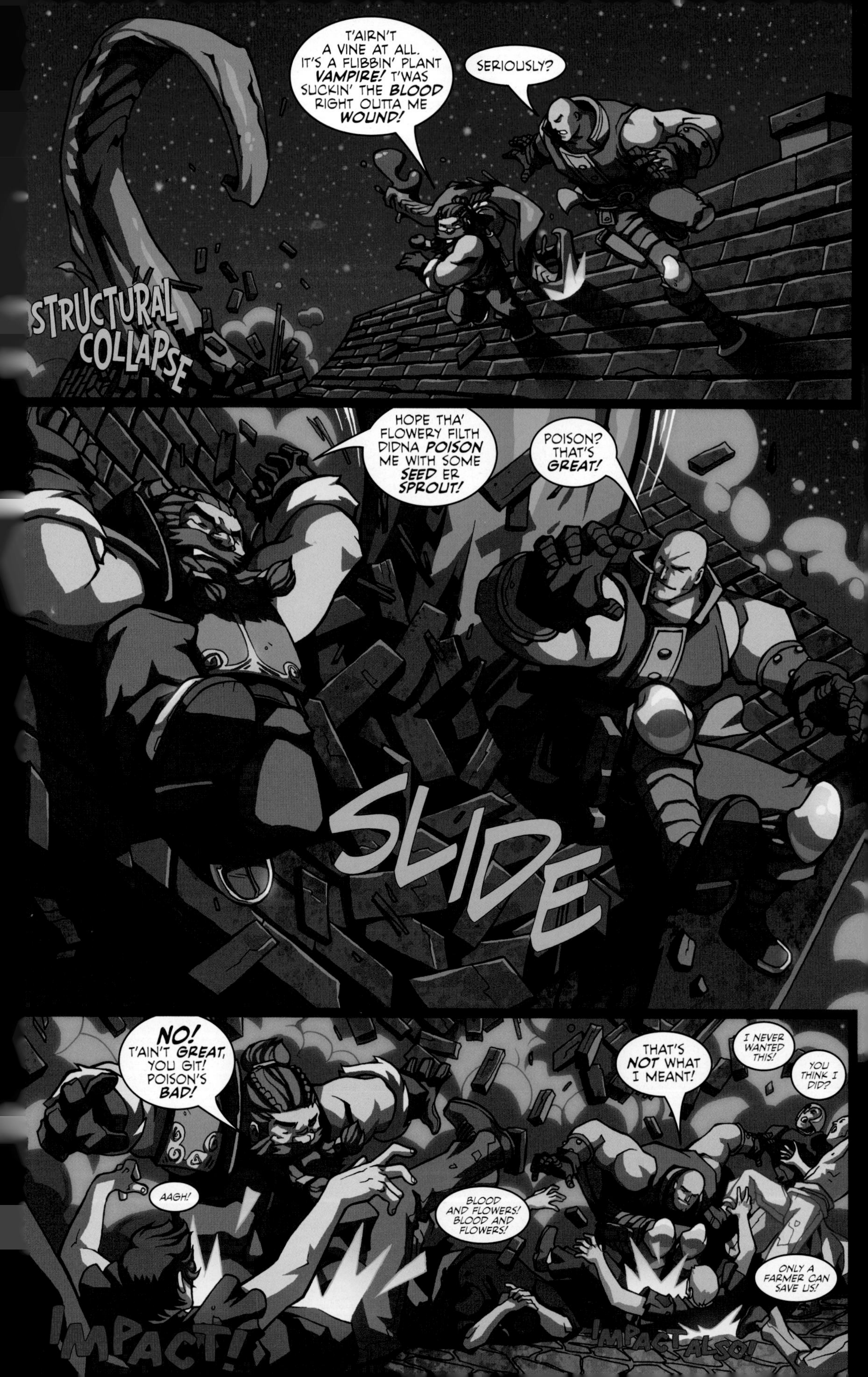

T'AIRN'T A VINE AT ALL. IT'S A FLIBBIN' PLANT **VAMPIRE!** T'WAS SUCKIN' THE **BLOOD** RIGHT OUTTA ME **WOUND!**
SERIOUSLY?
STRUCTURAL COLLAPSE
HOPE THA' FLOWERY FILTH DIDNA **POISON** ME WITH SOME **SEED** ER **SPROUT!**
POISON? THAT'S **GREAT!**
SLIDE
NO! T'AIN'T **GREAT,** YOU GIT! POISON'S **BAD!**
THAT'S **NOT** WHAT I MEANT!
I NEVER WANTED THIS!
YOU THINK I DID?
AAGH!
BLOOD AND FLOWERS! BLOOD AND FLOWERS!
ONLY A FARMER CAN SAVE US!
IMPACT!
IMPACT ALSO!

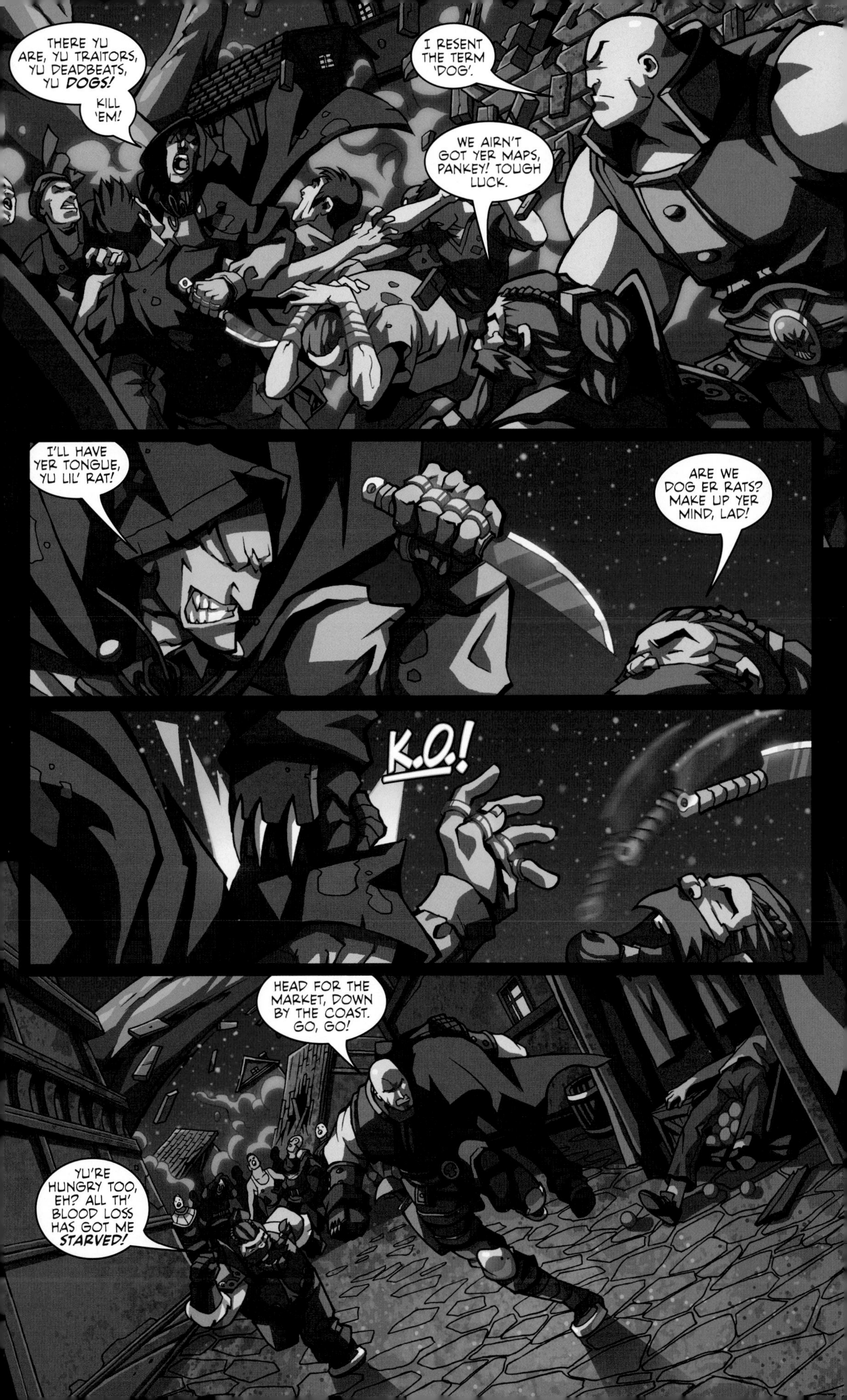
THERE YU ARE, YU TRAITORS, YU DEADBEATS, YU *DOGS!*
KILL 'EM!
I RESENT THE TERM 'DOG'.
WE AIRN'T GOT YER MAPS, PANKEY! TOUGH LUCK.
I'LL HAVE YER TONGUE, YU LIL' RAT!
ARE WE DOG ER RATS? MAKE UP YER MIND, LAD!
K.O.!
HEAD FOR THE MARKET, DOWN BY THE COAST. GO, GO!
YU'RE HUNGRY TOO, EH? ALL TH' BLOOD LOSS HAS GOT ME *STARVED!*

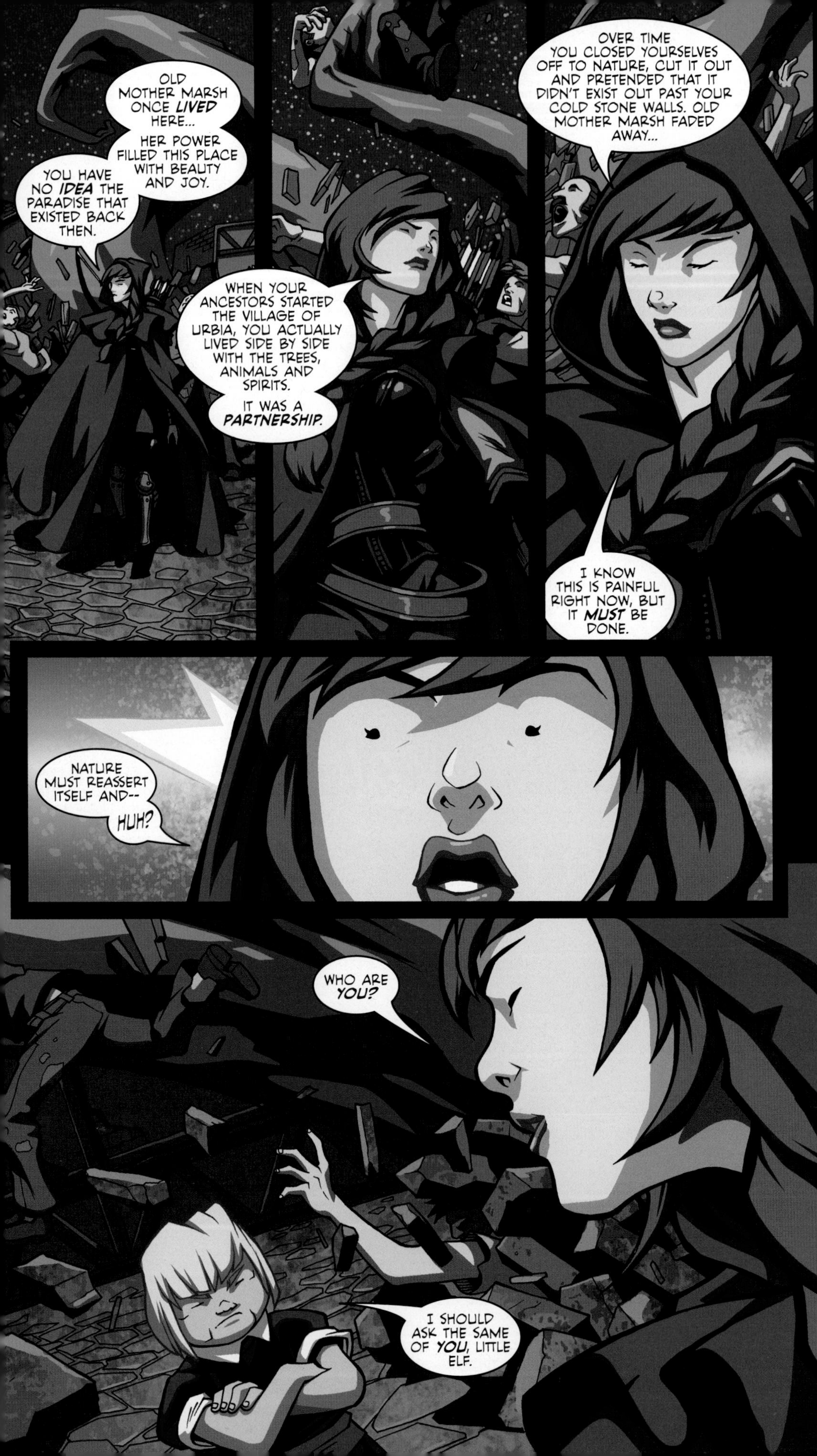
OLD MOTHER MARSH ONCE *LIVED* HERE...
HER POWER FILLED THIS PLACE WITH BEAUTY AND JOY.
YOU HAVE NO *IDEA* THE PARADISE THAT EXISTED BACK THEN.
WHEN YOUR ANCESTORS STARTED THE VILLAGE OF URBIA, YOU ACTUALLY LIVED SIDE BY SIDE WITH THE TREES, ANIMALS AND SPIRITS.
IT WAS A *PARTNERSHIP*.
OVER TIME YOU CLOSED YOURSELVES OFF TO NATURE, CUT IT OUT AND PRETENDED THAT IT DIDN'T EXIST OUT PAST YOUR COLD STONE WALLS. OLD MOTHER MARSH FADED AWAY...
I KNOW THIS IS PAINFUL RIGHT NOW, BUT IT *MUST* BE DONE.
NATURE MUST REASSERT ITSELF AND--
HUH?
WHO ARE *YOU?*
I SHOULD ASK THE SAME OF *YOU*, LITTLE ELF.

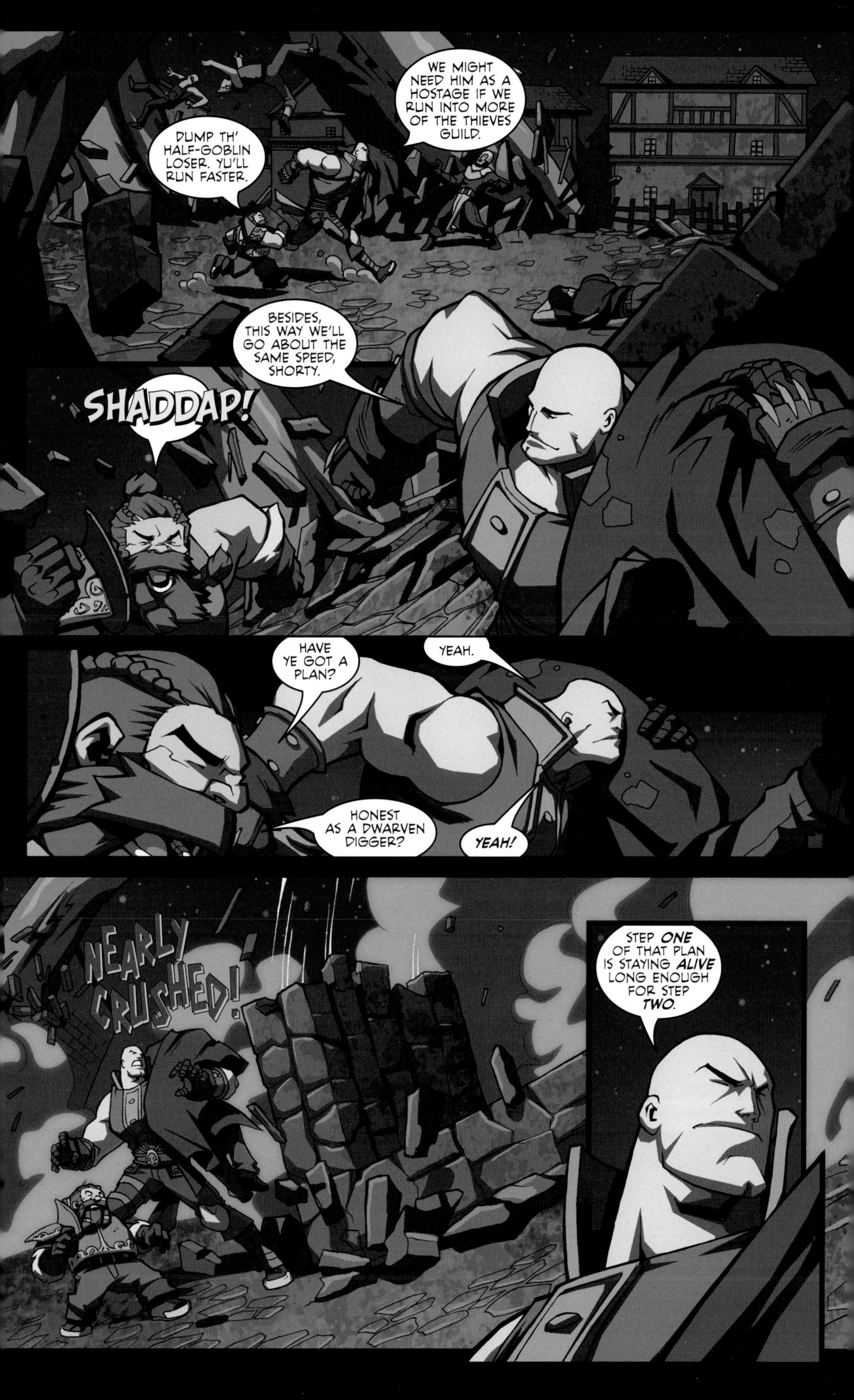
DUMP TH' HALF-GOBLIN LOSER. YU'LL RUN FASTER.
WE MIGHT NEED HIM AS A HOSTAGE IF WE RUN INTO MORE OF THE THIEVES GUILD.
BESIDES, THIS WAY WE'LL GO ABOUT THE SAME SPEED, SHORTY.
SHADDAP!
HAVE YE GOT A PLAN?
YEAH.
HONEST AS A DWARVEN DIGGER?
YEAH!
NEARLY CRUSHED!
STEP ONE OF THAT PLAN IS STAYING ALIVE LONG ENOUGH FOR STEP TWO.

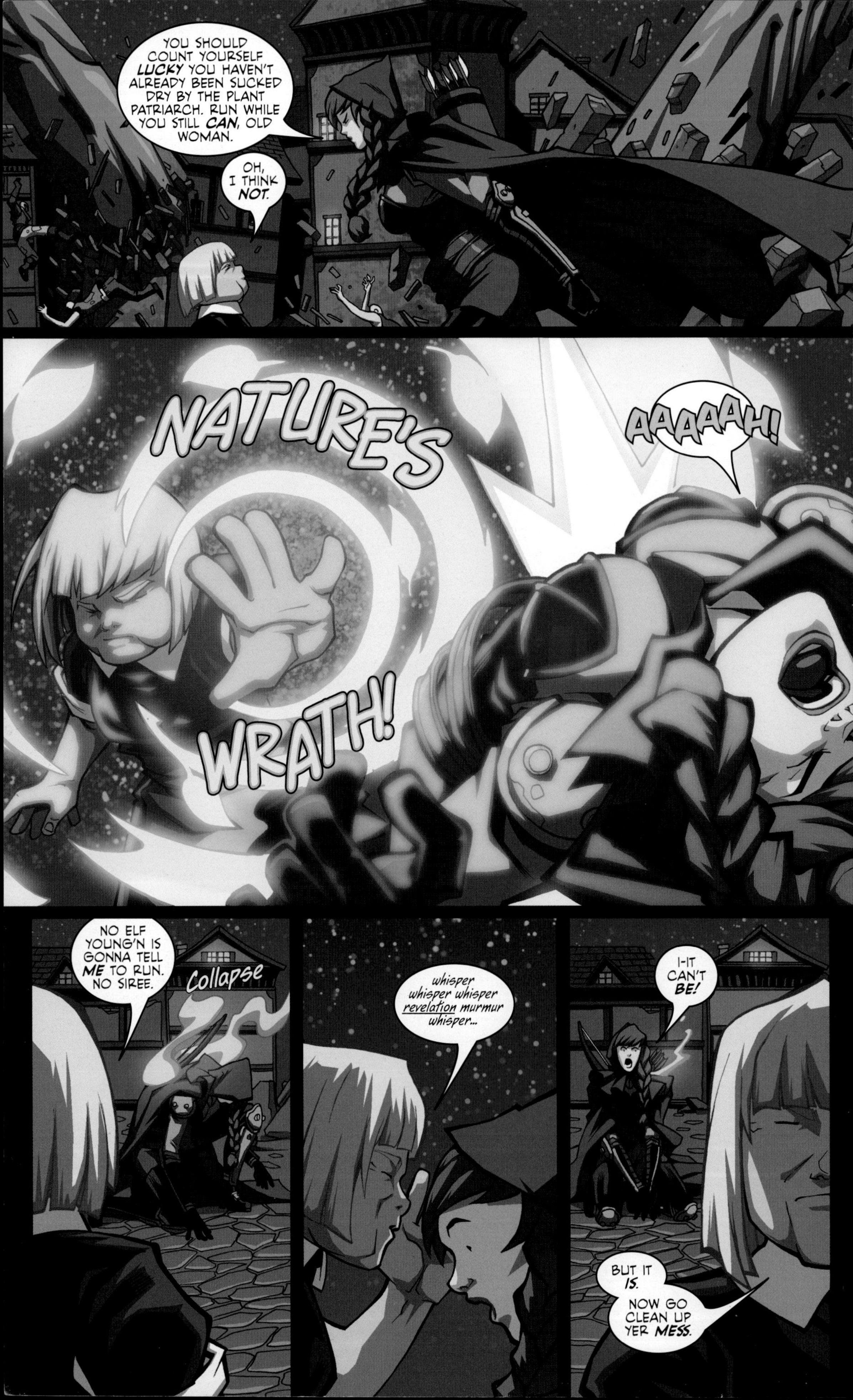

YOU SHOULD COUNT YOURSELF LUCKY YOU HAVEN'T ALREADY BEEN SUCKED DRY BY THE PLANT PATRIARCH. RUN WHILE YOU STILL CAN, OLD WOMAN.
OH, I THINK NOT.
NATURE'S WRATH!
AAAAAH!
NO ELF YOUNG'N IS GONNA TELL ME TO RUN. NO SIREE.
Collapse
whisper whisper whisper revelation murmur whisper...
I-IT CAN'T BE!
BUT IT IS.
NOW GO CLEAN UP YER MESS.

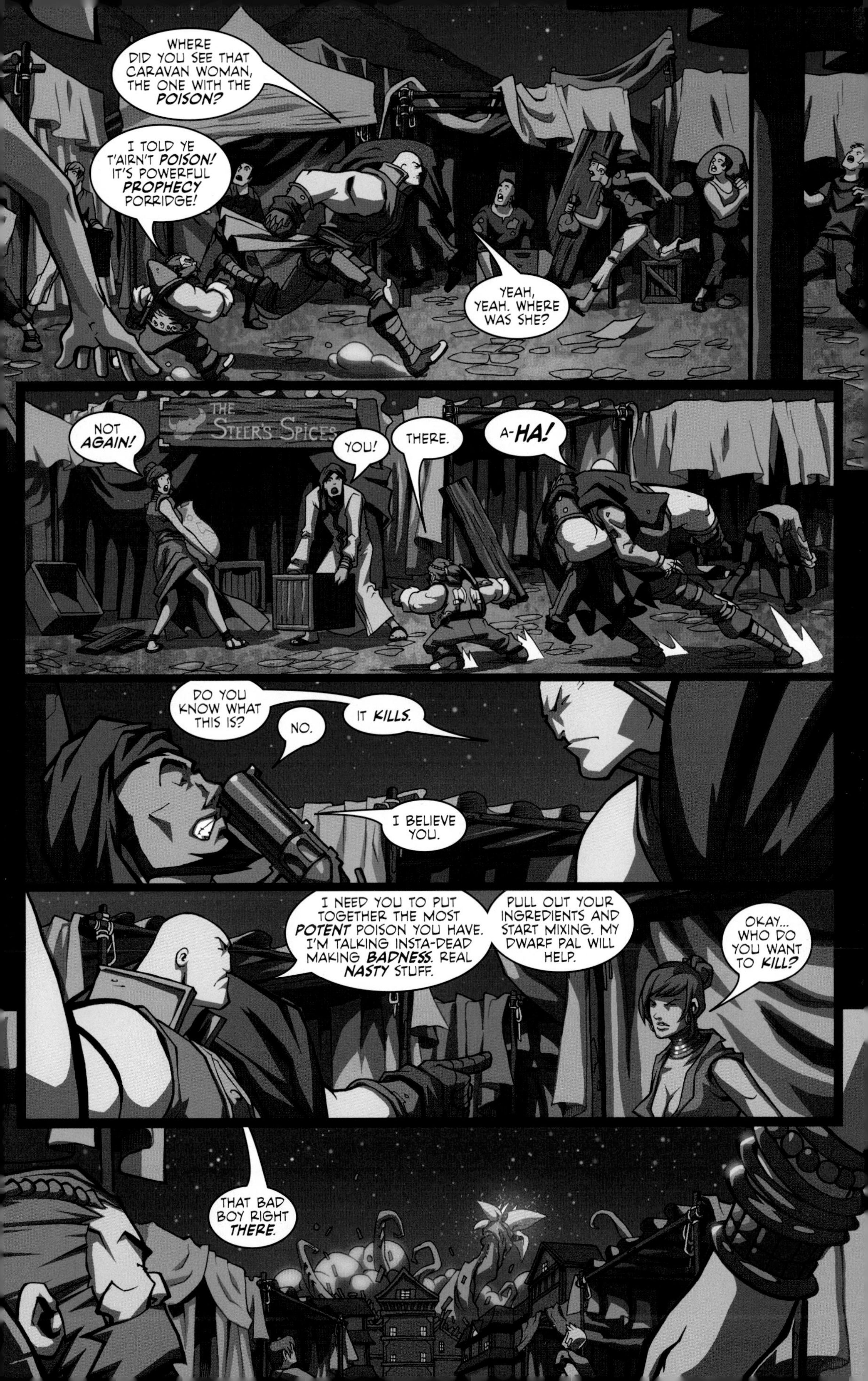
WHERE DID YOU SEE THAT CARAVAN WOMAN, THE ONE WITH THE POISON?
I TOLD YE T'AIRN'T POISON! IT'S POWERFUL PROPHECY PORRIDGE!
YEAH, YEAH. WHERE WAS SHE?
THE STEER'S SPICES
NOT AGAIN!
YOU!
THERE.
A-HA!
DO YOU KNOW WHAT THIS IS?
NO.
IT KILLS.
I BELIEVE YOU.
I NEED YOU TO PUT TOGETHER THE MOST POTENT POISON YOU HAVE. I'M TALKING INSTA-DEAD MAKING BADNESS. REAL NASTY STUFF.
PULL OUT YOUR INGREDIENTS AND START MIXING. MY DWARF PAL WILL HELP.
OKAY... WHO DO YOU WANT TO KILL?
THAT BAD BOY RIGHT THERE.

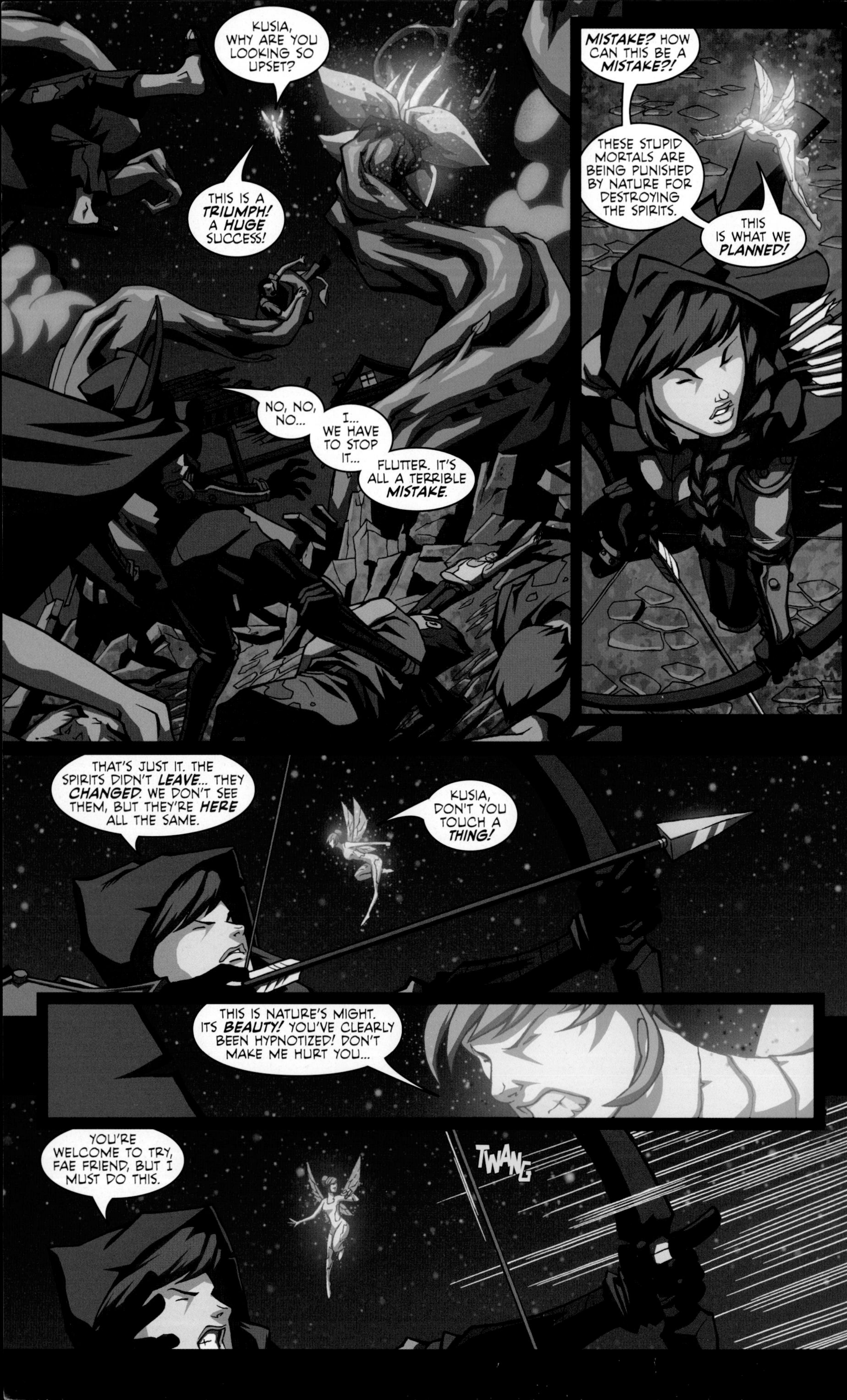
KUSIA, WHY ARE YOU LOOKING SO UPSET?
THIS IS A *TRIUMPH!* A *HUGE* SUCCESS!
NO, NO, NO...
I... WE HAVE TO STOP IT...
FLUTTER. IT'S ALL A TERRIBLE *MISTAKE*.
MISTAKE? HOW CAN THIS BE A *MISTAKE?!*
THESE STUPID MORTALS ARE BEING PUNISHED BY NATURE FOR DESTROYING THE SPIRITS.
THIS IS WHAT WE *PLANNED!*
THAT'S JUST IT. THE SPIRITS DIDN'T *LEAVE*... THEY *CHANGED*. WE DON'T SEE THEM, BUT THEY'RE *HERE* ALL THE SAME.
KUSIA, DON'T YOU TOUCH A *THING!*
THIS IS NATURE'S MIGHT. ITS *BEAUTY!* YOU'VE CLEARLY BEEN HYPNOTIZED! DON'T MAKE ME HURT YOU...
YOU'RE WELCOME TO TRY, FAE FRIEND, BUT I MUST DO THIS.
TWANG

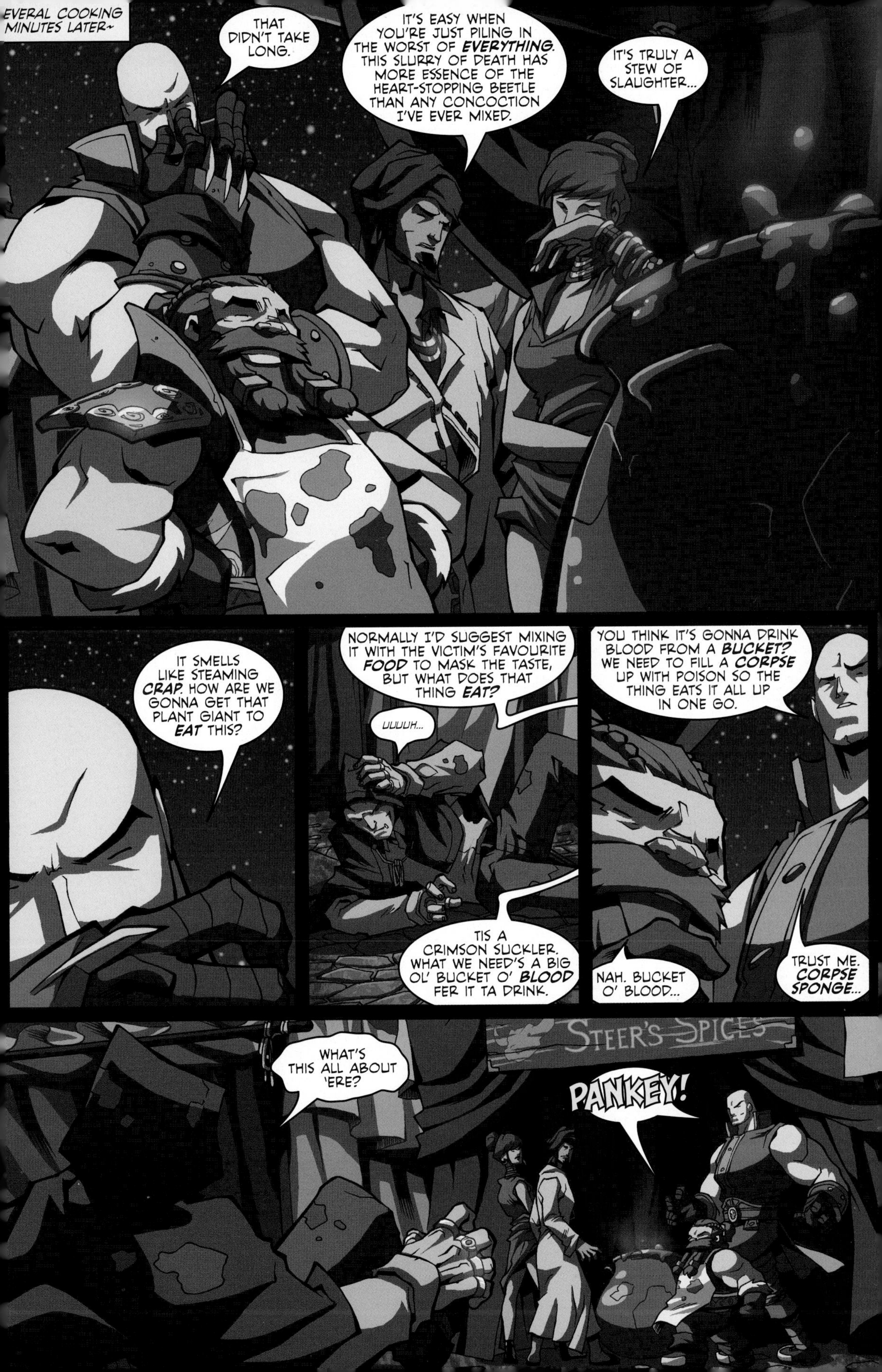
EVERAL COOKING MINUTES LATER~
THAT DIDN'T TAKE LONG.
IT'S EASY WHEN YOU'RE JUST PILING IN THE WORST OF EVERYTHING. THIS SLURRY OF DEATH HAS MORE ESSENCE OF THE HEART-STOPPING BEETLE THAN ANY CONCOCTION I'VE EVER MIXED.
IT'S TRULY A STEW OF SLAUGHTER...
IT SMELLS LIKE STEAMING CRAP. HOW ARE WE GONNA GET THAT PLANT GIANT TO EAT THIS?
NORMALLY I'D SUGGEST MIXING IT WITH THE VICTIM'S FAVOURITE FOOD TO MASK THE TASTE, BUT WHAT DOES THAT THING EAT?
UUUUH...
TIS A CRIMSON SUCKLER. WHAT WE NEED'S A BIG OL' BUCKET O' BLOOD FER IT TA DRINK.
YOU THINK IT'S GONNA DRINK BLOOD FROM A BUCKET? WE NEED TO FILL A CORPSE UP WITH POISON SO THE THING EATS IT ALL UP IN ONE GO.
NAH. BUCKET O' BLOOD...
TRUST ME. CORPSE SPONGE...
STEER'S SPICES
WHAT'S THIS ALL ABOUT 'ERE?
PANKEY!

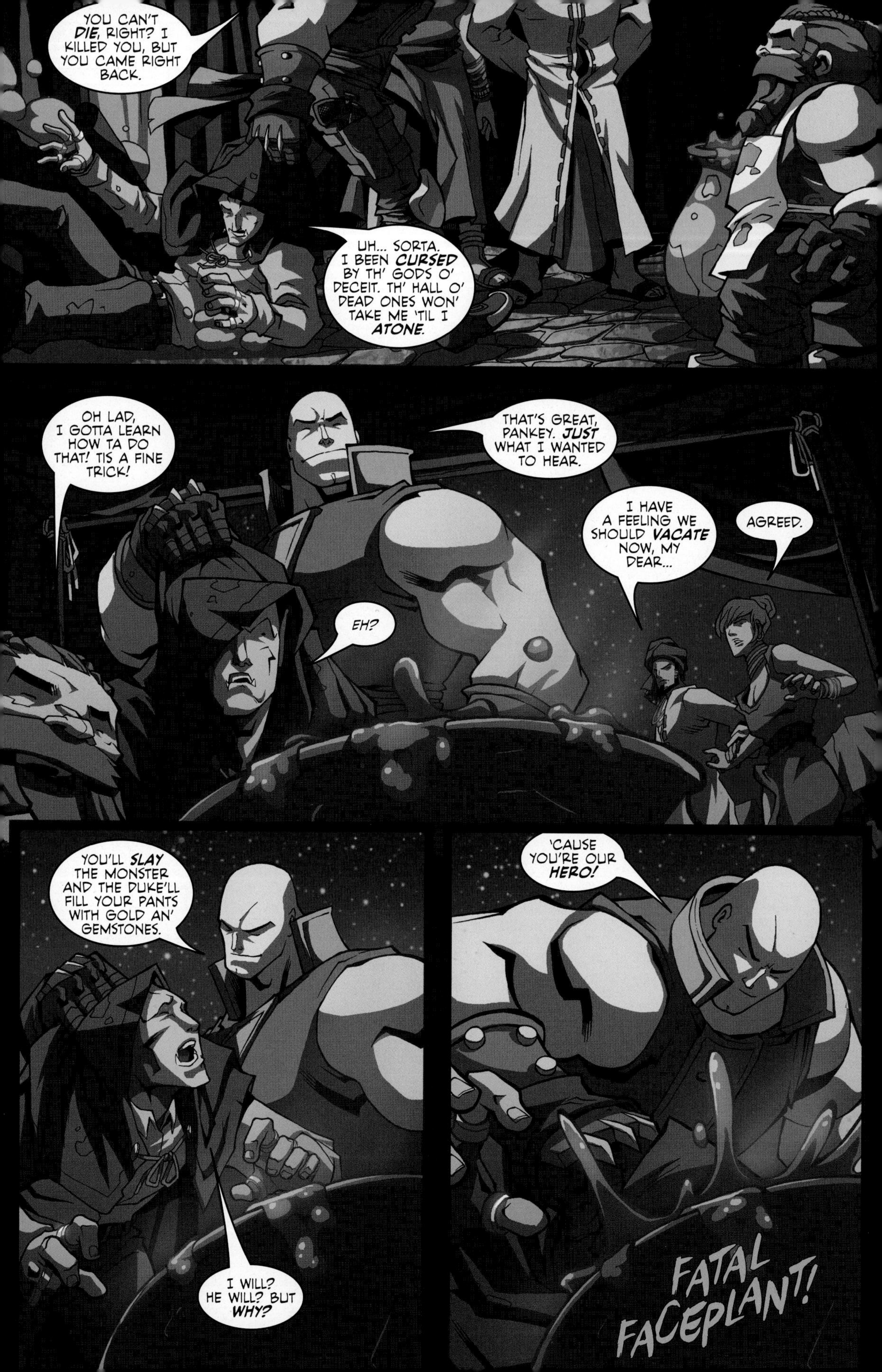

YOU CAN'T DIE, RIGHT? I KILLED YOU, BUT YOU CAME RIGHT BACK.
UH... SORTA. I BEEN CURSED BY TH' GODS O' DECEIT. TH' HALL O' DEAD ONES WON' TAKE ME 'TIL I ATONE.
OH LAD, I GOTTA LEARN HOW TA DO THAT! TIS A FINE TRICK!
THAT'S GREAT, PANKEY. JUST WHAT I WANTED TO HEAR.
I HAVE A FEELING WE SHOULD VACATE NOW, MY DEAR...
AGREED.
EH?
YOU'LL SLAY THE MONSTER AND THE DUKE'LL FILL YOUR PANTS WITH GOLD AN' GEMSTONES.
I WILL? HE WILL? BUT WHY?
'CAUSE YOU'RE OUR HERO!
FATAL FACEPLANT!

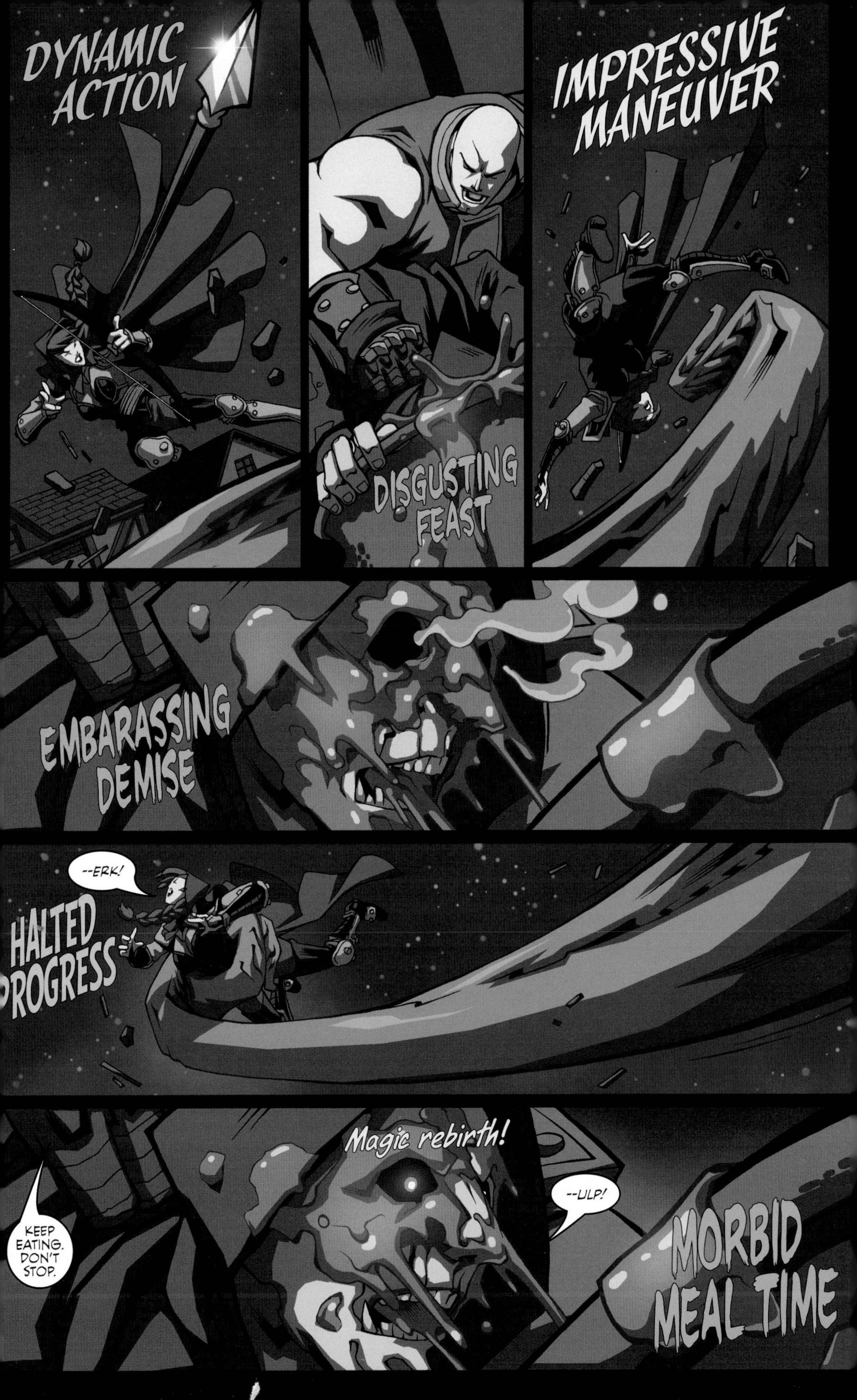
DYNAMIC ACTION
IMPRESSIVE MANEUVER
DISGUSTING FEAST
EMBARASSING DEMISE
--ERK!
HALTED PROGRESS
Magic rebirth!
KEEP EATING. DON'T STOP.
--ULP!
MORBID MEAL TIME

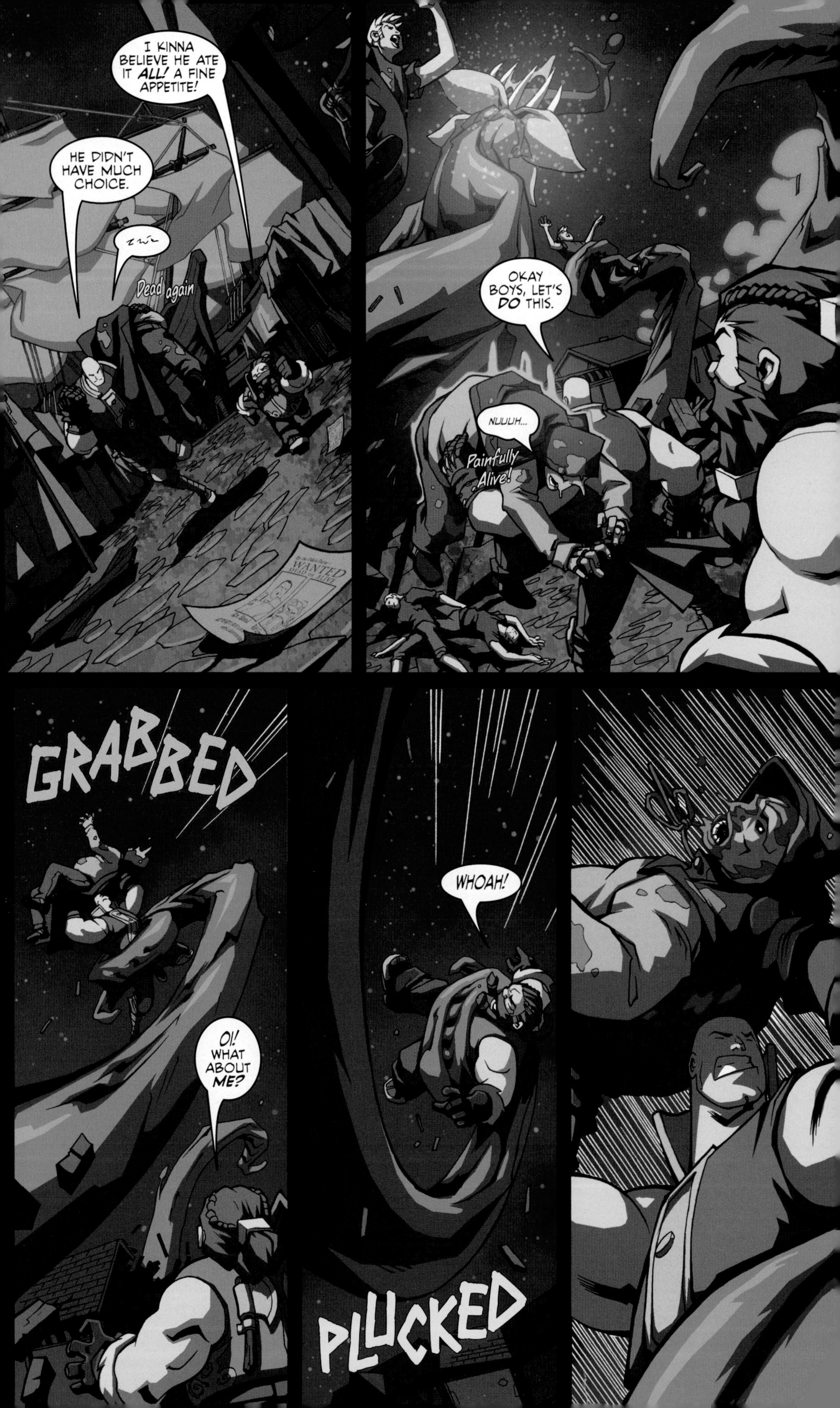
I KINNA BELIEVE HE ATE IT ALL! A FINE APPETITE!
HE DIDN'T HAVE MUCH CHOICE.
Dead again
WANTED
OKAY BOYS, LET'S DO THIS.
NUUUH...
Painfully Alive!
GRABBED
OI! WHAT ABOUT ME?
WHOAH!
PLUCKED

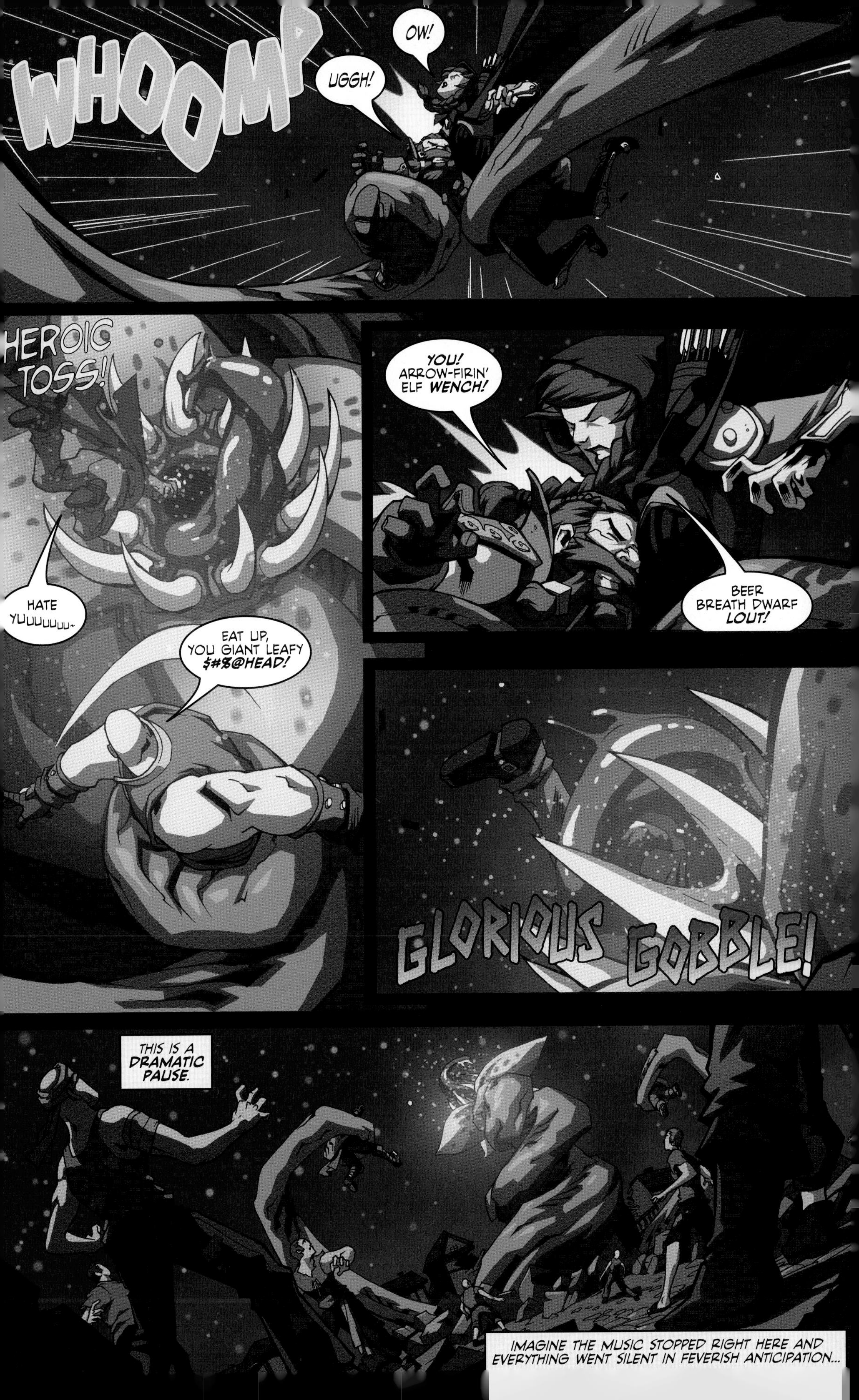
WHOOMP
OW!
UGGH!
HEROIC TOSS!
HATE YUUUUUUU~
YOU! ARROW-FIRIN' ELF WENCH!
BEER BREATH DWARF LOUT!
EAT UP, YOU GIANT LEAFY $#%@HEAD!
GLORIOUS GOBBLE!
THIS IS A DRAMATIC PAUSE.
IMAGINE THE MUSIC STOPPED RIGHT HERE AND EVERYTHING WENT SILENT IN FEVERISH ANTICIPATION...

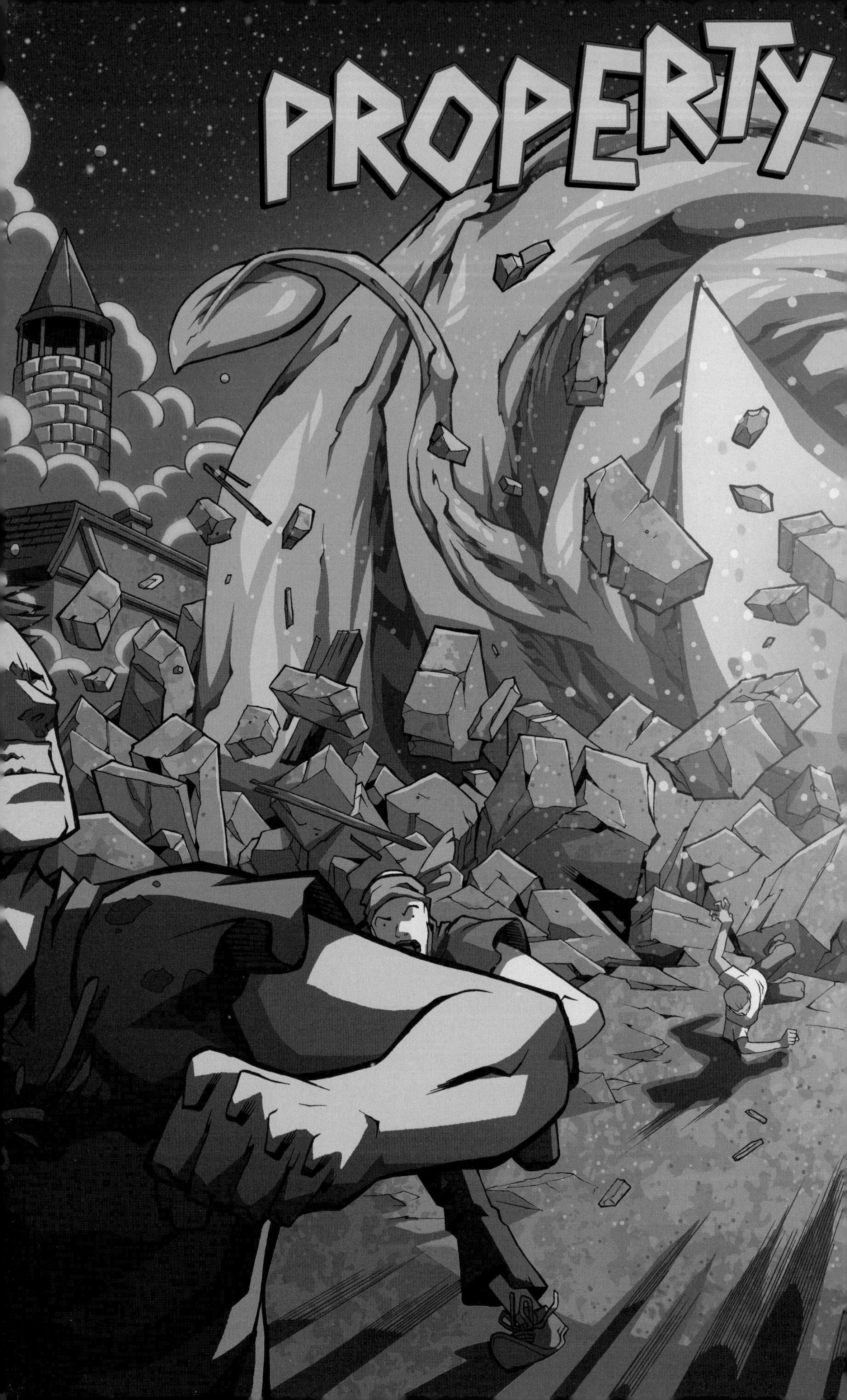
PROPERTY

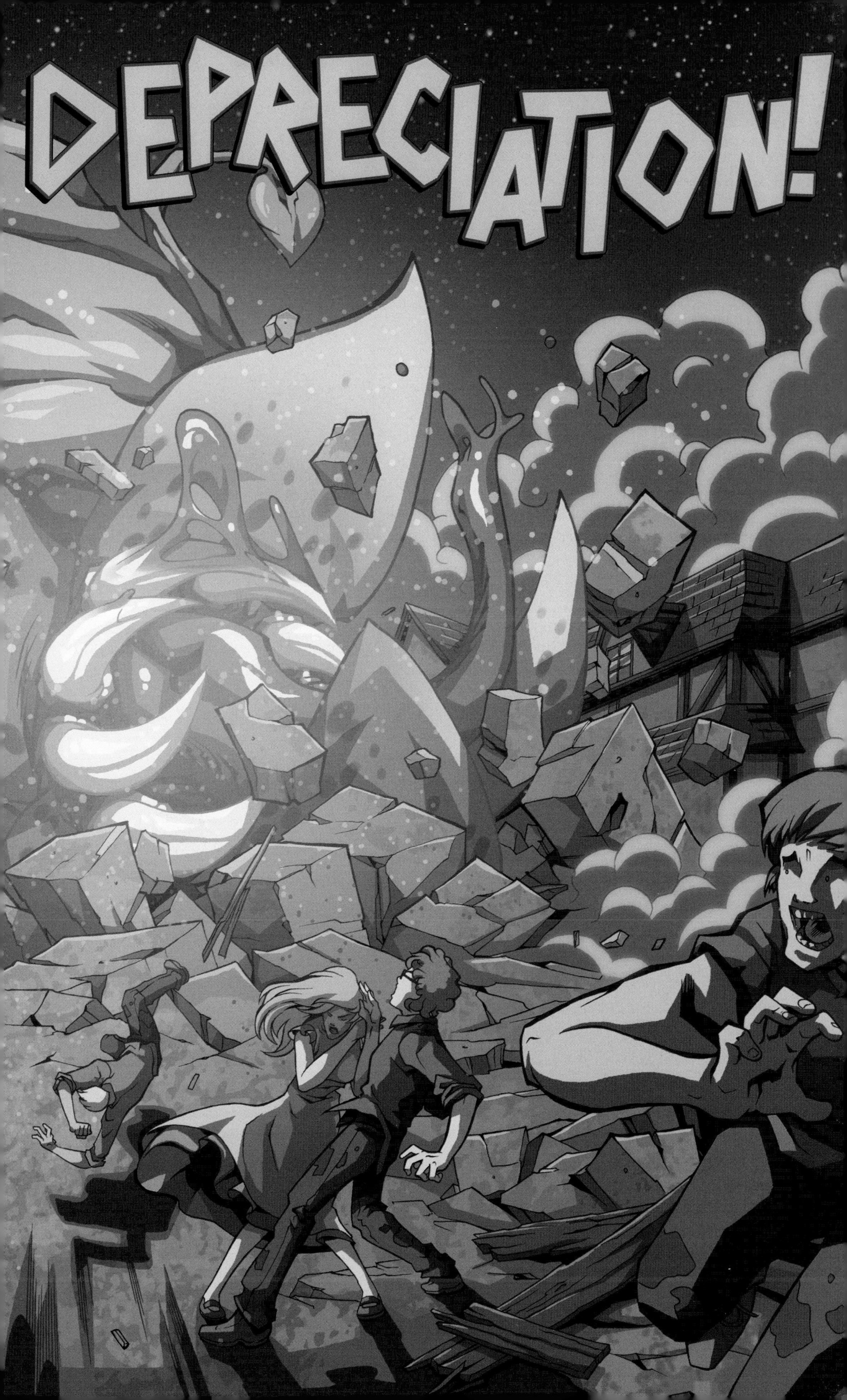
DEPRECIATION!

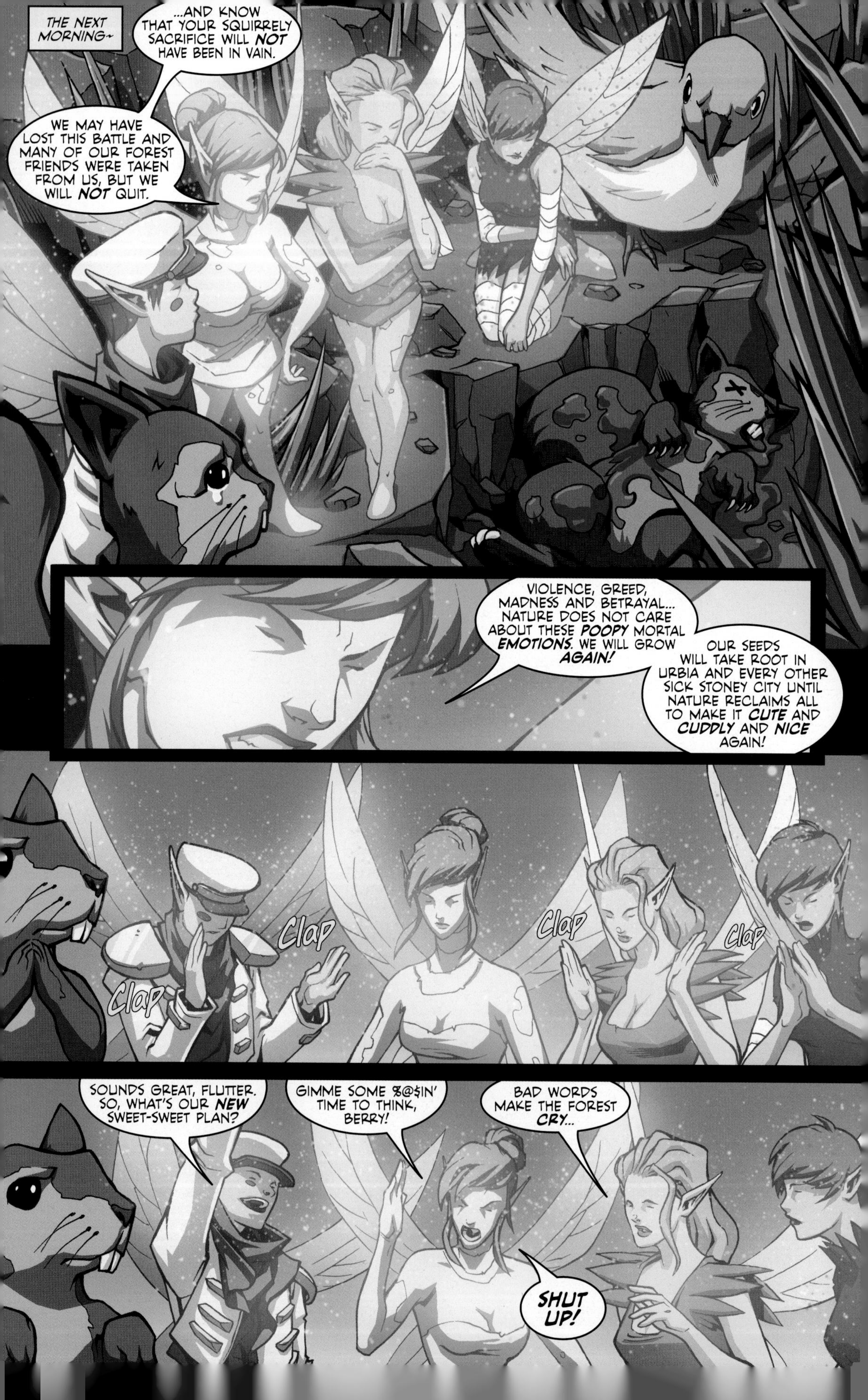
THE NEXT MORNING~
...AND KNOW THAT YOUR SQUIRRELY SACRIFICE WILL NOT HAVE BEEN IN VAIN.
WE MAY HAVE LOST THIS BATTLE AND MANY OF OUR FOREST FRIENDS WERE TAKEN FROM US, BUT WE WILL NOT QUIT.
VIOLENCE, GREED, MADNESS AND BETRAYAL... NATURE DOES NOT CARE ABOUT THESE POOPY MORTAL EMOTIONS. WE WILL GROW AGAIN!
OUR SEEDS WILL TAKE ROOT IN URBIA AND EVERY OTHER SICK STONEY CITY UNTIL NATURE RECLAIMS ALL TO MAKE IT CUTE AND CUDDLY AND NICE AGAIN!
Clap
Clap
Clap
Clap
SOUNDS GREAT, FLUTTER. SO, WHAT'S OUR NEW SWEET-SWEET PLAN?
GIMME SOME %@$IN' TIME TO THINK, BERRY!
BAD WORDS MAKE THE FOREST CRY...
SHUT UP!

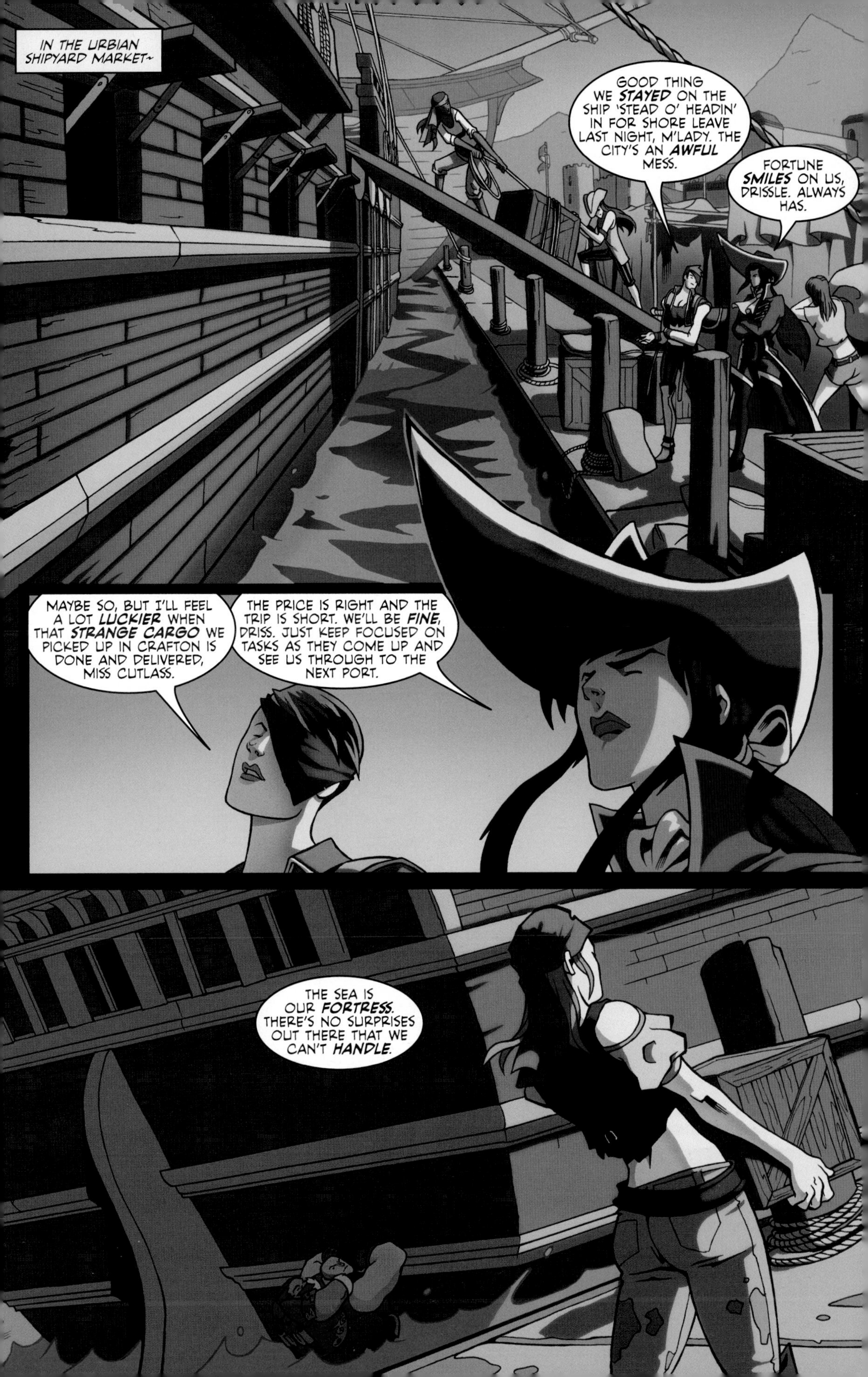
IN THE URBIAN SHIPYARD MARKET~
GOOD THING WE STAYED ON THE SHIP 'STEAD O' HEADIN' IN FOR SHORE LEAVE LAST NIGHT, M'LADY. THE CITY'S AN AWFUL MESS.
FORTUNE SMILES ON US, DRISSLE. ALWAYS HAS.
MAYBE SO, BUT I'LL FEEL A LOT LUCKIER WHEN THAT STRANGE CARGO WE PICKED UP IN CRAFTON IS DONE AND DELIVERED, MISS CUTLASS.
THE PRICE IS RIGHT AND THE TRIP IS SHORT. WE'LL BE FINE, DRISS. JUST KEEP FOCUSED ON TASKS AS THEY COME UP AND SEE US THROUGH TO THE NEXT PORT.
THE SEA IS OUR FORTRESS. THERE'S NO SURPRISES OUT THERE THAT WE CAN'T HANDLE.

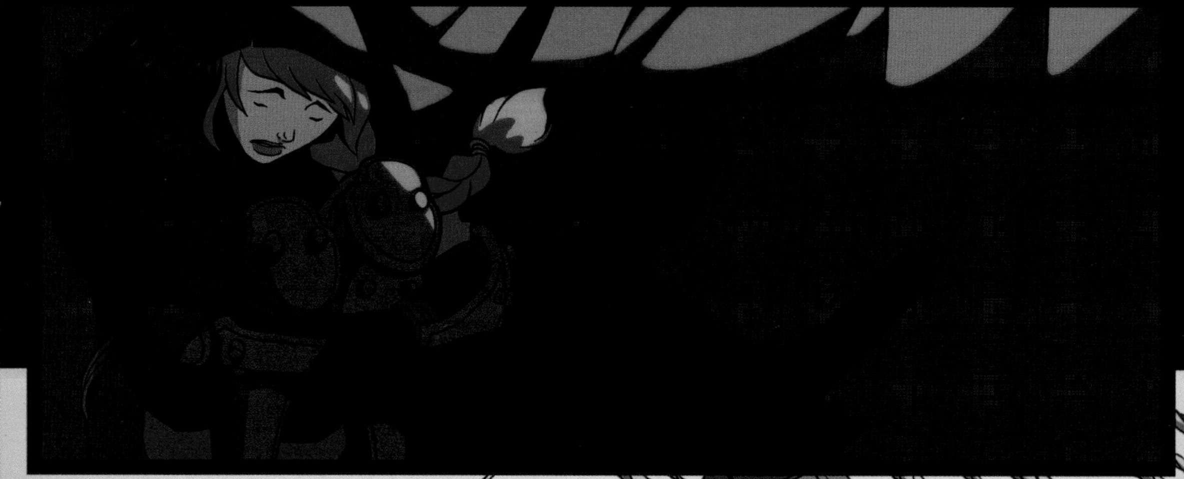

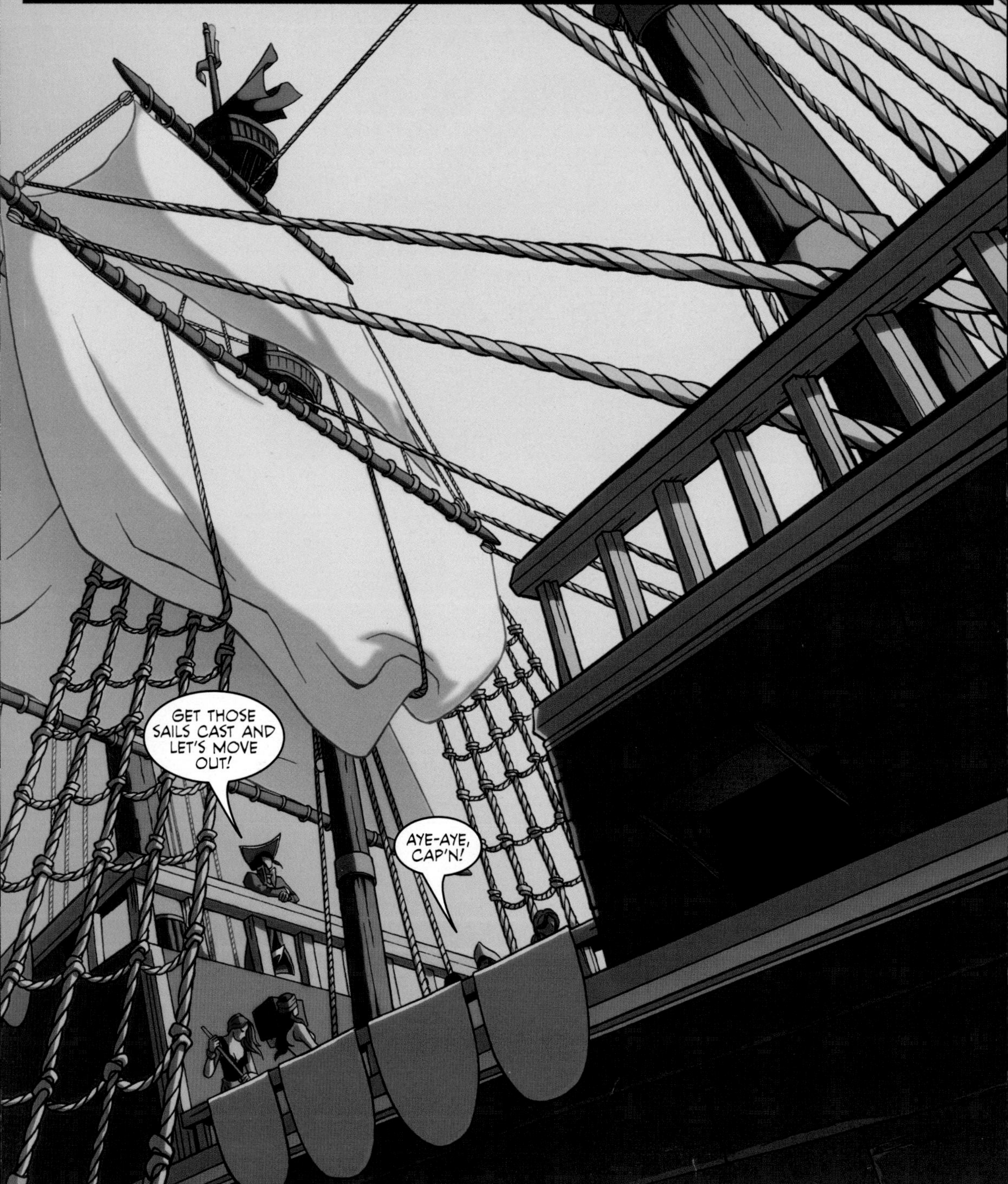
GET THOSE SAILS CAST AND LET'S MOVE OUT!
AYE-AYE, CAP'N!

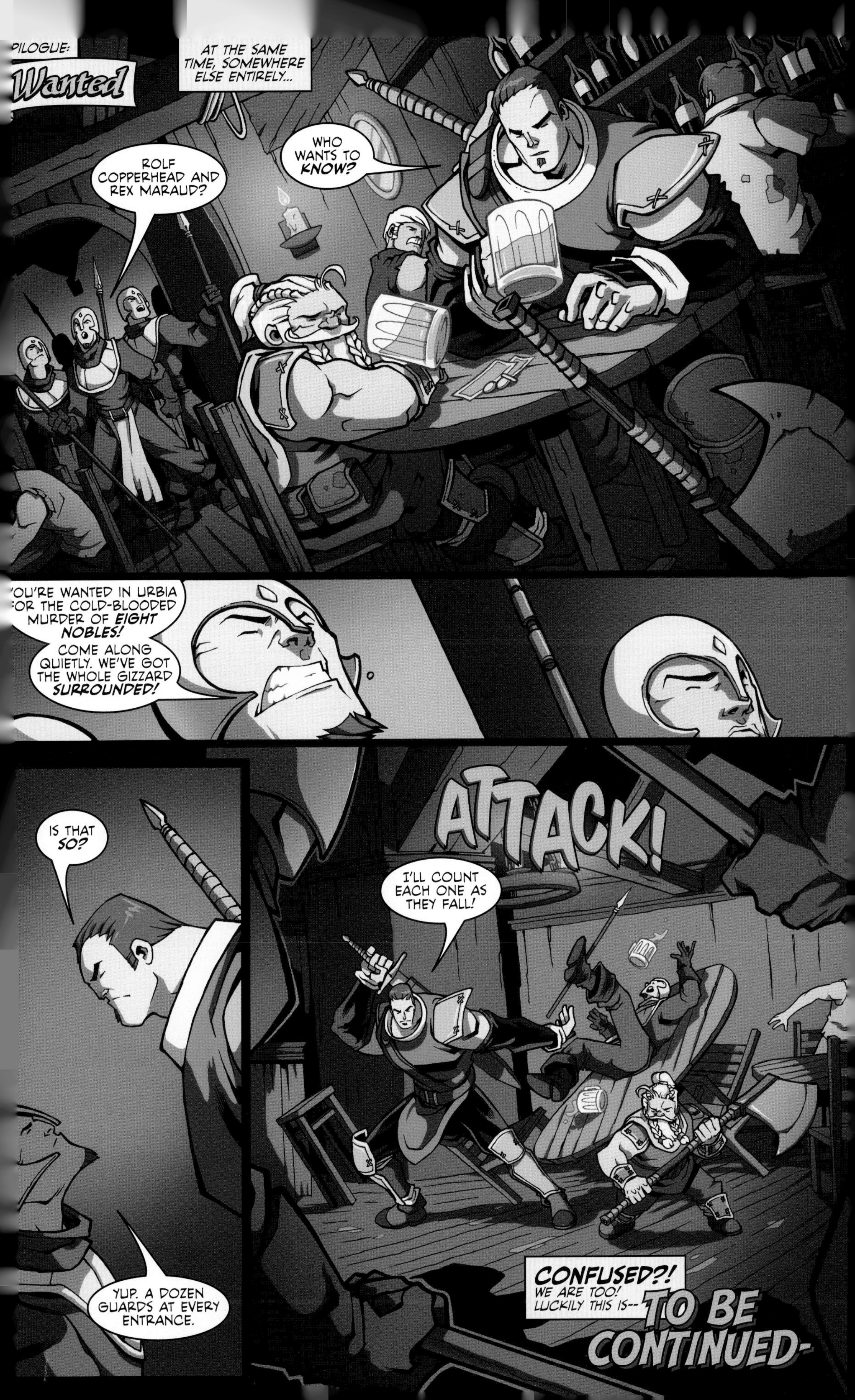
PILOGUE:
Wanted
AT THE SAME TIME, SOMEWHERE ELSE ENTIRELY...
ROLF COPPERHEAD AND REX MARAUD?
WHO WANTS TO KNOW?
YOU'RE WANTED IN URBIA FOR THE COLD-BLOODED MURDER OF EIGHT NOBLES!
COME ALONG QUIETLY. WE'VE GOT THE WHOLE GIZZARD SURROUNDED!
IS THAT SO?
YUP. A DOZEN GUARDS AT EVERY ENTRANCE.
ATTACK!
I'LL COUNT EACH ONE AS THEY FALL!
CONFUSED?! WE ARE TOO! LUCKILY THIS IS--
TO BE CONTINUED-

SKULL KICKERS
FOUR TAVERN TALES

After the original five issues of Skullkickers (happily collected in '1000 Opas and a Dead Body') were released, the creative team started pounding away on this second story arc. I was obsessed with keeping our fantasy hi-jinks on the shelves of comic shops everywhere even while we worked ahead, so I invited some of my favourite artists and writers to contribute short stories to a special issue. It became a fun interlude and gave readers a bunch of silly new adventures with our monster mashing morons.

Blood Curse of the Amazombies is written by Chris Sims, internet humorist and all around hilarious writer, reviewer and troublemaker. I have a distinctive feeling that Chris is going to take over comics as we know it at some future point and now I'll always be able to say that I gave his first big 'pro' break. The artwork is provided by Joe Vriens, monster artist extraordinaire. We've been friends for years and I knew his aesthetic would sync up well with the SK boys.

The Sklaag is written by Brian Clevinger, whose incredible humour and wit is on display in every brilliant issue of Atomic Robo. Every time I read a new Robo issue I'm jealously amazed at how effortlessly Brian seems to weave action, adventure, humour and emotion into his stories. The art is done by a guy named "Jim Zub". He's some kind of wannabe artist and, what the heck, I figured I'd give the kid a shot. I'm charitable like that.

Temple of Blech is written by Ray Fawkes. Ray's best known for his dark and emotional stories like Mnemovore and One Soul, but I've been friends with him for years and know that he has a dark and nasty funny streak a mile wide. I figured he'd make his short story hilariously violent and I wasn't disappointed. Scott Hepburn and Ian Herring lend their talents to the artwork and it's a perfect match. I've watched Scott's skills steadily grow over the years and am always impressed with his confident storytelling and character expressions.

The Cleavin' Part is written by Adam Warren, the amazing writer/artist of Empowered as well as the man behind the glorious Dirty Pair comics of my youth. Having him contribute a story, especially one so awesome, is a complete thrill. The artwork is provided by the infinitely versatile Jeffrey 'Chamba' Cruz. No matter what he does, the sense of energy and animated quality he brings to the page is top notch.

Enjoy!

ZUB

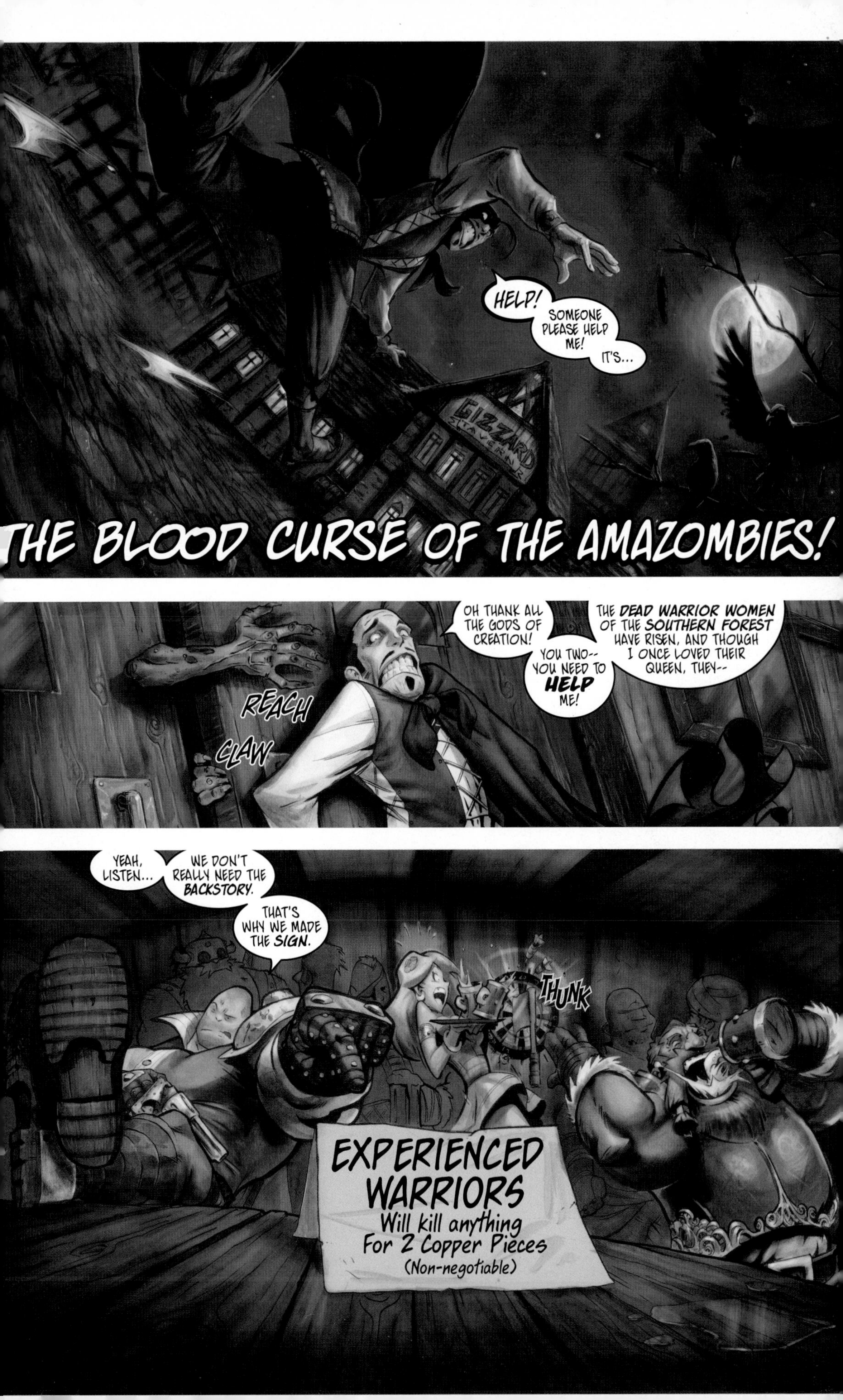
HELP!
SOMEONE PLEASE HELP ME!
IT'S...
GIZZARD'S TAVERN
THE BLOOD CURSE OF THE AMAZOMBIES!
OH THANK ALL THE GODS OF CREATION!
YOU TWO-- YOU NEED TO HELP ME!
THE DEAD WARRIOR WOMEN OF THE SOUTHERN FOREST HAVE RISEN, AND THOUGH I ONCE LOVED THEIR QUEEN, THEY--
REACH
CLAW
YEAH, LISTEN...
WE DON'T REALLY NEED THE BACKSTORY.
THAT'S WHY WE MADE THE SIGN.
THUNK
EXPERIENCED WARRIORS
Will kill anything
For 2 Copper Pieces
(Non-negotiable)

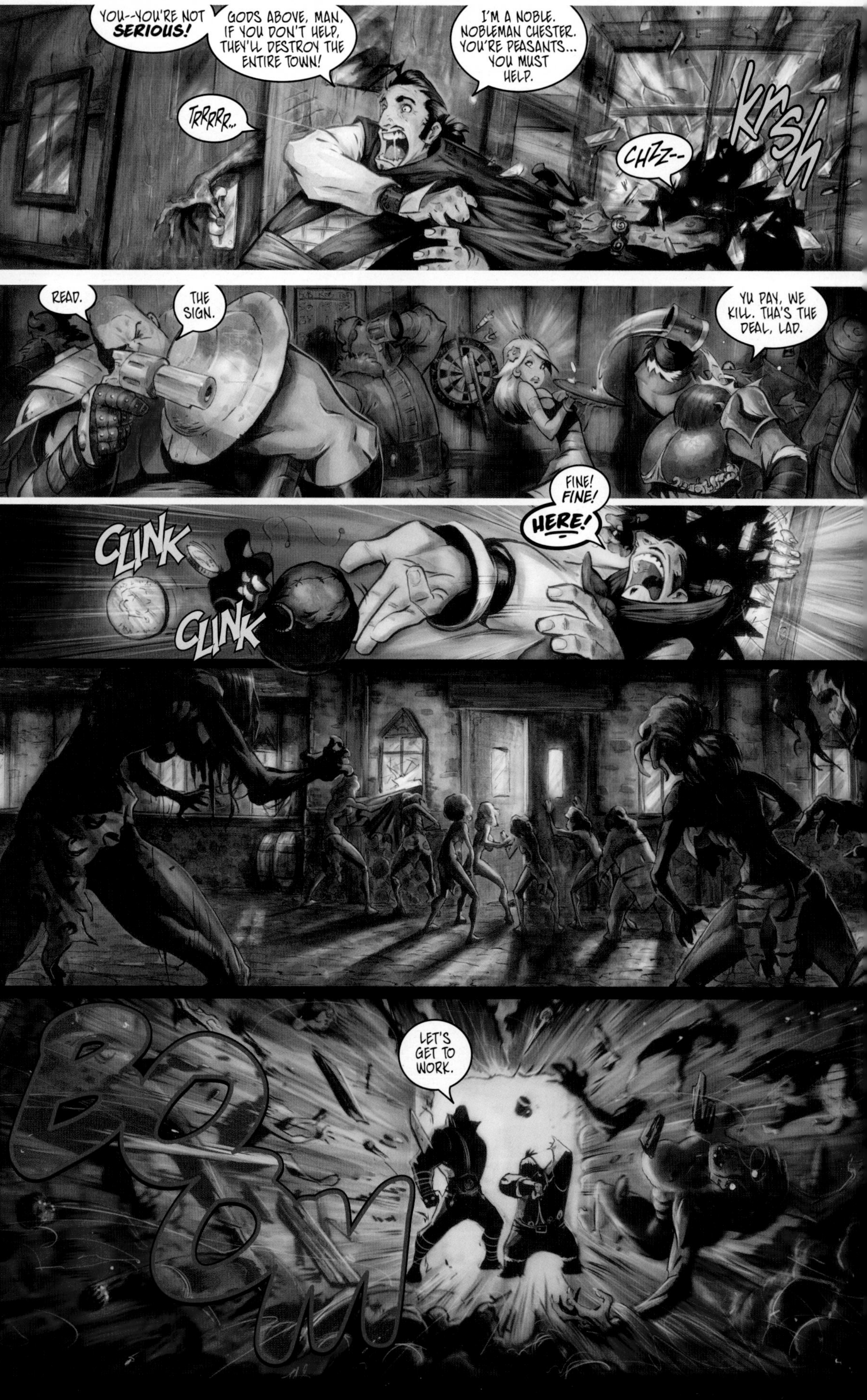

YOU--YOU'RE NOT **SERIOUS!**
GODS ABOVE, MAN, IF YOU DON'T HELP, THEY'LL DESTROY THE ENTIRE TOWN!
I'M A NOBLE. NOBLEMAN CHESTER. YOU'RE PEASANTS... YOU MUST HELP.
TRRRRR...
KRSH
CHZZ--
READ.
THE SIGN.
YU PAY, WE KILL. THA'S THE DEAL, LAD.
FINE! FINE! **HERE!**
CLINK
CLINK
LET'S GET TO WORK.

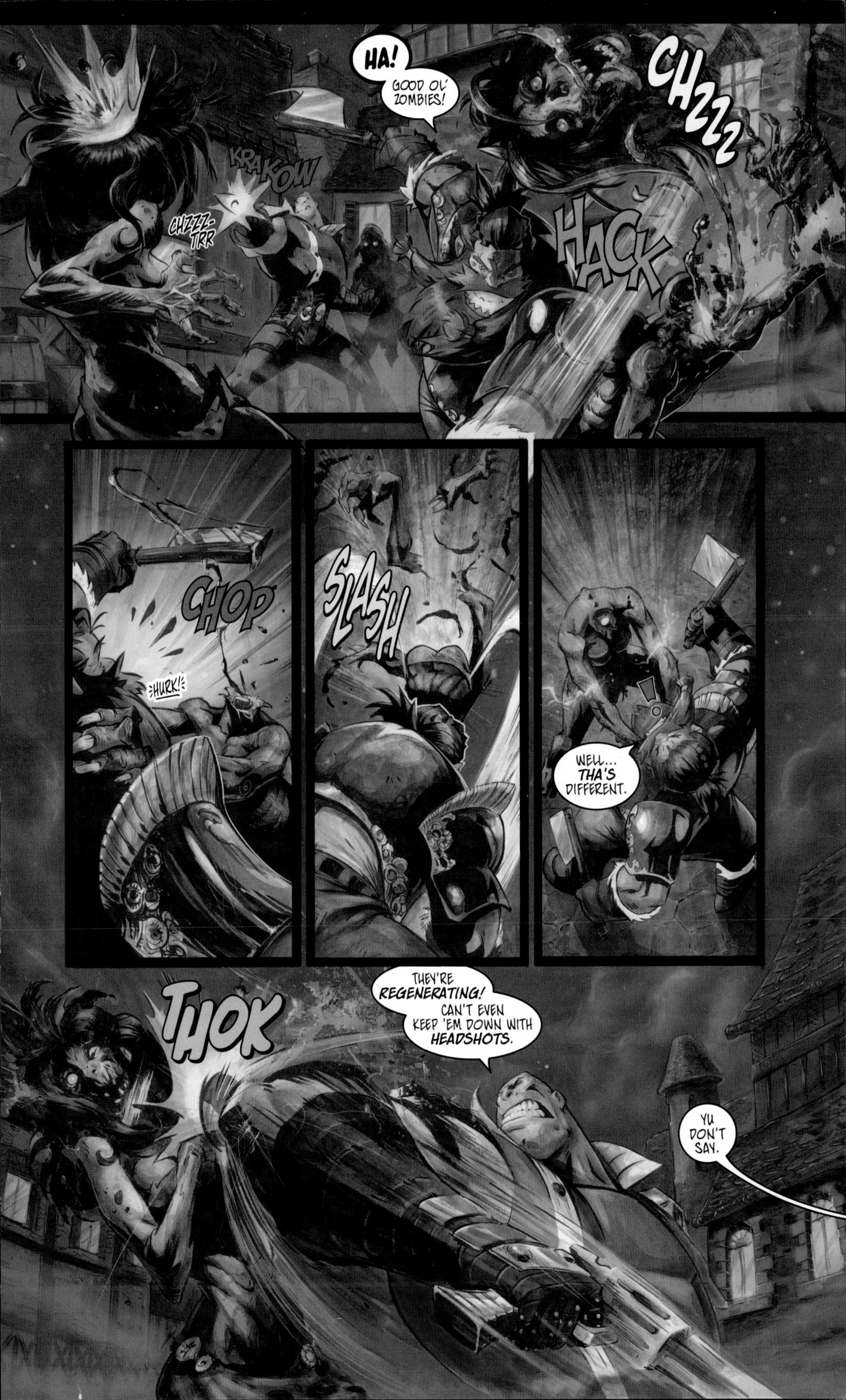
HA!
GOOD OL' ZOMBIES!
CHZZZ
KRAKOW
CHZZZ-TRR
HACK
CHOP
HURK!
SLASH
!
WELL... THA'S DIFFERENT.
THOK
THEY'RE REGENERATING! CAN'T EVEN KEEP 'EM DOWN WITH HEADSHOTS.
YU DON'T SAY.

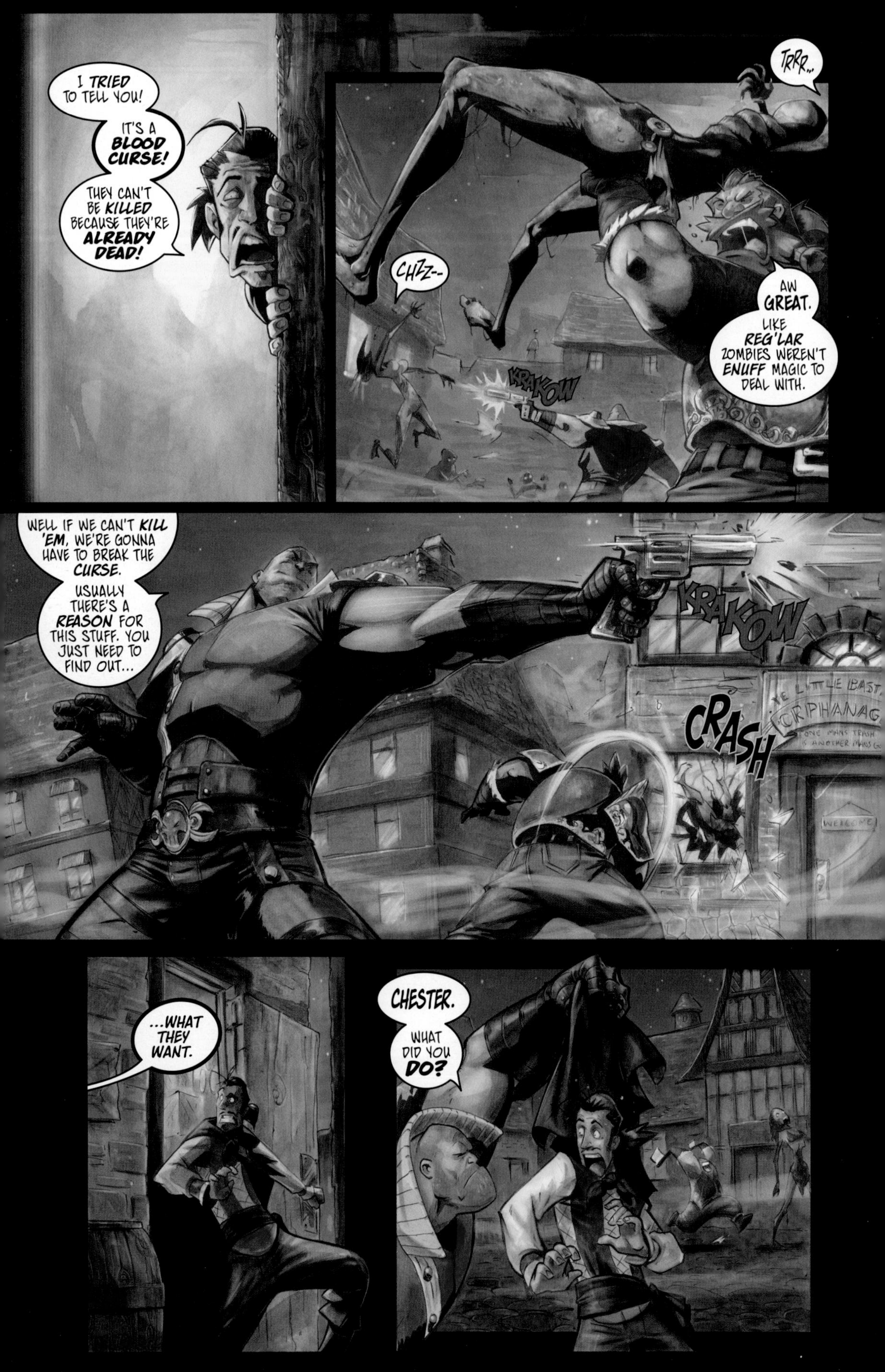
I TRIED TO TELL YOU!
IT'S A BLOOD CURSE!
THEY CAN'T BE KILLED BECAUSE THEY'RE ALREADY DEAD!
TRRR...
CHZZ--
AW GREAT.
LIKE REG'LAR ZOMBIES WEREN'T ENUFF MAGIC TO DEAL WITH.
KRAKOW
WELL IF WE CAN'T KILL 'EM, WE'RE GONNA HAVE TO BREAK THE CURSE.
USUALLY THERE'S A REASON FOR THIS STUFF. YOU JUST NEED TO FIND OUT...
KRAKOW
CRASH
...WHAT THEY WANT.
CHESTER.
WHAT DID YOU DO?

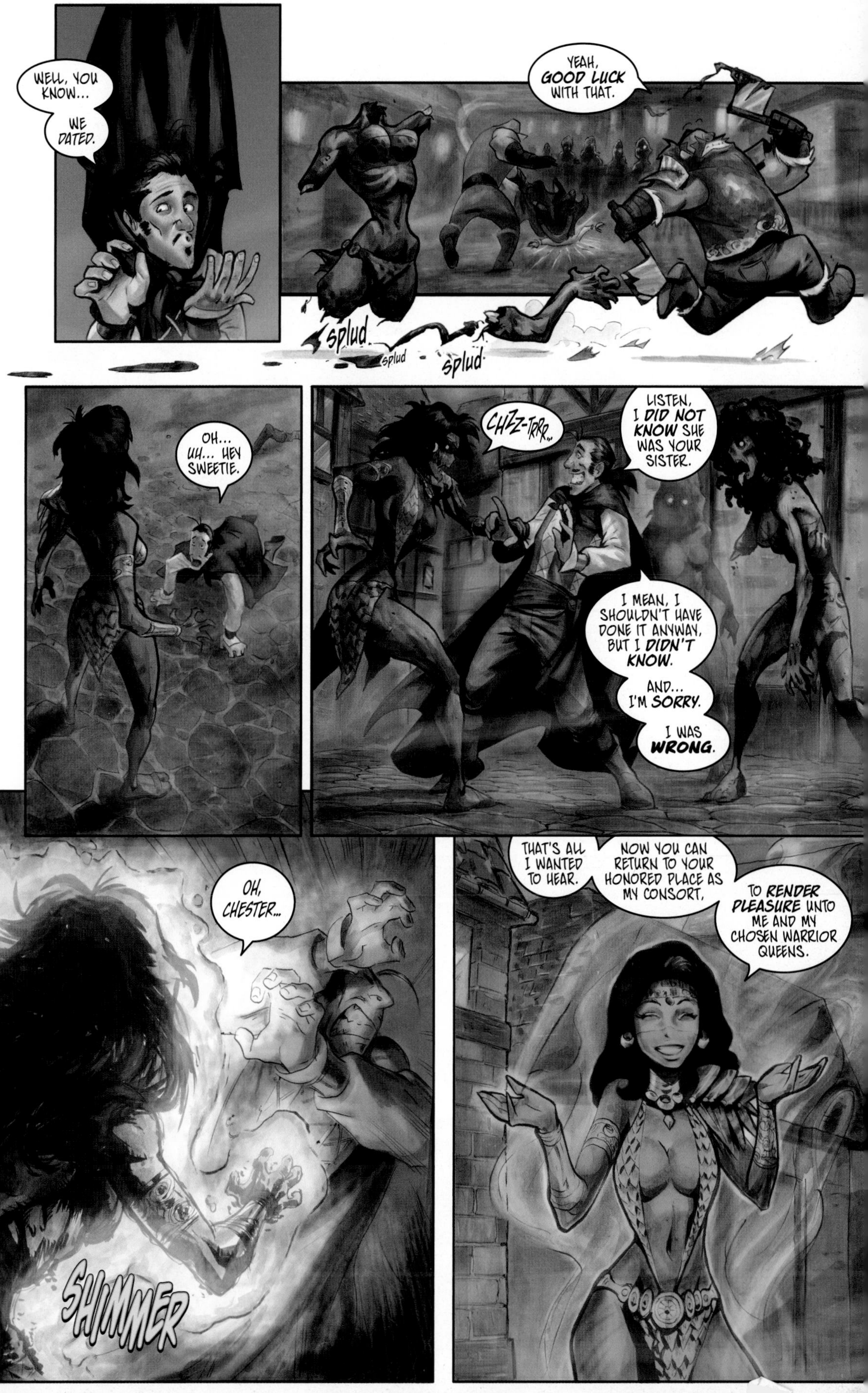
WELL, YOU KNOW...
WE DATED.
YEAH, GOOD LUCK WITH THAT.
splud
splud
splud
OH... UH... HEY SWEETIE.
CHZZ-TRRR...
LISTEN, I DID NOT KNOW SHE WAS YOUR SISTER.
I MEAN, I SHOULDN'T HAVE DONE IT ANYWAY, BUT I DIDN'T KNOW.
AND... I'M SORRY.
I WAS WRONG.
OH, CHESTER...
SHIMMER
THAT'S ALL I WANTED TO HEAR.
NOW YOU CAN RETURN TO YOUR HONORED PLACE AS MY CONSORT,
TO RENDER PLEASURE UNTO ME AND MY CHOSEN WARRIOR QUEENS.

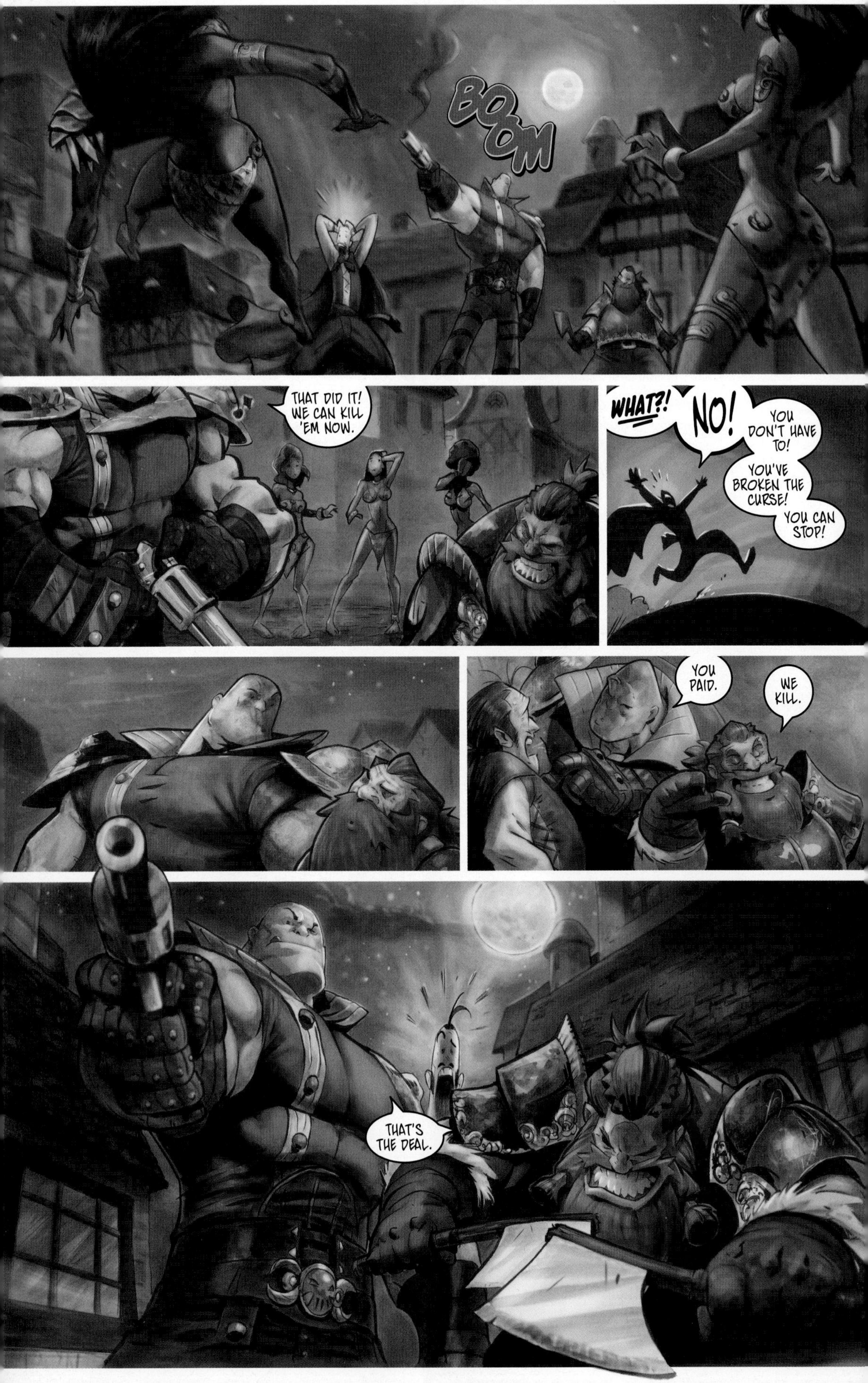
BOOM
THAT DID IT! WE CAN KILL 'EM NOW.
WHAT?!
NO!
YOU DON'T HAVE TO!
YOU'VE BROKEN THE CURSE!
YOU CAN STOP!
YOU PAID.
WE KILL.
THAT'S THE DEAL.

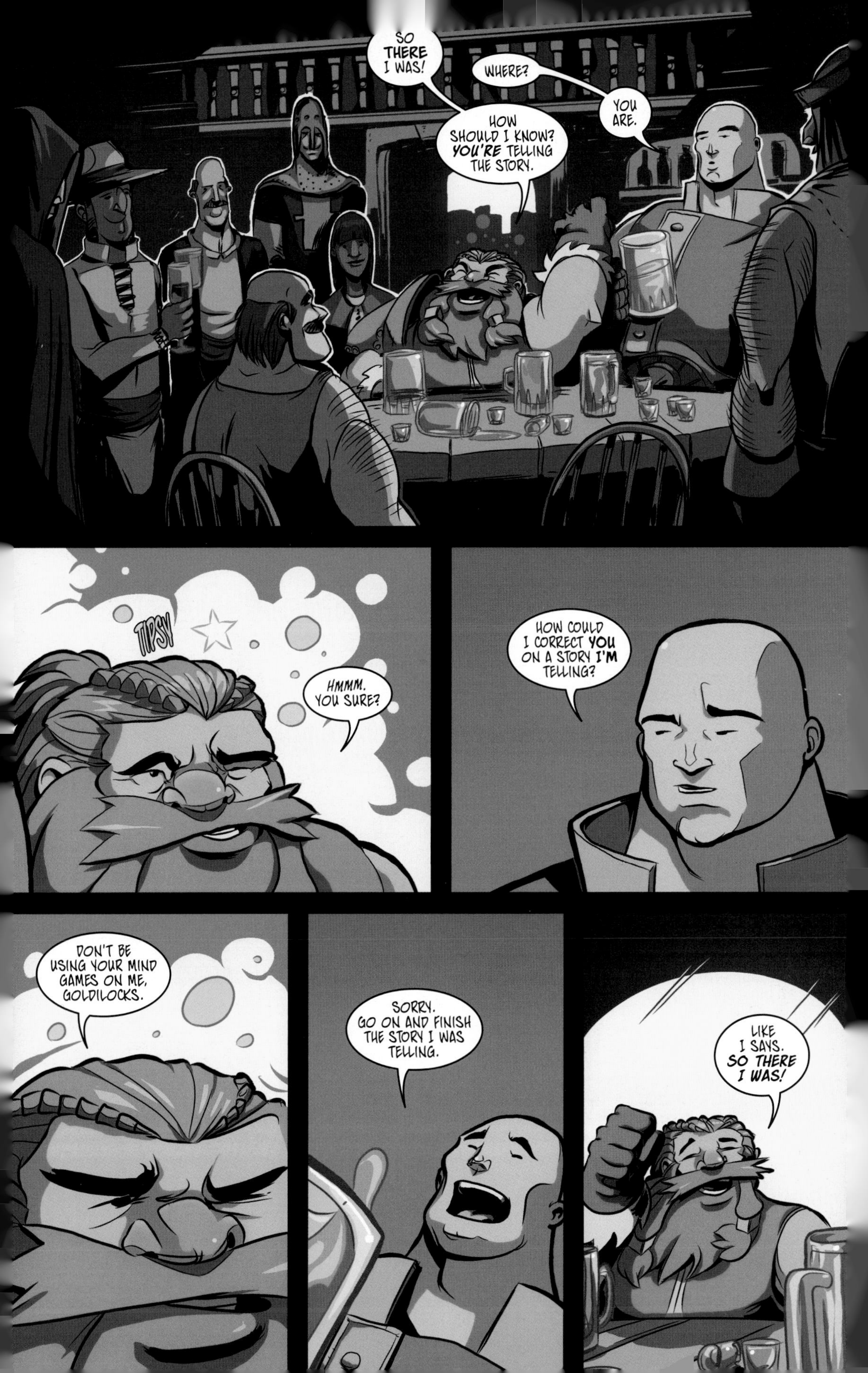
SO THERE I WAS!
WHERE?
HOW SHOULD I KNOW? YOU'RE TELLING THE STORY.
YOU ARE.
TIPSY
HMMM. YOU SURE?
HOW COULD I CORRECT YOU ON A STORY I'M TELLING?
DON'T BE USING YOUR MIND GAMES ON ME, GOLDILOCKS.
SORRY. GO ON AND FINISH THE STORY I WAS TELLING.
LIKE I SAYS. SO THERE I WAS!

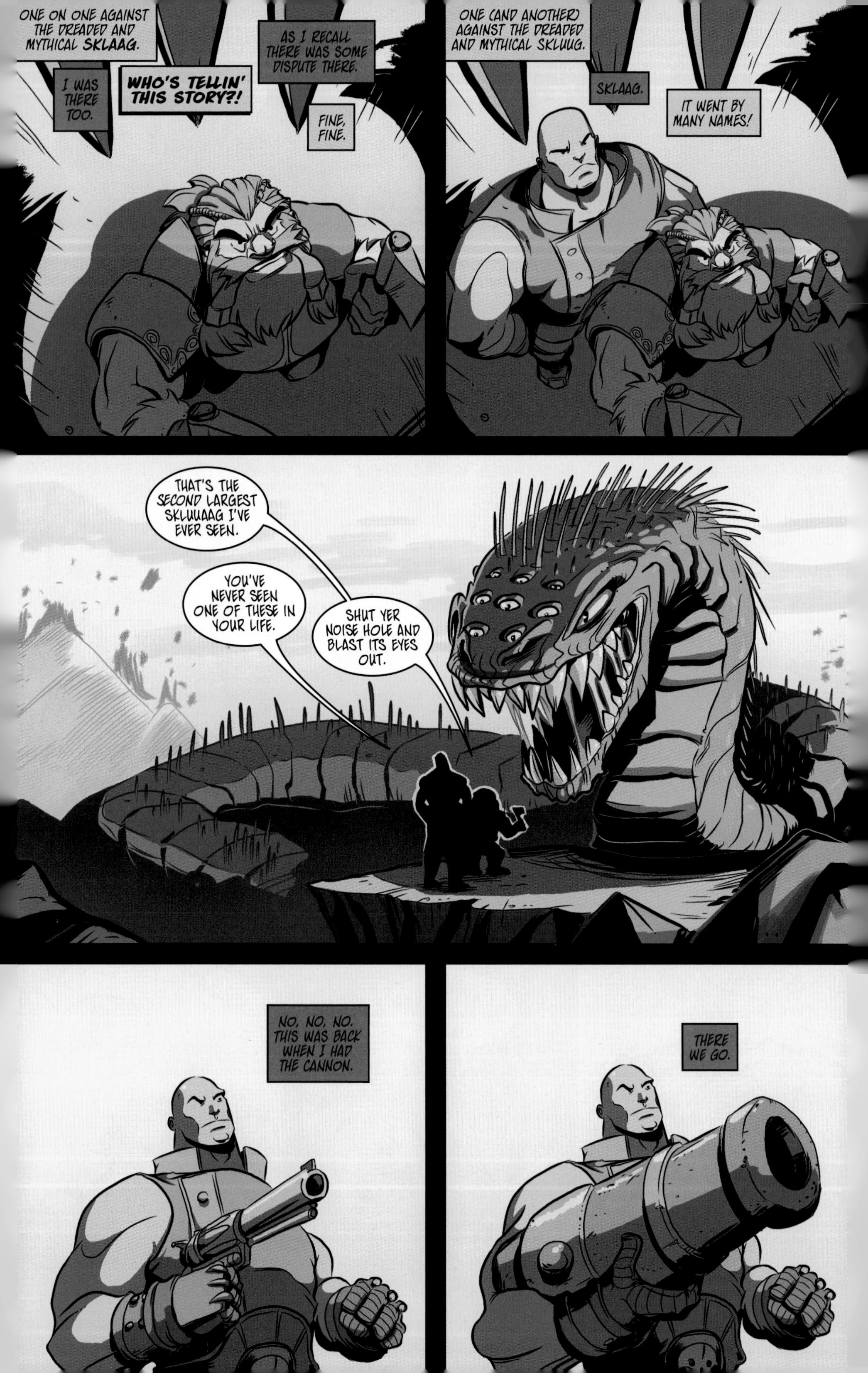
ONE ON ONE AGAINST THE DREADED AND MYTHICAL SKLAAG.
I WAS THERE TOO.
WHO'S TELLIN' THIS STORY?!
AS I RECALL THERE WAS SOME DISPUTE THERE.
FINE, FINE.
ONE (AND ANOTHER) AGAINST THE DREADED AND MYTHICAL SKLUUG.
SKLAAG.
IT WENT BY MANY NAMES!
THAT'S THE SECOND LARGEST SKLUUAAG I'VE EVER SEEN.
YOU'VE NEVER SEEN ONE OF THESE IN YOUR LIFE.
SHUT YER NOISE HOLE AND BLAST ITS EYES OUT.
NO, NO, NO. THIS WAS BACK WHEN I HAD THE CANNON.
THERE WE GO.

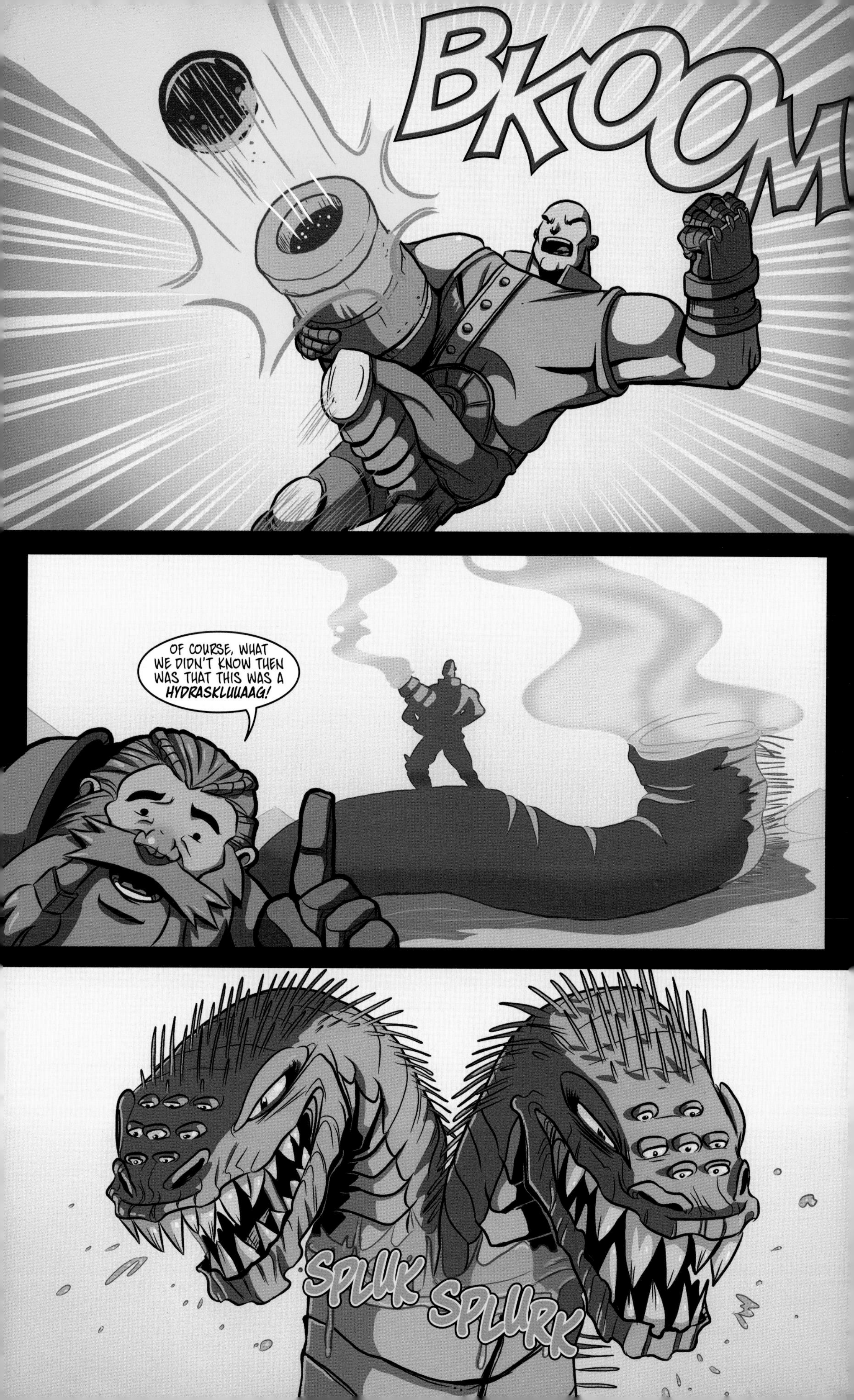
BKOOM
OF COURSE, WHAT WE DIDN'T KNOW THEN WAS THAT THIS WAS A HYDRASKLUUAAG!
SPLUK SPLURK

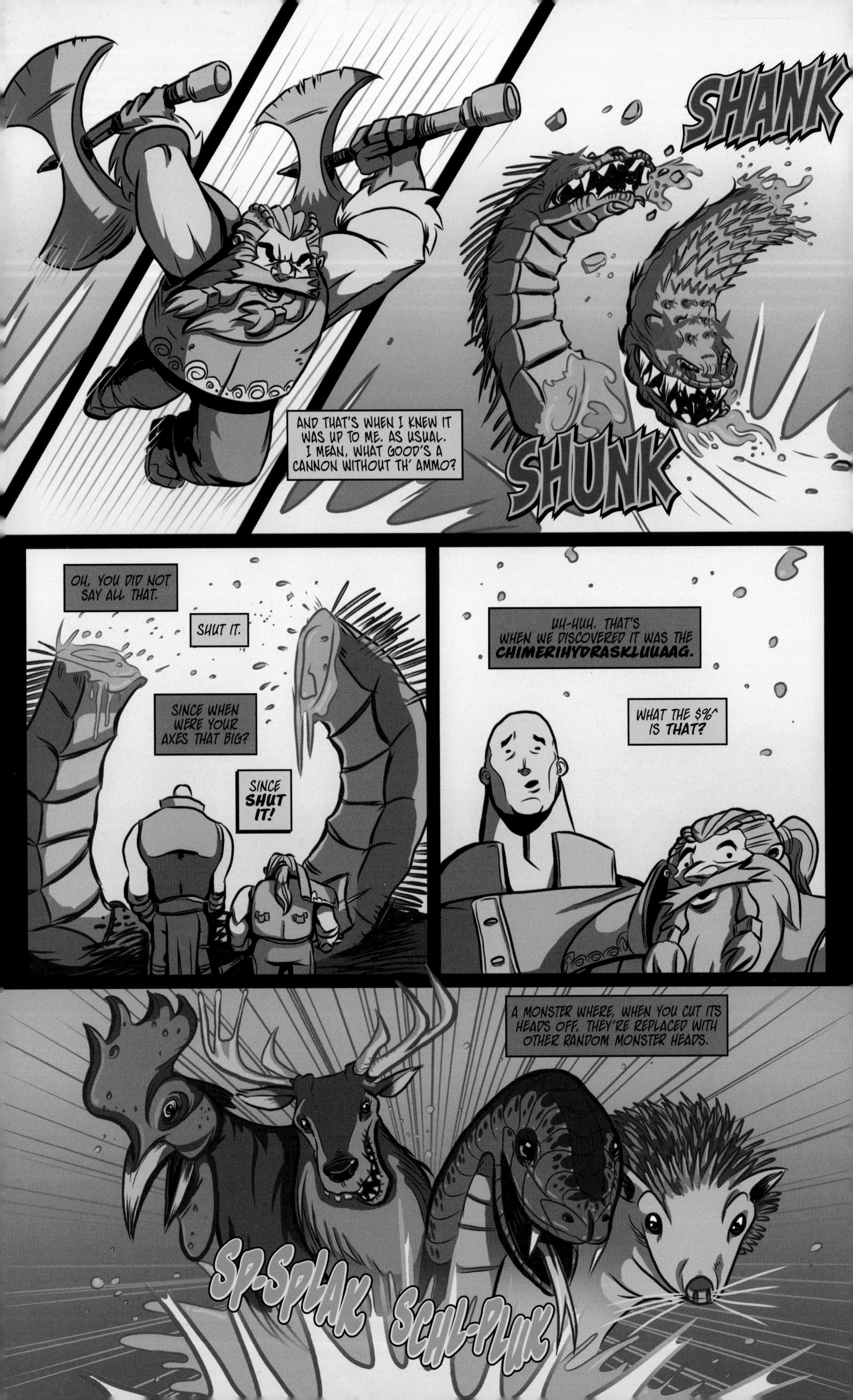

AND THAT'S WHEN I KNEW IT WAS UP TO ME. AS USUAL. I MEAN, WHAT GOOD'S A CANNON WITHOUT TH' AMMO?
SHANK
SHUNK
OH, YOU DID NOT SAY ALL THAT.
SHUT IT.
SINCE WHEN WERE YOUR AXES THAT BIG?
SINCE SHUT IT!
UH-HUH. THAT'S WHEN WE DISCOVERED IT WAS THE CHIMERIHYDRASKLUUAAG.
WHAT THE $%^ IS THAT?
A MONSTER WHERE, WHEN YOU CUT ITS HEADS OFF, THEY'RE REPLACED WITH OTHER RANDOM MONSTER HEADS.
SP-SPLAK
SCHL-PLUK

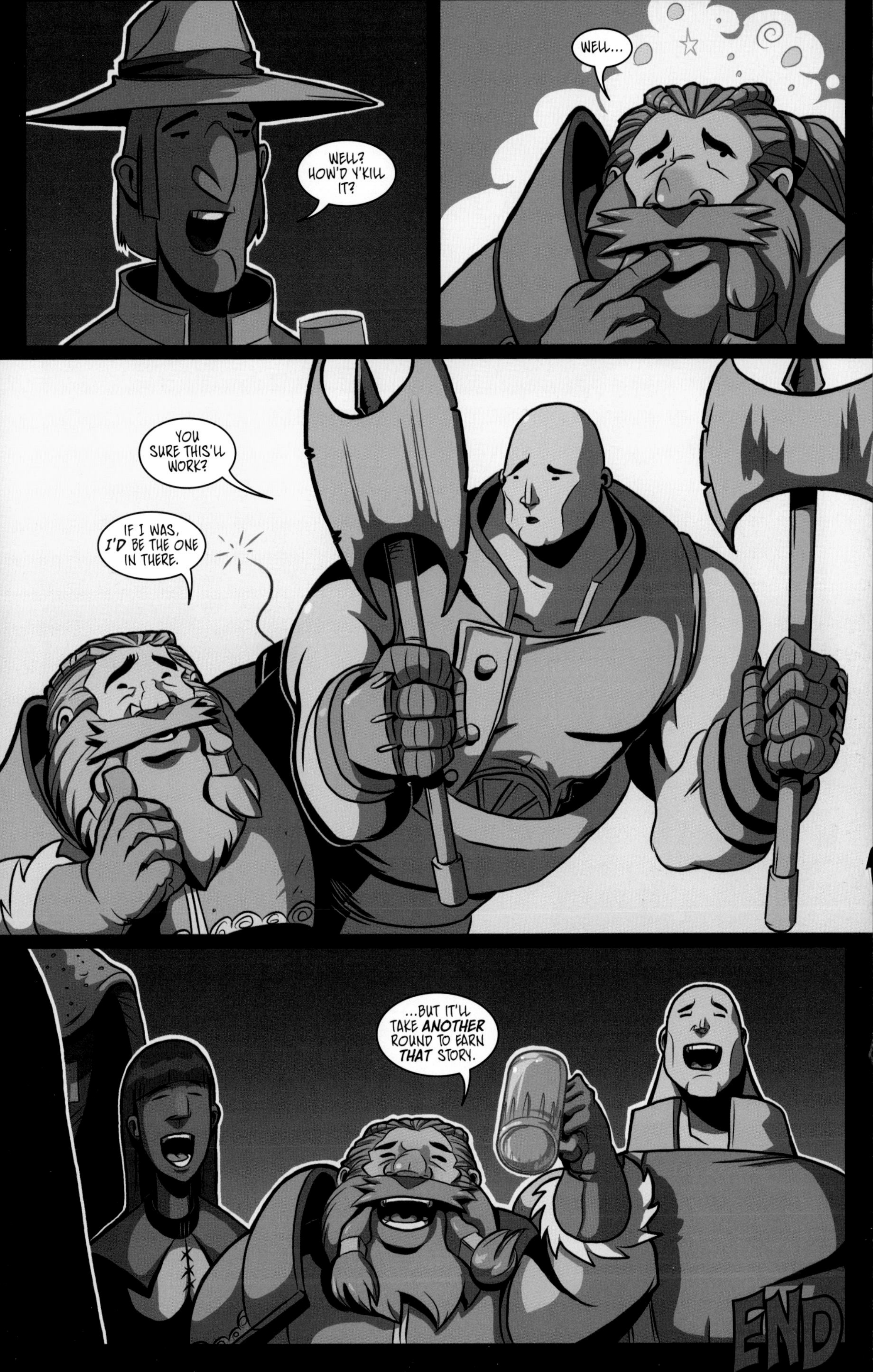
WELL? HOW'D Y'KILL IT?
WELL...
YOU SURE THIS'LL WORK?
IF I WAS, I'D BE THE ONE IN THERE.
...BUT IT'LL TAKE ANOTHER ROUND TO EARN THAT STORY.
END

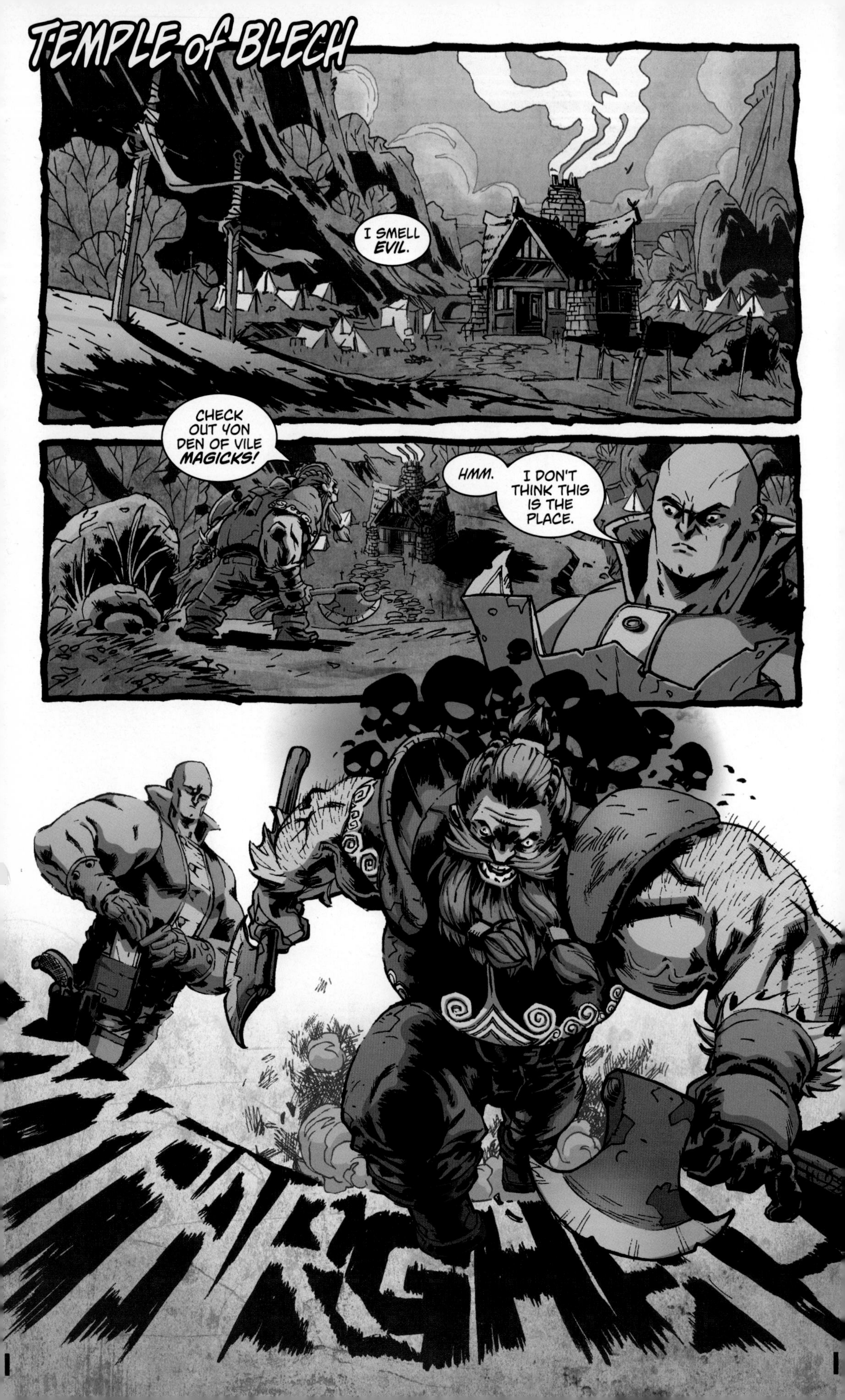
TEMPLE of BLECH
I SMELL EVIL.
CHECK OUT YON DEN OF VILE MAGICKS!
HMM.
I DON'T THINK THIS IS THE PLACE.

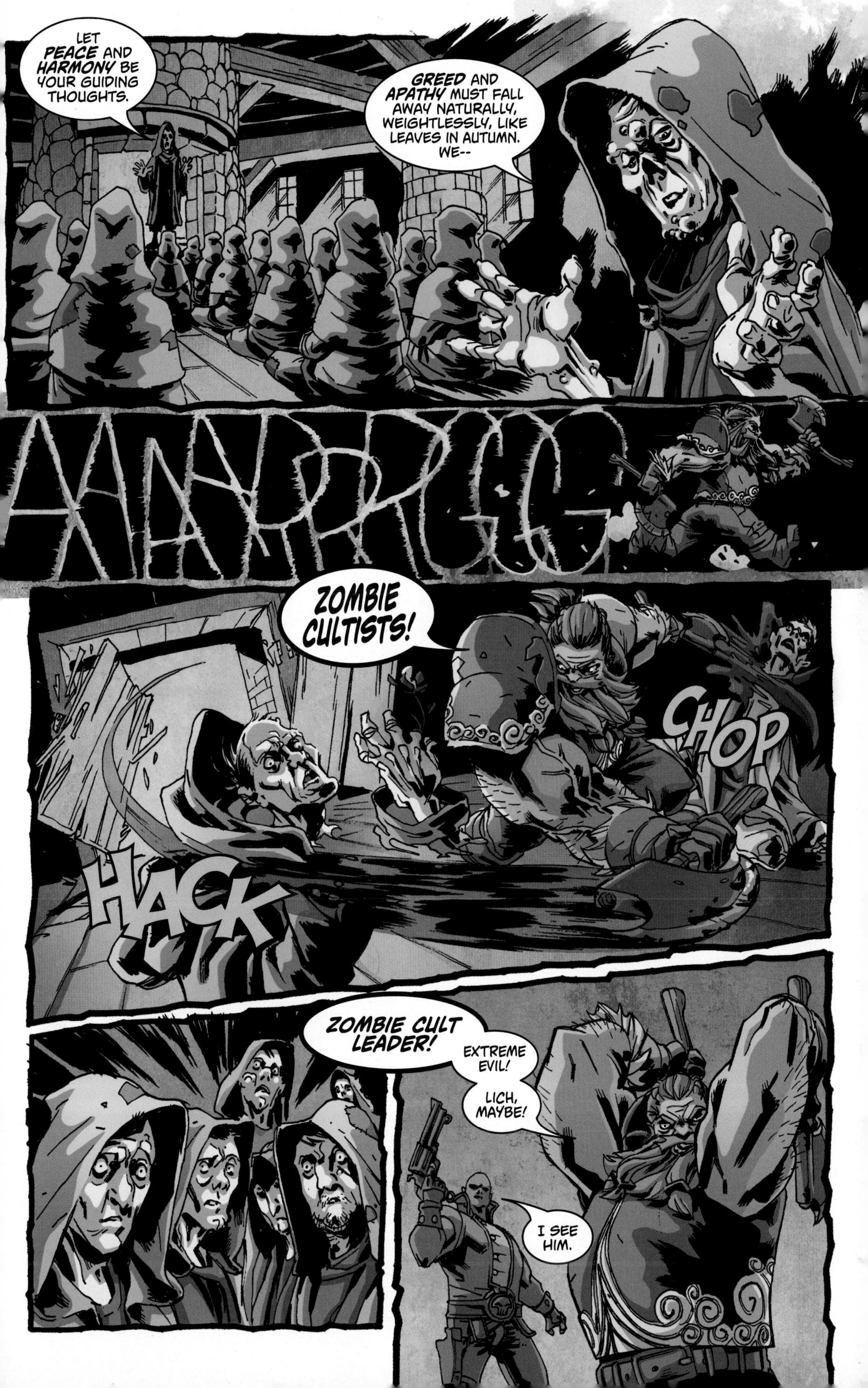

LET PEACE AND HARMONY BE YOUR GUIDING THOUGHTS.
GREED AND APATHY MUST FALL AWAY NATURALLY, WEIGHTLESSLY, LIKE LEAVES IN AUTUMN. WE--
AAAARRGGG
ZOMBIE CULTISTS!
CHOP
HACK
ZOMBIE CULT LEADER!
EXTREME EVIL!
LICH, MAYBE!
I SEE HIM.

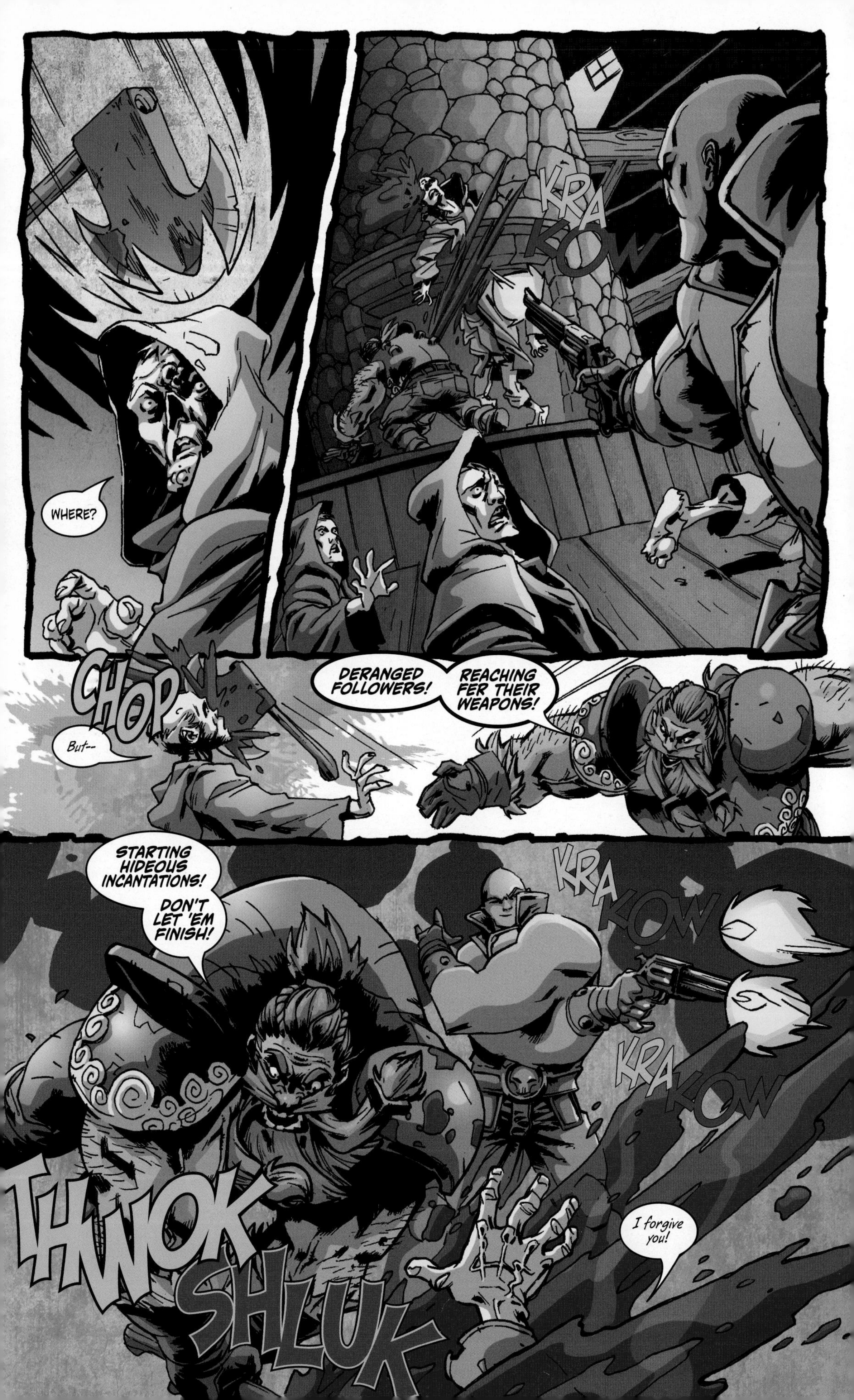
WHERE?
KRA KOW
CHOP
But--
DERANGED FOLLOWERS!
REACHING FER THEIR WEAPONS!
STARTING HIDEOUS INCANTATIONS!
DON'T LET 'EM FINISH!
KRAKOW
KRAKOW
THWOK
SHLUK
I forgive you!

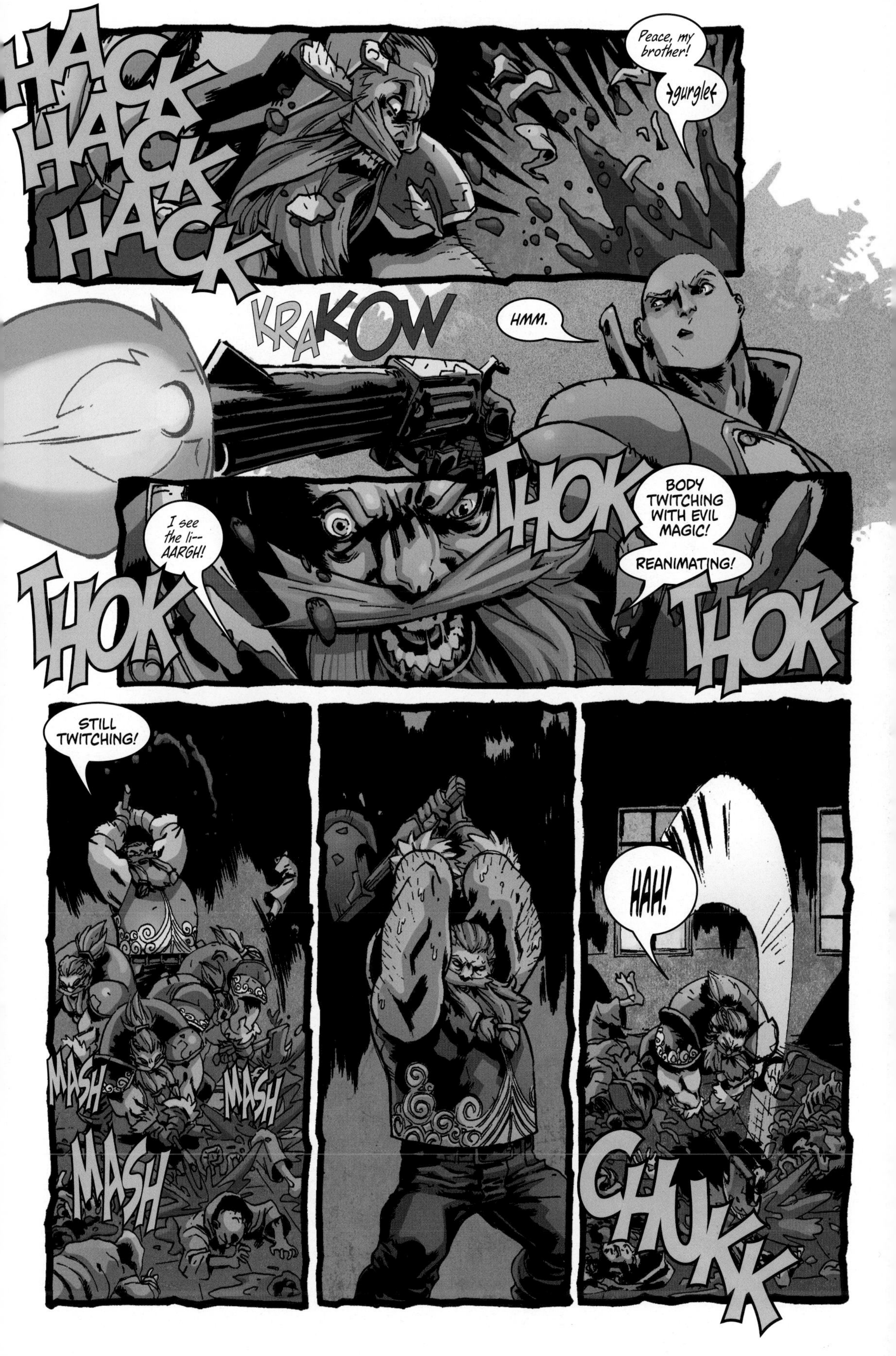
HACK
HACK
HACK
Peace, my brother!
gurgle
KRAKOW
HMM.
THOK
I see the li-- AARGH!
BODY TWITCHING WITH EVIL MAGIC!
REANIMATING!
THOK
THOK
STILL TWITCHING!
MASH
MASH
MASH
HAH!
CHUKK

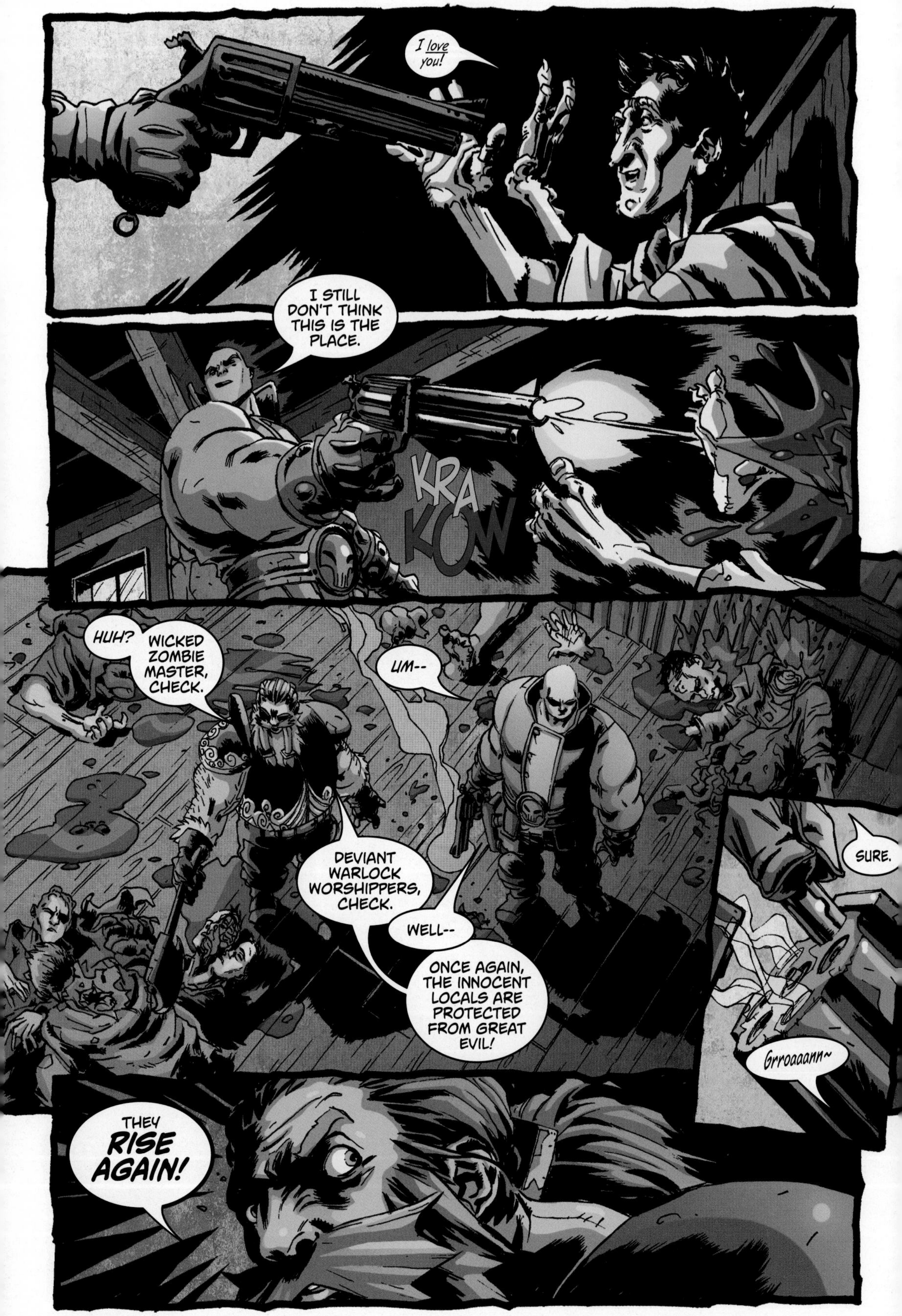
I love you!
I STILL DON'T THINK THIS IS THE PLACE.
KRA KOW
HUH?
WICKED ZOMBIE MASTER, CHECK.
UM--
DEVIANT WARLOCK WORSHIPPERS, CHECK.
WELL--
ONCE AGAIN, THE INNOCENT LOCALS ARE PROTECTED FROM GREAT EVIL!
SURE.
Grroaaann~
THEY RISE AGAIN!

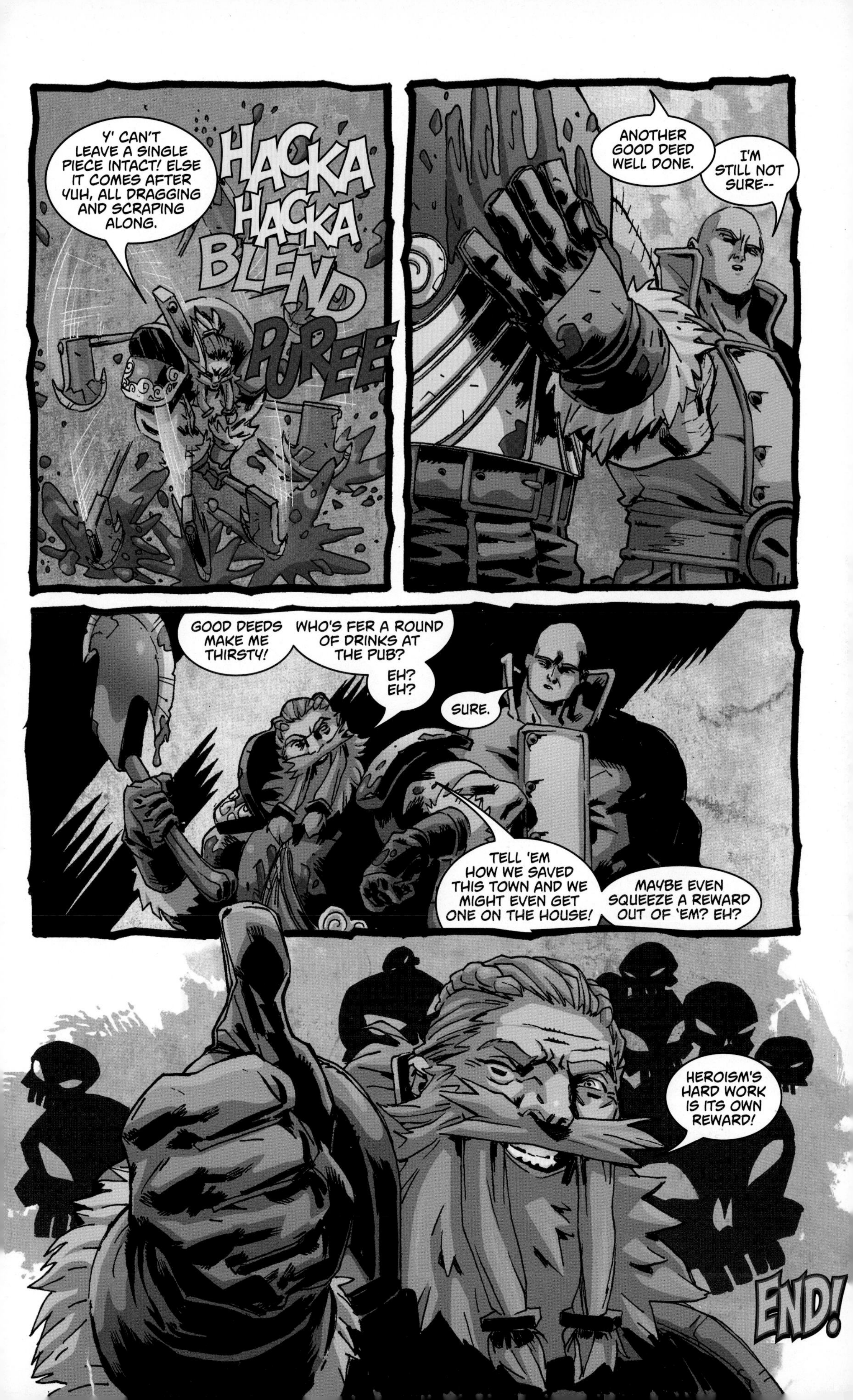
Y' CAN'T LEAVE A SINGLE PIECE INTACT! ELSE IT COMES AFTER YUH, ALL DRAGGING AND SCRAPING ALONG.
HACKA HACKA BLEND PUREE
ANOTHER GOOD DEED WELL DONE.
I'M STILL NOT SURE--
GOOD DEEDS MAKE ME THIRSTY!
WHO'S FER A ROUND OF DRINKS AT THE PUB?
EH? EH?
SURE.
TELL 'EM HOW WE SAVED THIS TOWN AND WE MIGHT EVEN GET ONE ON THE HOUSE!
MAYBE EVEN SQUEEZE A REWARD OUT OF 'EM? EH?
HEROISM'S HARD WORK IS ITS OWN REWARD!
END!

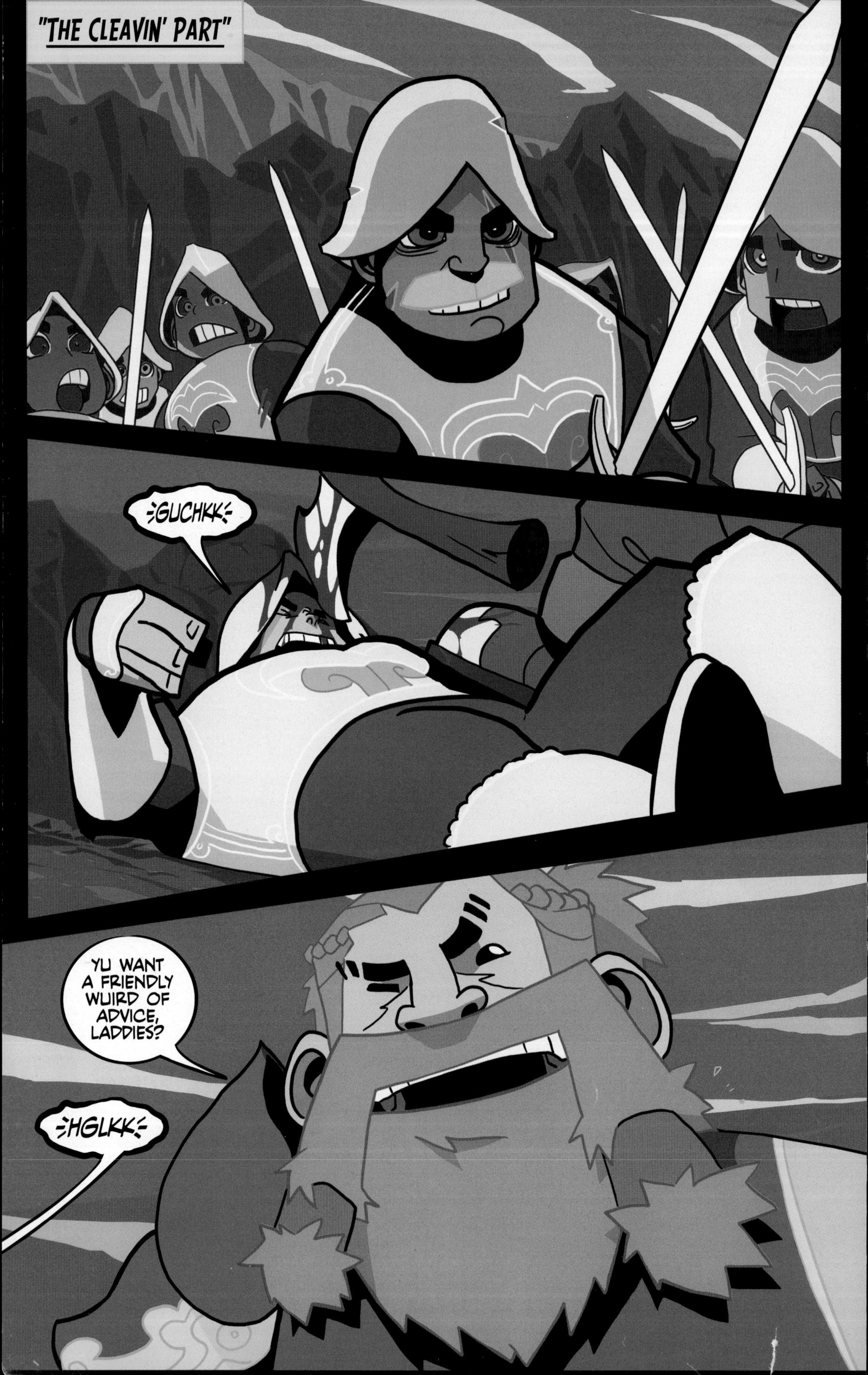
"THE CLEAVIN' PART"
GUCHKK
YU WANT A FRIENDLY WUIRD OF ADVICE, LADDIES?
HGLKK

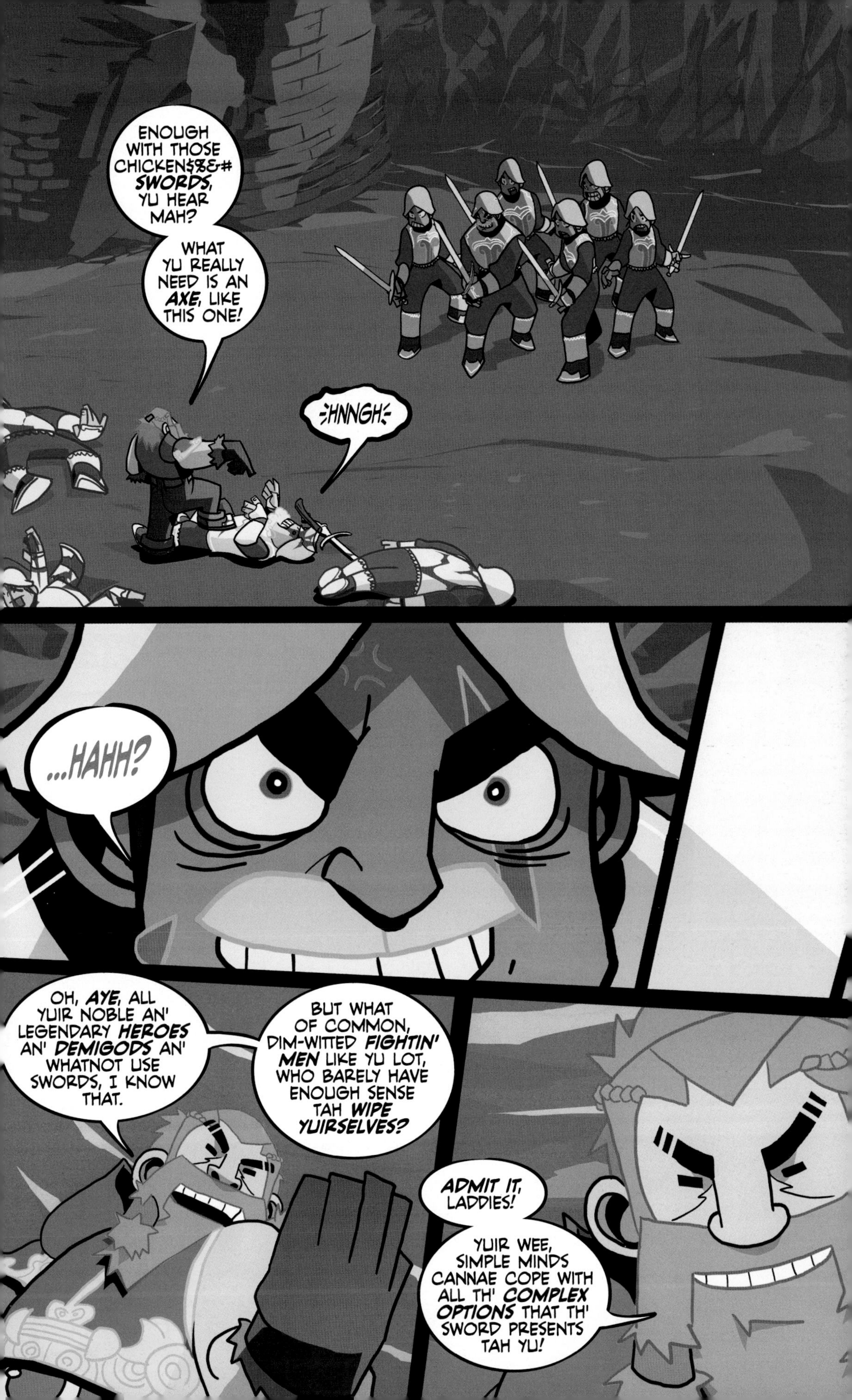
ENOUGH WITH THOSE CHICKEN$%&# SWORDS, YU HEAR MAH?
WHAT YU REALLY NEED IS AN AXE, LIKE THIS ONE!
HNNGH!
...HAHH?
OH, AYE, ALL YUIR NOBLE AN' LEGENDARY HEROES AN' DEMIGODS AN' WHATNOT USE SWORDS, I KNOW THAT.
BUT WHAT OF COMMON, DIM-WITTED FIGHTIN' MEN LIKE YU LOT, WHO BARELY HAVE ENOUGH SENSE TAH WIPE YUIRSELVES?
ADMIT IT, LADDIES!
YUIR WEE, SIMPLE MINDS CANNAE COPE WITH ALL TH' COMPLEX OPTIONS THAT TH' SWORD PRESENTS TAH YU!

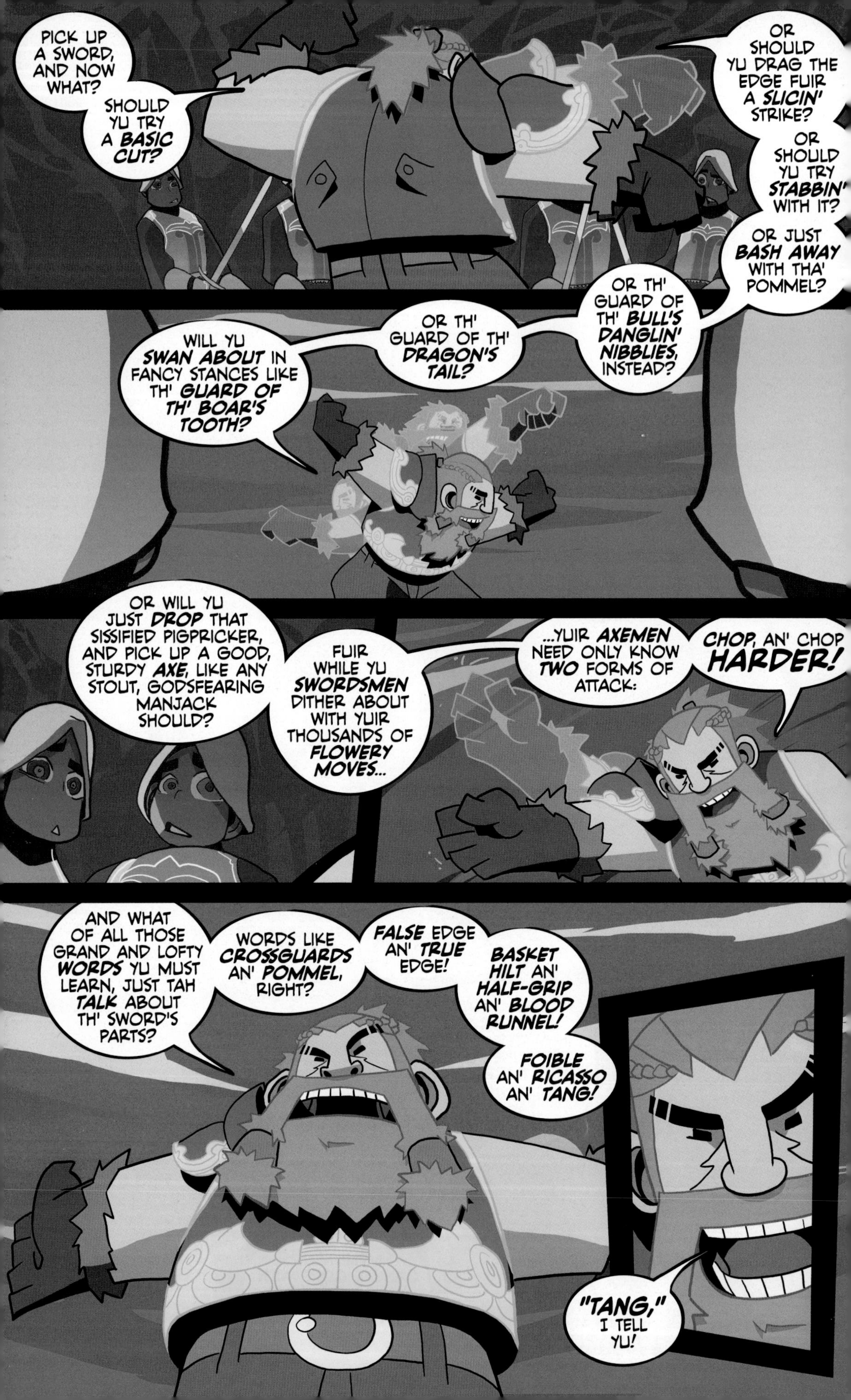
PICK UP A SWORD, AND NOW WHAT?
SHOULD YU TRY A BASIC CUT?
OR SHOULD YU DRAG THE EDGE FUIR A SLICIN' STRIKE?
OR SHOULD YU TRY STABBIN' WITH IT?
OR JUST BASH AWAY WITH THA' POMMEL?
WILL YU SWAN ABOUT IN FANCY STANCES LIKE TH' GUARD OF TH' BOAR'S TOOTH?
OR TH' GUARD OF TH' DRAGON'S TAIL?
OR TH' GUARD OF TH' BULL'S DANGLIN' NIBBLIES, INSTEAD?
OR WILL YU JUST DROP THAT SISSIFIED PIGPRICKER, AND PICK UP A GOOD, STURDY AXE, LIKE ANY STOUT, GODSFEARING MANJACK SHOULD?
FUIR WHILE YU SWORDSMEN DITHER ABOUT WITH YUIR THOUSANDS OF FLOWERY MOVES...
...YUIR AXEMEN NEED ONLY KNOW TWO FORMS OF ATTACK:
CHOP, AN' CHOP HARDER!
AND WHAT OF ALL THOSE GRAND AND LOFTY WORDS YU MUST LEARN, JUST TAH TALK ABOUT TH' SWORD'S PARTS?
WORDS LIKE CROSSGUARDS AN' POMMEL, RIGHT?
FALSE EDGE AN' TRUE EDGE!
BASKET HILT AN' HALF-GRIP AN' BLOOD RUNNEL!
FOIBLE AN' RICASSO AN' TANG!
"TANG," I TELL YU!

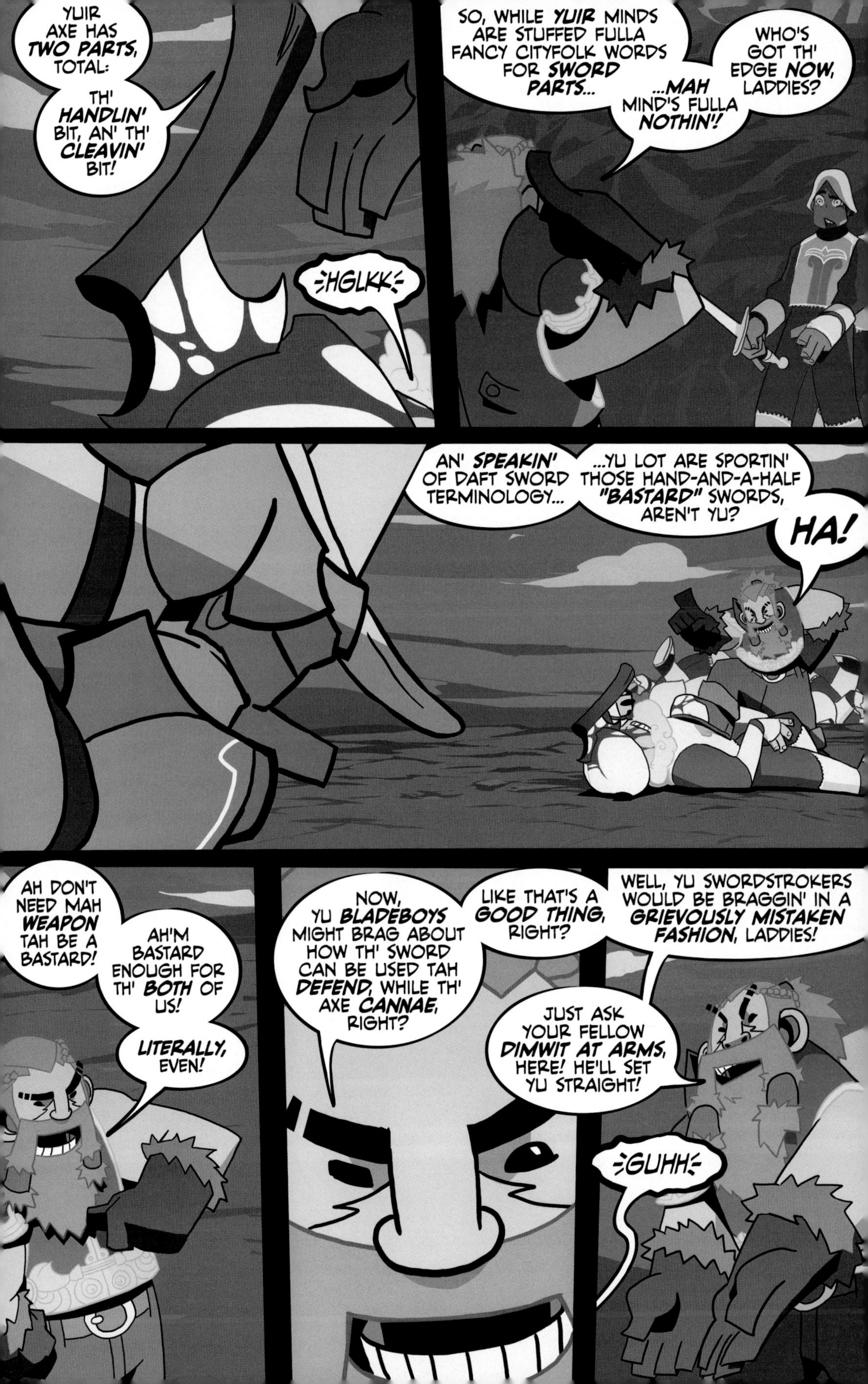

YUIR AXE HAS TWO PARTS, TOTAL:
TH' HANDLIN' BIT, AN' TH' CLEAVIN' BIT!
HGLKK
SO, WHILE YUIR MINDS ARE STUFFED FULLA FANCY CITYFOLK WORDS FOR SWORD PARTS...
...MAH MIND'S FULLA NOTHIN'!
WHO'S GOT TH' EDGE NOW, LADDIES?
AN' SPEAKIN' OF DAFT SWORD TERMINOLOGY...
...YU LOT ARE SPORTIN' THOSE HAND-AND-A-HALF "BASTARD" SWORDS, AREN'T YU?
HA!
AH DON'T NEED MAH WEAPON TAH BE A BASTARD!
AH'M BASTARD ENOUGH FOR TH' BOTH OF US!
LITERALLY, EVEN!
NOW, YU BLADEBOYS MIGHT BRAG ABOUT HOW TH' SWORD CAN BE USED TAH DEFEND, WHILE TH' AXE CANNAE, RIGHT?
LIKE THAT'S A GOOD THING, RIGHT?
WELL, YU SWORDSTROKERS WOULD BE BRAGGIN' IN A GRIEVOUSLY MISTAKEN FASHION, LADDIES!
JUST ASK YOUR FELLOW DIMWIT AT ARMS, HERE! HE'LL SET YU STRAIGHT!
GUHH

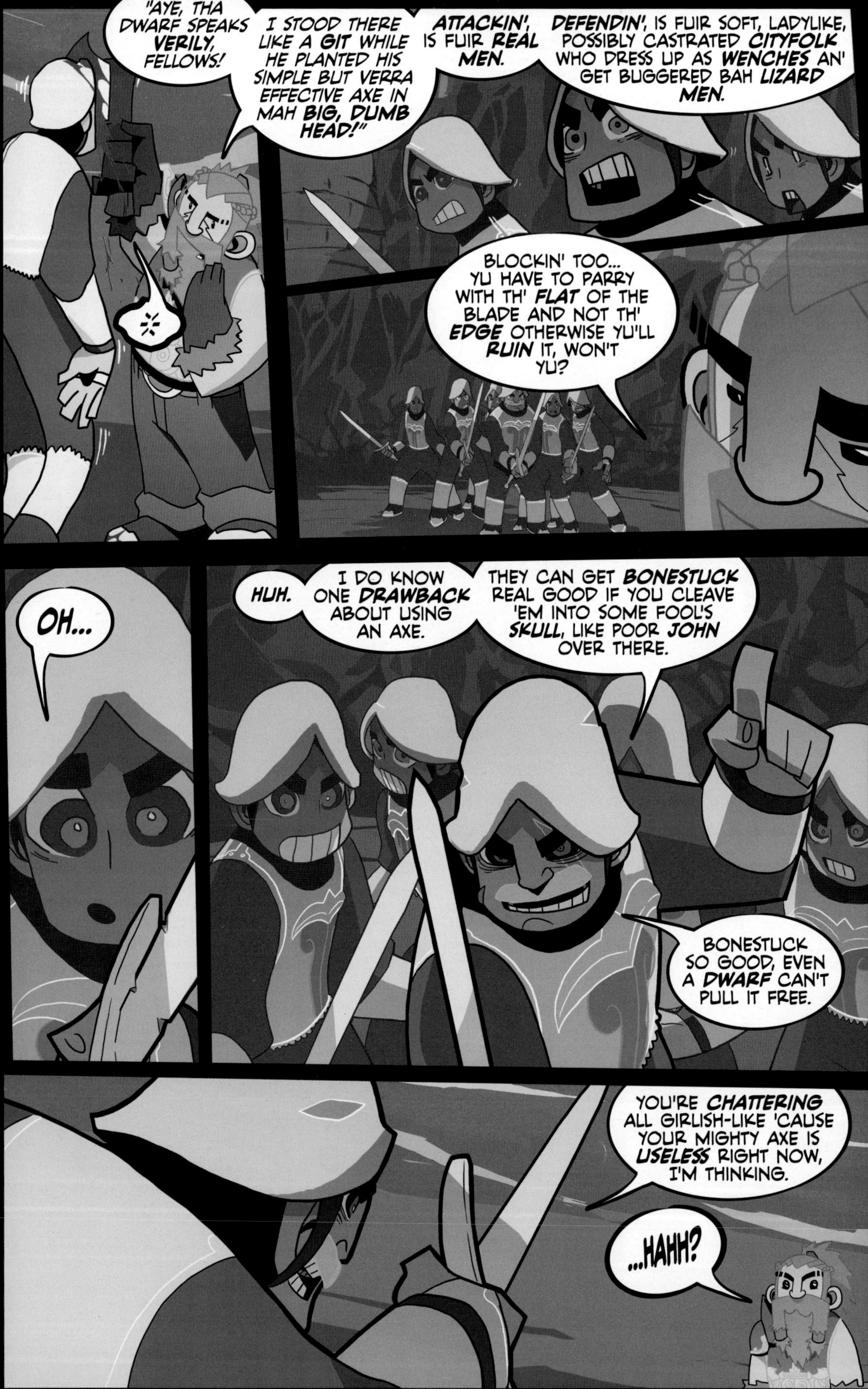
"AYE, THA DWARF SPEAKS VERILY, FELLOWS!
I STOOD THERE LIKE A GIT WHILE HE PLANTED HIS SIMPLE BUT VERRA EFFECTIVE AXE IN MAH BIG, DUMB HEAD!"
ATTACKIN', IS FUIR REAL MEN.
DEFENDIN', IS FUIR SOFT, LADYLIKE, POSSIBLY CASTRATED CITYFOLK WHO DRESS UP AS WENCHES AN' GET BUGGERED BAH LIZARD MEN.
BLOCKIN' TOO... YU HAVE TO PARRY WITH TH' FLAT OF THE BLADE AND NOT TH' EDGE OTHERWISE YU'LL RUIN IT, WON'T YU?
OH...
HUH.
I DO KNOW ONE DRAWBACK ABOUT USING AN AXE.
THEY CAN GET BONESTUCK REAL GOOD IF YOU CLEAVE 'EM INTO SOME FOOL'S SKULL, LIKE POOR JOHN OVER THERE.
BONESTUCK SO GOOD, EVEN A DWARF CAN'T PULL IT FREE.
YOU'RE CHATTERING ALL GIRLISH-LIKE 'CAUSE YOUR MIGHTY AXE IS USELESS RIGHT NOW, I'M THINKING.
...HAHH?

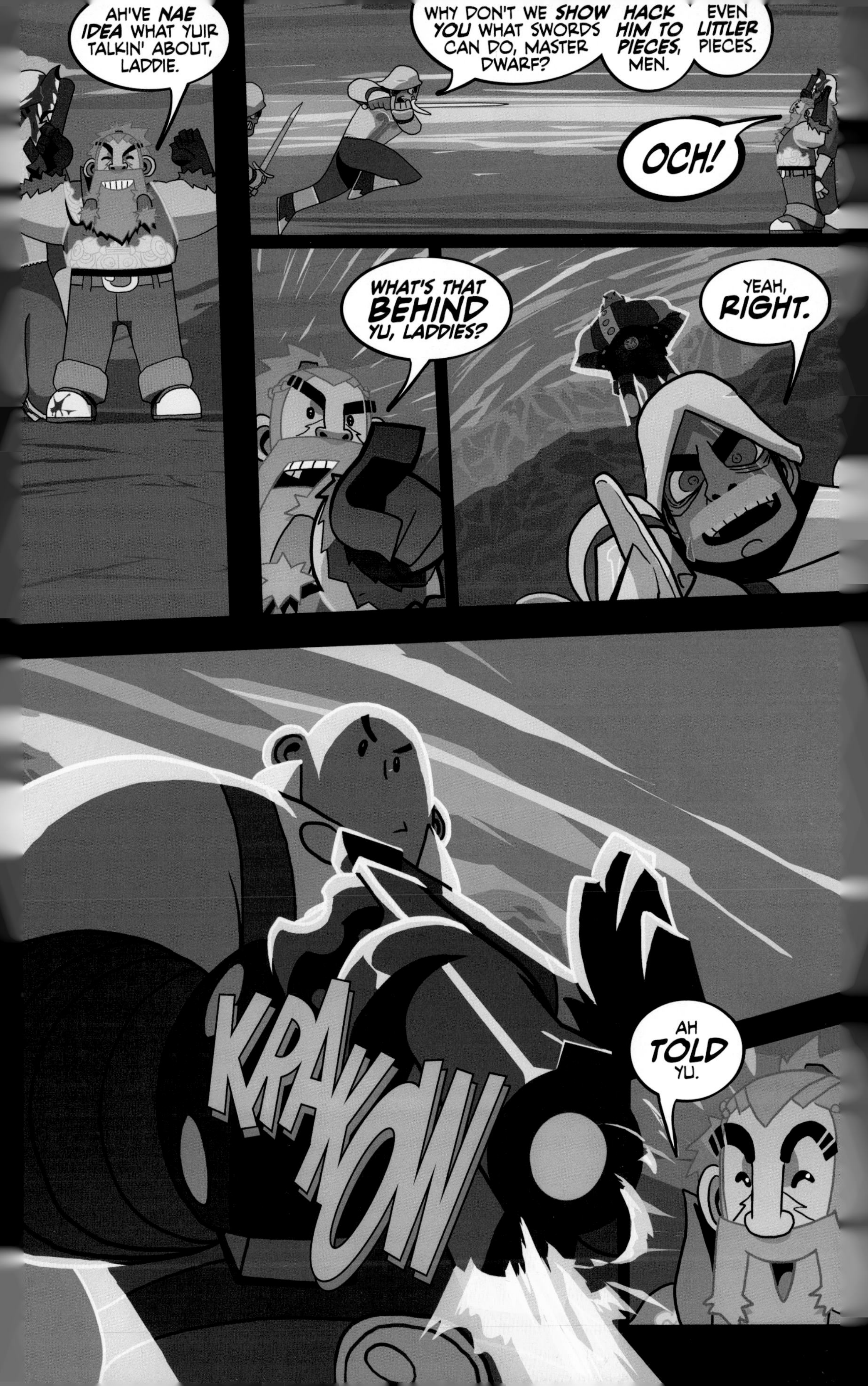
AH'VE NAE IDEA WHAT YUIR TALKIN' ABOUT, LADDIE.
WHY DON'T WE SHOW YOU WHAT SWORDS CAN DO, MASTER DWARF?
HACK HIM TO PIECES, MEN.
EVEN LITTLER PIECES.
OCH!
WHAT'S THAT BEHIND YU, LADDIES?
YEAH, RIGHT.
KRAKOW
AH TOLD YU.

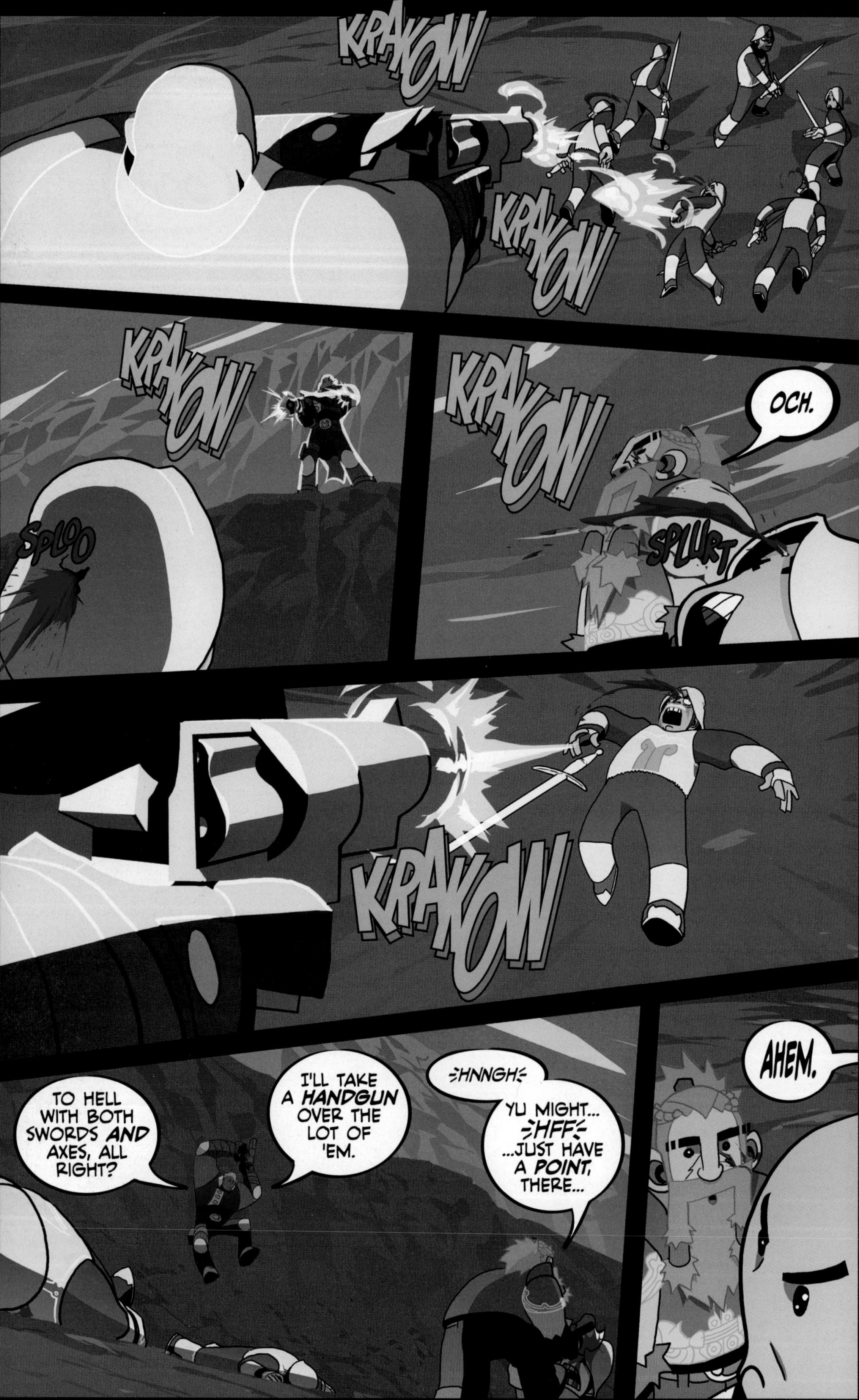
KRAKOW
KRAKOW
KRAKOW
SPLOO
KRAKOW
OCH.
SPLURT
KRAKOW
TO HELL WITH BOTH SWORDS AND AXES, ALL RIGHT?
I'LL TAKE A HANDGUN OVER THE LOT OF 'EM.
HNNGH
YU MIGHT... HFF ...JUST HAVE A POINT, THERE...
AHEM.

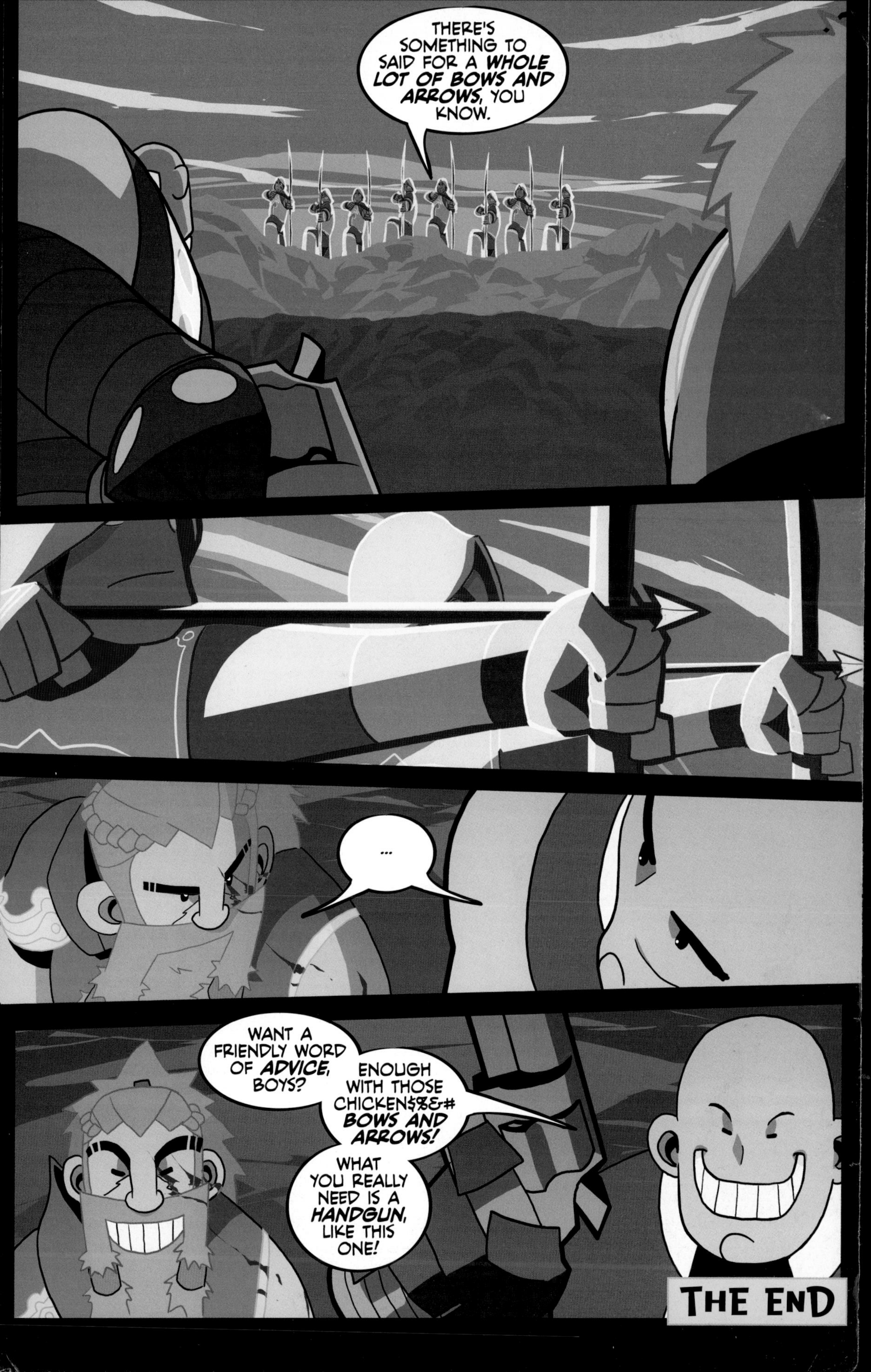
THERE'S SOMETHING TO SAID FOR A *WHOLE LOT OF BOWS AND ARROWS*, YOU KNOW.
...
WANT A FRIENDLY WORD OF *ADVICE*, BOYS?
ENOUGH WITH THOSE CHICKEN$%&# *BOWS AND ARROWS!*
WHAT YOU REALLY NEED IS A *HANDGUN*, LIKE THIS ONE!
THE END

SKETCHES

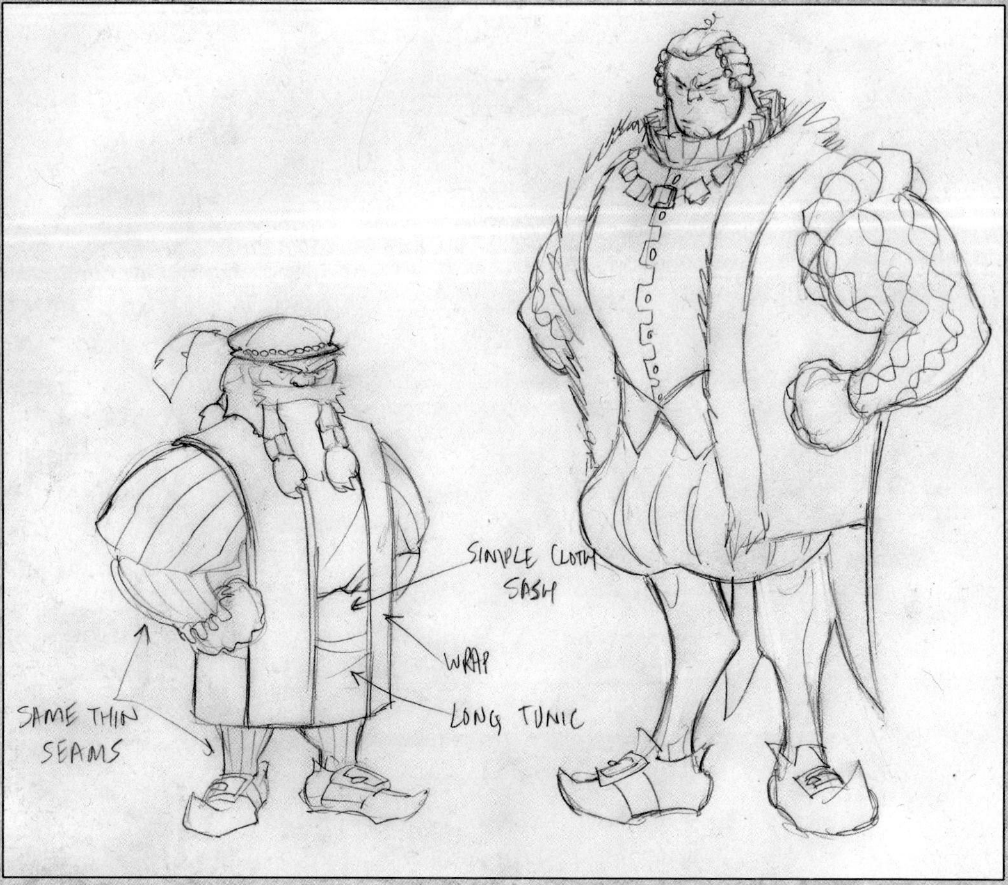

SIMPLE CLOTH SASH
WRAP
LONG TUNIC
SAME THIN SEAMS

Above: Noble costume designs for our mercenary morons by Chris Stevens.

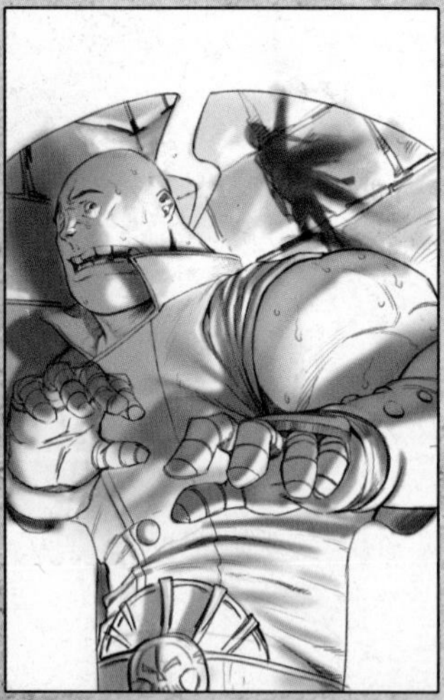

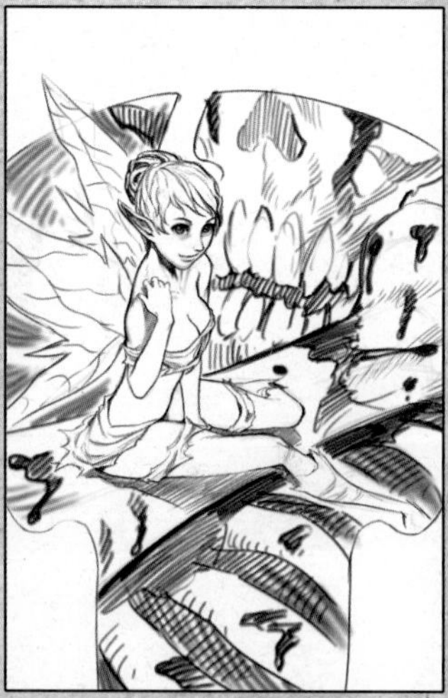

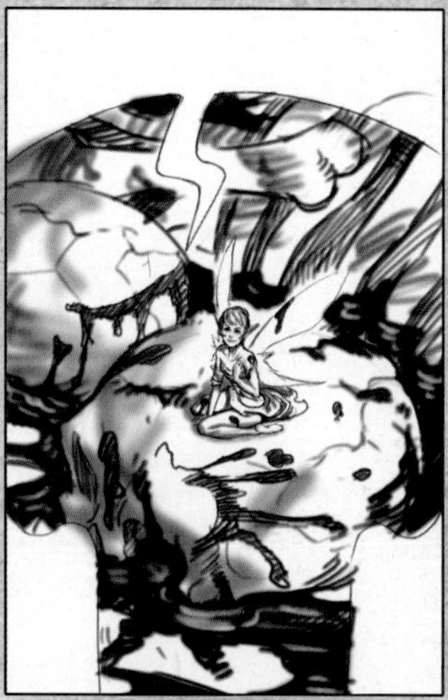

Above: Cover rough options by Saejin Oh.

As always, the art team delivered the goods on this arc, taking my crazy ideas and molding them into something entertaining and enjoyable. With each issue I feel like our storytelling abilities and comedic timing improve, bit by bit.

-ZUB